The Malacca Incident

The Malacca Incident

JACK NEWMAN

Copyright © 2024 Ben Collopy

The moral right of the author has been asserted.

All rights reserved.

All characters and events in this publication, other than those clearly in the public domain, are fictitious and any resemblance to real persons, living or dead, is purely coincidental.

No part of this publication may be reproduced, distributed, or transmitted in any form or by any means, including photocopying, recording, or other electronic or mechanical methods, without the prior written permission of the author. For permission requests, contact Jack Newman – JackNewmanNHI@outlook.com.

ISBN: 979-8-878-48492-3.

Book Cover by Augusto "Ace" Silva – BlesseD'Signs.

This book is written in the style of a techno-thriller. It seeks to blend espionage, war and military fiction with a particular focus on accuracy and the technical details of tactics, systems and mechanics. As such, a focus on real-world tradecraft and technology is a primary focus of this book. Wherever possible, efforts have been made to make the events and details described in this book as close to the real thing as possible. Despite these efforts, some creative liberties have been taken for the sake of the story. I hope you enjoy it, and please feel free to reach out with any feedback.

JackNewmanNHI@outlook.com

Cheers, Jack

ACKNOWLEDGMENTS

The creation of this book began three years ago at Christmas, following a discussion with my partner and dad on the difficulty of finding good thrillers to read. What started as a hobby and idea quickly grew, and through much trial and error, this book has grown from a couple of thousand words to a complete 120,000-word-plus novel. As my first work, it isn't perfect, but it's also not bad. Learning to write as an author and storyteller is something that I hope to refine and improve as I write more books in the future. I have, wherever possible, tried to be as accurate and as close to the real world as possible. This hasn't always been possible, and in some cases, I have deliberately altered language and details for narrative purposes.

Without the support of numerous members of the Australian Defence Force, both active and retired, this book wouldn't be the book it is. I want to give a massive thank you to all the members who were willing to provide their advice and expertise. I also want to thank the team at The Expert Editor, whose advice has been invaluable in improving and propelling my writing forward – especially Daphne, whose support and guiding hand have helped immeasurably. Lastly, and most importantly, I want to thank my partner, Nicole, who not only acted as my sounding board but reviewed the entire book and worked with me to make it what it is. Thank you, my love – without your support, I wouldn't have got here.

INTRODUCTION

100 Nautical Miles West of Christmas Island – Indian Ocean

The missile burst from its launch tube in a fiery display of smoke and sparks. The bright exhaust cone of the missile left a grey wispy tail of smoke as it crawled skyward, its powerful engine fighting against its own weight and the forces of gravity, the roar of the rocket shattering the calm, pre-dawn quiet.

Captain Jonathan O'Donnell pulled the binoculars away from his face to watch the weapon streak away. Only moments before, he'd watched the missile door of a fellow Arleigh Burke destroyer open smoothly before ejecting the missile. Now, he had to rely on the advanced cameras tracking it. He was quietly pleased at the non-eventful launch but was still on alert for any abnormal activity. There'd already been too many last-minute changes and surprises for what should have been a routine operation, but for now, everything ran smoothly.

Around him, the bridge was a hive of organised activity, with sailors watching screens and officers sounding out orders. Jonathan had always preferred to see things with his own eyes, and there was a certain thrill in watching a missile being fired or seeing his orders carried out in person – something he couldn't get from a monitor or over the radio. From his elevated position on the bridge, Jonathan could monitor the majority of the vessel comfortably; numerous monitors, consoles and screens were scattered around the open space. Here, he was responsible for the safety and navigation of the ship, but right now they were virtually stationary. If he wanted to track the flight, and hopefully, the ultimate success of the missile, he needed to head below.

Turning to the officer of the deck, he saluted quickly before announcing, 'Officer of the deck has the con!' his voice crisp and authoritative.

The officer, a young blond man in his early thirties, responded automatically, 'Officer of the deck has the con, aye sir!'

Jonathan turned sharply. Taking long, precise strides down the narrow hallway leading from the bridge, he descended several narrow stairways, seamen standing aside and saluting as he passed. He returned each with a quick smile and a salute of his own. His sailors were his people and his responsibility, and he treasured their lives over his own, but he was still the captain, and if he formed too many emotional connections, it could affect his decision making. For his sake, and the sake of his crew, he preferred to keep a degree of distance.

He was headed to the combat information centre, or simply the CIC, the brains of the combat ship, with direct information links to a dizzying array of data sources, from radars to satellites. The flight information for the missile would be directly piped into the CIC. From there, Jonathan could make split-second decisions, potentially between life and death, while keeping track of multiple threats, the running of the ship and information beamed from across the world. He descended the last flight of stairs and, swiping his pass against the secure room's lock, waited for the approving *beep* to let him in. The space inside felt like something out of a science-fiction movie, with gleaming screens, low lighting and numerous sailors wearing headsets. The room truly exuded a sense of power, but what Jonathan didn't know was that events were already spiralling outside of his control.

The missile streaked high into the sky, quickly climbing above thirty thousand feet, its booster engine burning the precise amount of fuel it had been loaded with. As it reached its zenith, the booster shut off and the roar of the engine was replaced, for a second, with blissful nothingness. This silence was quickly shattered as the powerful scramjet took over, absorbing air at speed to create combustion and push the missile forward. In seconds, it was travelling five times the speed of sound, well over seven thousand km/h. Faster, smarter and with a longer range than any hypersonic missiles previous, this was a new class of cruise missile. It could fly faster than any conventional weapon, but unlike other similar weapons in development, it could also fly further and change course as needed, avoiding anti-aircraft systems. It was quick, durable and nimble – an extremely deadly combination. By comparison, regular cruise missiles were slow and cumbersome. A hypersonic missile could reach a target in seconds, whereas a cruise missile might take minutes, ultimately giving the enemy valuable seconds to prepare a defence. Even more frightening, there was no viable defence against a hypersonic missile. They were simply too fast to shoot down with current defensive weapons systems. The United States of America had now found itself in an increasingly dangerous arms race. Nations all around the world were chasing the technology – but America's rivals, Russia and China, were the real concern for defence planners. These two nations were openly hostile to America and her allies. By 2022, both Russia and China had successfully tested numerous hypersonic prototypes, putting them firmly in the lead in this new arms race. America's allies, meanwhile, had started making their own plans. Nations such as Japan and Australia were pursuing their own hypersonic projects. However, realising the need for strong allies, America had joined forces to develop the missile currently in the air. Australia and America had signed a new defensive alliance in 2021 – awkwardly named AUKUS – but with it, a host of new technology, and shared funding, had been put into action.

From the moment the missile's scramjet had been fired, heat had begun to build on the missile's sleek outer ceramic surface. The friction of the air collided with the piercing power of the weapon as it cut through the morning sky.

As he entered the CIC, Jonathan was greeted by his executive officer, referred to simply as "XO".

'How are we looking, XO?'

'Fine, sir. A clean launch, and everything is reporting as expected,' Lieutenant Commander Christopher Baker replied. A highly affable man, he was well-liked and respected throughout both the navy and the ship, relaxed and always featuring a broad grin. Jonathan had come to rely on him over the years. He'd been immediately impressed with the man's ability to organise and keep the ship running like a well-oiled machine. Over time, a strong friendship had developed between the two men as they faced various crises together. He specialised as a naval flight officer, responsible for airborne weapon and sensor systems. 'She's flying high, smooth and looking pretty, sir.'

'Show me,' he ordered.

The XO simply pointed to a large monitor with the missile's flight path and location. The missile showed itself as a small pointed blue arrow. Its speed was immediately apparent, as the scale of the display showed from the launch position all the way into the Arabian Sea.

'If you don't mind me saying, sir, it's a hell of a thing to watch – terrifying, in a way. No way I'd want to see that coming at me. Blink and that would be that.'

'You're not wrong there, XO. Luckily, this one is ours. If this test goes well, we might actually be fielding these bad boys not too long into the future. The idea of a missile that actively avoids interception has its perks, if you ask me. Data feeding in nicely?'

'Yes, sir. We've got a constant stream of info. Guess all the extra sensors jammed into that thing are doing their job. Plus, there is always the internal storage; if we lose connection, we can just download on recovery.'

Jonathan nodded. He knew the idea of "recovery" wouldn't be as simple as the XO suggested, but this missile was supposedly so manoeuvrable they could choose exactly where they wanted it to come down.

'How long till the next manoeuvre?' Jonathan asked. There was a range of scheduled turns and changes planned to test the capabilities of the missile.

The XO checked his watch, 'About sixty seconds, sir. She did the first two easy enough. After that, we expect a splashdown in ten minutes, where pick-up will be waiting.'

'Good,' was all he mustered. Slowly, he let the pressure and stress loosen around his eyes and neck. The manoeuvres it was conducting were really just simple course corrections, but they were easily the most hazardous part of the flight – other than the launch, of course.

The XO knew him well enough to notice the signs of worry. 'No need to worry, sir; we've got this.'

Jonathan nodded, appreciating the supportive words, although not necessarily feeling reassured. He kept his gaze steady on the tracking screen, looking for anything that could suggest a problem.

Unknown to Jonathan or the rest of the crew tracking the missile's progress, a tiny hairline fracture was forming on the missile's ceramic heat shield. The sharply pointed arrowhead nose-cone of the missile was designed to slice through the air, creating a buffer for the rest of the missile to pass through. But, as with all hypersonic flight, the friction of the air against the sleek body generated extreme amounts of heat. Such a small defect would not be of concern for a conventional rocket or missile, but the tiny crack on this new prototype, invisible to the naked eye, slowly widened and grew into the internal casing. Tiny amounts of heat quickly seeped into the missile, slowly increasing the temperature. The crack widened as the integrity of the casing degraded further. A simple yet highly engineered metal plate inside the casing was the first component to suffer. Unlike the outer ceramic shell, this basic metal composite conducted heat, and did so effectively – an oversight in the design. Within a few seconds of the heat touching the plate, it had begun to weaken and glow. Fuelled by the constant flow of superheated air, the missile's fate was now sealed. One simple wire was the final straw. It connected the brains of the missile, its advanced motherboard, with the rest of its systems. This wire was a simple fibre-optic wrapped in rubber. The searing heat of the metal plate ate through it readily. A tiny sensor noticed the sudden rise in temperature and flashed a warning, but it was already too late.

Back aboard the USS John Basilone, a little red warning flashed on the screen of a technician monitoring the flight: *Temperature Warning.*

He raised his hand quickly, getting the attention of his supervisor, 'Ah, sir?'

Jonathan and the XO noted the alarm in the man's voice. Both began walking towards him. 'What have you got, son?' the XO asked.

'Temperature warnings, sir. Looks like an internal sensor.'

They'd been briefed on danger signs, and this was certainly one of them. It had only taken a couple of seconds for both Jonathan and the XO to cover the short distance to the technician, but unbeknown to them, those seconds were the last moments they'd had to stop the missile's demise.

'Commence shutdown!' came Jonathan's immediate order, cutting across his XO. The order had only just left his lips when the little blue marker that represented the missile vanished from their screens.

Jonathan knew the answer before he asked. 'Status?'

The technician paused, confused suddenly, but intelligent enough to understand what had happened. 'It's gone, sir. Nothing on scopes, no data arriving.'

'Did it complete its manoeuvre?' the XO asked.

The technician paused again, speaking quieter now, unsettled, 'I don't know, sir. We lost the signal before it finished.'

Events inside the cramped compartment of the missile, which was now well over the Arabian Sea, had taken a drastic turn. The heat building against the metal plate had consumed the insulating rubber on the wire, and the fibre-optic inside the rubber hadn't stood much of a chance, rapidly heating before simply – and somewhat anticlimactically – snapping. With the connection broken, no commands were received, no information shared. The sensor equipment, communication and propulsion had all been left without guidance or a way to send a distress signal. Essentially, the brain had been separated from the rest of the missile, so it had simply defaulted to its safety measures and shut down.

There was no explosion or scattering or debris. The scramjet engine turned off, and the missile began to glide, effortlessly. The speed dropped immediately, but the missile was still travelling at a frightening speed. The air friction reduced and the world around the missile went quiet as it continued to soar. It flew past its intended point of collection, across busy shipping lanes and a wide beach, and over land. However, despite the missile's superior gliding abilities, gravity had the final say. Slowly, its altitude decreased. Its maiden flight would be terminal.

Kuh-e-Birk Protected Area – Iran

Hashem Mohammed had awoken early to catch the morning sunrise in Kuh-e-Birk. The area was formally designated a "protected area", a type of national park in the

Islamic Republic of Iran. It was a mixture of large sand dunes and isolated oases; it even had an ancient fort built into the hillside. And it was far from the city – just how Hashem liked it. He'd travelled with his friends from the southern city of Shiraz. The idea had been simple: a reprieve from city life, away from studies, bosses and family. He slowly unzipped the tent, making sure not to wake his companions. The campfire had all but died away, but with a few extra pieces of tinder, he was able to get a small flame started, enough to boil some water. He waited quietly in the cold morning darkness, shivering. Pouring the steaming hot liquid into a small travel mug, he began the short walk up a nearby hill. It was still predawn, and he wanted to catch the sunrise, but he stepped carefully to avoid tripping over some unseen rock or shrub. As he crested the hill, only slightly out of breath, he noted that the valleys below remained hidden under the darkness, still awaiting the sun's rays. He found a large rock to perch upon and proceeded to sip his tea slowly, enjoying the quietness and coolness of the morning, feeling the sleep melt away from his core. Slowly, he saw the first rays of sunlight break through the mountains across the horizon. Dashes of light blue were replaced by brilliant yellows, reds and oranges. He wasn't particularly religious, but the sight still awed him. If there was a god, he was here. As the sun emerged from behind the earth, the valleys around Hashem began to reveal themselves, a light frost sitting on the sand of the dunes around him, little critters scampering around collecting the morning dew. A glimmer caught his eye, reflecting the sun's rays. A shimmer blinded him momentarily before disappearing. He squinted and looked towards the origin of the light. Another quick shimmer, this time closer. He focused his eyes, catching sight of something zooming along between the sky and the dunes, contrasted with the blue sky behind. It was moving fast, low to the ground. With a sudden realisation, he realised it was flying too low; it was going to crash. A large dune in front of him caught the object first. A puff of sand was thrown up into the air, with the object seemingly bouncing off the top before disappearing down into the valley of sand behind it. A dull but deep thunk rang out across the valley. He hadn't even realised he'd spilled his tea until some of the burning liquid touched his bare leg, causing him to shout in alarm before cursing his own clumsiness. He turned to look back at the impact site before running down the hill to collect his friends.

After much cajoling and a few false threats, he managed to rouse Saayd and Bilal, both of whom were none too pleased to be awoken so early.

'C'mon, you idiots, something fell from the sky in the next dune!'

The two gave him a sceptical look, 'If this is another trick of yours to get us to go on more hikes with you, Hashem, just remember this: there are two of us and only one of you.'

Hashem gave him a look of feigned hurt.

'Bilal, I would never! But let's be serious, you could use some more exercise.' His wide grin cracked into a broad smile.

'Come here, you donkey,' Bilal chased.

Saayd sighed. It was too early for this. They set off up the hill, and Saayd had to admit, it was quite a beautiful sight, the morning sunrise across the dunes. Bilal and Hashem were already running down the other side of the hill. He shrugged, following the other two, who were shouting, laughing and teasing their way across the rocks and sand.

The distance to the crash site had been longer than they expected, the sand softer, making each step a physical effort. By the time they had crested the final dune, they were all panting with exertion, Bilal and Saayd complaining even louder than before. But all that quickly faded. Looking down the reverse slope of the dune, they could see it, laying still amongst the sand. The dune they were now atop had a small crater on its peak. The sand splashed in every direction. Hashem figured the object must have bounced before landing further down in the valley. There was no smoke or fire, but bits of white and silver panelling were strewn around the surrounding area, each piece reflecting the sun's increasingly hot rays. They flew down the dune, hoping to get a closer look, any feeling of fatigue or hunger forgotten in the excitement. The closer they got, the more details came into view. Hashem recognised it as a missile almost immediately, having seen more than his fair share during his mandatory military service, although he had to admit this was not like any missile or rocket he had ever seen. It had a sleekness to it. Each side was sharp – cutting, almost. The shininess of its coating caught his eye. But it wasn't in perfect condition; the tail section had almost certainly snapped off, and the pointed nose looked dented and somewhat mangled, half buried in the soft sand. Bilal appeared more excited than the others, moving in closer, trying to examine the details.

'This is not Iranian. Look, the writing on the side is in English,' he pointed out.

Saayd made a hmmmm noise, hand on chin. 'You know, brothers, this could be worth something. It does look valuable, and it is not very large. We could probably carry it.'

'You know someone who would want to buy this?' Hashem scoffed.

'My uncle knows some people,' he replied thoughtfully. 'Bilal, try and lift it.'

Bilal immediately bent down and tried to scoop it up before rapidly pulling his hands away, 'Ahh, the damn thing's hot!' he exclaimed, sucking on one of his fingers.

'Well, let's go get some breakfast and come back when it cools down! We'll bring a rug so Bilal doesn't burn his little fingers!' Saayd grinned at them. It was hard to disagree. Hashem could feel his stomach rumbling, and more than an hour had passed since the object had fallen from the sky.

They had just started their trudge back when a faint thumping noise began to echo across the dunes. They all looked around, confused by the noise, which was seemingly coming from everywhere and yet nowhere as it reverberated off the sand dunes around them. It started to grow louder with each moment, the thumping becoming more distinctive. Hashem was the first to recognise it. 'We should run!' he yelled at his friends.

They all started to move, fear suddenly fuelling their flight. But it was already too late. Before they could crest the dune, two black buzzing aircraft zoomed over their heads, throwing sand into their faces. The thumping helicopter blades overwhelmed every other sound, making it almost impossible to hear each other. Sand blasted against them, blinding all three, the sting of the fast-moving granules beating against their skin. Then, the gale suddenly lifted, and they were relieved to find the sand dropping back to earth slowly, the roar of the engines receding.

Hashem looked up, spitting sand from his mouth as he saw them: two black helicopters hovering a short distance away, missile pods and cannon aimed at them. A surge of fear washed over him in that instant. Little did they realise they'd simply be the first victims in a long list of casualties, all fighting over the same broken missile laying in the Iranian desert.

CHAPTER 1

Canberra – Australia

Daniel Blackburn, or Danny to his friends, was sweating furiously, his heart pounding and breath ragged. He was pushing his body in the early morning light, fighting against the urge to slow down and make the pain and suffering stop. But he couldn't – not now. He was close, and every step he took was one closer to the end. He had to make it!

The final part of the track had almost killed him, the gentle slope of Commonwealth Bridge over Lake Burley Griffin in Canberra. His poor fitness and the slight incline were a bad mix. Danny's eyes remained locked on his feet and the ground below them, his exhausted state pulling his head and body into a hunched trudge. If he'd had the time to stop and take in the sights around him, the picturesque Canberra morning would have wowed him. The huge artificial lake sat below him with perfectly still, almost mirror-like water, while blossoming trees and historic government buildings dotted the popular pathways around the manicured centre of the city. But Danny trudged on, panting loudly.

'C'mon, DANNY!' one of them yelled, egging him

onward.

'Almost there, mate!' yelled the other.

There they are, he thought. His pain and suffering was all their fault. Their stupid ear-to-ear grins waited for him. He only had to reach them.

Danny had moved to the Australian capital of Canberra a few months previously. He'd taken a job working for the United States Department of Defence on a joint project with the Australian Defence Force, specialising in advanced hypersonic weaponry. Moving across the world down to Australia had been an exciting change, and he'd found the Aussies friendly and relaxed. Making fast friends, some of his colleagues had talked up their fitness routines, and before Danny had had a chance to catch himself, he'd managed to be goaded into an early-morning run, failing to consider, of course, that both of his colleagues were active military personnel and undoubtably fitter than he was. It wasn't that he was overweight – but, now that he was in his mid-thirties, Danny had fallen into the trap of office work and afternoon lounging.

How did I end up here? Danny wondered. Thinking about it now, it seemed obvious that Danny may have been set up by his newfound friends. The Australian sense of humour was still somewhat lost on him. He'd have chided his mistake if he wasn't so focused on breathing and not dying. The worst, and most humiliating, part was that the run they'd taken him on wasn't even that long or difficult. The picturesque loop around Canberra's artificial lake was no more than three miles in total, and mostly flat and paved. But if there was ever a reminder that his nine-to-five office life had caught up to him, his gasps for air were sufficient. Part of his brain promised to never let himself slip this far out of shape again. His legs burned, the stitch in his side raged and his breathing was more of a desperate pant.

One thing Danny had failed to consider was the power of the brutal Australian sun. It had made itself known halfway into their run, the warm glow hitting his back and quickly heating his body. By the time they'd reached the final section at Commonwealth Bridge, the sun's full power was cooking him, exhausting him even more. Not that it seemed to bother his two climatised friends. He cursed himself again.

He started to hear clapping and cheering over the sound of his own laboured breathing.

'Yeaaahhh, DANNY! Few more steps, mate!'

He pushed himself the last few metres, his legs wobbling with each step, threatening to collapse under him.

Staggering to a stop in front of his so-called "friends" – evil assholes, really – he almost immediately doubled over, panting. His face was red with effort and sweat drenched his clothing. Taking a moment to raise his head, Danny saw his friends' smiles beaming down at him, seemingly unaffected in the slightest by the morning run.

The two were an odd mixture, one Australian, one American, both military to their core. Sidney Hawkins, undeniably Australian from his accent, greeted him first, 'Killed it, mate!'

'Yeah, Danny, good work. A few more runs and you might be able to keep up with us … Our warm-up stage, at least,' ribbed Jesse Edwards.

'Hey Jesse, what do you say to round two? I'm feeling fresh, how about you?' Sidney said, voice full of mirth. Danny had noticed Australians tended to give everyone a nickname. Sidney quickly became Sid, and he'd not once been called Daniel, only Danny.

'Yeah, I think that would be quite refreshing – what do you say, Danny?'

He simply looked back at them, 'You guys suck,' he managed between breaths.

They both burst out laughing.

Danny admitted self-defeat and enlisted a recently learnt Australianism, simply saying bugger it and flopping down on his backside, then resting his back against a pole behind him.

The others took a more sympathetic tone, Sidney taking the lead. 'Ah, don't worry, Danny, we'll sort you out. A few more of these and you'll be able to keep up with us, no problem.'

Jesse chimed in, 'Look, you kept up with us for a while there, and we didn't go easy on you. You did good.'

Danny didn't feel like he'd done that well, or that more exercise was on the cards. All he knew was that he was going to be sore for the rest of the day, and probably the next.

After a bit more teasing, Danny was eventually hauled to his feet by his newfound friends. His breathing had returned to normal, and he didn't feel like he was about to throw up, so there was that. Still, his legs felt like they were on fire. They all walked gingerly back to their starting point, a small carpark next to the bridge. Canberra was starting to come alive. While it was still early morning, more people were out, going for walks, heading to work or exercising like he just had. The city was a strange spot for the capital of the country. With barely over four hundred thousand people, it was hardly a city at all, but it was jam-packed with government employees, buildings and well-managed, expansive broadways. The biggest difference was the sheer amount of bushland both in and surrounding the city. Danny liked it, but he still couldn't get used to the scorching heat the Australians seemed to shrug off so easily.

Sidney and Jesse bantered back and forth with Danny. They were going to get a large breakfast somewhere, but all Danny wanted was a shower. A loud ringer interrupted their chatter as they headed towards their vehicles. Danny had purchased a sleek black BMW 3 Series sedan, while Sidney and Jesse had both settled for Australian pickups, although the Aussies called them "utes". To Danny, they were just smaller, almost adorable versions of the larger American trucks.

Sidney had kept his phone on him, and he answered it almost immediately, his tone transforming from joking to formal immediately. 'Yes, sir, right away.'

'That doesn't sound good,' Jesse murmured, giving Danny a worried look.

Sidney hung up. 'Sorry, fellas. Looks like breakfast is cancelled; they need us back at JOC ASAP. Sounds like they've been trying to call all of us for the last thirty or so.'

Danny unlocked his car and retrieved his phone. Sure enough, he'd had at least five missed calls within the last twenty minutes. This definitely wasn't good.

'Any idea what it's about?' Jesse asked.

'Nope, not the faintest. But that was the boss, and I was told ASAP, so it's serious.'

'Alright, back to the office then. Danny, you'd better wash up, mate, we can smell you from here. Don't want to be working in some crisis with you stinking up the place,' Jesse called out over the roof of Danny's car.

Danny gave them both a middle finger as he got in his car.

He didn't get far before his phone rang again. 'This is Danny,' he answered. The number was marked as private.

A familiar, sharp voice barked back at Danny, 'Where the hell have you been? I've been trying to contact you for the last half-hour!' Internally, Danny sighed. He could never win with his boss. 'Well?!' the man demanded.

'I was going for a run, Mike. I just got back to my car.'

'You think I give a shit, Danny? Get into the office ASAP.'

There it is, always a trap with this guy, he thought. Still, he did sound more worked up than normal; something had clearly gone wrong.

'What's going on, Mike?'

'You'll find out when you get here! I want you here, now!' Mike yelled down the phone.

Michael "Mike" Clayton was a constant buzzing problem for Danny. A mid-level manager whose career had peaked. He ran the American part of the team Danny was a part of. He was the worst kind of manager, unable to make any meaningful decisions, petty and lazy. Danny had quickly learnt how to avoid the man, when possible.

'On my way,' was all he could muster. There was no point trying to argue with Mike. He'd still go home, shower and get changed. Mike would be just as frustrating, whether he was there right this second or in a half-hour.

'Good, the Australians are already in a fit. We'll need to handle that,' said Mike. Danny doubted they needed to "handle" anything.

'Sure thing, Mike.' He hung up, knowing his sarcastic tone would be lost on his boss.

Turning the ignition, he felt the pleasant rumble of his new car coming to life. Revving the engine, he backed the car out and sped off, the gravity of the events occurring around him not yet known.

***

The fresh change of clothes and shower had somewhat revived him after his torturous morning run, although he still felt a little weak at the knees. As he cruised out of Canberra, rows of pine trees and native forest whizzed by. His one guilty pleasure had always been fast cars, a pile of speeding tickets standing as a testament to Danny's antics. With a freshly brewed coffee in hand, Danny savoured his morning commute to work, the rich coffee beans creating a pleasant aroma throughout his car. He noted that he did feel more awake than usual today; maybe morning exercise was better than he'd realised. Not that he'd tell his colleagues that.

Danny had started his career as an aerospace engineer, finding his niche working on new and cutting-edge technology. He'd taken a slightly unorthodox career change at age thirty, when a colleague offered him a role as an intelligence analyst working with the department of defence. Despite the pay cut and change in work, Danny had been immediately drawn to the challenge of intelligence work and hadn't looked back, quickly climbing the ranks to become a senior analyst and then team leader. He was young for his peer group but seen as highly capable, his knowledge of weapons technology making him the point of contact for numerous other researchers and analysts throughout the defence and intelligence community. When the offer to work on a new project in Canberra, Australia had presented itself, he'd leapt at it. Danny found his outgoing personality fitted well with the Australians, and he'd quickly felt right at home, venomous snakes and insects aside.

With a tinge of regret, he arrived at his destination, HQJOC – or JOC – short for Headquarters Joint Operations Command, one of Australia's primary and most modern military facilities. He drove up to the entrance. Numerous armed guards greeted him, checking over his car and his ID. He smiled back at them pleasantly; he'd been working here long enough to know that he was a recognised face. Danny had always enjoyed getting to know people, no matter their position. To him, people were people, and all had interesting backstories and beliefs to be explored. He checked the time on his dashboard as he waited for the standard security inspection. A good hour had passed since Mike had called. Man, I bet I won't hear the end of this, he thought.

It was now mid-morning, and the Australian spring was quickly turning into summer. He knew from experience that his new black sedan would be turning into an oven before too long. The heat was something that Danny still hadn't quite adjusted to, but at least it meant formal suits weren't a popular business choice. Most office workers and analysts preferred collared shirts and chino pants to full jackets and ties. Stepping out of his airconditioned car, he was immediately assailed by the warm air. He grabbed his coffee and bag and headed straight for the entrance, eagerly seeking refuge from the heat. A few winding turns and security checkpoints later, Danny found the nondescript door he was looking for. He swiped his card and entered, immediately wishing he hadn't.

The room was filled with frenetic energy. People in both military uniform and business suits were moving around the floor; others were speaking in small huddles or tapping away furiously on their keyboards. There was a certain speed at which people moved, a heightened level of noise that replaced the regular hum of activity. Danny realised this wasn't a normal day. 'Oh boy,' he muttered to himself.

The space looked like a NASA control room, with massive TV screens showing information feeds, including live TV broadcasts and tactical inputs directly from military, while the rest of the space was an array of workstations and offices, all facing the displays mounted on the walls.

Danny had barely taken a step towards his desk before the familiar Texan drawl of Mike boomed over the hum of the room, distinctly separate from the surrounding Australian accents.

'Where the hell have you been?!'

At six feet tall, with short white hair and a rough, squared jawline, Mike cut an imposing figure. He rarely cracked jokes, and a smile from Mike was as elusive as a blue moon, often broody or indecisive, sometimes both. Danny had seen glimmers of a more responsive and capable version of Mike, maybe from his youth, but those glimpses were as rare as his smile. The Mike striding towards Danny was at best uninterested, at worst a bully. Somewhere along the road of his life, Mike seemed to have lost his spark for life, leaving behind an angry human.

By the time Danny had spotted Mike in the crowd, the man had already closed the distance between them.

'Shit, Mike! I got here as fast as I could – you know, it's not just a quick drive over.'

Now that they stood face to face, Mike appeared strangely indecisive, stuck somewhere between boiling anger and relief. For a split second, Danny thought the man might try and hit him. But just like flicking a switch, he changed course, simply saying, 'Come with me. We need you up front with Ata.'

Danny had a million questions, between the random early morning calls and the frantic action around room ... His curiosity burnt bright at the best of times, but right now, it was flashing bright red. 'Mike, what's going on?'

'Ata will brief you,' was all he got in return – a short, dismissive reply from the back of Mike's head. Looking around at the large monitors on the walls, Danny caught sight of a tactical map showing the position of a number of military vessels near Christmas Island, northwest from Australia's western edge. Danny was very familiar with those ships and the exercise they were meant to have commenced later today; it was part of his project. A small lump formed at the back of his throat.

Mike escorted him, rather unnecessarily, to a small pod of desks that represented Danny's little team. Sidney and Jesse were already hard at work on something and didn't even look up at their arrival.

Athena Papadopoulos – or Ata, as she preferred – was an Australian geospatial intelligence analyst and the fourth and final member of their team. Of Greek descent and in her early thirties, Ata was easy to like, quick-witted, smart and fiercely capable; she was one of the best team members Danny had ever worked with. As they approached, Mike loudly exclaimed, 'We've found him, Ata.'

She swivelled in her chair, looking up from three large monitors, grinning, 'Ah, his majesty, so nice of you to join us.'

Danny shrugged while grinning back, 'Yeah, I know. I got here as fast as possible. What's going on? Why is everyone running around?'

Ata looked up at Mike, an annoyed scowl on her face. 'C'mon, Mike! You haven't told him?'

Mike shrugged dismissively. 'I'll leave the briefing in your capable hands; I want an update in an hour, confirm the status of the prototype.'

Danny's ears pricked, a knot now forming in his gut to go with the growing lump in his throat. *That isn't good*, he thought.

Ata audibly sighed once Mike was out of earshot. 'Man, he's a real prick sometimes.'

Danny grunted his approval and sat down. 'So, what is going on?' he asked again, hopefully for the final time.

'Well, you'll love this.' She turned one of her monitors to face Danny, gesturing to a range of data on the screen. He immediately recognised one set as telemetry tracking data and glanced over to find multiple lines of code and error logs on the other screen. Ata simply watched Danny silently ingest the information, eyes darting across the feeds on the screen, his finger underlining where he was reading.

He recognised it all immediately. 'Ata, why am I reading telemetry from our missile, from … this morning?'

She gave him a slight nod, 'So… for reasons beyond me, orders seem to have come down.' She pointed upward with her finger. 'From up top. To commence the test early. But that's not even the best part.' She pulled up another screen, 'Check the coordinates.'

Danny followed the data logs, the changing latitudes and longitudes appearing with each line. He did some quick mental gymnastics and the sinking feeling in his gut grew bigger. 'Ata, where did they launch this thing? This isn't the planned route.'

She pulled up one last screen showing the track of the missile against a map, the line clearly heading out over the Indian Ocean before turning northwest towards the Iranian coastline.

'What the fuck …' he breathed. Not only had they conducted the test without the knowledge of the joint American–Australian team, his team, but they had changed the flight path completely. Whoever had ordered this clearly didn't care.

Danny already knew something had gone wrong. He doubted he'd have been called in and found the room in a panic if the test had gone as planned. 'Show me the final logs.'

She already had the list ready and pulled it up right away. He could see the critical errors at the bottom, followed by endless repeated attempts by the tracking software to reacquire a connection to the missile.

Danny frowned, rocking back into his chair and spinning in a small semi-circle. 'So, we lost the prototype.' He then added, 'Someone changed the flight path, the timing and basically everything about the test – and, cherry on top, they lost the prototype.'

The original test was meant to be a fairly routine joint test with the Australian Defence Force, demonstrating the prototype's capabilities when fired from a sea-based platform, a Virginia Class attack submarine. It was meant to launch directly to the west, ensuring it would avoid any major shipping routes and the prying eyes of other interested parties. But, by launching the missile to the northwest, someone had ensured that it would fly past India and head directly towards Iran, while also passing over major shipping routes.

'Pretty much, but that's not the best part. We don't know what went wrong, or where the remains of the rocket are.'

Danny blinked, nodding his head while he processed the information. After a short, silent pause, he said, 'Okay, so we're all on the same page: we've fired an experimental cutting-edge missile, worth hundreds of millions of dollars – no, sorry, billions of dollars – and now we can't figure out if it exploded into a million pieces or is out there somewhere.'

Ata grinned this time. 'Yep, that about sums it up. Oh, and no one told the Australian side of the changes.'

'Right … And that went down a treat, huh?'

The Australians were jointly funding the development of the missile technology, and as part of the project, were meant to have joint control and equal say in decisions. Their little team was a key part of that system, made up of half Australian and half American personnel. Even Mike was technically sharing the responsibilities as their boss, as he had an Australian counterpart. The unilateral decision to alter the destination would have shaken this equality badly.

'Okay, so exactly which brainiac decided to alter the test?' Danny asked.

'Not a clue, but it looks like we're getting saddled with the clean-up.'

'Alright, what about these two, what are they doing?' Danny said, pointing to Jesse and Sidney.

'So, Sidney is listening to maritime traffic throughout the region to see if he can pick up anything mentioning debris or lights in the sky.' Sidney gave him the thumbs up as he chewed on an energy bar, headphones securely covering a portion of his head. 'And Jesse is running point on allied and friendly shipping in the area, seeing if they picked anything up on radar.' Jesse returned a bored look; he was clearly not loving the task. Danny chuckled. A small bit of revenge for the morning.

'I know we've just started, but so far, we've got nothing. The search is just too massive, and we don't know enough,' Ata finished.

'Alright, Ata. I'll get cracking on the technical data and telemetry from the test. I guess you'll stick with the geo?'

'You know it,' she confirmed.

Today was going to be a long day. Unknown to Danny, back in the Iranian desert, the rumble of heavy machinery and military equipment had begun to echo over the dunes.

CHAPTER 2

Kuh-e-Birk Protected Area – Iran

The heavy Chinook CH-47 transport helicopter thumped across the desert dunes of Kuh-e-Birk, its dual rotor blades slicing through the hot desert air with impressive ease. It flew fast and low, throwing up clouds of sand as it swept across the sandy peaks below. The helicopter was fully loaded: men filling all available seats, gunners manning door guns. It had a purpose, and speed was of the essence.

It wasn't alone, either. Two additional helicopters flew ahead of the slower, heavier Chinook, screening the area ahead for possible threats. They were smaller but far more deadly, the angular design of the Cobra gunships making them look like massive, angry wasps. Loaded with rocket pods and a twenty-millimetre cannon on their noses, the two gunships could decimate any threats at close range. The small grouping was not all that it seemed. The aircraft were old – far older than many others flown around the world. Hobbled together with makeshift replacement parts and ingenuity, the aircraft operated far beyond what the lifetime of their airframes should have allowed. Despite being American designed and built, these aircraft flew under a different flag, sold to this country when the Americans had once been considered close friends, prior to the overthrow of the Shah in 1979. The Islamic Republic of Iran Army Aviation, known locally as the Havanirooz, had worked tirelessly and with no small amounts of innovation to maintain the decades-old aircraft.

Colonel Kamran Rostami of the Iranian army sat close to the cockpit of the Chinook, ignoring the rattles and groans of the aged airframe he was flying in. His mind was focused on the mission ahead, and the opportunities that lay beyond it. He was surrounded by a multitude of soldiers, scientists, engineers and men in suits. A curious mix for a military mission, but if the intelligence report he now held in his hands was correct, something valuable lay in the desert before him.

The radar had picked up faint signatures of something entering Iranian airspace, its altitude dropping steadily. At first, it was considered a glitch, but the clear trajectory of the object as it descended changed things. The quick actions by one radar operator to determine the object's speed and likely landing location had sparked immediate interest. It was travelling quickly but losing speed, and its likely landing location had nothing of value. The conclusion was that either something to threaten Iran was occurring, like an incursion, or something was happening that the owners of the object hadn't intended. Either way, a taskforce was needed to investigate. In Rostami's mind, a real opportunity existed to represent not only himself but his unit and branch of the Iranian armed forces. Normally, the upstart Islamic Revolutionary Guard Corps would have been assigned to a mission of this importance, but Rostami's unit had been closer, and his reputation had preceded him. The moment the hurried order to deploy had hit Rostami's desk, he'd been a relentless force of nature. Within thirty minutes, his small taskforce had been deployed from Mashhad international airport. He knew, as did the leaders of his country, that if a drone or other piece of technology had crashed in their lands, it could be used to their advantage. Previously, American drones had been salvaged, much to the benefit of Iranian technology, and it was hoped this could be achieved again. Or, if the Americans or Israelis were foolish enough to try something, his force would be there to respond. His gut told him it would be the former. The only question would be whether the object had survived the landing. He knew speed would be of the essence: if the Americans, or any of the other Western nations, had lost a piece of their precious technology, they'd want it back. It was going to be his job to get there before them.

He stood up and looked through the cockpit, watching the sand dunes and rocky outcrops flash by. Rostami was a hard man, disciplined and precise, with a reputation for achieving the impossible, even if it was at the cost of the lives of the men around him. He was, at his core, a nationalist; he had dedicated his life to the advancement of his nation's goals. In his view, the lives of his men were simply tools to be used for greatness. Death in the name of Iran was an honour.

One of the pilots turned around, visibly startled upon seeing Rostami towering over him, his muscled neck and broad shoulders making for an imposing sight. Swallowing quickly, recovering, he pointed to a spare pair of headphones hanging from the roof of the aircraft. Rostami slipped them on. Immediately, the near-deafening noise of the aircraft was drowned out, to his hidden relief. He tapped the mic to make sure it was working.

'Go for Rostami.'

His headphones crackled to life, 'Colonel, message from escort Cobra lead,' the co-pilot announced.

'Understood, connect me.' The line crackled as the pilot switched bands. He waited until the pilot gave him the thumbs up signal, 'This is Colonel Rostami receiving.'

The voice on the other end sounded strained as the man fought the noise of his aircraft, 'Colonel, we are approaching the coordinate now.'

'Copy. Give me an update once you have a visual.'

He didn't have to wait long. 'Cobras on station, colonel. We have eyes on something in the sand; it appears to be some kind of missile or drone. It seems to have hit one of the dunes and crashed into a valley.'

Rostami almost smiled. His gut had been right; there was something in the sand, and it was his to recover. The radio crackled again before he could reply.

'However, we also count three – I repeat, three – unidentified individuals at the site. They appear to be leaving.'

A flash of alarm swept over him, the hairs on the back of his neck standing tall, 'Are they armed?' he demanded immediately.

'Negative, sir. They appear to be wearing civilian clothing.'

That could mean a lot of things, Rostami thought to himself. If they had taken something from the object, his efforts could be in vain. They'd need to be dealt with.

'Maintain a perimeter around the site until we arrive, Cobra lead. Ensure the unidentified intruders do not escape, is that understood?'

'Understood, colonel. Cobra lead and support commencing overwatch and security. Over and out.'

The colonel tapped the pilot on the shoulder, 'ETA?'

The man didn't need to check his instruments; the Colonel had been asking every couple of minutes, 'Ten minutes, sir.'

***

The Chinook eased itself onto the soft surface a short distance from the apparent crash site. The other two gunships continued to circle above, looking for any potential threats. Rostami watched from the cockpit doorway as the sand was blasted away from the aircraft by the beat of its rotor wash. The once-clean site became a hazy fog of sand, visibility disappearing with every dispersion. Yet, the pilots were experienced and perfectly judged the landing, meeting the surface with only the slightest bump. They immediately started shutdown procedures, slowing the rotors to stop the sand cloud building around them. The various air intakes would need a full clean when they got back to base, they both knew. Rostami didn't wait for the sand cloud to dissipate. He strode into the cargo hold of the large helicopter, issuing orders to his squads.

'First squad, secure the crash site. I want this site locked down and concealed as soon as possible. Begin scoping locations for defensive emplacements. Second squad, locate and secure the unknown individuals. I want them alive, but if they are a threat, neutralise them. Understood?' Both lieutenants managing the squads saluted, a flicker of fear and respect in their eyes.

The rear door to the helicopter slowly lowered, a wave of sand immediately entering the confined cargo bay, irritating everyone's eyes and giving the once-clean space a hazy hue. Rostami strode out onto the soft sand, feeling his feet sink ever so slightly into the ground. The rotors had slowed considerably, and the air was clearing enough that he could examine the immediate terrain. Sand dunes, mixed with rocky outcrops. The land was almost featureless, no trees or shade. The oppressive heat made him feel like he had entered an oven; beads of sweat were already forming across his forehead. Not that it bothered him – and if it did, he wouldn't show it. His persona was strength above all else. Nothing would shake the image he'd crafted for himself.

Moving a short distance away, he crested the peak of a dune overlooking the small valley below. One of the squads had already made their way down, their footprints slowly fading in the sand as a gentle breeze swept across it. The object was unmissable. An anomaly against the featureless landscape. A gleaming piece of metal, reflecting the sun's light and laying peacefully in the sand, its fins clearly visible.

Rostami knew immediately it wasn't a weapon of his country. No, this was something far more valuable. He'd studied the weapons of war of his enemies for years, and this, this was unknown to him. He felt a surge of excitement building inside him. It was something new.

Behind him he could hear the rhythmic thumping of feet pushing against the sand and a small but noticeable squeaking sound. His quiet inspection was quickly disturbed by the excited exclamations of the crowd of scientists and engineers gathered at the peak.

'Woah! That's different! Doesn't look like any missile I've ever seen!' exclaimed one of the civilians.

Another one, an older, more quietly spoken man, said, 'It must be a prototype of some new missile. It's hard to tell from here, but it's much more angular than most Western cruise missiles, and it's much smaller …' He trailed off, hand on chin in contemplation.

Rostami listened intently, concealing his interest. If these supposed specialists couldn't identify it immediately, it could well be even more valuable than he suspected.

A hurried summons from one of the impatient soldiers escorting the small group of civilians sent them storming down the dune. He'd give them time to make their assessments, even if part of him wanted answers now. 'Patience,' he chided himself.

Rostami continued to observe silently from his elevated position. Soldiers hurriedly setting up camouflage netting, digging holes, and hauling crates and other equipment to the site. It wouldn't be long before they controlled the entire site, and hopefully had enough of a presence to keep any prying eyes away. Still, they were awfully exposed out here in the desert.

Assuming the object was American, it wouldn't be long before they identified the crash site, even with the camouflage efforts. US military satellites or reconnaissance flights would eventually identify the site. He had to act quickly, determine the object's nature and, if it had value, protect it and transport it to a safer location. He hoped they wouldn't be in the desert for long. But assuming the owners of the object did know where it was and wanted it back, what would, or could, they do?

If it was the Americans, his great fear would be drones. He doubted his country's ability to protect against them. They'd be able to shoot down any helicopters under thirteen thousand feet, but against aircraft and drones, he was defenceless. He wouldn't put it past the Americans. They did have shoulder-launched Misagh-2 MANPADs, which gave him a small sense of safety. Still, until reinforcements arrived, he knew they were largely alone.

He knew what needed to be done next. Pulling out a large, encrypted satellite phone, he dialled a number he had become all too familiar with over the last few years. He hoped the line was as secure as advertised.

'What do you have for me, colonel?' a sharp, nasally tone demanded without a greeting.

'We have secured the site and confirmed that something has fallen. It looks like some kind of missile, but we do not recognise its make and model yet. We'll have more information within the hour. Please let his eminence know.'

The voice on the other end paused. 'Good, colonel. I will expect updates hourly; do not concern yourself with his eminence. I will inform him as required. Focus on the task at hand. You know the consequences of failure.'

Rostami gritted his teeth, trying to hide the boiling anger growing in his chest. The confidence of this man, this worm, to speak to him this way. He would make sure he dealt with this lack of respect, but not now. He had to play the game a while longer. 'I understand. I will report back within the hour.'

'Good. I am sending one of my men, Merada, out there to observe. See that he is given the respect and authority he expects.' The line clicked dead, the other man hanging up before Rostami could respond.

Colonel Rostami clicked his tongue as he returned the

satellite phone to his pocket. He was playing a dangerous game, and he knew it. But, if he didn't, his country would bear the cost. He had to act. But no one was above suspicion, especially those with power. He'd need to be careful, especially around this "Merada". He returned his gaze to the crash site, mulling the possibilities and threats that could arise before reinforcements arrived. He knew he had to move the missile from its crash location – it was too exposed to stay here, and the desert was unforgiving to both humans and machinery. But without heavy lifting equipment, he was stuck amongst the desolate dunes.

His attention was suddenly pulled away by the sound of shouting and cursing. Turning around, he could see a small group of men being hauled along by his soldiers, one of his men seemingly holding a cloth against his mouth, nursing a slight injury. He grunted with satisfaction. One less loose end to deal with.

***

Hashem struggled against his captors, arguing that they had nothing to do with the crash site. The soldiers had caught them as they had tried to pack up their tents and run to the car. The moment the helicopters had appeared, they knew they had to leave. But they'd been too slow. Saayd had hit one of the soldiers when they'd tried to stop them. It had been a good hit as well; the solider had gone down, his lip split. But that had just made everything worse. They'd all received a beating. And in the end, they'd been captured regardless. He and his friends were thrown onto the soft sand at the feet of an imposing man who Hashem figured must be in charge. Prostrate, he looked up from the ground imploringly, searching the angular facial features of the man towering before him. He looked into the eyes of the figure, seeing only darkness, a deep sense of fear rising within him.

Hashem blurted out quickly, 'Please, sir, we have nothing to do with this. We were camping nearby and saw it land!' He pointed down the slope towards the crash site.

The imposing man stared down directly into Hashem's eyes, analysing his face but remaining silent and expressionless. The silence continued on for what felt like an eternity; he could feel a sense of panic washing over him, his desperation becoming increasingly uncontrolled.

The man frowned at Hashem then turned to one of the solders. 'Take them away. I will interrogate these spies once the site is secure.'

Mention of the word "spy" hit Hashem like a hammer. He knew full well that being considered a threat to his nation carried a swift and likely painful end.

The soldiers hauled Hashem and his friends up, and the imposing man turned around to face the crash site. Hashem called out as he was dragged away, 'Please, sir, I beg you, we are not spies, we are innocent! Please!'

His calls fell on deaf ears. The soldiers hauled Hashem and his friends away from the site and past a sand dune. A small tent was being erected away from everything else, isolated and secluded. It filled Hashem with a deep sense of foreboding.

CHAPTER 3

Tehran – Iran

Ming Fang woke suddenly to an incessant buzzing next to his head. He rolled towards the irritating noise, swatting at his bedside table with his hand to silence the racket, his mind still cloudy from the aftereffects of sleep and his late-night activities. When it didn't stop, it took him a couple of seconds to realise that the noise was his mobile phone. As he opened his eyes, the light from the window in his room beamed painfully into his eyes. Ming groaned. He could already tell that today was going to be a long day. The room seemed to sway and roll as he tried to right himself. This hangover was going to be difficult.

Finally grasping his buzzing phone, he pulled himself into a sitting position, swinging his legs over the side of bed. It was no small effort. His head started to throb, and his eyes hurt from the sunlight. His stomach gurgled unhappily, rebelling against it contents. He looked down at the device in his hand, recognising the number as one of the official lines from the embassy down the road from his apartment. He grimaced, wondering if any of his antics last night had been seen and reported to the ever-watchful officers at the embassy. Not that he could do much about that now. He answered cautiously, putting effort into his tone to sound awake and alert, the opposite of how he actually felt, a sick, uncomfortable feeling rising in his throat.

'Yes?'

An overly formal voice replied. He didn't recognise it but suspected it was one of the officers, probably some admin officer. 'Report immediately to the office; your presence is required now.'

While not uncommon to be summoned at short notice, it was rare that he would be called in without some idea of what the meeting would be for, and to be called in at such short notice … Checking the time, he realised it was still early morning – no wonder he still felt a little drunk. Whatever was going on, it must be important.

He let a short silence hang on the phone call as he thought it through, the gears in his brain turning slowly. 'I'll be there in thirty minutes.'

The respondent replied robotically, 'Your presence is required as soon as possible,' and hung up.

Ming felt uncomfortable, and not just from his hangover. Being summoned early in the morning out of the blue normally meant something bad had happened. A small part of his mind wondered again if he'd been caught out finally. Pulling himself to his feet, he swayed uncertainly, his body's balance confused by all the alcohol he'd put in his system. Dropping his phone on the bed, he threw out one of his arms to balance himself on the wall. He could feel his stomach churn and a slight sweetness spread throughout his mouth. Experience had taught Ming what to expect next. Half stumbling and half running, he darted to the bathroom adjoining his bedroom, falling to his knees before the shiny white porcelain of the toilet, and heaved. Yeah, it was a rough start.

A shower, a couple of massive glasses of cold water, some aspirin and an energy bar started to breathe some life back into him. His mind felt less cloudy, and he could feel his focus returning, his mind returning to the phone call. He donned a more businesslike attire, dressing in a simple yet presentable black suit. Under the jacket, he wore a simple holster against the small of his back, holding a loaded QSZ-11 pistol from his bedside. When tucked into the belt of his pants and covered by his jacket, it would be well hidden from the casual observer. With one final glance in the mirror, he exited his apartment.

The chaotic streets of Tehran felt familiar to him after the last few months. Yet he still hadn't adjusted to the constant, beating heat, only made more uncomfortable by his hangover. The constant din of the city – honking horns from impatient drivers, people talking on phones and street vendors selling their wares – seemed to rattle through his brain in one painful arc. Despite it all, he loved it. The smells, the heat, the chaos. It gave him a sense of danger and adventure, and it scratched an itch that he'd never been able to get rid of. From a young age, he'd realised he wasn't built for an office job and longed for a sensation, a thrill – for danger. Much like a drug addiction, Ming had increasingly sought more dangerous and exciting ways to challenge himself, but with each new level of danger, he found himself becoming less excited and increasingly bored by things that had once made his heart beat in fear.

Ming had been identified as a student of heightened intelligence and physical skill at a young age. Surveillance of the many thousands of schools across China was commonplace, with officials searching for talented individuals. By the time Ming had graduated, he'd been offered a role in China's elite Ministry of State Security. He'd leapt at the opportunity, never looking back.

It had been clear through his early training that he had the drive, determination and charisma ideally suited to intelligence. People liked him, and his disarming personality made getting information surprisingly easily. The only concern of his trainers was his apparent disinterest in ideological studies, but coming in top of his class, it soon became a simple footnote in his file: Lacks ideological conviction.

Hong Kong had been his first assignment, where the growing independence protest movement led by students had threatened to become a full-blown revolt. Tasked with infiltrating the various protest groups and identifying the central leaders, Ming had been amazed to see the near-fearless nature of the protestors who, despite the odds, would regularly face off against tear gas and rubber bullets. He'd quickly found himself on the front lines of the various protest skirmishes, revelling in the excitement of the confrontation with police, all the while feeding vital information back to his handlers.

Looking back on his fond memories of his early days in Hong Kong, he felt somewhat despondent. In the couple of years that had passed since then, he had been deployed around the world, from the South Pacific to Europe and now the Middle East. His burning desire to feel the rush of adrenaline was increasingly hard to satisfy, and he had gone to increasing lengths to get his next buzz. Ming had learnt to hide his desires from his handlers and superiors in Beijing, who he feared would remove him from field duty if they ever discovered the risks he was taking, not in the name of the MSS or CCP but for his own desires.

Moving through the street, he cut an unexceptional figure through the crowd, with average height and a slim build. His Asian features were no longer uncommon in this part of the city. The world had grown smaller, and numerous trade links, wars and mass movements of people had made people of Asian heritage a regular sight in Tehran. It worked to his advantage, allowing him to move unnoticed amongst crowds, receiving only casual glances here and there. Soon forgotten.

As he moved, he was constantly scanning, looking for anything out of the ordinary. Something out of place, someone looking at him with too much interest or perhaps someone like himself, trying to hide their true purpose. It was practically second nature to him, something he never really turned off or was even aware of. Every reflective surface was a means to get another angle. Subtle pauses to check his phone or his watch or tie his shoe, taking quick, casual glances at his surroundings. Walking through the bustling streets, rubbing shoulders with random people, he felt at ease; this was his world, whether those around him knew it or not.

As he rounded the last corner, Ming could see the Chinese Embassy dominating its surrounds. Located in the diplomatic sector of Tehran on Movahed Danesh Street, the sprawling complex was hard to miss. The size of the building matched China's growing influence and ambition in the oil-rich region.

Avoiding the main entrance, Ming slipped up a side street, where there were fewer eyes and cameras. Patterns were always a problem in his line of work, and avoiding them took a concerted effort. Technically, he was employed at the embassy on official business as an IT specialist. It was a useful cover for his actual job. His comings and goings from the embassy wouldn't raise any eyebrows.

He swiped a key card against a small panel and pulled open a nondescript door attached to the embassy's outer wall, entering a small closed-off room, of sorts. A single reinforced glass booth stood inside, with an unsmiling, rigid guard manning the computers, a rifle visible on the wall behind him. The guard was the gatekeeper of the embassy; anyone who wanted in through this entrance had to get past him first. Ming had tried numerous times to get the stoic guard to smile and crack his hard exterior. Nothing had worked. He wondered what the man was like outside of a work setting, but the thought was fleeting.

He held up his pass identifying him as a staff member and waited for the guard to open the solid metal door separating him from the interior courtyard of the embassy. Instead of opening the door, the guard picked up the phone and dialled an unknown number. Ming couldn't hear what he was saying but assumed it was the guard informing someone of Ming's arrival. His interest spiked further. Well, guess it's urgent after all, he thought.

The morning hangover had finally started to fade into the background, but he knew he'd need food and coffee to keep him going. As he stood silently waiting for the guard, he tapped his sidearm, reassuring himself that it was there. A small but loud thought penetrated his head again: What if they know what I've been doing? But it was impossible – he was always careful. Ming had always enjoyed some of the finer things in life, and it had become apparent to him early in his career that his meagre salary wouldn't cut it. In light of his risk-taking approach to life and need to get information for his superiors, Ming had quickly established relationships of benefit with a number of underworld figures. His bosses didn't ask, and he didn't tell. But his desire for more extreme experiences had increasingly taken him to deeper, darker parts of the criminal underworld. If his actions were ever found out, he wasn't sure what would happen, but it probably wouldn't include his ongoing freedom.

The guard put down the phone after a short conversation. Ming watched him as he moved to click the button to open the inner door. He figured if the guard moved towards the other button, the one he'd identified as locking the external door, he would have enough time to jam it open and make his escape. For now, though, everything was in order.

The door slid open silently, the guard returning to his best impression of an emotionless statue. Stepping across the threshold, Ming left behind the guard and his own lingering thoughts, his curiosity getting the better of him and driving him onward. Inside the compound was one large multi-storey building looming across a litter of smaller ones. Compared to the brown and dusty streets of much of Tehran, the Chinese Embassy was a mixture of pleasant greenery and manicured walkways, the noise of the city slightly muffled behind concrete walls.

He hadn't taken more than a few steps into the open compound before a door flew open in front of him. Ming didn't flinch; he'd been expecting it. A slight but poised woman in a black suit strode out with a hard stare on her face. 'Officer Fang! You were expected ten minutes ago!'

Like all intelligence officers around the world, Ming had a case officer, or as he thought of it, a babysitter. Liu Tien was a fierce and unbending babysitter. If she wasn't checking up on him, she was requesting written reports or additional information on anything he provided. It felt like a very abusive relationship to Ming. But he knew there was no point fighting her; in many ways, she controlled his future. He gave her a broad smile, followed by a relaxed "sorry" expression and a brief shrug of his shoulders.

'Apologies, boss. The traffic was worse than expected.' She knew he lived within walking distance, but she wouldn't question him, at least not in public anyway. He'd worked long and hard to charm her, slowly gaining some freedoms and liberties other officers wouldn't receive.

She ignored his explanation, turning around and walking back through the door she had just come through. 'Follow me,' she called over her shoulder. Ming followed, more curious by the second.

Liu led Ming through the surprisingly spartan interior, taking him into the secure bowels of the building. Behind numerous secure doors was a small conference room with a large monitor mounted on the wall. Another officer sat in the room – one of the team's intelligence analysts, if Ming remembered correctly. A large satellite image was on the screen, seemingly controlled by the computer setup in front of the analyst. Ming couldn't see anything of interest, just rolling sand dunes. But then again, from his experience, the most uninteresting location could often hide the most nefarious operations. His curiosity grew.

He didn't have to wait long. Liu gave the analyst a curt nod, and the briefing started. 'At 0600 hours this morning, an unidentified American weapons system crashed into the Kuh-e-Birk Protected Area in the Iranian desert. Our satellites have been tracking a small flotilla of American and Australian ships south of Indonesia and spotted the launch.'

Ming started making mental notes, prepping questions for the end of the briefing.

'Based off its flight speed and the range of the missile, it is likely a new type of hypersonic cruise missile. Luckily, one of our naval vessels patrolling nearby in the Gulf of Oman was able to track the missile for a number of minutes before it lost contact. It appears that this missile is faster, smarter and has a longer range than anything we have seen before. It is possible that it is even beyond the capabilities of any missile that we possess.' A pointed statement from the analyst. This weapon could be both a threat and an opportunity.

Speed, range, capabilities – the questions built up in Ming's mind.

'It appears to have suffered some form of failure mid-flight. We suspect the plan was to terminate the flight somewhere south of Iran, as there is an American ship in the area that could easily conduct recovery. However, once the failure occurred, it appears the missile continued to glide.'

Ming turned his attention back to the monitor, taking renewed interest in the image. The analyst manipulated the image, zooming in. A small, silver spear-like object appeared against the brown sand.

'Shortly after entering Iranian airspace, the object continued to descend and slow before coming to a rest, most fortunately, I might add, in an area of soft sand dunes, likely reducing damage to the missile.'

Ming could only guess how quickly and easily a piece of experimental tech would shatter into a thousand pieces if it hit anything hard. They were very fortunate indeed.

'The Iranian military mobilised no more than thirty minutes later, deploying a strike force to secure the site. A larger military convoy has just departed to further reinforce the site and, potentially, move the object.' Another satellite image flashed on the screen, showing a line of twenty or so vehicles moving along a highway.

Ming checked his watch. It was now close to 0900 hours local time; the Iranians had moved fast.

'At this stage, we have not identified any reaction from American forces, and we believe they may be unaware of the missile's suspected survival.'

Ming had to ask, 'How can we be sure?'

'There is a E-3 Sentry aircraft currently patrolling out of Bahrain; however, it is continuing on a known flight path and has not deviated from its course. Additionally, other vessels or facilities in the region show no signs of action or enhanced readiness.'

He still wasn't satisfied. 'Satellites?'

The analyst shook his head, 'No movements or repositioning of space-born assets, and no drones have been identified in the area either,' he said, beating Ming to his next question.

Out of questions, Ming let the analyst continue, 'Our biggest question and concern is the state of the missile. There is likely damage we cannot see from the above shots – hopefully, the Iranians won't try and disturb it.'

The image changed to show the same place as before but altered, little dots moving around, netting and tents being assembled.

Liu stepped in now. 'If this missile is as cutting-edge as Beijing thinks it is, it will be of significant value to China. Beijing has ordered us to assess the missile and determine its current state.'

He could already foresee a few problems with just appearing at an Iranian military operation site. 'Not sure the Iranians will appreciate my presence,' he said questioningly.

'It's been taken care of. A representation has been made through official channels at the highest levels, and we have been permitted to send a representative … for a fee.'

Ming knew that meant someone had been bribed. Not an uncommon approach. China was seen as having a blank chequebook by many opportunistic nations and officials across the world. A small "fee" or "administration cost" was often applied to grease the wheels of bureaucracy, and China, for its part, was more than happy to deploy its wealth for its own means. Money, and people's greed for it, opened many doors for Ming, regardless of how wealthy or powerful many of those doors already were.

The briefing continued for a while longer, Ming asking questions and getting answers from either the analyst or Liu. By the end of it, he was armed with enough knowledge of the operation, and enough technical aspects to understand hypersonic missiles.

Liu summed up Ming's mission, 'Get to the site, assess the object and report. If it's worth recovering, lay the groundwork. We need to get there as quickly as possible. The Iranians will likely want to move the object soon. We want to make our decision before that happens.'

As he walked out of the embassy, Ming had largely forgotten about the lingering effects of his hangover, turning his mind to his new mission. A new type of ravenous hunger was building within him. The desire for adventure and excitement. A funny world he lived in. He chuckled to himself. But it was his world, and he loved it.

HQJOC – Australia

Ata threw her hands up in disgust, 'That's it, I'm calling it!'

Danny swivelled around in his chair, looking towards his other team members and noting that the clock on the wall read a quarter to seven.

'Yep, I'm out,' Sidney chimed in. 'Pub?'

'Now, that's a great idea,' Jesse said.

The team was at its wits end for the day, and if Danny was being honest, he was too. The constant searching without result was taking its toll, but something in him wouldn't let go, not yet. 'C'mon, guys, it's got to be out there somewhere,' he offered weakly.

'Nope. Sorry, Danny. We're not getting anywhere here; it's beer o'clock, and you're coming as well,' Ata said firmly.

He felt pained, 'I can't, Ata. It's out there somewhere. I've got a heap of leads to go over.'

'Danny, look, we all want to find it as much as you, but we've been at it for over twelve hours now, and we are no closer now than we were this morning. Mike has already buggered off, and you and I both know he'll be breathing down our necks tomorrow no matter what. Let's get out of here, have a beer. We're not going to find it tonight.'

Danny groaned, leaning back into his chair. 'Alright, fine.' A small sense of defeat washed over him, Ata's words breaking his determination to keep going. He seemed immediately aware of how tired and hungry he was.

Ata smiled, 'Good, and I've already invited Lee, so now you really don't have a choice.'

'What? When did you do that?' he stammered.

'Wouldn't you like to know,' she said with a grin, picking up her bag.

'Man, this feels like abuse,' Danny mumbled.

The rest of the team stood expectantly, waiting for him now. Sidney and Jesse each gave him a grin.

Danny looked back at them, holding his hands up in mock surrender, 'Alright, alright! Let me finish this up and I'll join you guys,' he said, jerking his thumb at his computer.

Ata raised her eyebrow, 'If we don't hear from you in thirty minutes, Danny, we're sending a rescue team.'

'I'm coming, I promise!'

They seemed satisfied and departed as a group, leaving him behind.

Danny turned back to his computer, where another random readout of flight data from the failed test flight sat on the screen. He'd been searching for something, anything that seemed out of place. But, other than a momentary spike in temperature before it lost all signal, everything else appeared normal. He kept reading, getting sucked back into his work. A sense of personal responsibility for the project stuck with him, and its failure irked him. Thirty minutes passed without Danny realising.

It wasn't until an email popped into his inbox that he realised the time. The subject line read *Call me! URGENT!* The email address was very familiar.

He got up and quickly walked out of the secure zone to retrieve his phone. It was already ringing. He quickly answered, feeling worried that something was wrong.

'Hey, what's up? Is everything okay?' he asked urgently.

The female voice responded brightly, 'There you are! I've been told by a little bird named Ata that you're in desperate need of rescue.'

He laughed, the sudden release of concern replaced with a jolt of happiness. 'Yeah, you could say that – it's been a day!'

'Well look, I'm heading down to meet Ata and everyone at the pub for a drink, and I think it would be wise for you to join me – and hell, I'll even buy you a drink. How's that sound?' Her voice sounded light and humorous.

A small part of him rebelled and screamed that he had to stay and solve the mystery of the missing missile, but that part was washed away by a large wave of relief. 'You know, I think that's a fucking great idea. I'll pack up now and meet you there. And hey, love you loads.'

Leah Rhodes, or simply Lee to anyone who knew her, laughed, 'Alright mister, if I don't hear from you in thirty, I'm sending in a rescue force to drag you outta there. Love you more!'

She hung up before Danny could protest that his love was stronger, a game the two shared.

His tardiness to meet his colleagues hadn't gone unnoticed, and a barrage of text messages and missed calls waited for him. Flicking through the messages, he gave a small smile, seeing the threats and cajoling of his friends.

They were a good bunch, a good team.

Sighing contentedly, he turned around and re-entered the secure room, locking his phone away again. He walked past all the desks and monitors until he reached his own, then bent down to pick up his backpack. Pausing, he looked across his desk with slight disgust. Post-it notes, empty coffee cups and random leftovers littered his workspace. He hadn't realised how focused he'd been, letting the junk build up around him. He quickly dumped everything in the trash and was about to leave when one of the night-shift analysts decided to strike up a conversation.

'Heading off, Danny?' the man asked.

'Yeah, doesn't look like this problem will get solved any quicker by hanging around.' There was a slight twinge of regret in his voice.

The analyst didn't directly respond to Danny, clearly running on a preconceived thought. 'One thing I don't get, I understand the plan was to recover this thing, but surely it's a bit dangerous, testing so close to a place like Iran?'

Danny responded politely, wanting to leave, 'Well, it wasn't meant to be anywhere near Iran; that all got changed on us at the last minute. It should have been relatively simple. Anyway, I'm …'

The man spoke over Danny, 'Yeah, okay, but like, how far can these things fly anyway? Like, what if it kept flying into Iran?'

'I mean, this can fly a good distance. It's a ballistic missile, after all.' He paused, thinking, a light bulb flicking on in his brain. They'd spent most of the day working under the assumption that the missile had crashed or failed near the point where it lost signal. But what if it hadn't? Without input from the motherboard or a controlling warship, would it have kept flying? He didn't know the answer. His polite annoyance was sidelined.

'*Shit* … Maybe …' Danny muttered to himself. He quickly sat back down and picked up his desk phone, ignoring the analyst.

'What?' the confused-looking analyst asked.

Kingston – Canberra – Australia

Fighting her way through the crowded bar with her beer, Ata managed to return to her colleagues and had just placed the cold glass to her lips with anticipation when her phone announced itself with a loud *buzzztttt*.

She lowered the glass regretfully. Danny's name flashed on her screen.

'You'd better be on your way, Danny,' she muttered before she answered the phone. 'Where are you?' she demanded loudly, the rest of the team cheering loudly for Danny to hear.

'I'm coming, I swear! But one thing first.'

So, he hadn't left yet. 'Danny, I've called in the big guns. Lee will find you; she has collected a specific set of skills, honed over many years …'

'I'm coming, I'm coming!' he protested again. 'But one last thing I've got to ask, I swear.'

Ata sighed, 'Alright, what is it?'

She could almost hear his silent cheer. He spoke quickly, 'Did we do any searches beyond the expected crash site? Like, over land, into the Middle East, maybe?'

Ata had to be careful speaking over an unprotected line. She decided to step outside to hear him better and get away from any prying ears.

The warm afternoon air was refreshing compared to the packed bar. 'Not really. I mean, we obviously had more extreme scenarios, but we can't cover everything, geospatially speaking – gotta pick our collection zones.'

'Right, so hear me out here. What if it kept flying? Not under power – obviously that didn't happen, otherwise we would have been able to track it. But what if it glided from the moment we lost its signal. No traumatic break-up or explosion. I don't think we have any recent modelling on its glide ability; it was always seen as a backup capability to scramjet after all.'

'Danny, careful. Unprotected line, remember,' she cautioned.

'Right … sorry. But what do you think?' he insisted.

She groaned, knowing full well he was suggesting they more or less expand the search. Meaning more trawling through lines of data and imagery. 'Look, Danny, I get it. I want to find this thing as well. But we can't do anything about it now. Let's have another look tomorrow. There will be more information then anyway. There should be some additional passes and a patrol or two that should get us more data. Danny, come get a beer.'

She could hear him deflate a little, 'Yeah, alright, I'm coming. Sorry, Ata. It just struck me we could have been looking in the wrong spot.'

In a more conciliatory tone, she said, 'Hey, it's a good idea. We'll sort it out tomorrow. But right now, its beer o'clock.'

'So, you're buying?' he replied quickly.

'Ha, alright fine, first drink's on me. But you have to get here soon, otherwise Leah's gonna dump your ass.'

'Coooooommmminnnnnngggggg,' he drew out before hanging up.

Ata chuckled, returning to the bar. Her cold beer was still there, undrunk. 'HE'S COMING!' she announced, lifting the glass. The group cheered back.

CHAPTER 4

Iranian Airspace

Everything had moved quickly after the briefing. Ming rushed back to his apartment, throwing a few necessities like extra clothing into a tan-coloured backpack. He'd donned some khaki outdoor pants and a professional-looking white business shirt. As he appreciated himself in the mirror, he decided he looked quite the adventurer. He shot off a few key messages to associates letting them know he was leaving town. As he left, he was careful to set up several nearly indistinguishable markers around the apartment. If anyone tried to get in while he was away, he'd know. Backpack over his shoulder, pistol tucked away safely, he ducked down the stairs and into a waiting car. From there, it was a straight shot to Mehrabad Air Base in Tehran, where an Italian-made Agusta-Bell 212 helicopter was waiting.

That had been an hour ago. It was now reaching late morning, and Ming's ears popped suddenly as the helicopter rose over the jutting mountains below. Beneath the oversized headphones he wore, the thump of the rotor blades was muffled but still loud enough to create a constant, almost soothing rhythm. Peering out the plexiglass window, he watched as the vast, arid and mountainous terrain of Iran clipped by below. Bleached rock and sand coupled with craggy valleys dotted the terrain below, hostile and deadly. He didn't relish spending any more time here than necessary. The memory of a recent desert survival course he had attended still lingered in his brain. The desperate thirst for water, mixed with the relentless heat from the sun, with no shade or protection; it had left a lasting impact. He preferred to stick to cities. The bustle and energy of millions of people packed together in a small space was hard to beat. Ming could simply disappear if he wanted to, lose himself in the noise and crowd of people. Plus, the various luxuries one could find in the darkest corners of any metropolis were always a delightful pursuit.

He wasn't the sole occupant of the helicopter. A number of other people were squashed into the small cabin. Ming had given them a curious assessment when he boarded, concluding that they were a mixture of officials or technical experts. They didn't challenge his spot on the flight, and he didn't bother them.

Ignoring the other passengers, Ming pulled a small, rugged laptop from his bag. Angling his computer away from the person sitting next to him, he brought up imagery of the crash site and some analysis pulled together by an analyst in Beijing. Flipping through the slides, Ming paused on the satellite imagery from the crash site. It was the same image he'd seen in the brief, but here he could take his time to examine it. The site appeared to be a hive of activity, with numerous military vehicles surrounding the site. None of the images showed the missile itself, as the Iranians had thrown camouflage netting across it the moment they arrived at the site. Ming wasn't sure what awaited him, but he wished he knew more about the missile or prototype or whatever it was. No-one seemed to know exactly what it was; clearly this was something new.

Assuming the object was intact and the Iranians hadn't

damaged it further, he still had to get photos of it and get them back to the experts in Beijing. Only then could they assess its value and decide whether it was worth recovering. There was no point worrying about the politics of convincing the Iranians to give it up; he'd have a part to play, he was sure, but ultimately, officers at the embassy in Tehran and back in Beijing would handle that. His job, his primary focus, was to get eyes on the missile and get intelligence back to the expert who would assess its worth. As he sat in the helicopter, Ming felt more like a delivery boy than a trained and deadly intelligence officer.

He pulled up a map of the country, looking at all the ports, airports and roads. Ming was already very familiar with the infrastructure of the country he'd been assigned to, but he liked concocting plans, even if they were never used. What would be the best way to get the missile out of Iran? And keep the Americans in the dark? He didn't have an immediate answer, but there were a lot of options.

The only looming question was whether the Americans knew where their missile had fallen. The analyst back in Tehran had seemed relatively confident they didn't know. But Ming doubted that would last. In his mind, it was safer to assume the Americans would figure out the final resting place of their precious missile soon enough, if they hadn't already. Their satellites missed very little. The answer was simple enough: the missile would have to be moved, and soon. But how to keep the Americans unaware of China's involvement? An idea started to form in Ming's mind as he looked at the map on his computer, and he grinned. Yes, *that could work*, he thought.

He didn't realise it yet, but powerful decision-making gears were already turning in Beijing. His part to play in the whole affair had only just begun.

KH-11 – Low Earth Orbit

High above earth's surface, USA-186, a KH-11

"Kennen" variant satellite, was travelling at a blistering speed, gliding peacefully through its low earth orbit. Launched by the National Reconnaissance Office in 2005, the satellite was part of a highly advanced Keyhole series of satellites operated by the American Government. With highly sophisticated cameras, the Kennen series satellite took extremely detailed images wherever it was directed.

Set on a pre-programmed trajectory, it began its orbit across Iran. The earth's glistening blue surfaces were soon replaced by the darker reds and browns of the desert. USA-186 continued peacefully across Iran, paying no mind to the events unfurling below. Its cameras went about their job dutifully, collecting images of the harsh desert, as they had done every minute of every day since launch.

By sheer luck, and unbeknown to the people below, USA-186 glided peacefully across Kuh-e-Birk, snapping thousands of images as it went. Each image was catalogued and timestamped, with precise coordinates attached. The images were beamed back to earth, where they sat inside massive server racks inside the National Geospatial Intelligence Agency, or NGA. Most of the image frames would never be viewed by a human eye; they'd sit unnoticed, ignored. But they wouldn't be useless. The NGA servers would hold the images indefinitely, making them available to analysts across the American intelligence community and beyond. They'd eventually be uploaded into a geospatial software tool called ARCGIS, where the imagery would form a new, updated map, not unlike the constantly updating Google Maps or Google Earth imagery. For now though, the Kuh-e-Birk images sat waiting.

One day, USA-186 would burn up on re-entry, meeting a fiery and perhaps fitting end, its work completed without complaint or fault. It would remain unknown to the vast majority of humans below. But its contributions to the intelligence world would be almost incalculable.

AWACS – Strait of Hormuz – Hours Earlier

The Boeing E-3 Sentry departed from Al Dhafra Air Base in The United Arab Emirates. Soaring into the crystal-clear sky, the crew settled in for a routine patrol. The large aircraft was essentially a retrofitted commercial plane, but with advanced surveillance equipment. A large circular "rotodome" radar dominated the aircraft, sitting between the wings on the top of the grey superstructure. Inside, the passenger seats had been replaced with rows of computers and other sensitive instruments, known as an Airborne Warning and Control System or AWACS for short. The E-3, capable of detecting and identifying both airborne and ground targets for hundreds of kilometres, excelled at collecting information. Its primary purpose, however, was to act as a mobile command centre, using its superior battlefield vision to direct squadrons during battle and identify incoming threats. It was both the eyes and brains of the US Air Force, capable of flying more than 7000 kilometres, or up to eight hours, without refuelling. Patrols on E-3s could be long, drawn-out affairs.

For the crew of the E-3, this was just another patrol. They hadn't been informed of the missile test, nor had they been tasked with monitoring the progress of the test. Had they been, they would have tracked it with ease, giving live updates on its progress, even after it had failed. Instead, they went about their tasks, blissfully unaware of the events unfolding around them. The flight path took them in a broad, sweeping line up the Persian Gulf before hugging the Iranian border and swooping back along the Gulf of Oman. The total flight time would be well over six hours – longer if they spotted anything of interest.

Senior Airman Michael Kim was settled comfortably in his chair, the gentle vibration and rumble from the plane engines mixing with the quiet hum of the computers surrounding him. As an airborne intelligence operator, the enormous power of the E-3 was at his fingertips. He'd taken the role looking for some excitement, but now, a couple of months into his first overseas deployment, the reality of the job was hitting home. The long hours spent staring at a computer screen felt annoyingly similar to a regular desk job, except of course, he was crammed into a large plane flying through the sky. In his mind, the only major difference between this job and flying commercial was the lack of cute stewards with food and drinks. He sighed at his monitor. At least the pay was good.

'What are your odds today, man?' asked another operator sitting opposite Kim.

Kim stretched. 'I reckon we're flying this one alone today. Just the usual crap: you know, "Death to America" and all that,' he replied, raising his hands into the air and making quotation marks with his fingers.

They had a running bet for each patrol for how the Iranians would react to their presence. It was a bit of a 50/50 chance whether the Iranians would simply hurl abuse at them over the radio, or, if they were feeling a bit frisky, send up some fighters to keep an eye on them, potentially even threaten to shoot them down. So far, Kim was ahead of everyone else in the crew, having successfully picked the last three responses correctly, and was starting to get a reputation.

'Awww, man,' the operator groaned.

Kim grinned, 'Picked the other one, huh?'

A sudden red blip caught the corner of Kim's eye. A small cluster of them had appeared in the top right of his screen. Manipulating the display through his console, he examined the electronic signature of the aircraft. Their suspected make, model, flying speed and height had been picked up in a matter of microseconds and were all visible to Kim, live.

'Looks like we have something. Geez, these guys are really hugging the ground.'

The other operator was immediately curious, 'Whatcha got?'

'Check this. Got at least three helos – looks like two old

Cobra gunships and a Chinook. They're flying low and hauling ass.'

'Did they just come into range?'

'Looks like. My guess is they've come from Mehrabad, based off their trajectory. Straight as an arrow!'

'We'd better get the LT over here,' the operator said.

Kim looked up and caught the eye of his immediate superior, a second lieutenant. The man quickly made his way over.

'What have we got?'

Kim pointed to his monitor. 'Looks like three Iranian helos making a beeline through the Iranian desert. They're flying low and fast.'

The second lieutenant paused for a moment, taking in the information. 'Alright. Any indication where they're headed?'

Kim shook his head, 'Not yet, we've only been tracking a couple of minutes, but based off their current flight path, they'll be out in the middle of nowhere. If they change course, they could head to one of the central or south cities or airbases, but with the data I've got right now, I'm not sure where they are going, sir.'

'Training op, maybe?' the other operator standing at Kim's shoulder suggested.

'Maybe,' the lieutenant said. 'Keep an eye on them. This is out of the ordinary enough that someone back in Washington will be interested. Anything else going on?'

Kim took a quick look across his other data feeds. 'Heightened chatter on Iranian military comms, but nothing too extreme.'

'Alright, keep on it,' the lieutenant ordered. 'I'll get everyone on this.'

Once he was out of earshot, the other operator lamented, 'We'll be up here for hours now.'

Kim grinned. 'Hey, look on the bright side: the Iranians might decide we are snooping too closely and try to get rid of us. You could finally win.'

The operator didn't seem convinced, 'Uh-huh.'

For the rest of the patrol, Kim watched as an increasing number of aircraft and vehicles converged on a random point in the desert. By the end of the flight, he'd searched the location and everything close by. But, as the wheels of the E-3 touched down, he felt no closer to understanding what had happened. If the team had been forewarned of the test flight, or even its failure, the surge in activity might have made more sense. For now, it remained nothing more than a noted anomaly, written into a post-operational brief.

CHAPTER 5

HQJOC – Australia

Danny yawned as he walked towards his computer, coffee in hand. He felt relaxed and ready for the day ahead. It was day two for the team. Their failure to locate the missile still weighed on Danny, but it only fuelled his drive to find an answer.

Mike popped his head around his office door, apparently having seen Danny walk by. 'Better have more to show today than yesterday, Danny. I want results!'

'Sure thing, Mike,' Danny replied, a hint of annoyance in his voice. Mike didn't even seem to hear, as the phone in his office rang suddenly. He darted back behind his door, his movements more frenetic than normal.

Mike's general attitude constantly irked Danny, but he knew better than to engage. He'd had more than a few conversations with Leah, discussing Mike and his various ticks. She always seemed to be able to break down what was happening, analyse the psychology of Mike's actions. She'd become the dependable rock in his life after only a few short months, and he couldn't picture a future without her now.

Putting down his bag, he realised he was the first one in

the office for a change. The shift from the night before was just clocking off. One of the Australian analysts called out to him, 'Hey Danny, spotted a report that might be of interest. Sent it across to your inbox. Let me know what you think, mate. Looks like some kind of strange activity in Iran.'

That piqued Danny's interest. He couldn't remember the name of the analyst – Ben something. 'Thanks, I'll have a look,' he mumbled over his computer screen. As he double-clicked on the email, his attention was immediately spiked.

One by one, the different members of the team trickled in, and Danny started briefing them on the plan. There was a new pile of reporting that they had to reach, satellites that had to be tasked and data to go over. It would be another busy day, but the team was highly capable and worked well together.

He skimmed the report before quickly rereading it in detail. He wasn't immediately sure what he was reading; it didn't mention the missile, the test flight or anything related, but as he read, the smallest glimmer of an idea began to form, fortifying itself in his brain. Preferring to have a paper copy, he quickly hit print but kept reading at his computer.

USCENTCOM//E3 Sentry//Callsign: Sentinel//Priority Traffic//0900HRS UTC//02JUL25
START:
Sentinel Flight conducted scheduled surveillance patrol across Arabian Sea AO BRAVO. Flight observed unusual Iranian military flight moving to estimated coordinates (29.857015, 58.206694). Additional Iranian military ground units subsequently observed arriving at the location by 1100HRS UTC. Location previously unrecorded as site of interest or military exercise. It remains UNKNOWN why Iranian military units moved to this location in force.
END.

The rest of the report consisted of data readouts, other

observations made by the E-3 on its patrol and radar information, all of which would be valuable in time, but for now, the gears turning in Danny's head focused on the summary. The first thing that struck him was the flight time of the E-3 sentry: too late to catch the missile flight, roughly an hour or so after it disappeared. *Another fuck up*, he thought. Changing the test last minute had caused no end of issues, and this was just one more in a long list. Either way, it didn't matter now. He tried to suppress his annoyance; it would only cloud his ability to analyse the information.

The E-3 sentry crew had certainly thought the activity was strange in itself, numerous Iranian military units converging on a random spot in the desert. It was possibly an exercise, but the movement of considerable equipment and troops to a random spot early in the morning without prior warning was strange. A little voice at the back of his brain whispered, 'Could it be the missile?' His first instinct was to deny the thought, but it stuck. He did some quick calculations. Could the missile fly that far? Looking at the scrawled calculations, he decided it could, but he would have to test them to be sure.

Next was a quick Google search of the coordinates. 'Kuh-e-Birk Protected Area,' he mouthed wordlessly. It seemed to be some kind of Iranian National Park, although with far more sand than his idea of what a national park should hold. And it was remote. A small village named Keshit was the only real human settlement. There certainly weren't any military facilities, except maybe an ancient fort, although he doubted it counted as "military". A quick search showed no other instances of previous interest in the area. He leant back in his chair, his index finger tapping his upper lip. They needed more. It was something, but it was wildly further away than he'd expected.

Danny was so engrossed that he didn't even realise the team had come back. 'Whatcha got there, Danny?' Ata asked, peering at his monitor. He startled, jumping slightly in his chair.

Ata laughed, 'Woah there, didn't realise you were in the zone! Here, take this.' She offered Danny a large coffee. He greedily accepted it, removing the lid and smelling the rich contents inside. A long black, just how he liked it: one sugar and no milk or cream.

After a moment, he recovered. 'Thanks. Hey, check this out.' He pointed at his monitor, taking a sip of the coffee. The yellow and red Iranian desert was still there.

Jesse and Sidney both joined them, curious at what Danny had found. 'Doesn't look like much of a holiday spot, Danny – where is it?' Sidney asked.

'This is the Kuh-e-Birk Protected Area inside the Islamic Republic of Iran. It's some kind of national park or nature reserve. But yesterday, an E-3 sentry spotted a sudden and unusual build of Iranian military forces at this location. It's never come up previously as a military site or anything like that. I've emailed everyone. Go have a read for yourself, but I think it might be something.'

Ata was the first to catch on to Danny's somewhat cryptic explanation. 'You think the missile landed there, don't you?'

Danny grinned, appreciating how quickly Ata had figured it out. 'I ran the numbers, and it should be possible for the missile to glide that far. We're missing some telemetry data, but assuming it didn't suffer any major damage, it could have made it. Plus, the activity was so out of place that the E-3 crew felt the need to report it. It's just a shame they weren't airborne when the test flight happened; we could have avoided all this pain trying to find the damn thing!'

Ata had a thoughtful look on her face, while the other two had returned to their own desks to check the report themselves.

'Where did you get this, Danny?' Ata asked after she'd had a read of her own.

Danny shrugged, 'One of the shift analysts spotted it last

night and sent it over. I only just got to it.'

'It could be something, Danny,' Sidney mused, 'but it's a bit thin on its own. We'd need to get more from the area to confirm anything.'

Danny nodded again, 'You're not wrong, although this is more than we had yesterday. With this, we can target our searches and at least figure out if the missile landed there – worst-case scenario, we at least confirm it didn't make it.'

Jesse jumped in next. 'The bigger problem here is that if what you're saying is correct, it means the Iranians have the missile.'

They were all quiet again, the implication sinking in.

Ata broke the silence, 'Alright, let's not get ahead of ourselves. We don't know enough yet. Let's say Danny's theory is right. We still have to prove it. But this won't be enough to convince anyone.' She pointed to the printed report in Sidney's hands. 'Especially now that we cannot access it. We're going to have to engineer the information. Second-source it.' She continued, 'So, let's check the satellite coverage for the area – Sidney, that's you and me. Jesse, you got SIGINT?'

'You bet,' he answered.

'I'll pull everything together for the briefing,' Danny added. He and Ata were technically the same level of seniority, but the team had found itself a good groove; if one of them had a good idea, they'd all listen. Danny didn't mind at all that Ata had taken the lead. There wasn't anything to argue against. It was a solid plan and the same one he would have suggested. He just felt happy he'd managed to convince them this was worthwhile. Maybe it was simply the fact that this was a better lead than anything else they'd seen over the last day and a half.

'Let's get to it,' Danny said, a deep sense of relief washing over him. He finally felt they had something worthwhile to chase.

***

It was mid-afternoon before they'd managed to pull everything together to brief Mike. Ata had been particularly excited when they'd finally got the most recent satellite shots, only a day old. The little isolated camp in the desert was impossible to deny.

'Weird design,' Sidney had commented once they had the image. 'They've surrounded this central X-shaped structure with everything else. All the other structures are arranged in a circle – and look at the emplacements, a second wider outer ring. Whatever the point of this camp is, it's all focused on that central structure.'

'Kinda like they're protecting something? A piece of advanced missile tech maybe?' Ata said, grinning.

'Hey, just saying, it fits the picture we're painting,' Sidney replied. The team really felt like they were onto something.

Now for the hard part: convincing Mike. He'd responded to their request with feigned interest, but as Danny began his briefing, he seemed to perk up.

'We didn't initially examine this area, as we believed the missile had still ditched somewhere in the ocean, but assuming it didn't, this is one possible flight path it could have taken.' Danny had a map of the region, the numerous different flight paths overlayed.

'We've looked across all these different paths and found nothing to suggest the missile went this way. Except one.' He flicked to the satellite image of the Iranian camp.

'This was captured yesterday by a KT satellite. Not only did this camp spring up suddenly, but movement was first detected within hours of contact being lost with the prototype. A lucky E-3 in the region spotted a flurry of activity.'

Mike spoke for the first time, 'So why didn't we have this sooner?' he asked, an accusing tone in his voice as he pointed towards the E-3 report on the screen.

Luckily, Danny had a good answer for that, 'Simple answer. Time zones. This was published as I was heading out the door. We didn't actually know about it until this morning, so most of what you're seeing here was worked up today.'

Mike grunted, not exactly letting it go but accepting it. 'Alright, so your recommendation?'

'We need more information. Task another E-3 patrol, additional satellite coverage, check SIGINT from the area – hell, even HUMINT. We need anything. After that, if it is there, we'll need to decide if we can recover or destroy it. But, as the Iranians are there right now, we have to accept that we might already be too late.' He didn't mean to sound so doom and gloom, but it was the truth.

Mike moved in his chair, looking a little uncomfortable, 'Uh, thank you Danny… and Ata,' he added hastily. 'Can you send me everything? I'll do a review, then we have our team leaders brief in an hour. I'll raise it then and we can go from there.'

Ata didn't like that response at all. It had the sound of inaction that only a bureaucrat could muster. 'What do you want us to do, Mike? We can start sending out taskings now, and we'll need to brief Maia.'

'Yes, thank you, Ata,' Mike replied, clearly annoyed. 'Don't worry. I'll push this at the meeting and we'll go from there, but first, get me the report in full. And no further action without my say-so. Okay?'

'Mike, we really can't sit on this,' Danny protested.

'And we won't! But first I make sure everything matches just how you say it does, and then we can push this up the chain. I'm sure you've all done great work, and please Danny, thank the team for me. That'll be all.' The distinct tone of condescension was impossible to ignore.

Just like that, they were dismissed.

'The fuck is that guy's problem?' Ata muttered as they left his office. 'Like, how much more could we give him? I know it's not completely solid, but it wouldn't take much to confirm. We have the resources to figure this thing out. Plus, he hounds us constantly for a result, then he gets one, and what, it isn't what he wanted?'

'Look, let's get everything ready. We'll get all our requests and plans developed, that way, when Mike finally pulls his finger out, we're ready. He'll just look like an ass this way.'

Ata didn't seem very convinced, but equally, there wasn't much else for them to do right away, 'Yeah, alright.'

The hype of the day washed away, the team were left feeling empty and somewhat dumbfounded; they had felt they like they were truly onto something.

Danny watched them go one by one, his own heart sinking. He walked over to Mike's office – maybe he'd be able to make the man understand – but as he neared, he saw that the lights in his office were darkened. The man had packed up for the day and gone home, the urgency of their request ignored. With a bitter taste in his mouth, Danny grabbed his bag, walking out the door.

The White House – United States of America

Quinton Davenport stared down at the intelligence report on his computer screen. The document had been forwarded to him by a colleague. Multiple pages of data and satellite imagery dotted his screen, but it was the short, to-the-point summary that had caught his eye, and to Quinton, it was earth-shattering. He reread it again:

It is likely the prototype missile has entered and landed inside the Islamic Republic of Iran. The unusual and unexplained build-up of Iranian military equipment at this previous unrecorded location, coupled with the intersection of a possible flight path, suggests the missile may have successfully glided beyond its programmed flight plan. While not confi—

He looked away, the summary half read. He had seen enough.

Even excluding the multiple pages of tactical readouts, the mere suggestion that the missile could have fallen into Iran's hands was catastrophic. He was partly responsible for it, and he'd sure as hell get the blame for it.

As the national security advisor, he held a position of considerable power within the White House and the United States Government. He'd exhausted considerable political power and effort convincing the President to alter the military exercise at the last minute, suggesting the test could be used to build support back home – assuming it was successful, of course. But also, it would send a stark warning to America's enemies. Quinton wanted the world to see that the United States would stand up for itself and had the means to do it. But the test had failed, and badly. But that in itself wasn't a problem. Missile tests failed all the time. They could simply try again. The problem was the report he was now reading. He'd done some quick comparisons with the missile's flight plan and where it had disappeared. He didn't know the specifics of the missile, but he knew it could fly halfway around the world with ease. If the Iranians – or worse, the Chinese – had found their missile, he'd be to blame, and he couldn't, *wouldn't* allow that. He'd worked too hard, called in too many favours and made a host of enemies to get to his position.

Quinton was used to getting what he wanted, switching between bullying, charming and cold cunning as the situation required. His political ambitions and thirst for power had driven him forward throughout his career, and now, finally, after decades of work, he sat in the White House, mere metres away from arguably the most powerful position on the planet. But it wasn't enough, it never would be, and the political games he now had to play were more complex and challenging. He loved every second of it, but in equal measure, he grew more and more frustrated with each day that he was unable to progress his own plans.

His boss, the President of the United States of America, was a deceivingly complex political operator, often presenting an outward appearance of disinterest or ignorance, when in reality, he was calculating and planning, weighing up pros and cons according to his own future, and that of America.

Quinton's ability to gain access to the President as the national security advisor was never a problem, but convincing him to take a particular course of action was a different matter. The President had selected Quinton to be his security advisor late into his presidential campaign, with Quinton's credentials as a hawkish and sometimes unbending proponent for American power earning the President key support amongst certain members of his party. Quinton had realised, perhaps too late, that the President didn't necessarily share Quinton's beliefs – or, in fact, come anywhere near them. Quinton had been used, politically speaking. Once that realisation had hit home, his sense of comfort and power had quickly washed away. He had to prove his worth, because at the end of the day, he was expendable to the President. And the missile test had been the perfect tool.

Quinton had never been a military man; he had never served or seriously considered the idea. His world had been a mix of academia and politics. He wasn't sure when it had happened, but he'd realised in his earlier years at university that his views didn't mesh with the majority. He often found himself taking the harsher, more hardline approach to debates, quickly earning himself a reputation as a hardcore conservative hawk. Some people had called his views dangerous back then, even labelling him a warmonger. It hadn't taken long before he had begun to relish the way he stood out from the crowd, the way they looked at him with anger or even hatred. It had set him on a path he hadn't looked back from. Sitting in his comfortable chair in the White House, he could easily and comfortably summarise his views as *America, above all else*. Numerous articles, essays and think-pieces had been written under his name and his stewardship, often calling for the use of nuclear or chemical biological weapons if needed. Many had been appalled, but in his mind, America was under threat from all corners, and it was up to him, and a few like-minded individuals, to protect it, not to rely upon networks of alliances or outdated institutions and ideals.

Focusing back on the report on his computer screen, the sense of impending doom felt immense. He'd wasted considerable energy, and more importantly, political power convincing the President to change the exercise at the last minute. He'd managed to get the President's ear just before the test, away from any dissenting views, most notably the joint chiefs. He'd offered the idea as a mere thought bubble, laying the hook for the President to get snagged on. It hadn't been easy, but the President had eventually gone for it, with one catch: he'd made Quinton take responsibility for the success of the test. At the time, Quinton hadn't given the idea of failure a second thought, but now, everything was on the line. At best, he could just lose his job, but the report on his computer could mean the end of his career and aspirations. Something he wouldn't allow. The President would know the test had failed, but he couldn't know the missile might have fallen into enemy hands.

'Alright,' he said to himself. He had to assume the worst. *The Iranians likely have it*, he thought to himself. There was no point dwelling on the issue now; he had to find a way to fix it. He prided himself on reacting quickly to changes, leaving past decisions behind.

As the national security advisor, Quinton had considerable resources at his fingertips, but he'd need to keep this as quiet as possible and include as few people as possible.

Picking up the phone, he dialled a number he had committed to memory from regular use.

'Hey, Dick, I need you here ASAP.' He didn't wait for a response. The man would be here soon, and he specialised in quiet work, the kind that didn't attract prying eyes.

He'd fix this, no matter what.

Kuh-e-Birk Protected Area – Iran

The helicopter began its descent. Ming grinned as he

looked down on the flurry of activity below. The site he'd seen only a couple of hours earlier on the satellite images was completely changed now. Numerous vehicles had arrived; tents had been erected and emplacements dug. The landscape appeared almost hospitable with so much human activity.

With a gentle jolt, the helicopter landed, and the side doors were flung open seconds later. Sand immediately blasted into the cabin. Covering his eyes and closing his mouth, Ming stumbled out of the helicopter cabin as quickly as possible, keeping a low crouched walk away from the wash of the helicopter blades. The other passengers followed right behind, with some coughing and spluttering, clearly having inhaled sand. Ming moved a good distance away and stood off to the side, away from the sand cloud and the small group but not far enough he couldn't join them if needed. Someone shouted an order and the small group started moving. He decided to follow. No one had greeted or intercepted him yet, so he just moved along with the others like he belonged there.

A rough path had been created by numerous people walking the same route. The moment Ming stepped off the path, sand would suck at his feet, making him sink into the soft ground. A sudden whine of engines forced him to look over his shoulder, where he saw the helicopter lifting skyward.

There goes my escape route, he thought.

He picked up the pace to keep up with the small group. It was a short walk to the main camp site, but the baking heat of the desert was already taking its toll. Every breath felt like he was inhaling air from inside an oven. Sweat beaded across his brow; his clothes were absorbing the moisture that his body was rapidly losing. He was glad to have his aviator glasses; without them, he was doubtful he'd be able to see at all, given the glare of the sun.

The group was led down a small slope into the encampment, passing at least two sandbagged weapons emplacements. Ming peered at them with feigned disinterest, spotting what looked like anti-aircraft guns and shoulder-launched missile launchers. He noted everything. The group came to a sudden stop at a small tent just on the outskirts of the site. A gruff-looking soldier with a clipboard appeared to be directing them where to go. He stayed at the rear of the group, listening intently. There was no point trying to separate himself now; it would undoubtedly catch the eye of the various guards around them. Still, the man went about checking names off a list, and it gave Ming a moment to examine his surroundings.

He couldn't see the crash site, but he could guess where it was. He'd spied a large tent structure as they'd entered the camp. Seemingly erected in the middle of the site, it formed a large cross shape with multiple entrances. Based off the cables and cooling units attached, it was clearly the most established structure on the site. He mentally compared the site to the satellite images he'd seen. The Iranians had made considerable progress in the few short hours since they'd arrived. He checked his watch. It was just past midday.

Numerous different tents and temporary structures had been erected across the site; desert camouflage netting had been thrown across just about every surface. Every effort was being made to conceal the site. He doubted it would do much in the long run but respected the effort.

Only a couple of people remained in front of Ming, the rest having been checked off. He shuffled forward. There were a few heavy transport trucks parked under some netting to his right and what looked like some kind of communications centre near them. It sure was a lot of equipment they'd moved over here. No doubt the Americans or Israelis would spot all this activity soon enough. A sense of urgency formed in his head.

'Name!' the guard barked at Ming.

He hadn't realised he was at the front of line and was momentarily startled, but he recovered quickly. 'Ah, yes. Hello. My name is Mr Bao, I'm here to meet a Mr Merada,' Ming replied in perfect English; no point playing his hand

and revealing that he could speak Farsi right away.

The soldier looked immediately on guard, dropping his right hand to touch his holstered sidearm.

Seeing the sudden, hostile response, Ming figured he wasn't expected. 'I am a delegate from the Chinese embassy in Iran, and I have been requested to provide advice and assistance for this operation.'

The soldier didn't appear to understand what he was saying, instead repeating in Farsi, 'NAME!'

Ming took a step forward, pointing toward the clipboard, 'B-A-O', he spelt out slowly, still in English.

The guard took another look down at his clipboard, a look of confusion on his face.

'Do you think you could find a Mr Merada? I was informed that he would meet me,' Ming continued. He could see the man recognising the name Merada but not much else. He had begun to unholster his sidearm. *Here we go*, Ming thought, turning his body sideways from the soldier, making himself a smaller target. He knew he could disarm the man easily enough, but it would also give him away as being more than just some official. Plus, it could result in getting kicked off the site.

A head suddenly popped out of the tent behind the soldier, followed by a sharp, belittling order. The solider immediately returned his sidearm and looked abashed.

The small, bespectacled man strode confidently from the confines of the tent, hand outstretched, and speaking slightly accented English, 'Mr Bao! My sincerest apologies. I did not realise you had arrived! I had ordered someone to warn me.' With a surprisingly firm grip, he shook Ming's hand vigorously.

Ming quickly adopted the relaxed and apologetic tone of an official. 'Mr Merada, I assume? Sorry for any confusion. I was unsure where to go when I arrived.'

Merada scowled at the guards. 'You caused nothing of the sort. This idiot will be dealt with, don't you worry! Now, let's get you settled. I assume you are interested in a tour of this site?'

Ming's first impression of Merada painted a complex picture. Merada seemed to speak quickly, starting a new sentence almost before finishing the last one, his eyes constantly on the move. He reminded Ming of a weasel. Yet, this man could be valuable. Merada worked within the Iranian president's office as an advisor and seemed to hold some political favour. If Ming could win him over, he could be useful to the mission.

'Well, all I have is in this bag. I am as ready for a tour as I'll ever be,' Ming replied cheerily.

'Excellent! Come! I am eager to hear your impressions of our little operations here.' Merada immediately took off, already beginning to discuss at length the various features of the site. Ming hurried to keep up.

***

The tour rounded out Ming's mental image of the site, reconfirming both the satellite images he'd seen and the quick assessment he'd made the moment he'd arrived. The camp had been set up in a largely circular layout, with supporting infrastructure erected around the central X-shaped tent. It looked like a rough track had been bulldozed to the site so heavy equipment could be brought in. Throughout the tour, Merada never stopped talking, constantly pointing out minor features of the supposedly superior Iranian operation. Ming didn't have to agree, but he made sure to remain the polite and attentive guest.

After almost an hour, the tour came to an end, and Ming was sweating profusely. Merada had circled them back to where they'd first met, where the same soldier remained at his station. The only spot Merada hadn't shown Ming was the central tent. 'Mr Merada, thank you for this wonderful tour; it is truly an impressive operation you have here. I will be sure to report this back to my nation …' Ming paused. 'But I cannot help believe we are missing the final part of the tour, and the reason why I am here.' He pointed towards the well-guarded tent behind them.

Merada's constant smile seemed to drop only for a second before returning, but his look had a certain slyness to it. 'Yes … indeed, I do understand your interest, but as I'm sure you are aware, the contents of that particular tent are very, very sensitive. Perhaps you would be able to share something that might demonstrate how your nation may assist mine, Mr Bao?'

He'd have to give Merada something. Luckily, he was prepared. Slipping his backpack off his back, he fished around inside it before pulling out a manila folder. He handed it over. 'As a sign of goodwill, Mr Merada, we are happy to inform you that we had the good fortune of having a ship in the region that was able to get a fleeting read on the device, and satellites confirmed something had landed. Our early assessment is that whatever has fallen into the desert here is some type of experimental missile.' Ming didn't mention that the more sensitive data had been omitted, including the missile's operating speed. The Iranians might want to keep the missile for themselves if they understood its potential.

Merada flicked through the pages; technical data, and a glossy low-resolution satellite image. It wasn't much, but it was enough. 'There is a lot more, Mr Merada. My country is happy to provide as much technical assistance as possible.' The underlying message: *China knows what is laying in the sand, we want to know more.*

'Very well, follow me, but I should mention, Mr Bao, there are some who are strongly opposed to your presence here. You are lucky the president values his relationship with China. But such friendship does come with … certain costs.' Ming read between the lines as he followed Merada. Pockets would have to be lined, starting but surely not ending with Merada's. That was fine by Ming; it wouldn't be his money or his promises to keep. He was just the messenger.

'But, of course, my nation understands the cost of business. If I may suggest, sir, assuming this technology is what we think it is, China has considerable experience taking advantage of Western technology. If we can offer assistance – economically, technically or militarily – to help you take full advantage of this fallen technology, we will be forthcoming.'

A smile flashed across Merada's face. 'I believe we can benefit each other nicely here.' His greed was poorly concealed; Ming could see it written all over his face.

The reality was that China was exceedingly wealthier than Iran, and coupled with Western sanctions, Iran was facing a dire economic situation. Men like Merada, those with influence but perhaps not as much wealth as they would like, would always be willing to work with China. It had worked many times in the past, and it would work into the future. Threats of violence or intimidation were often far less useful than indulging simple human greed.

They reached the final, central tent, where two armed soldiers were standing by the entrance. 'Shall we?' Merada said, holding open the entrance for Ming, who wasted no time moving inside.

Stepping past Merada into the air-conditioned interior, Ming couldn't help but feel impressed. This random patch of desert had been converted into what looked like a fairly sophisticated laboratory and command centre. Desks and computers had been assembled in neat rows, while engineers and soldiers moved between them with purpose. Bright low-hanging lighting was attached throughout the space, giving it a clinical feel. But in the centre of the room, the prize lay quiet. Surrounded by what looked like rubberised matting, it seemed comically out of place, jutting out from the ground, sand cradling it. Numerous wires had already been attached to it, and a group of civilians spoke animatedly, clearly excited. It was easy to forget he was in the middle of the desert – well, almost. Despite the air-conditioning, the space was still stiflingly hot.

Merada brought Ming right up the missile, showing it off. His eyes were gleaming with excitement. 'This is what you were looking for?' he asked.

Ming nodded, 'It is indeed.' His mind was working overtime, taking mental notes and trying to catalogue everything he could see. It wasn't entirely necessary, but his ability to recall even the smallest details had saved him before. Still, he wore a small hidden camera in one of his shirt buttons as a backup; it would record everything, but without audio.

'As you can see, it appears to be almost completely intact,' Merada commented, a smile stretching across his face. 'And with our state-of-the-art facilities, we will be able to unlock its secrets in due course.'

Ming doubted that, but he didn't say so, preferring to let Merada boast. 'Oh?' he asked innocently.

'Our scientists believe this is a new type of missile, possibly one of the new hypersonic class of weapons! With this technology, the Americans and Israelis won't dare to threaten us anymore.' Merada spoke with clear pride.

'What makes you say that?' he knew, of course, but he wanted to get as much as he could from the man.

He turned to face the missile again. An engineer was busy attempting to open a panel on it, and Ming wanted to get every shot he could. Merada's explanation sank into the back of his subconscious as he watched the engineer carefully. The techs back in Beijing would gobble up all the images he could get, and from learnt experience, they always wanted more, better angles, better picture quality. The engineer struggling to open the panel pulled harder, and the little piece of metal groaned slightly as it gave way. The metal bent, flying open with a loud *clang*. A supervisor swore at the man in a hushed tone, telling him to be careful. Merada remained oblivious as he prattled on. With the inner workings exposed, Ming could see numerous circuit boards, wiring and other components. To him, it was all a mystery, but no doubt what he was seeing would be important, and from what he could tell, it looked mostly intact. A very good sign.

He switched his focus back to Merada, trying to recall the conversation. 'Mr Merada, I have no doubt Beijing will be very interested in the progress of your scientists. Although, I wonder if maybe the support of our people might speed up the process, allow both our nations to benefit from this technology?' The question sounded sincere enough, but in reality, neither Ming nor the Chinese Government trusted the Iranians. Especially with something as seemingly advanced as the missile laying sadly in the sand in front of them.

Merada hesitated only momentarily, processing Ming's comment and constructing a reply, 'Well, I see no reason why we couldn't work something out, but it would not be for me to say, of course.' A weak answer, but Ming sensed an opening.

'If you would allow me, Mr Merada, I could take some photos and send them back to my people – we could have some advice ready within the hour.' Another sensible and seemingly innocuous offer.

Merada seemed to wring his hands, unable to come up with an immediate rebuttal.

'NO!' a sudden voice growled from across the tent, startling Merada. Ming turned quickly to face the origin of the voice.

Ming had seen photos of Commander Rostami before, but they paled in comparison to the man standing before him. He was a truly imposing figure. Merada failed to hide his surprise and stammered a response. 'Uh ... Ah, commander! It is good you are here. Let me introduce you to our guest, Mr Bao, from the Chinese embassy.'

Rostami contemplated Ming with a piercing stare.

'I am fully aware of our guest, Merada, *and* his speciality ...' he intoned. Clearly not much got by this man.

Merada seemed lost for words. Ming decided it was time to step forward. Raising his hand in greeting, he said,

'Commander, it is a pleasure to meet you. My country extends its thanks for allowing us to view this weapon you have acquired.'

'I'm sure it does, Mr Bao. I'm sure it does,' Rostami replied frostily, letting an awkward silence hang in the air as he refused to take Ming's offered hand. 'Tell me, what have you learned so far thanks to Mr Merada's … generous tour?'

'That you have quite an impressive operation happening here, and in such an inhospitable part of the world,' Ming replied quickly.

'It is impressive. Would you say we have sent some of our best people?'

'Most certainly.'

'Well, then, would you say we have this entire situation well in hand?' he said, waving causally at the missile.

Rostami's angle was clear enough. He wanted no involvement from Ming or the Chinese Government. 'That isn't in doubt, sir. I merely suggest that by using both our countries' resources, we could take advantage of this technology quicker, and use it against our shared enemies.'

Rostami wasn't buying it. 'Hmm, a generous offer, but completely unnecessary. My country will of course share its secrets in due time.'

Rostami waved his hand dismissively, 'Now, if you don't mind, we have work to do here, and as you can see, this is a very fragile piece of equipment. Wouldn't want untrained individuals damaging it.'

Ming ignored the pointed jab, preferring to remain the gracious guest, 'But of course, thank you again for your time.'

Rostami signalled for one of the guards to escort Ming out, but Merada stepped forward instead, 'Please, allow me. Shall we get some refreshments, Mr Bao?'

Ming smiled, 'Please.'

There was no doubting who was in charge of the operation here, but Ming suspected Merada had significantly more influence in the halls of Iranian powerbrokers. Still, Ming was in Rostami's backyard, and he'd have to be careful.

Merada took Ming into his own private room in one of the tents. An hour later, Ming had every last detail he needed. A deal could be struck with the Iranian president for the missile, but it would come at a particularly high financial cost, not to mention benefit to certain individuals. But China would happily pay it. Using the bathroom as an excuse to separate himself from Merada, Ming quickly logged into his secure laptop, wrote a quick brief and uploaded the numerous images captured from his hidden camera. With a single click, the information he had gathered blasted off to a computer in the Chinese Embassy in Tehran. In thirty minutes, it would be in Beijing, and in an hour, it would be with the head of his organisation.

CHAPTER 6

Beijing – China

Chang Wonqin exited his armoured limousine into the dreary Beijing afternoon, his driver hurrying around the large black car to provide Chang an umbrella against the beating rain. Chang didn't care about staying dry; he wasn't one to worry about minor issues such as getting a little wet. He had more pressing matters to attend to. Only an hour before, he'd received an intelligence report from the Chinese Embassy in Tehran. The mostly unedited document from a field officer in Iran was starting to make small waves amongst Chinese officers, and the information held in that report represented an opportunity for China that a little rain wouldn't hold back.

As the minister for state security, Chang had enormous reach and political sway within the Chinese Government and Chinese Communist Party. But he was also only one member of the larger politburo, and his power did have limits. However, if his plan worked, those limits may soon begin to disappear. But first, he had to get to a meeting with the president of the Chinese Communist Party and the People's Republic, and he had to get to that meeting before anyone else could whisper into the president's ear. He was not under the illusion that the information he now held would stay within the confines of his department. There were many eyes and ears throughout the Chinese Government, all with competing loyalties.

Several hurried phone calls between various aides later, Chang had managed to arrange an extraordinary meeting with the president – a considerable feat in such a short timeframe.

Chang had spent his life working for the Chinese Communist Party. He wasn't the son of one of the powerful old guards; in fact, he was the first person in his family to achieve anything beyond an early death for their country, as far as he could tell. Now into his early fifties, Chang had slowly built his own personal power base. He'd aligned himself with the current president of the People's Republic early on, and he had reaped the rewards for it, attaining increasing seniority within the party and security services.

He hurried up the steps of Zhongnanhai, the headquarters for the president and communist party, in the old Imperial City, with his driver desperately trying to keep up. Chang had to admire the sense of raw power and importance of the decadent city. Armed guards stood to attention and held the large, decorated wooden doors open for him. The building was truly a palace, not some utilitarian office. Chang paid the guards and the opulence around him little attention, focusing on the briefing he was building in his mind. He wouldn't trust this to any analyst or senior executive; this was his role, his information.

He was quickly ushered into one of the larger meeting rooms, which was really more of a situation room, inside the sprawling palace complex. The space was not dissimilar to the types of rooms often seen in American movies, expect the walls had significantly more listening devices and photos of China's founding leader, Mao Zedong, apportioning the walls. An assorted crowd of generals, politicians and other powerful bureaucrats had been hurriedly assembled. It was more people than Chang had expected, but he wouldn't let his surprise show. Information must already be leaking that this was to be an important meeting, he decided, eyeing the room carefully.

Personally, Chang would have preferred a one-on-one meeting with the president, where he could present his course of action and recommendations without interference, but that type of meeting was exceedingly rare. Time with the president was fiercely fought over between the various politburo members and other ministers.

There was also a benefit to having all the different representatives in the room. Chang's plan was not a simple one, and the support and endorsement of the security services, People's Liberation Army and, most importantly, the Politburo Standing Committee, a select group of the seven most powerful politburo members, would be crucial. However, the current president was extremely powerful in his own right – more so than any previous president. Political anti-corruption campaigns had weeded out rivals and dissenters, leaving the president more capable of acting unilaterally than any before him. If the president made a decision, it would be supported. The trick, as far as Chang was concerned, was to present only one suitable option. If he gained the endorsement of the president, his own power would be elevated.

The president presided over the meeting. Not one for overt formality and processes, he cut straight to the point once Chang had taken his place at the large, polished table. 'Minister Chang, we've all had time to read the attached briefing.' He held up a two-page report for added effect. 'If you'd be so kind as to provide a full briefing on the operation and bring everyone up to date on our options.'

Chang could be a highly eloquent and charismatic speaker when he wanted to, but for this room, he adopted the tone of a formal briefer, copying the style of intelligence analysts he'd received briefings from in the past. He took his time, using the imagery captured from the field officer in Iran to illustrate any key points. Overall, it took less than ten minutes. The room remained silently beholden to his words. A good sign. As he neared the end of his briefing, he decided to try a slightly unorthodox move and recommend a course of action prior to the traditional discussion at the end. Although it would be out of the norm, it could give him the advantage he needed to get his proposal across the line.

'Comrades, we have a substantial opportunity ahead of us. If we can take advantage of it, it could provide us the edge we need over the Americans. There are three broad options available to us.' He held up three fingers on his right hand. 'Firstly, we can allow the Iranians to keep the missile and try to support them, offering our scientists and knowledge, perhaps. However, this will make us reliant upon them and, as we know, they are hardly reliable allies. Our second option is that we do nothing, but given the opportunity to expand our capabilities, I believe you will agree that this would be a mistake.' Chang looked around the room, taking note of each member and whether they were nodding their heads in agreement or making disapproving signs. The president's eyes remained locked on him, unmoving. 'Or … we can seize this opportunity.' He closed his fist for added effect. 'Our agents in Iran have confirmed that the Iranians would be willing to trade this technology for certain economic and military support. This path has more risks, and it would demand considerable support from all branches to return this object to our territory, but gentlemen, I believe you will agree with me when I say there is only one true option available to us here today.' He wouldn't go so far as to suggest what action they should take. That was for the standing committee and, more importantly, the president to dictate, but his short speech had framed their options clearly.

The lights brightened as the presentation came to an end, and the president opened the floor for a decision, saying quietly, 'Gentlemen?'

Unsurprisingly, the generals of the People's Liberation Army were the most enthusiastic. The most powerful of them spoke first. 'If this missile, this prototype, is what Comrade Chang suggests, we must take it for ourselves.'

The navy followed suit. 'The irony of taking this technology from the Americans and defeating them with their own missiles. It is too perfect!'

'Our planes can be dispatched immediately to pick it up,' a representative of the air force exclaimed, clearly excited.

The president let the conversation continue for a few more minutes, seeing a clear consensus amongst the assembled members. As the head of the party and the central military commission, his decision would be absolute. 'Comrades, it appears we are in agreeance. We shall take this technology for ourselves. I will lead a small working group to manage this operation. We shall succeed. We must, for our country, and for the future of China. But we must tread quietly. It is not to our benefit to loudly announce ourselves like the Americans. This is not to be discussed outside this room – is that understood?'

Everyone in the room nodded. The air was thick with the promise of consequences should they fail to obey the president's instructions.

Chang smiled internally. With his agent already in place, his involvement, and that of his organisation, would be unavoidable. The military would fight over this, but it didn't matter. In Chang's mind, their petty power plays were nothing compared to the opportunity this presented for his own personal gain, and that of his country.

The White House – United States of America

Richard Vanderhoe – or "Dick", as Quinton preferred to call him – was a tall, imposing figure with jet-black hair and a matching suit. He looked every bit the shady character that he was. Quinton used him to get rid of problems, whether they be pesky reporters or misled officials. Dick was effective – and he was quiet, something Quinton valued more than anything else. He'd already proved his worth more times than Quinton cared to admit, but more than that, he had connections to parts of the world that Quinton could never go near. Private military contractors, intelligence organisations – hell, even foreign intelligence and criminal groups weren't off limits. Dick was Quinton's problem solver, and he was good at it.

'You see this?' Quinton gestured in disgust at his computer monitor.

Dick moved with a strange stillness to him. Quietly spoken, he didn't laugh or display much emotion. Whenever he cracked a small smile, it always had a sinister edge to it, like he was enjoying a personal, unspoken, twisted joke that no one else knew about.

Dick read the report in silence, Quinton fidgeting in his chair beside him. He always felt uncomfortable with Dick in the room. Maybe it was the fact that the man could probably snap Quinton's neck in a heartbeat if he wanted to. Quinton had saved him years ago from an embarrassing court martial following the deaths of a family in Afghanistan. He'd read a report on the actions Dick had taken to eliminate a terrorist cell and had adopted a sympathetic stance – in his eyes, Dick was being punished for the mistakes of some stupid civilians who got in the way. They didn't call it collateral damage for nothing. Plus, the after-action report had shown just how resourceful and capable Dick could be. Pulling some strings, he managed to make the charges disappear and had brought Dick on to work for him. Still, Quinton couldn't dislodge the feeling that every time Dick looked at him, he was picturing some form of horrible torture being inflicted on him.

'The prototype?' Dick asked quietly, tilting his head slightly but not looking away from the screen.

'Of course, it is, what else could it be?'

Dick stood up straight, his hand on his chin, ignoring Quinton's tone. 'Hmm. Alright, what do you want done?'

Always to the point. 'I want it sorted. We can't have the president finding out about this.'

'Other people will figure this out,' Dick pointed out.

Quinton gritted his teeth. 'Which is why we are going to classify the shit out of this report.' He always felt like he had to do everything.

'And the prototype?'

'What about it?' Quinton snapped back.

'The Iranians would love to parade this across the country.'

It annoyed Quinton to be made to look the fool, but the man was right. 'We have assets we can deploy, don't we? I don't give a fuck what you do, Dick. *Get rid of it.*'

'Any means necessary?'

'Any means, Dick; I don't fucking care if you drop a fucking missile on it.'

Dick's right eyebrow rose. It wasn't often that Quinton was so transparent in his language. But he nodded in agreement and made to leave.

'Wait!' Quinton suddenly called out. 'The final decision goes through me on any action we take. We have to do this shit properly.' The unspoken implication that Quinton didn't trust Dick wasn't lost on either of them.

'Understood,' Dick said formally.

'And Dick, move fast, this could fuck us both. Do you understand?'

The man nodded slowly in acknowledgement, glancing back at Quinton in a cool, unemotional state.

'Damn, that guy gives me the creeps,' Quinton muttered to himself once Dick had closed the door behind him.

There was no point in putting all his eggs in one basket, either. He trusted Dick to get the job done, but he didn't trust him completely. Always better to have multiple options. He picked up the phone and dialled a long international number.

A jumpy voice responded immediately. 'Yes?'

'It's me again. I need you to do something for me,'

Quinton said simply.

The person on the other end made some kind of movement, the noise coming through the phone receiver. 'Umm … Hi. Yeah sure, what do you need? Did the report help?'

Quinton didn't like the man's weak, almost snivelling tone, 'Yes, it was very useful, thank you. But that's what I'm calling about. We need to keep a lid on this for as long as possible. We'll need to organise a response, and we can't have too many people interfering. They'll just get in the way and jeopardise things. So, I need you to keep things sorted down there? You understand?'

The man seemed to stammer, 'Yes, of course … How though?'

Quinton sighed audibly, not even trying to conceal his annoyance now. 'Make sure that no more information or reporting gets loose. Like I said, keep a lid on it.'

The person at the other end sounded somewhat uneasy. 'I'm not sure if I can do that, Quinton …'

'You have to. This is a matter of national security, and you are part of the inner circle here. You wouldn't have sent me that report otherwise, right? I don't care how you do it, but keep your people in check.' Quinton tried to sound reassuring, but he wasn't sure he hit the right tone.

'I'm sticking my neck out here …' Evidently not.

'And I appreciate it. Look, we all have to play our role here. Remember what I said before: we can't trust our allies on this one. We've got to keep it as quiet as possible. The whole reason I reached out to you is because I trust you completely. Remember that.'

The person sounded slightly more at ease, 'Yeah, I know. I've got your back. We go a long way back, don't we?'

He really didn't want to go down memory lane right now. 'That's right. You let me know the moment you hear anything, okay? I'll let you know if we need anything from you on this end.'

'You got it – and hey, I appreciate you giving me this

responsibility. It means a lot.'

He hung up without answering. People were a fucking pain in his ass sometimes. He didn't mind suck-ups from time to time, but the person on the other end was barely useful. Still, overall, he felt better. He had put his minions to work. Soon enough, everything would be under control.

At least, he hoped it would be.

Lennox Gardens – Canberra – Australia

Danny let the warming rays of the Australian sun wash over him. A gentle cooling breeze occasionally disturbed the leafy green trees that decorated the park. The large, artificial Lake Burley Griffin sat only a few metres away, its dark waters lapping soothingly against the bank while families and couples sat around the grassy park, playing sports, laughing. Danny smiled to himself; this was the life.

A figure approaching from the distance caught his eye, one he recognised instantly. The smile on his face widened as Leah approached.

He couldn't help but look her up and down, appreciating her figure, the way her dark hair bobbed slightly as she walked, and the cheeky grin that never seemed to leave her face.

'Should I do a dance for you?' Leah asked in an accusing tone, clearly feeling Danny's gaze.

'You won't hear a no from me,' he replied with a chuckle.

Laying down next to Danny on the small picnic rug, she sighed, resting her head against his shoulder. 'Honey, you couldn't afford me,' she said without a trace of humour.

'I don't know. I can be pretty persuasive,' he smiled, holding up a cracker with a slice of brie on it.

'It's a good start, but you'll have to keep the snacks coming.'

'I'll see what I can do.' He quickly loaded up another cracker with quince paste. The sound of laughter somewhere off in the distance was carried their way by the wind. In this moment, Danny could feel all the tension from the days prior melting off his shoulders.

'You know, this has got to be one of the best moments of my life, right here, right now …'

'With me?'

'With you,' he confirmed, a low warmth to his voice.

He could feel her smile, her hand squeezing his leg lightly.

A deep sense of love washed over him, and despite having only been with Leah for a couple of months, he couldn't think of anyone else he'd rather be with.

'You know, we might make an Australian out of you yet,' Leah said with a laugh.

'Hey, if we could have more days like this, I don't think I would mind that at all!'

Life was good. He was in love, the weather was beautiful, and the troubles of work were long forgotten.

Unbeknown to Danny, another set of eyes gazed upon the couple, but the click of the camera's lens was lost in the gentle breeze.

CHAPTER 7

Berkley – Washington – United States of America

The early morning glow entered Quinton's bedroom, waking him almost instantly. He was accustomed to working late hours and rising early in the morning, a habit he'd developed early in his career, partly driven by his desire to get a head start on everyone else. Although, this morning he felt like he was recovering from a hangover. He hadn't slept well. Nightmares of fallen missiles and sand had haunted his dreams. Despite it being a new day for him, it was still only late afternoon in Iran. There was still much to do.

Quinton owned a rather large home in upmarket Berkley, keeping him close to his academic roots but, more critically, close to the White House. He even kept a small townhouse in George Town for when he felt he needed to remain even closer. In his mind, there was a certain value in being the first person in the office, the first person to get their opinion out, the first person to act, no matter the reason.

As he woke further, he quietly moved downstairs to get a coffee, trying not to wake his wife. His thoughts lingered on last night's news. There had been a flurry of activity – phone calls, meetings, decisions. But now, in the early morning funk, doubts began to drift in. Without some feeling of action, he felt increasingly powerless, unable to change or influence actions on the ground. It was a feeling he hated. Despised. He needed a sense of control more than anything.

The machine before him dinged pleasantly, announcing the arrival of his steaming hot coffee. The rich aroma filled his nose, temporarily blocking all thoughts of the missile as he savoured the smell. A sudden gentle knock on his rear kitchen door startled him. Momentarily annoyed that his morning ritual had been disturbed, he moved quickly to unlock the door.

There was only one person who'd be knocking on it this early in the morning.

Sure enough, as Quinton stepped outside, pulling his robe around him, he spotted Dick standing in his backyard. Quinton guessed he hadn't slept last night. But that was the man's role: get the job done, no matter what, no matter the personal cost. Late hours were to be expected.

'What do you have for me?' Quinton said as he sipped the coffee, feeling the slight burn as the liquid entered his mouth. They'd had more than a few meetings like this in the past. His house had a large backyard and was secluded from public eye. It was perfect for meetings that needed to take place without prying eyes, or ears.

'The report has been handled; it won't be a problem,' Dick responded in a matter-of-fact tone.

Good, Quinton thought, although that was the minimum he'd expected. 'Alright, what else?'

'An armed Reaper drone has been dispatched; it will be over the site in two hours. Once it arrives, we will be able to get eyes on the location.'

Quinton nodded as he listened. Dick was good. He'd anticipated Quinton's expectations and planned accordingly. He hated to admit it, but without this man,

Quinton wouldn't have anywhere near the reach he now did. How Dick organised everything – well, Quinton didn't really care. As long as it was done, and done quietly. He had to protect himself first after all.

'It isn't at risk from Iranian anti-air?' Quinton asked. The last thing he wanted was another piece of advanced American tech lost to the Iranian desert.

'No, we are using a CIA-funded operation that has been collecting intelligence against the Iranians for the better part of a year now. Their anti-aircraft systems still haven't recovered from the cyberattack we launched a couple of years back. Their airspace is open.'

'Good. Is the drone armed?' A pointed question with significant implications.

Dick nodded, 'Full complement of air-to-ground Hellfire missiles.'

Well, that would give him more than a few options if needed. He mulled it over as he took another sip of his coffee. 'Call me at the office when it's ready. I want confirmation on this thing before we decide next steps, understood?'

Dick nodded again.

'Oh, and Dick, prepare some kind of cover in case we do need to launch some kind of strike – call the site a terrorist training camp or something like that. Never hurts to have more than one plan in place.' Quinton had to smile to himself. Not a bad plan, overall; they could have this cleared up sooner than expected.

Dick, for his part, remained largely emotionless. Quinton thought he might have seen the hint of a raised eyebrow when he'd mentioned the option to strike the site, but for the most part, Dick simply continued to loom creepily over Quinton, his expression completely neutral.

'Understood, sir.' If Dick had any misgivings or input, he didn't volunteer them. He'd learnt long ago to keep his own opinions to himself, particularly around his current boss.

'Excellent, now get out of my yard,' Quinton said, dismissing him. The sense of unease always built up the longer he was with the man.

As he returned to his kitchen, he felt more at ease. Action, *a plan*. Soon enough, this threat would be eliminated, and he could get back to his real goals, free of petty distractions.

Standing under a large oak tree outside Quinton's house, a lone secret-service agent watched Dick open the gate to the backyard and quietly enter an enormous black Escalade. The agent noted the time mentally before continuing his vigil, gently releasing his grip around his service weapon.

Kuh-e-Birk Protected Area – Iran

A tortured scream echoed out across the desert. Ming shivered in discomfort. He'd been summoned to an isolated tent away from the rest of the camp, escorted by an unsmiling guard. Two more soldiers with rifles stood stoically at the tent's entrance. Another pained scream sounded from inside. Whatever was happening in there, Ming was sure he didn't want to be a part of it.

A wave of fear washed over him. Was he about to face a similar fate to the poor person inside? He didn't know. He didn't relish torture; the act of willingly and intentionally inflicting pain on someone was normally the pastime of narcissistic psychopaths, in Ming's experience. To him, it was something to be avoided. He forced himself to focus, letting his training take hold, calming his mind. If this was a life-or-death scenario he was about to walk into, he'd need to be ready to act.

Another scream rolled out of the tent flap, followed by muttered, panting words he couldn't make out, but the tone seemed clear. Someone was pleading.

They stood outside the tent, Ming waiting for the guards to usher him inside. He had an inkling of why he'd been summoned.

The report he'd written back to his embassy had travelled like lightning. News that the missile was intact, and secured, had increased the importance of Ming's mission a hundred-fold. Everything went from being a possibility to being a reality. Numerous calls and emails had followed, with Ming trying to answer as many questions as possible, providing insight where he could. He'd even suggested a plan to get the missile out of Iran, although he doubted Beijing would proceed with his plan of action. The latest communication he'd received only minutes before made the next steps clear. Beijing had given the green light, and everything now had a momentum of its own. Working through Merada, the embassy had made a highly lucrative offer to the president. Merada would, of course, be getting his own reward.

Ming's orders were simple enough: remain at the site, determine what would be needed to transport the missile and then finally escort it all the way back to China. Ming wasn't going back to the city anytime soon. He'd very quickly gone from being a simple pawn to a powerful bishop in the game of chess playing out around him. The only real question he had was whether Rostami knew of the machinations occurring behind his back. If he did, it could derail everything – or worse, it could cost Ming his life.

The flap of the tent was pulled aside suddenly, and another grim-looking guard exited, taking a deep breath before glancing at Ming. He motioned for Ming to enter without much enthusiasm. Steeling himself, Ming walked forward slowly, trying to present an air of confidence, even though, just below the surface, he was readying himself for an attack. It was a feeling he was unaccustomed to. Normally, he felt sure and confident in himself and his actions, but this had an ominous feel he didn't like. He could still feel his pistol pressing against the small of his back. It gave him a small degree of comfort; he wasn't completely defenceless.

The guard motioned to Ming, and the guards escorting

him gave him a gentle but firm nudge towards the tent's entrance. He steeled himself, taking a big breath. Stepping past the guard and into the gloom of the tent's interior, Ming was immediately assaulted by the extreme temperature difference inside the small tent. All the ventilation flaps were securely fastened, and without any fans to circulate the air, the tent had become an oven, oppressive and humid. Moisture clung to the materialled roof of the tent. Ming guessed it was done purposefully, to create a punishing environment for its victims. He immediately started to sweat, and he took another breath. A gross mixture of sweat and blood hung in the air; the unpleasant odour assaulted his nostrils. The next breath he took was through his mouth. The sensation of hot air could still be felt entering his throat and lungs, but at least he didn't smell it.

His eyes adjusted to the dim light quickly. The space inside the tent was simple enough – just one large rectangle with some tables and chairs packed against the sides. A couple of sheets hung in a corner, concealing what lay beyond. In the middle, the figure of a man was slumped on a crude metal chair, arms and legs tied down. His shirt had been removed and his chest appeared covered in sweat, blood and cuts. He appeared unconscious; a small mercy, perhaps. The only sign he was alive was the slow rise and fall of his chest. Ming didn't have the faintest idea who the figure was, but he knew one thing: he didn't want to be next.

'Mr Bao, thank you for joining me. I do apologise for the conditions.' A harsh, familiar voice spoke suddenly from behind him.

Colonel Rostami had his back turned to Ming. He was cleaning his hands on some rag. He spoke with a slight accent, but his English was perfect. Ming hadn't seen him immediately upon entering the tent, as his eyes had needed time to adjust, but the sudden awareness of his presence made the hair on Ming's neck stand on end. Looking past Rostami, Ming could see a number of painful-looking instruments and blunt objects sitting on a small table. Blood was splattered across them; clearly, they had been used recently.

Ming shuddered involuntarily. He quickly controlled himself before Rostami turned, forcing his mind to focus. He'd need to be careful.

'Colonel, I must say, I wasn't expecting a summons. Might I ask why you have brought me here?' He emphasised the word *here*; he wasn't interested in playing nice.

The colonel smiled, looking down at Ming with focused, hunting eyes. A renewed scent of blood mixed with sweat washed over Ming. He tried to conceal his discomfort.

'Well, Mr Bao, I want to make sure we understand each other.' Rostami paused before continuing. 'You see, I'm a patriot of my country. My land. My people. I would do anything – *anything* – Mr Bao, to defend them. From threats external … and internal.' He began slowly walking around the small space in a semi-circle, keeping his eyes on Ming as he moved. A predator stalking its prey. 'This missile, or whatever it is, it may help my country defeat those that threaten it. The nations that threaten us, attack our facilities, murder our leaders. Do you understand, Mr Bao? Do you see we are under attack constantly?'

Ming nodded. Using a neutral tone, he said, 'I can see that, colonel.'

Rostami stopped walking. He was now facing directly into the tent from the entrance, effectively blocking Ming's only escape route. 'Good. So you may understand my suspicion at your presence here … Do you, Mr Bao, threaten my country?'

Ming didn't answer immediately. He was trying to decide on the right response. It was time for some truth. Rostami would see through anything else; the man was too intelligent. 'Colonel, my country has the same enemies as yours. If we can find ways to defeat our mutual enemies, does that not make us friends?'

Rostami remained quiet, examining Ming carefully. 'Perhaps … Yet, I expect your country would happily throw mine into the fire if it were to your benefit.'

Ming didn't correct him; he wasn't wrong.

There was no point trying to fool this man; Ming suspected only hard logic would work here. 'I believe we are both pragmatists, sir. Both of us know there is value in what is lying in the sand there.' He pointed down towards the crash site. 'My country has considerably more resources and knowledge available to exploit this boon.'

Rostami's eyes narrowed on Ming. Perhaps he'd overdone it.

'You are right, of course,' he said slowly, clearly enouncing each word. 'But if we were to give you the missile, you would not share all its secrets. Your nation would withhold the technology unless it benefitted your own plans. My nation will never be second best.' A ferocity seemed to build inside Rostami, and his next words were spoken in a low growl, 'Do you understand me?'

'I do.'

'I do not believe you do,' he replied coldly. 'See that man? He is one of my countrymen. We found him and his friends at the crash site when we arrived. They, Mr Bao, are not spies, or foreign agents – they were simply in the wrong place at the wrong time.' Rostami pointed to a corner of the tent. 'But, as you can see, we deal with any possible threats harshly.' For the first time, Ming noticed two pairs of feet sticking out from under the sheet, implying that the men beneath it were almost certainly dead.

Rostami continued, waving his hand towards the man in the chair, 'Mr Bao. Look with your eyes and see the damage we inflicted upon this innocent man, and ask yourself, if this is what I would do to an innocent man, a man of my country, then what would I do to my enemies, those who would take from my country?' Rostami kept his eyes fixed on Ming's. Ming resisted the urge to look away. What he saw in Rostami's eyes scared him. The deadly and cold face of a fanatic stared back at him. Ming forced himself to stay still; he could just imagine what the colonel would do.

Ming didn't have a hand to play here. Rostami stood directly facing Ming, his eyes remaining absolutely focused on Ming with a laser-like intensity. He was trapped, both logically and physically.

'I can deliver your message, colonel. But I am just the messenger,' Ming offered weakly. 'We are merely the servants to our leaders' decisions, are we not?'

The speed with which Rostami moved shocked Ming, and he wasn't ready. He should have been, but he wasn't.

The colonel pulled a knife from his belt. In a blur, he swung his right arm in a sweeping downward motion towards Ming. Ming could see the small blade cleanly leaving Rostami's now open hand, the cold steel flying towards him in slow motion. He tried in vain to react, but he was already too late. His mind waited for the thud as it entered his body. He could feel the woosh of the cold steel as it flew through the air, and he heard the impact as it entered flesh. But Ming didn't feel anything – no shearing pain, no wet flow of blood, nothing. It took him a moment to realise what had happened. The colonel, clearly an expert with knives, had flung the small weapon past Ming, missing him by a fraction. It had instead landed in the poor soul tied to the chair just behind him, hitting him squarely in the chest, right in the heart. The man in the chair let out a sad final breath of air before slumping down, motionless.

Ming tried to relax and rebuild his composure. He'd been too slow, but his hand had automatically gripped the sidearm against his back. The colonel walked past Ming silently, leant over the deceased man and pulled the knife from his chest with ease. As he cleaned the blade on a filthy rag, he spoke to Ming, not looking at him, 'Remember, Mr Bao, I am in control here. The desert is a dangerous place. We wouldn't want to lose you in this land. The missile is ours, Mr Bao. It is *mine*. And nothing – nothing – will change that.'

Ming remained frozen, hand gripping his sidearm, time moving by slowly. He wasn't sure what to do next. But, just like switching a light off, Rostami changed his approach, broaching a broad, sickening smile at Ming without waiting for his reply. 'I'm glad we understand each other, Mr Bao. My men will escort you back. I'm sure a helicopter will be here shortly to take you back to your embassy.'

The colonel followed Ming out of the tent. 'Clean up the mess and put him with the others,' he barked at the guards.

Ming turned and put on his bravest face. 'Thank you for that enlightening conversation, colonel.'

Rostami paused, examining Ming a final time before moving away dismissively. A sense of relief flowed through Ming. Relief at being out of the stuffy tent, and relief he wasn't the man being buried in an unmarked grave. The boiling heat of the desert was almost pleasant compared to the atmosphere inside the tent.

As Ming walked back to the main camp, his mind was working overtime, his heart pumping, the sense of danger receding. He normally relished this feeling, but the implications for his mission were clear, and Rostami was something that Ming had rarely encountered. He was a true believer, a fanatic – but worse, he was cunning, intelligent and highly capable. But, despite the colonel's threats, Ming knew he was not in total control. He hadn't mentioned Merada, or anything that was happening back in Tehran. He mustn't know yet, Ming thought. Merada had climbed aboard one of the transport helicopters a couple of hours ago to speak with the president and garner support in their deal to hand over the missile, while Chinese officials back at the embassy had been pulling overtime to reach an agreement. They'd all been successful, and Rostami didn't know. If he did, Ming was sure he'd be in the ground now. Rostami would be called away shortly, and when that happened, Ming would move. For now, he just had to make himself scarce.

HQJOC – Australia

Today, Danny was determined. The team had left deflated and sour after last week. Mike's outright dismissal of their findings had infuriated Danny, but it hadn't surprised him. Mike was ultimately lazy and risk-averse. Today would be different. He'd talked over his plan of attack with Leah, and her advice, which was almost sage, had fuelled him. As he strode through the security checkpoint, he knew they'd get somewhere today.

Tossing his bag on the floor next to his desk, he strode right over to Mike's office.

He gave a gentle tap on Mike's open office door. The man looked startled, and Danny realised that it didn't look like Mike had slept much. A flicker of hope surged inside him; maybe there was something major going on, maybe they were actioning their information.

'What do you want, Danny?'

Not to be dissuaded, Danny shrugged off Mike's rudeness, adopting a cheery tone. 'I just wanted check how the seniors took the info. Can we start digging and get some requests out?'

Mike sighed, 'Take and seat, and close the door, would you?'

This wasn't good, but Danny did as he was told.

Mike gave a slight pause, then using a soft, conciliatory tone, said, 'Listen, Danny, you and the team have done great work. I briefed everyone yesterday, but there were some concerns. Nothing that reflects on you or the team, of course – but it is safe to say they weren't convinced …'

'What do you mean?'

Mike held up his hand. 'Danny, please let me continue.'

Danny held his tongue, his mind racing.

'As I was saying, you've all done great work, but we have a problem.'

Danny raised an eyebrow.

Mike gazed back at Danny for a moment before sighing and looking away. 'Danny, this test is very important to some very powerful people, and they aren't very happy.'

He wasn't entirely sure what Mike meant by "powerful people".

'Now, given how important this test and the missile are, we need to make sure we are providing the best advice and information possible.'

'Mike, my job is to support this team and help develop this weapon system. I am tasked with providing intelligence and threat reports directly through this team and nowhere else – what exactly are you suggesting?'

His boss clenched his jaw tight, 'Danny, you need to work with me here. Do you get me?'

'I really don't. What are you saying?'

'Look, what I'm saying is we need to find this thing at any cost, you understand? Any cost?'

'I mean, that's why we're working so hard, Mike. That's why we gave you the brief. I just don't understand why it hasn't started a firestorm of activity.'

Mike held up his hand again. Danny bit his tongue; he could feel his anger rising now.

Mike continued, 'Which is why ... we need to make sure we know what the Australians know.'

'What?! They know the same as us, Mike! We share pretty much everything – how the hell would they know more about the missile *we* fired?'

Mike was now staring at Danny, his arms propped up against his desk with his index fingers meeting at his bottom lip. 'You never know, Danny; they could be hiding something from us. Hell, maybe they did something to the missile after they found out we changed the test parameters.'

It was madness, and Danny suspected Mike knew it. There was no way the Australians could have changed the missile's flight. 'Mike, I don't even know where to begin with that. I'm just going to pretend you never suggested it.'

'It's our technology, it's our missile! We're the ones doing all the work, they're just benefiting from it! That means, Danny, we decide what information and access they can and can't have!' Mike suddenly snapped.

The irony that they were sitting inside a secure Australian facility as part of a joint US–Australian team seemed lost on Mike. Not the least that both Danny and Mike were equal parts to their Australian counterparts. This was utter nonsense to Danny. It didn't even make sense, but Mike was pushing hard. Something else was coming.

'Let me be clear, Danny: I want to know everything – I mean everything – they report.'

'What the hell is this?' Danny replied, feeling the anger spreading from his ears and down his collar.

Mike continued, ignoring Danny, 'Secondly, you are not to share anything more with them, do you hear me?'

'No, Mike! I don't hear you!' Danny yelled back. He didn't care about being polite or controlling himself anymore; this was too much. 'You're talking about cutting our team in half, and then treating them like the enemy. Where is this coming from?'

'That's none of your business, Danny! You do as I say,' Mike shouted back, his face becoming redder by the second.

'Mike, I won't do this. This is wrong,' Danny said firmly. He tried with all his might to restrain himself; he needed to remain focused and rational.

Mike smiled at him, a sickly, evil-looking gleam in his eyes. 'Are you sure, Danny? I'm not sure someone in your position, someone who has embraced Australia so ... *fondly*, can stand back and stay impartial. You, Danny, have to prove yourself to your country. I've defended you, Danny. Did you know that? There have been some questions asked about your loyalty. Whether you can still be trusted. If you can't help me, I don't know if I'll be able to protect you for much longer.'

'I don't need or want your protection, Mike. Leave me out of this,' Danny replied firmly.

'But what about Leah? She needs you, right? You can't protect her if you are sent back home, can you? And Danny, you two do look so very happy. We wouldn't want anything to get in the way of that, would we?' The evil smile on Mike's face remained frozen in place as he flipped around the monitor of his computer, revealing a colourful picture of a couple cuddling at a park. Danny's temperature dropped instantly, his mind recognising the spot where he and Leah had been only a day before. His mind went into overdrive, a hundred questions all begging to be answered at once. How did Mike have this photo? Who took the photo? Why was Mike showing him this? What did he want?

Danny took a big breath and squeezed his hands tighter as he tried to quieten his mind. A vitriolic rage seemed to burn inside him. *How fucking dare he?* The violation of their privacy! Spying on him?! The threat to him and Leah wasn't even suggested – it was clear as day. A small part of Danny's brain tried to find some twisted logic to Mike's actions. Maybe he'd come across the photos some innocuous way? No, there was no way. This was wrong. His brain let out another warning; something was very wrong. Mike's behaviour was far beyond anything Danny would have expected. He needed to tread as carefully as possible now.

Through gritted teeth, he said, 'I'm listening.' It was all he could think of to give himself more time to process what was going on.

Mike clearly sensed a victory. 'Look, Danny, of course everything I'm saying is just hypothetical, but we can't be too sure, can we? I don't like this any more than you do, but orders are orders, right?'

Danny remained silent as Mike continued, 'All we need to do is keep track of everything the Australians are working on relating to the missile. It's your team, so it should be nice and easy. Just make sure you now send everything – data, reports, the lot – to me. Okay? Nothing ridiculous. Just an email a couple of times a day with updates. Nice and simple.'

The simmering rage inside Danny began to subside, replaced with another feeling, a cold uncertainty and confusion. Danny had assumed Mike was just trying to make him a scapegoat for the missile loss, but this, this was something else. It made him feel uncomfortable and uncertain. It must have shown on Danny's face because Mike gave him a hard look. 'I'll need an answer, Danny.'

If he'd had his phone on him, he would have recorded the conversation, but Mike had, of course, picked a location where Danny wouldn't and couldn't have it on him, the security requirements of his job keeping any electronic device behind lock and key. Maybe he was more cunning than Danny had given him credit for. Everything would be off the record, but the implications were real enough.

He was stuck, and they both knew it. He could refuse Mike here and now and deal with the consequences, or he could play ball and see what he could find out. He didn't know what was going on, but he had to find out – for his sake, and for Leah, his team and the project.

He released the tension from his balled-up hands and relaxed his body bit by bit. In a flat, cold voice, he answered, 'Alright Mike, I'll do it.'

Mike immediately brightened, any hint of malicious intent seemingly gone in an instant. 'Outstanding, Danny. I knew I could count on you!'

For Danny, the meeting was over. He began to stand while the now-pleasant Mike continued to chatter away.

'Return to work for now, Danny, and make sure this stays between you and me. No one else, you understand. Even the other Americans. We must keep the circle closed.'

The alarm bells were truly ringing now. Even if Mike was speaking some form of the truth, asking Danny to do something with no one to witness it, and telling him to keep it secret – it just didn't make sense. More than a few people in the intelligence community had been burnt this way before; it wouldn't happen to Danny. He wouldn't let it happen.

He left Mike where he sat without really thinking about it, his mind running at a million miles an hour. His team had arrived since he'd entered Mike's office. How long had he been in there? He couldn't really tell; his sense of time had been warped by his rage. He knew if he went to them now, he'd appear visually upset, and it would lead to more questions. He skirted his team, hoping they wouldn't see him, then he swiped his pass and darted out the door.

The corridor was clear outside. No Mike. He quickly retrieved his phone and found the number he was after. He needed allies, and fast.

He pressed dial, praying the person on the other end of the line would pick up. He tried to release his fists, realising they were balled tightly again. He felt ill, he felt mad. But most of all, he felt scared.

CHAPTER 8

Creech Air-Force Base – United States of America

The MQ-9A Reaper drone flew lazily through the clear midday sky. Invisible from the ground, a mere speck against the blue backdrop of the sky, its small propeller engine impossible to hear. The baking heat of the Iranian desert some 50,000 feet below was a distant concern for the aircraft.

The pilot shook her head, reading her vague orders, as she sat at Creech Air-Force Base, half a world away from her aircraft. 'How's it looking?' she said to the man next to her – her sensor operator, a tech sergeant.

'All quiet so far, LT. They don't have much radar coverage out here, and even if they did, I doubt they'd be able to spot us. Their air defence is trash,' the man responded without breaking eye contact with one of his numerous monitors.

They both sat inside a GCS, or ground control station, which was essentially a large, air-conditioned container. From there, they could send and receive information and commands from the Reaper drone. The pilot kept her hands on the controls; if she needed to, she could change direction rapidly.

Their shift had started off normal enough, conducting a standard recon operation, but the sudden arrival of a lieutenant colonel from the 489th Attack Squadron had quickly changed things. The original mission had been scrubbed and a new set of orders thrust into their laps. A mission coordinator had arrived soon after, immediately dialling an unknown person on a secure phone.

It wasn't abnormal by any sense, the pilot reasoned. Normally, it meant that some high-priority target had come up through intel or some unknown source. Their job would be to get eyes and, if needed, take them out. Still, she had been looking forward to a beer; the overtime wouldn't hurt though.

'Nothing on radar?' she asked.

'A few low-flying helos, but nothing for us to worry about. Only way they're shooting us down is if they scramble fighters, and we'll see them coming.'

'Good.' She turned her head slightly to speak to the lieutenant colonel standing at her left shoulder. 'Sir, we're coming up on the coordinates now. What are we looking for exactly? The orders aren't clear.'

'A military camp,' he replied simply, not really answering her question. 'Bring the feed up on the big screen.'

'Yes, sir, bringing it up now.' The sensor operator quickly manipulated his controls to focus the Reaper's powerful camera and senior suite on the desert below. The defined images of tents, vehicles and people in military fatigues quickly came into view.

'Weird place for a camp out here – pretty isolated,' the sensor operator quipped.

'Yeah, you're gonna get thirsty real quick down there, that's for sure. They must be trucking everything in. Long-ass drive,' the pilot replied.

'Shit, I'm thirsty now,' he replied with a smile, hinting at their aborted plans for beers after work.

The lieutenant colonel ignored their conversation as he

watched the display intently, conferring quietly with the mission coordinator. He'd placed a set of headphones on; they must have been connected to a different channel so that the pilots couldn't hear a word. Whoever was on the other end of the secure line was clearly important.

'Anything standing out down there? Missiles or weapons?' he asked the pilot, relaying the question from his headset.

'Let's take a look,' the sensor operator said, panning the camera and zooming in. 'Looks like a few poorly concealed emplacements – probably AA, nothing more than shoulder-launched systems at most.' He paused, 'Although, it kinda looks like they are pulling them down.'

The lieutenant colonel relayed everything quietly. 'Keep looking, we're after something bigger.'

'Okay …' The sensor operator panned the camera into the camp, giving the pilot a quick glance, one eyebrow raised. They weren't normally this in-the-dark. 'What about this? Looks like these guys are loading something onto a truck.'

'Where?!' the lieutenant colonel said suddenly, almost startling the pilot.

'Just there.' He pointed to his screen for the senior officer. 'Three large trucks, next to some big tent in the centre of the camp.'

The lieutenant colonel stood perfectly still, examining the image. 'Stay with the trucks. Any eyes on what's in them? You're certain they're loading?'

He flicked through different sensors, checking the infrared. 'Not seeing anything more on scopes.'

The sensor operator waited a moment, watching the activity carefully. 'Definitely loading; looks like they are moving some kind of crate or container in now. Pretty big and heavy. They're being super careful, and they're using a forklift.' He flicked through different sensors. 'Not seeing anything more on scopes.'

'There's a decent amount of armed vics down there –

escort, maybe? I'm seeing at least three armoured personnel carriers and like six, maybe seven, technicals.'

They stayed on the trucks, watching as the soldiers milled around, moving crates and packing down tents.

'These guys are definitely getting ready to move, sir.'

'Where do those roads lead?' the lieutenant colonel asked quickly.

The pilot yawed the Reaper drone, giving her sensor operator a better view of the camp.

'Looks like they've bulldozed a rough access road to the site …' He panned the camera further afield. 'Continues for a few hundred metres before it intersects with a dirt road. After that,' the sensor operator paused as he checked a local map, 'looks like it'll link up with the paved road. Highway 68. From there, they could pretty much move anywhere.'

A degree of energy and tension had started to build inside the GCS. Normally they spent hours looking at nothing; this was different. They'd only arrived on scene minutes before, and already there was movement. The lieutenant colonel was absolutely focused, while the Reaper crew still had no idea what they were looking for.

'They're moving,' the pilot announced suddenly. Three trucks were trundling out of the camp and along a makeshift road.

'Armed vics following. Forming a convoy,' the sensor operator said.

'Confirm we cannot see what's loaded in the trucks?' the lieutenant colonel said suddenly, clearly relaying a question from the secure line.

'Negative, sir.' The trucks had made their way along the access track, turning onto the more frequently used dirt road.

The pilot continued to make minor adjustments, giving them the best angle on the convoy and avoiding the sun so it didn't cast a shadow. They didn't want anyone to know that they were following. But, with perfect weather and zero clouds, the image was crystal clear.

'Anything else back in the camp?' the lieutenant colonel asked.

The pilot replied, 'We'd have to swing the aircraft back around to get a clean shot, but we are recording, so we can always review.'

The senior officer seemed annoyed at her response but held his tongue.

'Uhhh, I think they are splitting up,' the sensor operator said suddenly. The last truck in the convoy turned the opposite way to the first two, a small armed escort following closely behind.

'Oh yeah, there they go: one east, the others west, by the looks of it. We're going to need to figure out who to follow here; we can't cover both groups.'

The lieutenant colonel conferred with the person on the secure line for a few minutes. 'The truck we saw being loaded – which way is that one going?'

The sensor operator answered immediately, 'West, sir, with another truck and escorts in tow.'

'Follow that one,' he ordered hurriedly.

'Tracking,' the pilot said, gently altering the Reaper's flight.

The drone continued its lazy flight, its Hellfire missiles gleaming in the bright sun.

The White House – United States of America

Quinton felt good. Despite the chaos and stress of yesterday, he knew things would improve as he entered his office in the White House. He considered himself smarter than most people, and he believed that as long as his instructions were followed, no situation was too difficult to handle.

He'd only just put down his bag and checked his mail when his secretary called. 'Mr Davenport, Mr Vanderhoe is holding for you on the secure line. He said it was urgent.'

'Good, thank you,' he replied. Dick was loyal, he knew;

and he was good at what he did, but given the nature of the work he did, he was often the bearer of bad news. Quinton checked the time. Dick must be at the Pentagon by now, likely liaising with the Reaper team. There must be an update then; a degree of anticipation was building inside his stomach.

He swept up the secure phone in his hand without sitting, preferring to look out the window of his office at the cool autumn morning. 'Yes?'

Dick's cold, balanced voice responded immediately; he wasn't one for small talk or pleasantries, always straight to the point. 'We have eyes on the camp, sir, but there is a problem.'

Quinton tensed. 'Go on.'

'As the Reaper arrived on station, a number of cargo trucks were seen departing the camp. It appears they have loaded an unknown cargo, but they have an armed escort.'

'So?' Quinton didn't immediately see the significance.

Dick paused only momentarily, 'We can't know for certain what was loaded, sir, but we did witness one large crate being moved onto one of the trucks. It could have been the missile. But sir, they have armed escorts on the trucks – that suggests whatever it is, the cargo is important.'

'Right, any idea where they are heading?'

'No, sir. It's pretty remote, and their highways go on for hundreds of miles. Could be any location at this point.'

'Alright, and you feel confident the missile is on one of these trucks?'

'It's a possibility, sir, but we can't be certain. There is another problem, however.'

Quinton sighed, 'Which is?'

'The cargo trucks have split up; we will not be able to track them all.'

Quinton groaned, 'Goddamnit … knowing the Iranians, they'll try and parade our missile down the streets of Tehran, show it off to the whole damn world!'

Dick remained silent.

'Okay ... Which truck are you tracking now?' Quinton said, rubbing his temples.

'The one we saw loading the large crate, sir, it's the mos––'

Quinton cut him off, 'Yes, I know, it's the most logical.' He wouldn't say it, but it was the choice he would have made. Compliments never came easy to Quinton.

'What do you want to do, sir?' There was a slight edge to the man's voice – anticipation, maybe?

Right, next steps, he thought. 'Keep following the truck. I want to know where the hell it's going, and if we need to, you have authorisation to take kinetic action, but I want to know first.' The implications of a strike against foreign targets in a foreign country didn't even register in his brain.

'Follow the truck we saw loading the crate, sir?' Dick asked.

'Yes! You idiot!' Quinton felt exasperated. Did he really have to explain everything?

'Understood, sir.'

'Update me if anything changes.' He hung up, slamming the phone receiver back into its cradle, the good feelings of the morning evaporating and a sense of powerlessness quickly returning.

He sat there brooding for a moment before opening his inbox. Hundreds of fresh emails were waiting for him. He initially scrolled mindlessly before starting to read some of the more interesting reports. An hour disappeared rapidly as he consumed the morning's briefings. He always tried to keep his morning clear of meetings so he could read what he needed to. But now, he fidgeted at his desk, procrastinating, his mind racing as he explored the various possibilities. What if the Iranians paraded the missile around? How would he explain it? Could he protect himself? The questions were endless, and all without answers. A couple of hours had passed when his phone buzzed loudly.

'Yes? What do you have for me?' he answered coolly.

'We might have a complication,' Dick's unemotional voice answered. 'A Chinese Air Force transport has just come up on radar, appears to be making a scheduled landing at a nearby air base.'

Quinton's heart skipped a beat, '*What?*'

'Yes, sir. I don't think it'll be a problem. It was a scheduled flight, but we don't have a visual of that other transport truck, and it was —'

'Heading in that direction,' Quinton finished, interrupting Dick again. 'What's the name of the air base?'

A slight pause. 'Um … Zahedan Air Base,' Dick confirmed.

'How are we seeing this Chinese plane?'

'There is a E-3 sentry on station providing support over the Strait of Hormuz.'

'Dick, let me be fucking clear: turn that drone around and get eyes on the other truck. And tell the E-3 to fuck right off. Do you hear me?' He could feel the temperature around his neck and ears building quickly.

Dick paused. He knew better than to try and apply logic to his boss when he was worked up. 'Understood, sir. Re-tasking the Reaper. What do you want to do about the Chinese?'

'Just get eyes on the air base first, but Dick – get rid of the E-3. Understood?' Quinton knew exactly what needed to be done; the answers always came easily to him. There wasn't a need to reflect or reconsider. His mind was made up.

Zhongnanhai – China

Despite its enormous size, the gears of the Chinese Government could move quickly, especially when led by a small group of senior people. The Leading Small Group, as it was known by Western analysts, was one such group. Comprised of key PLA generals, government officials and, of course, the president's office, it was responsible for the key decision making for the entire operation. Logistics and operational work would be handled by their respective offices and agencies, but the decisions would be theirs. There were still politics within the group, but without so many middlemen and personal rivalries, issues were easier to overcome.

Once the images and reports from Iran had been confirmed, the path forward had been clear, and in a rare show of solidarity, both the military and security services agreed that the missile and the technology that enabled it must be seized.

Inside a secure, richly decorated room within the Chinese Communist Party Headquarters, the debate was well underway.

'Our office has drafted a proposal for the Iranians, offering them considerable economic aid, as well as sharing some key military technologies – namely missile and fighter jet tech. We have already engaged with their president's office and confirmed the terms will be favourable, especially with some additional financial support,' the head of the ministry of foreign affairs said.

As one of the weaker ministries within the Chinese Government, they leapt at any chance to appear useful. Chang knew that the actual agreement would most likely be hashed out by lower-level diplomats and intelligence officers, but there was no value in correcting the man. Rather, it would be better to demonstrate his own ministry's commanding position of power over the operation.

'Our field operative has continued to feed intelligence through the Tehran Embassy; we will be able to maintain constant awareness of the missile's location.'

'However, according to your man's report, this Colonel Rostami looks to be a problem,' the foreign affairs head inserted.

Chang responded confidently, 'Nothing to be concerned about. If you read further into the report, a suitable solution has been found. Our agents in Tehran have already made the approach to the president's office, and the colonel will be recalled.'

The foreign affairs head didn't push the point further. 'Very well.'

The head of the People's Liberation Army Air Force, an aged lieutenant general, stepped into the debate confidently. 'Comrades, the real question is, how do we get this precious cargo back to our lands? I suggest we aim for the shortest route and move as quickly as possible. There is no telling when the Americans will react, after all. Our air force can have suitable transport in Iran within the next couple of hours. After that, it is only a short flight. Safe and simple!' He slapped his palm against the oaken table for added effect, clearly feeling his argument strongly.

'I think we must be more careful, Comrades,' the slightly younger Admiral Tung, who represented the People's Liberation Army Navy, cautioned. 'Planes can be shot down easily; it would be a shame to lose this treasure to a single missile. The navy has modern, well-armed ships in the region; we can easily pick up the missile and transport it under guard back to our waters. The Americans wouldn't dare stop us!'

'Comrade admiral, I accept your vessels are powerful, but that plan will take time. We already have a transport plane heading to Iran we could use; this weapon could be in our hands in hours, not days,' the air force general rebutted.

News of a transport plane already moving alarmed Chang; for his plan, they needed secrecy at all costs. 'Comrade, this transport plane, I hope you have not made a unilateral decision and dispatched an aircraft without warning us?' He tried to resist the urge to scold the man like a child.

The general waved his hand dismissively. 'No, no, it is just a routine flight,' he paused, checking his notes, 'to some air base, Zahedan, but we could easily use it to transport the cargo.'

That was alright then. It wouldn't alert the Americans or

anyone else who might be paying attention. Chang nodded back at the man, accepting the response.

The debate raged on between the different arms of the military, all of whom sought to play the principal role and assert their power over the fallen missile. Chang sat in silence, amused at the debate. The army had actually suggested providing an armed escort across Afghanistan with the missile. Chang had a plan of his own, one that the president himself was aware of and had endorsed. But it never hurt to let the military men show off; they often made themselves out to be fools, as far as Chang was concerned.

The president ultimately broke up the debate, leaning forward in his large, comfortable chair and saying, 'Gentlemen, these suggestions all have value, and I believe each arm of the military has a key role to play, but I believe Comrade Chang has a proposal of his own he'd like to share.' The president gave Chang a subtle nod. The floor was his.

Chang kept his voice clean and commanding, 'As we all know, this is an opportunity we cannot miss. This technology may be the key to securing China's future.' The men around the room all nodded. 'However, we must be careful. The Americans and their allies will undoubtedly be looking for their fallen missile, and they will do anything to get it back. From what we can tell, they have not yet figured out where the missile fell, but it won't stay that way for long, so it is imperative that the missile is moved soon.' The men kept nodding; this was nothing they didn't already know. 'I suggest, gentlemen, we take a modified approach to what has already been suggested in this room.' An image of a cargo ship flashed up on the screens around the room. 'Let me introduce you to the Huang Shen. She is a simple cargo ship, and she has just docked in Iran.' Chang paused a moment for dramatic effect. 'In order to keep the Americans completely unaware of our acquisition of their technology, I propose that we transport the missile to the Huang Shen, which will then make her way back to China completely under the Americans' noses.' Chang stopped talking, giving his colleagues the opportunity to either support or challenge him.

The head of the People's Liberation Army spoke first, seeing an opening for his service's involvement. 'I think this is a wise plan, and for added security, we can deploy one of our special forces units to board the Huang Shen and provide some degree of protection.' Chang had no issues with that; it was actually part of his plan anyway.

The admiral nodded, stroking his chin. 'I can see its merit. Once we get this ship through the Malacca Strait, the Americans will be hard pressed to do anything about it, although the ship will be vulnerable until it makes it through.'

Chang had anticipated this. 'Comrade admiral, we do have some forces in the Indian Ocean and Arabian Sea, do we not?'

'We do. A couple of destroyers and resupply vessels I believe.'

'Perhaps we use those ships to distract the Americans, draw their forces away?'

The admiral was quiet for a moment. 'It is possible … what did you have in mind?'

Chang could smell victory. 'Perhaps something involving the Maldives? Something the Americans cannot ignore?'

'I think we can work something out.'

The air force general remained the last senior member to speak, but with both the army and navy sounding their support, there was little the man could do. 'Comrade Chang's plan is a good one. It certainly has its risks, and I am not sure if they are greater than simply sending a plane for this missile.'

It was a weak argument.

The president spoke up quickly, sensing an agreement had been reached. 'Comrades, it appears we have reached a consensus. This Leading Small Group will endorse

Comrade Chang's proposal to recover the missile.'

Chang smiled across the room. If the operation was a success, it would be a major victory for him politically.

Tehran – Iran

'YOU DID WHAT!?' bellowed Colonel Rostami at the well-dressed man in front of him, face a mask of rage, jaw clenched and a large vein pulsing on his forehead. 'You give away what has fallen from the sky? What God himself provides our nation?!'

'Colonel, calm down, lest I remind you who you are speaking with,' the stern, educated voice replied.

Rostami tried to calm himself, but all thoughts of self-preservation were overwhelmed by the rage he felt. He managed a single word, trying with all his might to hide what he truly felt, '*Why?*'

The man on the other end of the phone sighed. He really hated explaining himself, but Rostami was useful. Best to give him something to settle him down; it would be a shame to lose such a useful tool.

'Colonel, I don't usually need to explain the choices of his excellency; however, given your service and value to our nation, I will explain this. The Chinese are clever, and they understand what we require to remain powerful. They are offering us more than one damaged missile ever could.'

'What do you mean?'

'I mean, colonel, that the Chinese are offering us economic security, and support against the Americans – real, military support.'

'But, if we have the technology ourselves, the potential …'

'ENOUGH!' the man yelled. 'We could at best hope to learn some of this technology's secrets in time, but it would take years. It's more likely the Americans would figure it out and attack us. Plus, the Chinese have promised to share the results with us,' the man added quickly at the end.

'And you believe them? They will steal everything and give us mere crumbs!' Rostami fumed.

'Nonsense, why would they? They want us to be powerful allies against the Americans. It's not within their interests to keep knowledge from us.'

Fool, Rostami thought. He knew better, and he was under no illusions about who would benefit from "economic security". The leaders of his nation were corrupt and greedy. What really burnt was watching a powerful piece of equipment, something that could change his nation's fortunes, traded like a cheap piece of meat.

'They will betray us,' Rostami muttered through clenched teeth.

'Colonel, you are growing fearful in your old age. I do hope your usefulness doesn't wane.' The threat was implicit.

'I can assure you, I am more useful than you know.'

'Hmm … Either way, the deal is done. And the preparations are already underway to move the missile.'

Really, he'd been recalled to ensure he didn't intervene. That much was clear now.

CHAPTER 9

USS John Basilone – Indian Ocean

Captain Kate Douglas dismounted from the side of the Sikorsky SH-60 Seahawk helicopter the moment the landing crew opened the door. The wash of the rotor blades pressed over her, forcing her to hold onto her cap tightly while she moved across the wet deck of the ship, crouching low to avoid the blades of the helicopter above her. A group of windswept officers huddled like penguins at the rear entrance of the ship, trying to keep dry in the stormy conditions while they waited for her.

The huddled officers quickly separated and saluted as she approached. Each shook her hand firmly, showing her the respect of a visiting captain from a foreign navy.

She'd hoped to see the man she was here to see on the deck, but she wasn't surprised he was absent. He was the captain of this ship, and he would have a multitude of duties similar to her own to attend to. Plus, the stray tropical storm wasn't exactly a treat to be in.

'I assume the captain is inside, gentlemen?' she asked, returning the handshakes and salutes. Her shouting could barely be heard over the noise of the helicopter mixed with the sound of the stormy ocean below.

The most senior of the group nodded, 'Yes, captain, he's on the bridge. If you'll follow me, we can get you out of this weather.'

She followed the American officers into the ship, letting the natural roll of the waves guide her balance through the metal corridors. Years of experience on the ocean had given her sea legs of steel, and she walked confidently through the tight corridors of the rolling ship, demonstrating her seasoned years out at sea. The sounds and smell of the foreign ship were nearly identical to her own; the tinge of grease and oil mixed with the constant thump of people walking against the metal floors brought a certain comfort to her. In reality, she probably didn't need a guide or escort. She'd spent more than enough time on American Arleigh Burke destroyers to be able to navigate her own way to the captain's office. But she was still a foreign officer on an American ship. Removing the escort wasn't an option.

The group wound their way through the ship, moving quickly through watertight bulkhead doors and up narrow stairways. Junior sailors pulled themselves into corners and doorways to make way for the officers, and Kate saluted each of them as they passed. A sense of curiosity washed over each of their faces, the speed and purpose of the group of officers catching their attention. It only took a few short minutes before they arrived at the bridge.

The senior officer announced their arrival. 'Captain Douglas, sir!' he said loudly, standing to attention and saluting the turned back of the American captain.

Captain Jonathan O'Donnell turned quickly, saluting Kate first and then the other officers before a broad grin took over his face. 'Captain, coming on board bring back memories?'

'Only the ones I try to suppress,' she replied, grinning.

He moved in for a handshake and she made sure to squeeze his hand as tightly as she could. 'Can't help yourself, can you?'

'Not even a little bit,' she replied lightly. They'd developed a strong friendship over the years, bonding over the strongest of experiences: shit bosses. Kate had met Jonathan when she'd been seconded across to a vessel Jonathan was serving on as a lieutenant early in his career. A tyrannical senior officer had made both their lives hell for a few months, and their friendship had been forged through shared suffering. Years had passed since the beginnings of their friendship, and they'd both risen the ranks, making captain in the same year, almost in the same month. Still, despite the years and senior ranks, their friendship hadn't changed much, with each taking a chance to try and poke fun at the other and one-up them when possible.

Jonathan led her to his stateroom, dismissing the other officers to their duties. This conversation would just be between the two of them.

Kate sat down on one of the comfortable leather chairs she'd sat in many times before. Jonathan's stateroom was larger and far more richly decorated than her own spartan office: hardwood flooring, with richly coloured rugs, and nautical artwork covering the walls. In some ways, it was almost too easy to forget they were on a warship; the constant roll of the room was only a small reminder of their fluid location.

He offered her a drink from a small bar cabinet tucked into the wall, which she happily accepted. Just a beer for now. Normally, she'd have preferred a gimlet.

Jonathan sat down on a small couch opposite her. 'So, what happened? We were expecting you days ago.'

She sighed. 'Out of my control. Our Seahawk had to go in for repairs, and they held us back thinking it would be ready. As you can see, I'm here, *late*, with no Seahawk, hitching a ride on your bird.'

He chuckled, 'Alright Kate, hit me with it then. I'm guessing you're not here for the twenty dollars I supposedly owe you,' he said with a look of mischief in his eyes.

'I'll get my twenty bucks, don't you worry.' She smiled

back before shifting to a more businesslike tone. 'But you're right, this isn't a social call.' She leaned forward, 'I've got Canberra sending me increasingly pissed-off messages, asking about the test. What's going on, Jonathan? I know the test failed, but why have we got radio silence? Have we recovered it?'

He grimaced slightly before leaning back into the couch, swirling his drink in his hand. He looked her in the eyes, 'Just between us, okay?'

She nodded, 'Always.'

He paused. 'We don't know where it went.'

Kate was a little dumbfounded. 'How is that possible? Surely we have a last-known location, radar, black box? Something?'

Jonathan took a sip of his drink. 'Nada. Not a thing – no signal, no debris, *nothing*. It seems to have just vanished.'

'Okay …' she paused, thinking quickly. That explained part of the issue, but not everything. 'But that shit happens all the time – what happened to the original launch schedule? Why the hell did we fire it north-west?'

Jonathan sighed. 'We received a change in orders the night before the launch. No warning, nothing. They completely changed the plan, and the direction of the test flight. We weren't given a reason why, but the orders came down from the top.'

Kate was silent for a moment. 'Alright, so just ignoring the part of this where Australia was cut out of the decision-making loop and some big shot just changed the plans on us, what's going on? Right now? Why aren't we working together on this?'

'Kate, honestly, I don't have a fucking clue. We're getting mixed signals from Washington. Everyone seems to be running around with their heads cut off.'

'Right,' she said simply, taking a swig of beer. Clearly there were some major problems state-side. 'So, what's next?'

Jonathan didn't answer straight away but stood up and

went to retrieve something from his desk. He fished around for a couple of seconds before pulling a manila folder out. He handed it over to Kate.

'Again, Kate, this has to stay between us.'

This was interesting. Jonathan wasn't normally so cagey or worried. 'Of course,' she answered impatiently.

'We're getting reassigned. They're moving the three vessels here to search around the Arabian Sea, while we're getting tasked off Sri Lanka.'

'The whole task group? What about the rest of the exercises we're meant to complete?'

'Sorry, Kate. Our orders are final. Someone wants this missile found more than anything. Plus, there are a couple of Chinese PLAN vessels cruising around out there. I think they want more muscle.'

Kate sucked air in through her teeth. 'Shit, Jonathan. Canberra is going to hit the roof. But I get it, kinda … if the Chinese get that missile, we're fucked.'

'Yep,' he replied simply, quietly.

Kate finished the rest of her beer and placed the empty bottle on the small coffee table. 'Well, my turn for the bad news, but I guess it doesn't matter anymore anyway. I'm getting re-tasked. I think Canberra is pissed about being cut out of the decision loop when the missile test was changed. They've got us chasing illegal fishers up near Timor. So, I won't be riding shotgun this time.'

Jonathan nodded quietly. 'I'm sorry, Kate. You know I wouldn't cut you out if it was up to me.'

Kate gave him a smile. 'Don't sweat it. I know … Plus, you're the one that lost the multi-billion-dollar state-of-the-art test weapon. I just turned up late.'

They talked for a little bit longer before it was time for Kate to leave. They'd been friends for nearly two decades, and this hadn't changed that. But, for the first time, it felt like their countries might not be on the same team.

Just as she was leaving, she said, 'You hear anything or find this missile, you let me know?'

'I will, I promise. But listen, keep your head down. Something doesn't feel right about this; feels like we're playing catch-up and only have half the information.'

As Kate boarded the Seahawk back to her own ship, she noted that the sun had reappeared and the tropical storm had been replaced with a gentle breeze. Her mind wandered as she gazed out of the plexiglass window. There was something going on that was above her pay level, but she couldn't figure it out. The pieces didn't seem to fit. All she knew was that she was purposely getting drawn away from the action. Her orders were sending her in the wrong direction.

Type 052D Luyang Destroyer – Indian Ocean

The Type 052D Luyang destroyer cut graceful lines through the relatively calm Indian Ocean. Commander Li Zaoling watched the numerous large cargo vessels drift along on a straight and steady course, their holds packed with millions of dollars' worth of trade goods. His vessel, one of China's most modern and powerful destroyers, had been patrolling the waters around India for the better part of a week. The Indians had taken exception to their presence, regularly overflying his ship and keeping a close eye on them. Li didn't mind. China's role in these waters was ascendent; the quicker the Indians learnt their place, the better. Still, despite the attention of the Indians, the patrol had been frustratingly uneventful and routine. That was, until the communications officer had handed Li his latest orders.

He didn't comprehend the orders entirely. His ship, and two others in the region, were to make best speed toward the Maldives capital of Malé. They were to make their approach as obvious as possible and cut a direct path. Once near the capital, they were to secure a small area and await further instructions. Li looked down at a chart of the area, and as far as he could tell, there was nothing there. Finally, he shrugged. Orders were orders, and his hunch was there must be another operation going on and he was inadvertently supporting it.

He gave the orders quickly and precisely, 'Bring us around, heading 200 degrees, make best speed.'

The navigation officer hurriedly replied, 'Heading 200, making best speed, aye, sir.'

The ship rumbled underneath them as they turned. Li smiled to himself; this was the most interesting thing that had happened to them in a while. The addition of two extra PLAN ships was curious. It would be a considerable combination of firepower, but for what? It would certainly cause a stir with the Indians. No doubt they'd mobilise in short order. But considering the specific mention not to hide their direction, it was clear that command wanted others to see them. Well, there were ways to be visible.

'Bring the Star of the Sea online. I want full power. Give us the widest coverage across all bands,' Li ordered, referring to the powerful Type 346 radar mounted atop his warship.

'That'll make us highly visible, sir,' the radar control officer commented. They seldom used the radar for fear that other vessels would collect the highly prized data it gathered. With it, they could more easily understand the radar's capabilities, and even jam it.

'Don't worry yourself with that. Our goal is to be seen, like a moth to a flame.'

'Aye-aye, sir,' the radar officer responded, somewhat confused.

Li quickly scribbled down a message on a piece of paper and handed it to the communications officer. 'Flash reply, get this back to command.'

The man saluted and hurried off. Li turned his gaze back to the commercial vessels, his mind drifting as he thought about his orders.

American Embassy – Canberra – Australia

Danny had been to the American Embassy in Canberra more times than he could count. But this time felt different, like he was in trouble or hiding something. It was stupid. He was just here to talk with an old friend, yet it was the topic of discussion that had his stomach tied in knots.

The embassy itself was located centrally within Canberra, a short walk from the Australian Parliament building. A Georgian-style historic estate, it stood out with its red-brick exterior and beautifully maintained gardens. Danny normally loved coming here, particularly for events.

He made his way to the staff offices, moving past the soldiers acting as guards. Every smile, every glance felt like another dagger in Danny's back. 'It's all in your head,' he whispered to himself. At last, he came to his destination and knocked gently on the wood-panelled door.

'Come in,' came a pleasant yet authoritative voice from the other side.

Timothy Ward was the legal attaché for the FBI operations in Australia. Normally, his role was one of coordinator and diplomat, but he still maintained all the powers of a federal investigator, and he was a friend to Danny.

'Danny, how are you going? We missed you at the embassy dinner the other night. Too busy playing with your toys again?' Tim grinned at Danny, standing up from behind his small but well-decorated office desk.

'Ah, you know me, Tim: give me some tech to play with and I'm gone.' In reality, Danny had skipped the event to hang out with Leah.

'Don't I know it. Interest you in a coffee? Maybe something stronger?' Tim offered.

'Got a beer?' Danny asked hopefully.

'For you, always!' Tim spun around on his chair and opened a small cabinet behind his desk. A tiny little bar fridge had been neatly hidden behind it. Tim pulled out two Australian beers with the words *Coast Ale* printed on their labels in red and blue. In a practised movement, Tim pried the bottle caps off and passed one to Danny. 'So, what's this about? You sounded pretty out of sorts on the phone yesterday.'

Danny took a big sip of his beer, sighing. 'I need to run something by you. I feel like I'm losing my mind a bit here, and I didn't know who else to ask.'

'Shit, Danny, you know I've got your back. Hit me with it.'

He took another smaller sip before starting, 'What do you know about Michael Clayton?'

'Who? Mike? You mean other than the fact that he's a massive jackass?'

Danny snorted mid-drink. 'Yeah, other than that,' Danny added neutrally, looking down at this beer.

Tim paused for a second, thinking. Danny figured he had a file on just about everyone at the embassy. 'Career public servant, floated around a few different agencies, used to have a good reputation. Has some political connections back state-side. That's pretty much it. All I really know for certain is that it's better when he's not around, which seems to be often enough. He's your boss, right?'

Danny nodded, 'Yeah.' He could feel his phone vibrating in his pocket; he ignored it.

'What's happened, Danny?'

He started at the beginning, not really knowing where else to start. 'Mike pulled me into his office the other day. Nothing out of the ordinary. But he starts talking about some special project and how we can't trust the Australians. He goes on to tell me that I need to start providing him with updates on what the Australians know about a project we're working on. Tells me I cannot tell anyone else and that I can only report to him. I've never been asked to do anything like this before – I work in a joint Australian–American team, for God's sake.'

Tim frowned, 'That doesn't sound right. Obviously I don't know the details of your work, nor do I want you to tell me here, but could this be part of your work, if you catch my drift?'

'Tim, I'm just an analyst; I'm no spook, and Mike isn't either. Our project is jointly run. It doesn't add up.'

'And there has never been any kind of request like this before?' Tim asked.

'Never, but here's the kicker: he said there were questions being asked regarding my relationship with Leah, and that I needed to prove my loyalty to the US.'

Tim sat up, leaning forward to look Danny in the eyes. 'You familiar with the acronym "MICE", Danny?'

He shook his head.

'It stands for Money, Ideology, Coercion and Ego. It's standard counter-intel speak. Basically, the four primary methods to lead someone into betraying their country or spying for another. What you just told me sounds an awful lot like coercion.'

Danny felt a mixture of emotions – anger, fear and vindication at the same time. 'Fuck, man.'

'That's one way to put it. This is a pretty big deal, Danny. Even with just the information you've given me, we'll need to launch an investigation, and we'll have to involve the Australians.'

'Guess it wasn't just in my head,' Danny said.

'No way. This smells bad and looks bad; there are protocols for this kind of stuff, and it doesn't happen without being recorded and run down the chain. Who's the boss on the Australian side there?'

'Maia Tavonga. She runs the project jointly with Mike, although in reality she does all the work and is more senior.'

'Right, we'll need to speak with her. The Australians have resources we can use, and given it's a joint project, it'll be necessary for the relationship side of things. I'll run this up the chain in Washington. We're going to need to be briefed into your work as well, Danny.'

Everything was moving faster than Danny felt comfortable with, but he trusted Tim. 'Alright, what do you need from me?'

'At the moment, nothing. We'll need your help organising a meeting with Maia, but we have channels we can go through here. The key is keeping Mike in the dark for as long as possible. That means you need to play a role here. He can't suspect anything has changed, so you're going to need to tough it out, but document anything and everything Mike says, especially if he tries to pressure you.'

This was well out of his comfort zone, but he agreed uncertainly, 'Okay.'

Tim gave him a kind look, his beer forgotten. 'Hey, don't sweat it, Danny. We've got your back, and you did the right thing.'

Danny nodded, feeling better. 'Who do you think he's working for?'

Tim shrugged. 'That's the million-dollar question. Either he's out for himself, which is definitely possible given what we know about Mike, or someone got to him. We won't know until we start digging.'

He was about to ask another question when his phone rang again. 'Sorry, Tim, I'd better take this,' Danny said, holding up his phone. He excused himself and strode into the hallway outside, 'This is Danny.'

Ata's clear and distinguishable voice shot through the phone, 'About time, Danny. Where'd you go, man? We need you back here.'

'Sorry, Ata. What's happening?'

'There've been some changes.' Her voice sounded unusually cryptic.

It was strange enough to pique his curiosity again. 'I'll be there in an hour. Just wrapping up my stuff here.' He really hoped it wasn't something to do with Mike. He'd taken a risk coming straight to the embassy and leaving the team. It was now midday, almost eighteen hours since they'd briefed Mike. He poked his head back through Tim's door. 'I've got to go; there's something going down at work. You'll let me know what happens next?'

'Leave it with me, Danny. Just remember: keep your

head down. We've got your back.'

Back in his office, Tim looked down at the quickly scribbled notes he'd made. Normally, he'd need something more concrete to start an investigation, but he knew Danny, and he trusted his integrity. If something seemed off, it was good enough for Tim. He snatched up his desk phone.

It rang only a couple of times before it was picked up. 'Yo, Bobby, how's things state-side?'

The man chuckled. 'Ha! Good, Tim. Surprised you haven't been killed by the wildlife down there yet.'

'Don't even get me started. Every time I take a step it feels like life and death – but hey, got something to run by you.'

'Shoot.'

'You ever meet or heard of a guy named Michael Clayton?'

'Name seems familiar, but I can't say I've met him.'

'Right, well I've got some information that he's possibly up to no good, sharing information and interfering where he shouldn't be. Potentially leaning on key staff members down here on a special project.'

'Shit, okay. Want me to look into it then?'

'I think so, but quietly, yeah? Check phone records, bank accounts, that kind of thing. This one feels off, and my hunch is this guy might not be acting alone.'

'Understood, Tim. I'll put a rush on it, let you know what I find tomorrow.'

'Thanks, Bobby. Have a good night. Steak's on me when I'm back, yeah?'

'I'll hold you to that!'

Tim put down the handset. Looking back at his notes, he scribbled down, *Who's calling the shots?* before locking the notepad into his safe.

E-3 Sentry – Strait of Hormuz

Michael Kim stifled a yawn as he stared into his monitor.

Another routine patrol, but this time there was a friendly drone hovering over the site. It was common enough to support these kinds of missions, yet Kim couldn't help but feel a sense of satisfaction that his report had led to another mission. It was a rare thing to get feedback or follow-up in his line of work.

With interest, the drone began to move away from the site, heading east. He had a perfect 360-degree scan of the airspace around it. There wasn't much going on. Bunch of commercial aircraft, but no more military helicopters. There was a Chinese military aircraft arriving at an airbase a short distance away. He noted it, but it ultimately didn't pose a threat.

The sudden shift in the E-3's direction surprised him. Normally they flew along in boring straight lines for hours on end. This was a more substantial turn. He poked his head up. 'What's happening, LT?'

His CO shrugged in reply, 'RTB.'

That was weird. They were only halfway into their scheduled patrol. But it did happen from time to time; sometimes there was a mechanical issue or just something more important back at base, although it didn't normally happen while they were supporting another aircraft.

Already, his view of the Reaper drone was declining. The powerful AN/APY-1/2 passive scanned array system on top of the E-3 didn't have unlimited range. A tinge of disappointment washed over him; he'd wanted to see what the drone did, see if his work led to something more.

He took one last look at the skies over Iran as the Reaper dropped off his monitor. There wasn't anything too crazy, but another Chinese plane seemed to be landing in the south. Some kind of luxury jet, but still military-flagged. He noted it as well before moving onto his next task.

Creech Air Force Base – USA

'Visual coming up now.'

They'd abandoned the larger convoy to try and reach the third vehicle, but the decision to focus on the other vehicles had cost them time, and now they were racing to catch up.

The large air base loomed across the multiple monitors inside the GCS. 'Look for the convoy; we need eyes on that truck ASAP,' the lieutenant colonel ordered.

The Reaper crew went about their task quietly, scanning the different buildings and vehicles. The base was a hive of activity, only making identification harder.

'Got a fair bit of activity outside one of the hangars,' the sensor operator announced. 'Looks like a cargo plane, an Il-76. Lots of boxes being loaded into the rear. Can we swing around a bit so we can see its designation?'

'Sure thing, wait one.' The pilot adjusted the Reaper's heading slightly, giving the sensor operator a wider side view of the plane. 'Try that.'

A distinctive red star with lines on either side stood out immediately. 'Chinese Air Force, looks like. Wonder what they're doing here?' the sensor operator said, peering closely at his monitors.

'Beats me – what are we looking for here, sir?' the pilot asked. She still didn't feel any more informed of their mission or what they were looking for, and she hated being kept in the dark, especially when it impacted her ability to do her job.

'We're looking for the truck and its cargo. See if you can get a view into the rear cargo hold of that aircraft.'

She moved the Reaper further away, giving the drone's cameras a longer, lower angle towards the parked cargo plane.

'That's better,' the sensor operator said. 'Let's have a closer look.'

The Reaper's cameras zoomed in on the Il-76's rear cargo bay, the longer angle providing a clearer but not complete image just inside the rear of the aircraft. 'Definitely some kind of containers; kinda looks like the shit we saw them loading back at the camp, but I can't be sure.'

'Alright, log it and let's move on, see if we can find that transport truck,' the lieutenant colonel ordered while he relayed everything through his headset to the mystery person on the other end.

They kept scanning the base, checking any possible spot the vehicles could be stored or parked. 'What about that?' the pilot said, pointing to a large, open hangar a short distance from the Chinese cargo plane. 'Multiple vics inside. I count at least two transports.'

'I think we have a winner. See that tear in the canvas covering? Our truck had the same thing. Pretty unlikely to have two trucks with the exact same damage.'

'Is it still loaded?' asked the lieutenant colonel.

Luckily, the truck was parked with its rear facing out of the hangar. The sensor operator focused his cameras on the rear tray. 'Afraid not, sir. Whatever was in there has been unloaded. No indication where it was unloaded – it's a big base. But that cargo plane is nearby; it could have been moved aboard before we got on station.'

The senior officer frowned at the suggestion, clearly thinking through the possibilities. He returned to the rear of the GCS and spoke quietly into his headset. A growing tension hung in the air-conditioned space as the Reaper crew exchanged confused and worried looks. Something was wrong with their mission; they just didn't know what.

The engines of the Il-76 rumbled to life, the heat quickly showing on the Reaper's sensors as a bright white flash against the grey tones of the rest of the aircraft. 'Uhhhh, we've got activity from that Il-76. Engines are on – looks like they might be getting ready to move,' the sensor operator warned.

The pilot kept the Reaper on a steady heading, allowing it to look down the length of the runway.

'Shit. Okay,' the lieutenant colonel muttered. 'We're sure we can't confirm what's on board that plane?'

'Negative, sir.'

'She's moving,' the sensor operator said. 'If she's been

loaded with whatever was in that truck, it's about to get a whole lot more airborne.'

The cargo plane trundled slowly along the taxiway, heading for the closest runway. It would only be a matter of minutes before it took off.

The lieutenant colonel was distracted by a conversation going on with his headset, uttering lots of "yes-sirs" and "no-sirs".

'Can we strike the aircraft?' he said suddenly. The pilot was momentarily floored.

'Umm, technically, but once it takes off and gets up to speed, we won't be able to do anything – we're tooled for ground attack. But sir, that is a Chinese military aircraft. Are we cleared to engage?' She felt a lump in the back of her throat. She'd seen questions like the one just asked of her quickly turn into poor decisions.

The senior continued his increasingly sharp conversation through his headset. The sensor operator kept his powerful camera aimed at the cargo plane, his hand on the trigger for the targeting laser. The Reaper's Hellfire missiles weren't designed to target aircraft, but the tech sergeant could guide the missile in with the drone's laser.

'Are you sure, sir?' the lieutenant colonel said loudly, a bead of sweat dropping from his chin.

The White House – United States of America

Quinton snatched up the phone receiver the moment it started ringing, his mood foul. 'Well?'

'Reaper is in position, sir, but there is a complication.'

He squeezed a small rubber ball in his hand, his knuckles turning white, 'Which is?'

'The Chinese cargo plane has loaded something; we cannot confirm what, but it's now on the taxiway and about to take off.'

'How can you not confirm what is in it?' Quinton demanded.

'Well, sir, we think we've found the transport truck, but we did not see it get unloaded. Shots of the plane did show large containers like we saw in the truck, but we have no idea if they are the ones.'

Quinton wanted to scream at the man – why did he have to explain everything to everyone? He tried to remain calm. 'Dick, you're telling me you've found the truck, unloaded. And that a Chinese cargo plane is there at the same time, being loaded, and is about to leave? How the fuck don't you see what's happening?'

Dick didn't respond; he'd played this game before.

Quinton seethed into the phone line, 'Clearly, they have our goddamn missile. We. Need. To. Stop. Them. *Now!*'

'What are your orders?' Dick asked robotically.

'Is the E-3 out of range?'

'Yes, sir.'

'Then fire on the fucking plane.' The response came so easily and automatically to Quinton. He didn't stop to consider his state of mind or the possible repercussions. This was the easiest way to solve the problem at hand.

'Sir, are you ordering me to fire on the Chinese Air Force plane in a foreign nation?'

The ball in his hand was being squeezed tighter and tighter; he could feel the throbbing starting just above his right eye. 'Dick, if you don't fucking kill that plane, I'll see you arrested.' His voice was quieter now, but cold.

'Yes, sir. We'll call back to confirm.'

The line clicked off. Quinton slowly put the receiver back down, trying to breathe. The implications of his order had not yet been processed. 'Fucking amateurs,' he muttered.

'What?' was the pilot's first response. 'Repeat.'

'Remove safety, and target Il-76 with the laser.'

'Yes, sir!' the pilot confirmed, glancing at her co-pilot, who gave her a look that said *what the fuck?* Their recon mission had quickly changed to a strike mission. And against a foreign nation, no less. The co-pilot locked the laser designator onto the now slowly moving Chinese plane.

'Sir, to confirm, we are to strike the aircraft? We are not armed for air-to-air.'

'Correct, and that thing will be moving slowly even after take-off; just keep it lased.'

'It's moving now. Take-off is imminent,' the co-pilot announced, watching the II-76 moving along the runway. With a tell-tale tilt, the nose of the cargo plane picked up and the tail dipped. 'Airborne.'

'Prepare to fire,' came the order.

'On target,' confirmed the co-pilot.

'Fire.'

'Firing,' the pilot said, depressing the trigger on her flight-control stick.

Chinese II-76 – Iran

The pilot yawned as they taxied towards the runway. 'Talk about hospitality – wouldn't even let us stretch our legs!'

'You're telling me. They seemed pretty on-edge though, like they were expecting something,' his co-pilot said. They'd both been flying for nearly eight hours and were starting to feel the effects.

'They keep flying us like this, we'll end up falling asleep at 30,000 feet, you know,' the pilot complained. 'What do they think, that the plane will land itself?'

His co-pilot offered a grunt in agreement. 'Let's just get out of here. I don't know how people live in this god-forsaken land. Just sand and rock.'

'Aren't you from the West?' the pilot smirked as he keyed into his radio. 'Tower, requesting permission for take-off.'

It didn't take long. The tower gave them immediate permission. The pilot eased the throttle forward gently, increasing power.

'Good riddance,' the co-pilot muttered as the power of

the aircraft increased. Thirty seconds later, they were barrelling down the runway. The pilot pulled the yoke back on his controls and the nose lifted skyward. There was a momentary feeling of weightlessness before the power of the large engines propelled them upwards. 'And we are away,' the pilot announced with satisfaction.

'So, what the hell were we picking up anyway?' the co-pilot asked, jerking his thumb back towards the cargo bay.

'Just more shit the Iranians broke, man. They can't repair it, or they don't want to, so we end up hauling it back. Why the hell they get us to do it is a fucking mystery to me.'

The co-pilot was about to respond when an alarm started blaring through the cockpit. 'Fuck! Missile launch!' the pilot yelled.

'Could it be a false alarm?'

'Do you really want to stick around and find out?! *Fuck*, we don't have the altitude yet; I'm turning.' The pilot gritted his teeth as he pushed the control arms downwards, forcing the nose of the plane to immediately dip back towards the dark-yellowish surface.

'Flarr—'

The co-pilot never finished his sentence. The laser-guided Hellfire missile slammed into the right wing of the heavy transport aircraft, blowing it apart in milliseconds. Even if the plane had been higher, surviving the loss of a wing was nearly impossible. The pilot continued to hold onto the control stick as the plane spiralled down to earth.

The loadmaster strapped in the back of the aircraft simply watched as the side of the plane disintegrated in front of his eyes. The wall of the aircraft was replaced with a spiralling view of the sky and ground. The containers in the rear were quickly sucked out of the plane, commencing their own descent to the ground below. Seconds later, the plane finished its doomed descent, impacting the ground in a massive explosion.

Fire and rescue crews were immediately dispatched, but the moment they arrived, it was clear no one had survived.

Charred and burning wreckage was all that remained of the aircraft. The debris covered the landscape for miles.

Creech Air Force Base – United States of America

'Well, shit, that's gotta be a first,' the sensor operator said as they watched the fireball flash across their monitors.

The pilot was silent for a moment. 'Yeah, I guess so, using a Hellfire on an airborne target …'

'I mean, barely airborne, but I doubt anyone else has done it. Shame we won't be able to tell anyone, I'm guessing. Right, sir?'

'Not a soul. I hope that's understood,' the lieutenant colonel said without emotion.

'Yes, sir,' they both replied.

'Good, RTB, mission complete.'

'Well, beer?' the pilot said.

'I'm gonna need one after this,' her sensor operator confirmed.

The White House – United States of America

'Well?' Quinton asked impatiently into his handset.

'It's done, sir. Aircraft destroyed.'

Quinton punched silently into the air, 'Goddamn excellent! Like to see those bastards try and steal our tech now!'

'Yes, sir. What are your orders now?'

'Any chance that anything survived?' he said quickly.

'No, sir. The plane's a total loss. No survivors or surviving missile components, if it was on that plane. It's done, sir.'

'No "ifs" about it – the missile was on that plane,' Quinton corrected.

'Yes, sir. What are we going to say about this, sir? We destroyed a Chinese Air Force plane.'

It was a good question, but Quinton wasn't in the mood. He'd just won; his anger had been replaced with elation.

'Fuck 'em. If they can try and prove we did it, let them try. Their plane crashed on take-off; hardly surprising. I'll make sure the messaging is consistent over here.'

'Okay, sir.'

A sudden thought popped into Quinton's head. The other part of the convoy. He was certain that they'd destroyed the missile, but it was probably better to be safe than sorry. 'Dick, make sure we keep an eye on those other trucks, just in case, although it'll probably be unnecessary.'

'The other trucks, sir?'

'Yes, Dick, let's keep an eye on them. The Iranians can be crafty – you never know, they might have pulled the thing apart.' Quinton pushed that thought aside as quickly as he'd spoken it. Now wasn't the time to dwell; he'd just gotten himself out of a jam, and he'd done it largely by himself. He knew he was right. Still, a glimmer of doubt lingered.

Dick left a long pause on the other end of the call. The transport trucks would be long gone by now, but his boss wouldn't accept it as an answer – not now that he felt so accomplished. Dick had learnt long ago not to step on Quinton's self-aggrandising moments; he'd be the one to suffer. Better to simply agree with him now. Maybe Quinton would forget the order, as he'd done so many times before. 'Yes, sir, no problem.'

'Good. Let me know if we spot anything of concern.' Quinton hung up without waiting for the man's reply. Goddamn, he felt good. The fact that men had just lost their lives never crossed his mind.

CHAPTER 10

Bandar Abbas – Iran

Ming stretched his arms and legs out as he exited the cabin of the stiff military truck. They'd been on the dusty, often bouncy and uneven roads of Iran's interior for hours, and his body felt the worse for it. They'd arrived in the port of Bandar Abbas, of the Strait of Hormuz, a bustling location, with multiple ships docked and cargo transiting through the port every day. It was the perfect spot to hide in the traffic. Ming was half surprised that the Americans hadn't already tried to intercept them. He didn't complain, of course, but he wasn't going to make it easy for them either. Everything they could do to conceal the missile would be done. He just hoped it was enough.

    The truck carrying the precious cargo had wasted no time, immediately moving closer to the water, the covers thrown off while a crane latched its hooks on the large container. Ming shielded his eyes as he watched the crate get lifted in the air, swinging around slowly while it was hoisted towards a waiting ship. He smiled to himself, feeling a sense of satisfaction. The plan had come off so quickly, and flawlessly.

The Iranian soldiers around them still had a nervous look in their eyes. They were constantly eyeing the cargo and Ming, almost as if they were cursed. The news that a Chinese plane had crashed closer to the east of the country hadn't helped things. Ming had heard of it over the radio, but he had paid little attention.

Ming and a couple of Iranian soldiers had slipped out in the dark of the night, carrying the precious cargo in a lone truck. Rostami had been whisked away in a helicopter shortly after their unpleasant meeting. Ming had no doubt he would have tried to stop them if he had still been around. In Ming's mind, the smaller the target, the less protection, the greater the likelihood it would go unnoticed. A large, protected convoy screamed importance, and the last thing Ming wanted was American Hellfire missiles raining down on him.

Still, it had been a long drive, all the way into the night and well into the next morning. He felt dirty, tired and sore.

Looking across the port, Ming sighed quietly. The next part of the journey wouldn't be much fun either.

Their transport, a commercial vessel named the Huang Shen, wasn't anything particularly spectacular. A classic cargo ship, it was designed to haul and hold various containers and bulk equipment. The rust and derelict signs across its hull didn't fill Ming with confidence, but then again, it didn't have to be clean or modern – it had to blend in, and for that it was perfect. With its red hull, large white superstructure and a couple of old loading cranes, it was, if anything, one of the most common sights on the ocean. Plus, it was large, with lots of places to hide, and to fight, if anyone tried to board her.

The crunch of gravel behind him caught his attention. Turning quickly, he was greeted by a comforting sight. A small bus had pulled up, and a cluster of people were making a hasty exit. Ming knew exactly who they were; a security team had been assigned to assist him, as well as a small number of scientists and specialists who would examine the missile while in transit. Beijing hadn't wanted a second wasted.

He couldn't help but frown as the members of the security team, decked out in black combat clothing, approached him with heavy bags slung over their shoulders. He counted only six; he'd hoped for much more. What was worse, the larger group, at least eight in total, wouldn't be much use – they had decidedly civilian mannerisms, looking around, both nervous and excited. Still, it was better than nothing, he supposed. The other main question for Ming, however, was the crew of the vessel itself. They didn't have time to replace the crew, and doing so would create a lot of loose ends anyway. He'd have to settle for the civilian crew that normally ran the vessel. They were Chinese at least, and they had been informed that their vessel was needed by the state, with no further information on who or what it carried.

His goal now would be keeping the knowledge of what was in the hull of the vessel as far from the crew as possible. Only the captain would have an idea, and even then, it would be far from the truth. If all went off well, they would be none the wiser, and other, harsher measures could be avoided upon their return to China. Still, it would take at least eight days before they reached Fiery Cross Reef, and in that time, a lot could go wrong. He'd feel a lot better once they'd passed the Malacca Strait in seven days and were under the protection of the Chinese military. By his rough calculation, the quickest route along international shipping lanes would be 4,200 nautical miles – not a short route, by any measure. But, by hiding in plain sight amongst the thousands of other commercial crafts, they would be almost impossible to find. At least, that was the idea.

One of the overly serious, gruff-looking soldiers approached Ming with purpose, his eyes locked on Ming. When he reached Ming, he stood to attention suddenly, offering a perfect, swift salute. 'Mr Fang? I am First Lieutenant Jiang.'

Roughly Ming's height, but with a clenched jaw, angular

features and a military-style buzz cut, Jiang looked like a warrior. Ming had no doubt he would be able to best him in a hand-to-hand fight. The large muscles that were seemingly bulging through the man's black fatigues suggested significant strength. Ming outranked him, but only just. As a captain, he would call the shots, but with all the men and guns, Jiang would have the power. Both men knew it. The fact Jiang hadn't used Ming's military rank was evidence that Jiang wasn't going to let rank dictate mission. He would do what he believed best, even if Ming didn't agree.

Ignoring Jiang's failure to use his military rank, Ming decided to copy his stiff, military air, standing to attention and saluting with an equally formal reply. 'Welcome, first lieutenant. You have my gratitude for getting here so quickly; I was concerned I would be forced to escort the package by myself.'

'We're always available for China,' Jiang replied. A fiery intensity seemed to burn in his eyes. A true believer, Ming decided there and then; he'd need to be careful around this man. He'd never been much of a follower himself, preferring to make his own path. But, around the wrong people, Ming's flexibility could be misconstrued as weakness – or worse, disloyalty.

'Yes, of course,' he replied swiftly before moving the conversation forward. 'Tell me, how many men do you have, and what are your plans for the mission?'

Ming already knew the number of men Jiang had and could guess the strategy, but it was worth hearing it from Jiang, give the sense that Ming wasn't as well informed as he actually was. Plus, it could always reveal more about Jiang himself.

'Including myself, we are a team of six, but you will find my unit highly capable and well trained for this kind of operation,' he said, turning to gesture towards his men, who were still unpacking the bus. 'As you can see, we have come well prepared; should anyone try and interfere with our mission, they will be met with harsh consequences.'

Ming nodded. Jiang was cocky, but there was a certain confidence in his voice that made Ming believe he meant everything he said. Although, considering the size of the cargo ship, the roughly fifteen or so unknown crew members, and the lack of any real defence, Ming wasn't sure Jiang's men and bravado would mean much. Their best bet was to remain as quiet and uninteresting as possible.

'Your team will be more than enough, lieutenant. Once we are all aboard with our equipment, we will depart. The captain of the vessel is loyal and knows not to ask questions. But I cannot speak for the crew – we'll need to be careful around them,' Ming warned.

Jiang looked past Ming, examining the vessel that was to be their ride. Jiang's eyes darted across the breadth of the vessel, homing in on the various features. Ming could see him trying to look for the ship's weaknesses. A good tactical eye, Ming decided.

'We'll board immediately. Are we responsible for the civilians as well, Mr Fang?'

A pointed question. What he was really asking was whether they'd be Ming's problem or his. Ming suspected he didn't want anything to do with them, especially if it meant babysitting. It was an opportunity for Ming to build some good will and ensure he had some control over the people actually driving the ship. 'No, I'll take care of them. Get your men aboard, lieutenant.'

One of the civilians seemed to almost sense what they'd been discussing, detaching himself from the rest of the group and marching up to Ming and Jiang with an air of self-importance and misplaced confidence. 'Comrades, I assume one of you is in charge?' He looked between the two of them. Jiang remained silent, looking at the civilian. Ming cleared his throat. The civilian's eyes darted to him immediately. 'Ah, Mr?' the civilian asked, hand outstretched.

'Fang,' Ming confirmed, taking the man's hand. He received a vigorous handshake in reply.

'Comrade, it is so excellent to meet you. I am Chief

Scientist Sun, expert in aeronautical and experimental missile technology. Now! Tell me, where are we to go? And when can we get to work? I, and my staff, are eager to get started.' The scientist spoke so fast he was almost breathless.

'Ah, chief scientist. How fortuitous it is to have you join us … there is much work to do.' Ming paused for effect. 'The vessel we will be taking is just behind us, the Huang Shen.'

The man frowned, looking past Ming at the fading writing on the ship, reading its name to confirm that what he said was true. 'But sir, that is a container vessel – it is not fit for our work! Surely there is a more state-of-the-art military vessel available to us?'

It seemed the chief scientist was not someone who liked to do without his creature comforts. Ming smiled, 'I am afraid not. For our mission, utmost secrecy is required; we will have to make do. But that shouldn't be a problem for you and your team. Surely, a man as talented as you can still achieve what China needs from you?'

The man was flustered, caught between the thought of slumming it on an old container vessel and his own patriotic beliefs. 'I … of course! We will do what we can … in these conditions.' A look of distaste had spread across his face.

Ming immediately brightened. 'Excellent! Then, in the meantime, take your staff, and whatever equipment you have, and board the vessel, following First Lieutenant Jiang.'

This was followed by another swift salute. 'Yes, sir.'

The chief scientist promptly marched off, yelling orders at his small team. *Poor bastards*, Ming thought. The man would be a thorn in his side.

Jiang, who had been watching the interaction with a look of amusement, promptly saluted Ming before returning to his men. Well, he had control for now. He just had to maintain it. The chief scientist he could handle, but the hardened military man would be a bit trickier. Best to keep him busy.

Swinging his backpack over his shoulder, Ming gathered up his meagre belongings. He hadn't packed for a multiple-week adventure, but events had outpaced his planning. He'd have to make do with whatever he had on him and anything he could get from the ship.

He pulled his mobile phone out and turned it on. As he waited for the device to boot up, the searing heat beat down on him. The little smartphone dinged pleasantly, downloading a steady flow of alerts and messages. He'd ignore most of them for now; they could wait. Tapping the Signal application, he pressed his thumb against the fingerprint scanner, logging in. Despite the plethora of secure communication devices and radios, sometimes the most secure form of communication was a simple encrypted application. His message would just be another one of many, amongst millions of other people sending messages. The NSA would have a hard, if not impossible, time cracking the message.

Loading up now. Cargo secure, team arrived. Will depart within the hour. He typed quickly; Case Officer Lin would probably be fretting. He could already see she'd sent at least four messages looking for updates.

Sighing quietly, Ming marched towards the Huang Shen, following the soldiers and civilians.

HQJOC – Australia

Danny was practically out of the breath by the time he swiped into his team's secure area. He'd rushed through the various checkpoints and up a couple of flights of stairs to get back as quickly as possible. But, once he was through the door, he was surprised; the team was quiet, working away diligently.

'Alright, what's going on?' he asked, announcing himself to the group.

Ata was momentarily startled at his arrival. 'Oh shit, you're here.' She recovered quickly, adding, 'About time.'

She had a questioning look on her face. Danny knew he didn't appear his normal self. He still felt on edge after Mike's shakedown.

'Sorry, guys. So, what do we have?' he asked, trying to move the conversation forward.

Jesse chimed in, 'Two things, first.' He pointed to a large wall-mounted monitor that had the BBC World News playing. Danny read the ticker at the bottom of the screen.

'Plane crash?' he asked, eyebrow raised.

'Not just any plane – a PLAAF transport, and guess where?'

Danny gazed back at the TV. 'Shit … that's not Iran, is it?'

Ata grinned, 'Winner-winner, chicken dinner. And what's better, guess how far it is from our Iranian campsite?'

Danny groaned. 'Show me,' he sighed.

'According to Google Maps, only a two-hour drive,' Ata replied.

'That feels a bit too off to be a coincidence. Wait, so what's the second thing?'

Jesse pointed to another monitor. It showed a sandy-looking area, devoid of any activity, yet seemingly only recently abandoned. Tracks and rubbish appeared in small piles, slowly gathering sand.

Danny groaned again, 'Is that the camp site?'

'Afraid so. The latest satellite pass shows absolutely nothing as of 0600 HRS local time,' Jesse confirmed.

An undeniable sense of failure seemed to radiate inward towards Danny. Their lead was gone. He could feel himself deflate.

Ata was watching him. 'There's one more thing. That report you found the other day. We've all lost access to it. The whole team. I've even asked around; seems to have been removed or blocked or something.'

Danny sat down in a heap on the nearest chair. Part of him wanted to cry, wondering what was going on and why. It seemed almost comical; they'd poured their efforts into trying to find the lost missile, only to have it blow up in their faces. 'Does Mike know?' He dreaded talking to the man alone, but it was his job, and he wouldn't let Mike stand over any of the other teammates if he could avoid it.

Sidney perked up, 'Mate, he's been about as useful as a chook with its head cut off. Been a total frenzy since the news of the Chinese plane crashing, but he hasn't been tasking us, just creating a fuss.'

Typical, Danny thought. Mike was still a problem he needed to solve, but he didn't know how yet. One silver lining of the report and the camp disappearing was that at least there wasn't anything he would or could report to Mike. A small saving grace.

'So, Danny, we've been mostly spinning our wheels here for the day. What's the go with the brief? Do we have a green light, or yeah … what's happening?'

Time to break the bad news. 'I spoke with Mike earlier.' He knew the team wasn't going to like this. 'And he basically told me he couldn't convince the bosses the information was worth checking into.'

Ata was the first to respond. 'Bullshit – I bet he didn't even brief them. You saw how he was in the meeting.'

'I know, Ata, and I'm sorry I was out, but I still reckon we had something. We just need something more, something they can't ignore.'

'Like what?' Sidney asked.

'I don't know. I'm sorry, guys. We just have to keep looking at our other avenues. Let's try and figure out what the hell happened to our camp, and if we can't find anything, we go back to trawling through SIGINT to find something, *anything*.' It wasn't the inspiring talk he'd wanted it to be. But it was the truth.

The team looked slightly deflated, but they put their heads down and started working away, a quietness settling over the work pod.

Danny spun around on his chair, thinking. There had to be a way to figure out where the camp had gone. He looked down at the printed copy of the report he'd made earlier. The contact details for the intelligence officer were still scribbled on the bottom. He'd left a message earlier but never got a reply. He checked the time on his watch; it would still be early morning over there. He might be able to reach him. He picked up his phone and dialled the man's contact number. After a few rings, the line finally clicked.

'Michael Kim,' a voice answered.

'Good morning, Michael. This is Daniel Blackburn posted over at HQJOC in Canberra Australia. I left you a message yesterday regarding a report you published recently.'

'Hi Daniel. Guessing you mean the report covering the Iranian activity in the desert?'

'That's the one. It sparked a fair bit of activity for us, and I wanted to discuss what you found the other day.'

'No joke, we were watching the activity today with interest. Shame our patrol was ended early.'

'Sorry, you were up earlier?'

'Yep, routine patrol, but we wanted to swing back around the site, support the recon effort there as well.'

Danny knew he was missing something now. 'Sorry, Michael. When you say "recon effort", what do you mean?'

Michael suddenly sounded wary, unsure whether he should continue. 'Uhhh, I can't really discuss that, sir, if you're not across it. You know, "need to know" and all that.' It was a poor attempt at covering his tracks and they both knew it.

Danny didn't push it, but he pocketed the information. There were clearly other players in the game he wasn't aware of. 'I see. Well, my team provides support to new weapons systems. Long story short, we lost our missile in a test and have been looking for it since. It's been a couple of days now. And it's also why we're so interested in your report.'

'Yeah, right. Well I can't say we spotted anything like your missile. I saw some of the sitreps that were flying around. By the time we were up there, there wasn't anything for us to see really, just a couple of PLAAF aircraft in the area, but our patrol was cut short for some reason.'

'PLAAF aircraft?'

'Yep, same one that took a dirt nap earlier. Shame we weren't on station; we probably could have figured out what happened. The Iranians are claiming someone shot it down.' There was a mocking, humorous tone in Michael's voice.

Something about the aircraft stuck in Danny's brain. 'Right ... And the other aircraft?'

'Just some VIP transport, headed over to Bandar Abbas, if I remember correctly. Beats me why they'd head there. It's mostly just a large port.'

'Okay, and getting back to the camp, was there anything you could add for context? Just want to understand everything I can.'

'Look, not really. We were up on a regular patrol and then, out of the blue, Iranian helicopters started flooding the area. Watched it for a good few hours. Real mixture of military and civilian stuff heading out there as well. No idea why – it's just a bloody desert.'

'Right, okay, one last thing: what happened to your report? We can no longer access it.'

Now Michael sounded confused. 'What do you mean?'

'It's gone, no one can access it.'

The man groaned. 'Ugh, thanks for the heads up. I bet I've done something to get it taken down. Leave it with me, I'll get it fixed.'

'No problem. Thanks, Michael – and you said *Bandar Abbas* for that PLAAF aircraft?'

'Yep, dirty old port city on the Strait of Hormuz.'

'Thanks, Michael.' Danny hung up.

Something about the whole situation bothered him. Why was there a drone operating over the site that they didn't know about? Who was playing games and trying to keep them out of it? What was the deal with the Chinese aircraft? The questions just kept building up. He looked down at his notepad, reading the words that had been hurriedly scribbled down. *Bandar Abbas*. A quick Google search brought up the city, the port facilities, maps and photos. He started scrolling through, his mind processing the information. It was close enough to the campsite, but it didn't have any major known military facilities that would normally handle high-tech weapons.

'Hey Ata, do we have any recent passes on Bandar Abbas?'

'Maybe. I can have a look. Why?'

'Just a hunch,' he replied cryptically.

'Ah, sure. Give me a sec.' He could see a curious look on her face. 'Okay, so captured a day or so ago. Got high-res shots of a good part of the city, few military sites and the port area. How much of it do you want?'

'All of it.'

'What are you looking for?'

'Not sure yet. Not sure.'

***

Danny spent the rest of the day flicking through the imagery and avoiding Mike, who thankfully wasn't present for most of the day. It was late in the afternoon. Sidney and Jesse had already left when it finally clicked. Ata was the only other person left.

'Ata, check this out,' Danny said suddenly, breaking the deathly silence that had settled over their work area and making her jump.

'Geez, give a girl some warning, Danny.'

'Sorry, Ata, but check this,' he replied quickly.

She rolled across on her chair and he gave her a quick update on his chat with Michael. 'So, essentially, I've been looking at Bandar Abbas for anything out of the ordinary. It seemed a bit strange to have a Chinese jet landing around the same time as our camp was seemingly getting disassembled. Especially as this isn't a spot frequently visited by the Chinese.'

She nodded, following his chain of thought.

'I managed to get some CCTV footage from some street cameras, and I got a shot of this white bus leaving the airport. I searched around for a while but noticed there was a decent amount of activity occurring at the port. Sure enough, I found the same white bus pulled up at one of the docks, near some cargo ship. I had a look at AIS data, and it's apparently a Chinese-flagged container vessel called the Huang Shen.'

'Don't often fly in replacement crews on VIP PLAAF aircraft, do they?' Ata commented.

'No, definitely not. And get this, the Huang Shen was due to move through the Suez and head to Rotterdam, but, as of two days —' he paused to check his watch, 'sorry, almost three days ago, its plans changed.'

'Don't keep me waiting, Danny,' Ata scolded him.

He pulled up a display of the vessel. 'AIS tracking has the Huang Shen now travelling eastward, right for the Malacca Strait. Probably a couple of days out.'

Ata leaned back in her chair. 'So, you reckon something is on that ship then, don't you?'

Danny smiled, 'I know it's a bit loose, but there's one more part to it. From the first images of the desert camp, we spotted a bunch of military transport trucks, and before you say it, *I know, super generic transport that is used all over the country by the military.*' He held up his hands in mock defence. 'But get this. I count at least four of these same transport trucks.' He pointed to a truck sitting by itself. 'What do you notice about it?'

Ata leant forward, looking at the image, 'Got an awfully distinct mark across its bonnet,' she said finally.

'Exactly!'

He pulled up the original satellite image of the port, but this time, with a large red circle over a group of vehicles. 'Tell me that isn't the same mark on that truck.'

Ata sucked air inward, making a whistling noise. 'Fuck me.'

He smiled at her. The feelings of defeat washed away in an instant.

Ata was suddenly energised. 'We need to jump on this now! Like, *today*. If the Chinese have the missile – I mean, we're fucked sideways anyway – but we need to tell someone, now!' She paused, looking at Danny, 'How do you want to handle Mike?'

He knew the answer already. 'We don't. We go around him, straight to Maia.'

She grinned, 'Atta boy. Let me set it up. Hopefully she's still here.'

She was. The rest of that afternoon then subsequent night was like a blur to Danny. Desperately pulling everything together into a set of PowerPoint slides, they'd ventured up into Maia's office, who looked curious at their arrival. Danny didn't waste any time. Inside the cramped office, he broke down the satellite images and his logic, taking a now very attentive Maia through the journey of their discovery. As they neared the end, she seemed convinced.

'Danny, Ata, this is great, but I've got to ask, why am I only hearing about this now?'

Danny answered, 'We only just pieced it together, to be honest.'

Ata said scathingly, 'We briefed Mike on the camp a day ago, but he told us that he briefed you and nothing came of it.'

Maia raised an eyebrow, 'I see ... So, he hasn't seen this?'

'No, he's already left,' Ata confirmed.

She asked a couple more questions before making a decision. 'Alright, can I get you two to stick around? I need to run this up the chain.'

They both nodded, not realising just how quickly their information would run, or how far. Less than an hour passed, with both Danny and Ata working furiously to tighten up the report and briefing pack, before Maia popped back down.

'Alright, both of you, let's go.'

CHAPTER 11

HQJOC – Australia

Maia returned with a sheepish look on her face. It was now late into the afternoon. Most of the shift workers had switched over, and anyone working business hours was long gone.

Danny could already tell the slight glimmer in her eye would mean something bad for him.

'Alright, Danny. You got a briefing pack good to go?' Maia asked.

He nodded in reply, 'Yep, it's all here for you.'

Maia gave him an evil little smile. 'Great, bring it with you – and Ata, you're coming as well.'

'Wait, what do you mean? Where are we going?'

Maia gave a little chuckle. 'Well, Danny, the bosses thought your intel so absurd that it was probably worth sharing with the seniors. And lucky for you, the joint chiefs and heads of the ADF are scheduled for their quarterly catch-up. You've just made the last-minute addition.'

'*W-w-what?*' he stammered.

'There will probably be a few other higher-ranking officials and personnel on the call as well.'

Ata whistled through her teeth. 'Better you than me, Danny,' she said, giving him a pat on the back.

'Don't stress, Danny. Just do what you did with me. It's just a briefing.'

It didn't feel like just a briefing, but he mustered a small nod. 'Yeah, okay …'

It wasn't long before Maia led them into a large meeting room that was brightly lit and filled with senior officials. More casually dressed than the rest of the room, Danny felt out of place and desperately wished he had a tie and blazer. The eyes of every person in the room seemed to follow him, trying to figure out who he was and what he was doing in this room. Maia took a seat at the table, pointing Danny to a spare seat next to her. Only the most senior people sat at the table; the rest were on the chairs behind.

He shuffled uncomfortably in the chair, flicking through his notes and memorising what he'd have to say. He'd done countless briefings before – but never one so suddenly and to such a powerful audience.

The majority of the meeting wasn't anything remotely linked to Danny or the project, but as they neared the end, an unseen moderator announced them, 'As a last-minute addition, there will be short brief on the recovery efforts of the hypersonic missile test conducted earlier in the week.'

That was Danny's cue.

He stumbled initially, his brain fighting against panic, trying to create a clean line of logic to follow. But, once he found it, everything started to flow. He was a good speaker, and briefings were just structured speech, in many ways. The goal was simply to present the information, clear and unbiased. Give them the facts, explain his assessment. That was all he had to do.

His slides were thrown up on the screen with satellite imagery showing search patterns and trajectories.

'Ladies and gentlemen, as you are aware, the latest hypersonic test ended when contact was lost with the test missile. We have run numerous possible paths and trajectories and found nothing. No debris or hint the missile ditched. Given the range of possible crash sites, it is not impossible we will never find evidence of the missile. However …'

The next slide went up, showing the desert camp in Iran.

'Roughly three hours after contact was lost, a routine E-3 patrol over the Strait of Hormuz spotted the rapid movement of Iranian military equipment to a seemingly random location in the Kuh-e-Birk Protected Area. Additional satellite imagery identified the camp you now see. We've run a number of possible scenarios for this sudden movement, but none make much sense. The location is desolate, with little importance and no military sites of significance. The equipment deployed, however, is significant. Considerable anti-air emplacements can be seen, with substantial logistics and earthmoving equipment. Lastly, there is no chatter of exercises or drills. All we can see is a spike in Iranian military comms early in the morning.'

The slide changed, showing a zoomed-out view of the camp, with a large red line over it.

'If we overlay possible glide routes for the missile, we can see that it is possible the missile passed over or into this area.'

'Sorry, glide routes? Wouldn't the missile have ditched without propulsion?' a senior officer asked.

'Not this missile, sir. It's designed to glide as efficiently as we can make it, meaning it can travel huge distances,' Danny replied confidently.

The senior military man nodded, satisfied with the response.

'Our working hypothesis is that the missile crash-landed in the Iranian desert, where the Iranians mobilised to capture it.'

An audible groan went up amongst the people in the room. People started talking to each other, discussing the possibilities, before the room was ordered to quiet.

'Son, just to be absolutely clear, you're telling us that the Iranians have captured one of the most valuable pieces of cutting-edge tech developed in the last couple of decades? And perhaps even intact?'

The chairman of the joint chiefs was a blunt man.

'Perhaps initially, sir, but no, we don't believe so,' Danny replied, leaving a purposeful pause.

'Well, what are you suggesting then?' the chairman asked, annoyance penetrating his voice.

Another slide flew up on the screen. It was time to bring it home – hook, line and sinker.

'On the same day we lost contact with the missile, the same E-3 patrol picked up a Chinese PLAAF VIP aircraft heading for Bandar Abbas port. That aircraft was identified landing at the city; it was running dark, not transmitting publicly. Footage from some of the street cameras in the cities spotted a white bus moving from the airport. We managed to track it back to the port itself.

'A Chinese commercial vessel, the Huang Shen, was the only large vessel in port at the time. It appears they were initially destined to continue on but changed their plans rapidly on that same day, opting to return to China.

'Lastly, satellite overpasses of the port from that day identified one last interesting piece.'

A zoomed-in image appeared on the slide, showing a military truck with a distinct mark on the front.

'This truck was seen parked near Huang Shen, likely being unloaded. If we compare this image to one of the satellite passes taken earlier over the camp, we get this.'

A second image appeared next to the first, showing a truck with a similar mark on the front.

'They look the same!' someone in the room exclaimed.

Danny smiled, 'That's because they are. We've done the measurements, and it is identical to the other truck. Furthermore, the mark on the bonnet is the exact same size. Likely some defect or poor repair job. But this truck is sitting higher off the ground.'

'So it's lighter,' the chairman summed up.

'Exactly, sir.'

'Based on the available information, we believe the missile has been transported from the desert and loaded aboard the Huang Shen late in the afternoon. The arrival of the PLAAF aircraft at the port is highly unlikely to be a coincidence. It is probable that the Chinese have sent a team to escort the missile, loading it onto the Huang Shen as a cover to get it back to China in an attempt to keep us unaware.'

'Fuck's sake,' someone muttered, just loud enough for everyone to hear.

An American naval officer was a bit more forward-leaning. 'Where is the Huang Shen now?'

Danny's final slide went up, showing the last known position. 'Moving through the Indian Ocean as we speak; it should make the Malacca Strait in roughly forty-eight hours.'

The room erupted into discussion again. Danny began fielding a swarm of questions before the chairman of the joint chiefs took over.

'Alright, everyone. We have ships available in the region. But so do the Chinese. We won't make a decision here. But we will ensure there is a vessel able to respond if required.' He looked across to the American chief of naval operations. 'What do we have, Charlie?'

'The USS John Basilone is best positioned, but it's not close. It was reassigned a couple of days ago to conduct a search pattern to the south; the rest of the fleet have already moved further to the west. If the John wants to catch them, they'll need to make good time.'

The chief of operations for the Australian navy spoke next. 'We also have HMAS Hobart down in the Timor Sea – worst case, we can move to intercept her as she leaves the strait, but I don't like the look of those PLAN deployments. Hobart would be awfully alone.'

'Alright. I want a plan put together. When do we need

to decide to make an intercept happen?' the chairman asked.

'0600 hours Zulu, sir,' replied the American chief of naval operations.

'Right, everyone, I want options within two hours. Given the location, PACOM will have operational command, understood?' the chairman ordered.

The Australians wouldn't be left behind. 'We concur. We'll have options up within the hour. Op command will be led through HQJOC, we'll link up with PACOM.'

The chairman wasn't done with Danny. 'Mr Blackburn, one last question. Would you bet your life on this information?'

He didn't even pause to think about it, instead following his gut. 'In a heartbeat, sir.'

The senior man nodded. That seemed to signal the end of the meeting. Danny rose with everyone else, Maia mouthing *good job* as they left. It was late now. The afternoon hue had been replaced by the blackness of night. But, for many of them, sleep, loved ones and home would be a long way off. There was work to be done.

Central Military Commission Operations Room – Beijing – China

Vice Admiral Taosing Xaipi read the latest flash message. 'Commander Li is feeling confident,' he said to the room around him. Taosing, the operations commander for Chinese naval forces in the Indian Ocean, had initially raised an eyebrow at his orders. They were certainly more brazen than the middle-aged admiral was accustomed to. He now found himself in a large control room, where the screens at the front of the space were dedicated to various data feeds from around the world, with analysts on their own workstations spread throughout. The lighting was dim, without any hint of natural light.

'It's the eagerness of youth,' replied another, more senior officer, Admiral Tung.

'Indeed. But, for the task ahead, his brashness will come in useful.'

'It looks like the Americans have taken the bait,' another senior officer added.

'It does appear that way. However, at least one American destroyer is still of concern. The John Basilone is still heading towards Sri Lanka,' Taosing commented, his discomfort with the operation apparent.

'It is only one vessel. As long as their fleet is distracted, they won't have enough forces to react in time,' Admiral Tung replied confidently. As the overall commander of the People's Liberation Army navy, his say was final. 'However, just to be safe, make sure our profile on the ship and its captain are up to date. If this ship does cause us problems, we need to understand our adversary.'

'Of course, sir.' Taosing made a quick note, handing it to a waiting aide.

Admiral Tung nodded, keeping his focus on the large screen. 'What is our plan for reception once the vessel is through the strait?' He knew the plan, but he wanted to make sure everything was as he expected.

'Sir, once through the Malacca Strait, it will be met by one of our coast-guard vessels. The coast guard will board the vessel to conduct a routine inspection. We will transfer the cargo across, where it will be transported to our base at Yongshu Jiao. From there, a PLAAF transport will take ownership, and it will be transported back to China. We are moving additional coast-guard vessels into the region, and we have at least two destroyers enroute, just in case. Even if the Americans become aware of our plans, they will not be able to respond with enough forces. However, if all goes to plan, they will not realise anything has happened.'

'And what about the Australians?' Admiral Tung asked.

'They will not be of concern. Their vessels are much weaker than our own, and they wouldn't dare challenge us without the Americans. They are scared rabbits, sir.'

Admiral Tung stroked his white-bearded chin. 'Let us

hope so.' He was older than Admiral Taosing by at least a decade. Retirement was coming for him, and it would soon be time to step aside for the ambitions of the younger men around him. Taosing was hesitant but confident, with ample ambition and cunning. It was not his place to hinder the new generation, but he would need to be careful to moderate these men. They were untested in combat, part of the newer generation that knew of China as a powerful and modern state. The reality of conflict would come as a shock.

'How long until we expect the vessel to enter the strait?'

'At least three more days, sir. It is making good speed and should go unnoticed.'

'And what assurances do we have that the weapon is safe?' Admiral Tung knew the answer, but he wanted to make sure Taosing did as well.

'An MSS agent is aboard the vessel; his orders are to destroy the weapon should it look like it could fall. Plus, a small special-force detachment has been assigned. They will ensure the weapon is destroyed if needed. Four PLA soldiers are with him to protect it and ensure its destruction.'

Admiral Tung nodded. 'Good, now, let's review the plans for Commander Li …'

American Embassy – Canberra – Australia

Tim's contact state-side wasn't one to keep him waiting, and this time was no different. Phone records, bank accounts – the whole lot had been pulled and sent through late in the afternoon. Tim had stayed back in the embassy, going over the record. He'd also hoped to get Bobby back on the line, but it would be early morning in Washington.

Damn time difference, he thought, and not for the first time.

The bank account wasn't very interesting; no large unexplained deposits, just regular expenditure, like bills and shopping. The phone logs, on the other hand, were a lot more complex.

He'd been methodically scanning the miles-long

spreadsheet of phone calls made to and by Michael "Mike" Clayton. The man made *a lot* of calls – mostly to other government lines, although there were a few unknown mobile numbers and a bunch of calls back to the States, the majority all seemingly occurring during work hours. It painted the picture of a man who was spending more time talking than actually managing the team he was supposed to lead. But that was hardly a crime – poor practice, sure, but nothing illicit on the scale that Danny had suggested. Tim sipped his tea, a habit he'd picked up since coming to Australia. They seemed to love their tea and coffee in almost equal measures, and to Tim's surprise, he'd found himself a convert to tea, something he'd never indulged in back stateside. But he'd also fallen in love with the rich, milky Australian-style coffees. He'd miss them when he left.

His phone suddenly rang, giving him a start. He'd just clicked onto the last and final page of the phone calls – all the most recent ones, covering around a week.

'Hey Tim, it's Bobby!'

'Bobby! I was wondering when you'd get in and give me a call. Thanks again for sending all this through.'

'Hey, no problem. Have you read through everything already?'

'Financial done, just finishing the call log, on the last page now.'

'See anything strange yet?'

Tim paused; his friend was clearly fishing. 'No, not yet, just a middle-aged dude spending way too much time on the phone.'

Bobby chuckled, 'So you haven't seen it?'

'No ... what am I missing?'

'On that final page, check for a US landline number.'

Tim did a quick search and spotted it immediately. 'Got it.'

'Recognise it?'

Tim paused again. It did look familiar, but he couldn't figure out why. 'No, should I?'

'So, +1-202-395-0000 is a big deal. That number, my friend, is the placeholder number for none other than the White House itself.'

He felt a little stunned. 'What?'

'Yep, I basically spat my coffee across the room when I saw it.'

Tim didn't mention his tea. 'Why the hell is some mid-level nobody receiving calls from the goddamn White House?'

Tim could almost hear Bobby shrug. 'Beats the hell out of me.'

'And we don't know who is actually calling? Like, we don't know the real White House phone number?'

'We don't know *yet*.'

'Go on, Bobby, don't tease me.'

'I know a guy who can help us out. Should be able to see the call logs from the call-centre in the White House.' That meant a staff member, likely secret service or an administrative member of the administration.

'Shit, Bobby. I mean, this stinks to high hell – we'll need to find out.'

'I thought you'd say that, so I've already reached out to the guy. But listen, if this is what you think it is, we'll need to get this clearance up high, and I bet the Australians will want to know what the fuck is going on.'

'Yeah, you're not wrong. Alright, leave it with me. Looks like it's going to be a late night.'

'Okay, Tim. I'll let you know when I have something. This guy is solid – used to be one of us before he turned to the dark side. Hope you've got strong coffee over there.'

He would have to find some; the tea wouldn't cut it now.

'Oh, and did you hear about that plane in the Middle East?' Bobby added just before he hung up.

Tim had been locked away from the news for the last few hours. 'No, what happened?'

'Chinese military transport. Decided it liked the ground better than the sky, took a dirt nap. Whole crew dead.

Chinese are screaming foul play, saying we shot it down.'

'*Pfft*, they wish. No one would be that stupid. Cheers for this, Bobby. I reckon we're onto something here.'

Tim hung up, his mind racing. What was Mike doing receiving calls from the White House? And why? Best of all, who was contacting him? There was no way his actions towards Danny wouldn't be related to this number. It was too much of a coincidence.

He sighed before standing up and turning on the coffee machine. It was definitely going to be a long night here.

CHAPTER 12

Huang Shen – Indian Ocean

Ming sighed as he watched the ocean unfurl in front of him, small waves slapping against the bow of the vessel. They had been at sea for five days now, and the slow monotony of sea travel had well and truly become a reality for Ming. Without a job to do on the vessel, he largely spent his time moving between the cargo holds, where the prototype missile was being dissected and examined, and the bridge, where he was tolerated by the captain and crew. The engineers and scientists accompanying the voyage appeared excited enough, constantly talking in small, huddled groups and gushing over the data that was being pulled. All good signs, Ming figured, but he was worried his role in this saga was beginning to wane. Even the security force under Jian had more purpose than Ming did at the moment. They had set up defensive points around the vessel, ready to repel some imaginary attacker. Jian, meanwhile, looked at everyone with suspicion, particularly the crew of the vessel. But at least he had a purpose; Ming just watched.

He couldn't even report back to Beijing. The order had been to create a complete signal blackout while aboard the vessel. Nothing was to be transmitted outside of ordinary communications from the container vessel. Ultimately, they still didn't know what the Americans could intercept, and crossing through the Malacca Strait would put them under the microscope of the Australian facilities in Pine Gap.

The entire plan rested on stealth and mixing in with the regular commercial traffic. Even the slightest hint of something out of the ordinary could bring the Americans bearing down on them. Despite Jian's defensive preparations, Ming knew they wouldn't be able to resist any dedicated attempt to take over the ship. They could hold out, but they would eventually be overwhelmed. Their only real hope was to get through the strait before that happened.

But this was all worst-case scenario planning, Ming decided. At this stage, the plan was going perfectly – so well Ming almost wished something would happen. There was only one vessel that really stood a chance of threatening them. The USS John Basilone had maintained its position in the Indian Ocean, not following its sister vessels, which had been led on a wild-goose chase by the PLAN. But even still, every hour, they inched further away. Soon – by tomorrow, in fact – it would be impossible to catch them before they passed through the strait. One more day.

He decided to go down into the hull and check on the progress being made by the civilian crew. Pulling open the heavy bulk, Ming stepped over the threshold, his eyes immediately trying to adjust to the dim fluorescent lighting. He waited a moment before closing the bulkhead door, relishing the sea breeze for one final moment. With a heavy *thunk* and a squeaking noise, he closed and locked the door. The fresh air immediately dissipated into grimy, recycled air-conditioning. It was humid and stale, a collection of decades of use, rust and sweat. The entire vessel depressed him. Rust and muck could be found everywhere. Even areas that should have been clean, such as the kitchen and medical bay, showed the stains of age. Everything felt, looked and, worst of all, *smelt* old.

He slowly walked the tight metal corridors of the vessel, feeling the minor sway of the ocean as he walked. The first couple of days had been terrible for Ming and some of the other civilian members. Seasickness and the constant dull clanking noise of the ship had kept them awake and nauseous well into the night and earlier hours of the morning. But, eventually, they had become used to the slow roll of the vessel; even the identical hallways had started to become familiar.

Making his way through the maze of corridors, Ming finally arrived at the entrance to the cavernous loading area. One of Jian's stern-looking soldiers stood guard over the door, an QBZ-191 bullpup rifle slung across his chest. The man eyed Ming, despite recognising him, waiting until he was only a couple of feet away before nodding to him and opening the door. Ming supposed there was some kind of reasoning for it. More time to identify any weapons or ill intent Ming might have. He thought it was all a bit stupid – not like he could do anything here anyway. The level of inherent mistrust always bothered him.

As he strode into the loading area, he found it largely empty. Only a couple of containers had been loaded; the majority had been left on the dock back in Iran. Walkways and railings covered each side of the massive hall, running the length of the loading zone and ending at the bulkheads facing the front of the vessel. Dominating the space was the container that held the missile. Computers, desks, lights and a whole manner of other equipment had been rushed on board and were now set up to surround the open end of the container. Ming could see a number of civilian staff in the container, plugging in diagnostic tools and examining the various components. Others were working studiously away at their computers, and at all times, two of Jian's guards stood watching on either side of the loading area.

Entering the container, Ming was greeted by two of the scientists. The chief scientist was completely engrossed in something on a table he held too close to his face. He had grown to dislike the little man; prideful, yet highly introverted, he made for difficult company. But he was undeniably brilliant and, for Ming, easy to get information out of. He loved nothing more than to boast of his achievements, much to the annoyance of his colleagues.

'Gentlemen,' Ming said, announcing himself, 'how much progress have you made on the missile?'

The civilian staff hardly seemed shocked at his appearance. He'd been making regular visits and checking up on them. They were so engrossed in their own work that he was treated as more of an annoyance that had to be tolerated than a senior officer to be respected.

The chief scientist took his cue, speaking over his other two companions. 'We have only had a couple of days with the missile, comrade. But I can tell you now, there looks to be ample lessons and technology we can take from this.'

The other two men looked sideways at each other, clearly not as hopeful as the chief scientist.

'How do you mean?' Ming asked. He'd now have to provide some explanation.

'Well, you see, the missile is in surprisingly good condition for something that fell out of the sky.'

Ming looked down at the blackened and bent structure of the missile. Raising one eyebrow, he said, 'You sure about that? Looks pretty damaged to me.'

'All superficial. We can easily reconstruct this design based off the surviving architecture, but that isn't the most interesting part.'

Ming leaned in closer, undeniably curious now. All he could see was the dark interior of the missile. A small panel had been carefully removed, exposing the inner wiring and technology.

'We have only just gained access to the inner workings, and it looks like the central processing unit and motherboard have survived. This means we might be able to get access to its complete technical coding and specifications.'

So maybe all this effort had been worthwhile. Ming smiled. There could be nothing worse than getting this missile home only to gain nothing from it.

'When do you think you'll know? What's possible, I mean.'

Another voice appeared next to Ming's head, startling him and making him jump slightly.

'Yes, Chief Scientist Sun, when will you know?'

Jian had snuck up on them and been eavesdropping on the conversation.

The chief scientist, for his part, didn't seem surprised to see Jian there. Maybe he had seen him approaching and decided to continue talking. Or maybe he just preferred to have a larger audience. 'Well, assuming we can integrate with the American technology right away, and assuming there isn't some new, more powerful encryption than we have dealt with before, it should only be a matter of hours before we can start downloading from the missile.

That was a lot quicker than Ming had guessed. The team working on the missile was a specialist crew though. Experts in Western technology, but particularly in gaining access to it, understanding how it worked, and re-engineering it for China.

Jian spoke first. 'When you know, inform us at once.'

'Of course. We will double our efforts.' The chief scientist nodded and hurried back to his colleagues.

Ming doubted he'd double his efforts, but the man did appear eager to serve. Perhaps he was more experienced in dealing with senior executives and generals.

As he turned to leave, he shared a look with Jian. A level of ambivalence remained between them. Ming wasn't sure, but he suspected Jian was highly distrustful of him. He hadn't done anything to earn that, but perhaps it was simply who Jian was. Either way, it didn't matter to Ming; they only had a couple more days on this hunk of scrap – then, maybe then, Ming could go back to a more exotic lifestyle. Maybe Singapore or Bangkok. He'd always enjoyed the wild nightlife and vibrant cities. Danger could lurk around any corner if you knew where to look.

He nodded to Jian and walked out of the cargo hold, conscious of the man's eyes digging into the back of his skull.

Canberra – Australia

Danny felt like he had only just put his head on his pillow next to his catatonic girlfriend when his phone started buzzing. Leah groaned and he moved to pick up the phone, checking the time. Only two hours of sleep. The caller ID was hidden, but that didn't mean much in his line of work. Could be anyone. He swiftly moved out of the bedroom before answering the phone, his voice heavy with sleep.

'Hey, Danny, sorry about the late hour, but it's urgent.'

Even in his half-asleep state of mind, he could recognise Tim's Boston accent. 'That's alright, Tim. What's up?'

'It's about Mike. You got time?'

'Right now? I mean, I'm pretty wrecked, man.' Bed was desperately calling Danny back.

'I'm outside,' Tim said simply.

That changed things. The promise of more sleep faded sadly into the distance.

'Right. Coffee then?'

Tim looked wrecked. Clearly, he'd not slept at all. Danny couldn't help but feel a little guilty. He seemed shrunken almost, hugging the mug of coffee like it was his only lifeforce. He gave Danny the rundown, speaking in hushed tones to try and avoid waking Leah. By the end of the update, Danny felt sick to his stomach.

'The national security advisor? What the fuck, Tim.'

'Yeah, I know, but listen, I got some buddies of mine to dig around. There have been rumours floating around of some black-ops shit being run from his office. Real cloak-and-daggers kind of stuff. But, if the rumours are true, these ops might not have been cleared by the President. Which means, Danny, you're in a goddamn spider's web. And the spider is very powerful and very dangerous.'

Danny felt like he was going to throw up.

Tim must've sensed Danny's unease. 'But listen, if these are unsanctioned and Mike is trying to manipulate you, it means you're in the clear. You've done the right thing by coming to me. And it also means we need to formalise the next step. I've already pushed this upward to my bosses, and they've alerted the justice department. They'll be briefing the deputy attorney general later today. Which means, we need to start thinking about the Australian side. Get their attorney general and the Australian Federal Police onboard.'

This was all happening too fast. Danny could feel a sweetness in his mouth, and before he knew it, he was running to the kitchen sink, heaving out his guts. It wasn't quiet, either.

Leah stumbled out of the bedroom. The sight before her wasn't what her half-asleep mind was prepared for: Danny with his head over the sink, looking green, while Tim stood behind him, one hand on Danny's back and the other clasping a coffee. The sense of conspiracy was impossible to ignore. She wasn't one for bullshit.

Hands on hips, she said, 'I'm going to need an explanation here, boys,' a hint of mirth in her voice.

Danny looked up weakly from the sink to find his girlfriend's face staring back down at him, confused and slightly angry. He couldn't hide it from her any longer. After he had composed himself and everyone had a cup of tea in hand, they all sat down on the couch and Danny retold the story, leaving out anything that would compromise his job or Leah. She wasn't security-cleared, and she understood the limitations.

It took a while to bring Leah up to speed. With each turn, her outrage grew. By the time Danny had explained Tim's late-night arrival, it appeared she was ready to behead someone. Namely Mike.

'This is a load of bullshit,' she proclaimed in her uniquely

Australian twang. Danny had grown familiar with the Australian affinity to swearing – something that had surprised him when he first arrived.

'What are you going to do about this?' Her gaze was aimed directly at Tim. Danny felt almost sorry for him – except, of course, he had the same question.

Holding his hands up in mock surrender, he said, 'Hey, that's why I'm here. We have a path forward, but we need to talk to Danny's other boss, Maia, and get a criminal case rolling. Time is kind of working against us here.' He smiled gently, trying to deflect her icy stare.

'Well, why are you both still here? Go wake her up!' Leah replied, the fiery look still in her eyes.

Danny wanted to protest, but he had to admit, she was right – this was serious enough, and he hadn't even mentioned the report he and Ata had worked on overnight. The plan to wait for all the data and have a fresh morning was dead on arrival.

'She's right, Danny,' Tim chimed in. 'Get dressed, and let's get this ball rolling.' The tiredness had seemingly disappeared from his eyes and shoulders.

Begrudgingly, Danny rose. This was going to be a long day.

Leah followed him to the bedroom, where she found him getting dressed. 'Hey Danny, you should have told me earlier.'

He sighed, 'I know, but I wasn't sure what was going on, or what to do about it. He threatened me, and he threatened us – I was scared, babe.'

She moved in swiftly, tears in her eyes, and hugged him tight.

He hugged her back, resisting the urge to cry himself. Lifting her chin, he gave her a light kiss on the lips before pulling back slightly and smiling at her.

She smiled back. 'Good, now go get the bastard. If you need help burying the body, I know a good place,' she said, a cheeky grin on her face. Danny wasn't entirely sure she was joking.

Suburb of Reid – Canberra – Australia

The leafy upmarket Canberra suburb of Reid was pitch-black in the early morning, with large, overhanging trees blocking the streetlights. Danny drove in silence, Tim in the passenger seat. Maia's home was the only one with signs of life so early in the morning, with the entrance to her driveway lit up by the porch light.

She met them at the door and immediately directed them to her office, closing the door behind them once they were all inside. 'Alright, guys, why do I get the feeling you're about to complicate my world just that little bit extra?'

The home office space was clearly influenced by modern Scandinavian designers. Clean, modern wooden furniture, bright colours and lots of free space gave the room a comforting and professional feeling. Clearly a lot of love and care had been put into creating this space.

Tim kicked things off. 'Thanks for seeing us, Mrs Tavonga, this is a —'

She interrupted him with a smile, 'Call me Maia.'

Tim relaxed his shoulders a little and took a deep breath before starting again. 'As you can understand, this is a serious matter. It relates to Michael Clayton.'

She raised her eyebrow as though surprised, but Danny could have sworn he saw a small smile form in the corner of her mouth. 'Go on.'

'A day or so ago, Danny came to me with an interesting story regarding Michael Clayton.' Tim paused, looking over at Danny. 'Might be better if you explain this, Danny.'

He didn't really feel like retelling the story again, but he did anyway. 'Sure thing.'

Maia was already across the work he and Ata had been doing, but the news that Mike had been actively interfering was new to her. Her smile quickly faded as Danny started explaining.

By the time he was done, Maia's face had darkened and her eyebrows were drawn together; he'd rarely seen that expression on her face.

'Thank you for telling me,' she said, before quickly turning her attention to Tim, the stormy look still on her face. 'Obviously, this affects a lot more than just the individuals here. I assume the FBI has a plan?'

He nodded. 'The FBI has done some early investigative work and identified there's likely a conspiracy that is linked to Michael. In a few hours, a briefing will be given to the deputy attorney general, who will likely initiate a formal investigation. Given the links between our two nations and the obviously secret nature of the work being done here, we need to engage with you. Next steps will be engaging with the federal police and figuring out lines of effort. We wanted to meet with you first to ensure a tight lid is kept on this. We can't let Michael think anything is out of place. Otherwise, we risk spooking him.'

'So, you're saying you don't want Mike removed? Keep him working in the office? We also can't have him jeopardising this project, or the people in it.' She pointed at Danny.

'We have to. The linkages he's exposed back in Washington go extremely high up, and directly involve the national security of both our nations. If we keep Mike unaware, there is a good chance he'll inadvertently help us wrap this case up quickly. Plus, now we know he's dirty, we can watch him carefully and limit his ability to do harm.'

Maia frowned, 'I don't like it. If this man is willing to threaten or blackmail Danny, he could be willing to do a lot more to other staff members. We can't just remove our staff either – they have critical jobs. Plus, how do you suggest we keep track of him? We can't remove accesses without him noticing. He'll have free movement through one of the most sensitive facilities in the country.'

Tim was unrelenting. 'It's a risk, but from now on, his every keystroke, URL, email, phone call, even physical movement will be monitored. As for his presence in the facility, we have a plan for that. Mike will be called away to assist on a sensitive project. We just need to keep an eye on him for a day or two.'

Maia bit her lip. 'Okay, but what do we do about Danny? He's obviously expecting something from him.'

Tim didn't have a good answer for that. 'I mean, we could recall Danny to the States …'

Danny shut that down. 'Woah, look, I'm happy to tough it out and deal with Mike. I'm not interested in leaving behind the project – or Leah, for that matter.'

Maia gave him a thoughtful look, trying to analyse and determine the nature of the man in front of her. She paused for a moment before continuing, seemingly pushing aside a line of thought. 'Alright, gentlemen, let's park that for now. What are the next steps?'

'We'll take care of the federal-police angle and set up a taskforce. From there, the investigation side will take care of itself, but we'll work directly with you to manage Mike and arrange accesses to the facilities so we can monitor him. Additionally, we'll need a brief into the project you are working on to understand the charges we will level against Mike. But that can come later. The key will be to keep things as normal as possible and reduce the number of people who need to know in your office. We don't know who will share information with Mike – for all we know, he has tried to pull similar moves to what he pulled on Danny, but with others.'

Maia nodded, looking back at Danny. 'I think I have a solution to get you out of Mike's immediate focus. I was going to discuss it with you tomorrow …' She checked the time on her watch, 01:34. 'But it looks like we're there already. You're not going to like it.'

'What do you mean?'

'Ever been on an Arleigh Burke Destroyer?' she replied cryptically.

HQJOC – Australia

It was 05:42. Sidney yawned as he swiped his way into the compound. The early morning shift of the protective services officers guarding the facility gave him only the slightest hint of interest. The late-night call from Danny and then Ata had got him out of bed. But it was still a shock to the system. Without his morning workout, he knew his whole day was going to be off. Still, he did enjoy the early morning hue, the sky slowly turning a faint light blue as the sun made its presence known. There wasn't anyone on the roads, and he could get a carpark nice and close to the entrance.

The building seemed completely deserted as well, numerous corridors and rooms blackened by the automatic lighting that turned off when it didn't detect motion for a few minutes. It gave the building an eerie, haunted feeling as he traversed the corridors towards his pod. Only a couple of other night-shift staff remained at their computers, quietly going about their own business.

Plopping down in his chair and turning the computer on, he sighed to himself, hoping the early phone calls were actually something interesting – often, it was just someone overreacting. He found the email sitting at the top of his inbox, sent only a few hours earlier. 'Burning the midnight oil, huh guys?' he said quietly to himself. His voice sounded far louder in the empty space than it actually was.

At first, he wasn't sure what he was looking at, but as he read through the briefing slides, it started to come together. 'Holy shit,' he said, louder this time. Another voice made him jump in his seat.

'Whaddya got there, mate?' a raw American accent said. The word "mate" sounded oddly threatening.

'Wow, you scared me, Mike,' Sidney said, visibly surprised.

'Ah, sorry about that. Looks like you're working late, like me.'

It definitely wasn't late anymore, and Mike wasn't one to work early either. 'Yes, sir. I got a call from Ata to pop in and check something out, and help prepare briefing slides.'

Mike seemed to pause awkwardly for a moment, a deer in the headlights. 'Right, yes, that … Have you got a copy there?'

'Umm yeah, you haven't seen it?'

'Oh, I saw an earlier version; didn't see where she got up to. Wanna give me a quick update?'

'I only just got in, sir, but from what I can tell, both Danny and Ata seem to think the missile could have ended up on some Chinese cargo ship.' He pointed to some of the briefing slides for Mike to read.

Mike leant in closer to Sidney so that he could read from his screen. He licked his lips, and Sidney felt an unpleasant sensation, having him so close. 'Yes, good, good. No mention of a Chinese cargo plane?'

Sidney was a bit confused. 'No, sir, just the boat. Do you mean the one on the news? You think they're linked?'

Mike stepped back suddenly. 'Oh, no, no, no. Just wondering if they had covered it off at all. Now, you said both Danny and Ata worked on this?'

'Yes, sir.' Sidney was officially weirded out now.

'Good, good. Hey, do me a favour, shoot these across to me.' He locked eyes with Sidney, a weird frenetic look in his eyes. Mike didn't look like he had slept much – or, indeed, at all.

'Sure, no problem.'

'Thanks, Sidney.'

'No problem, sir.'

Mike stayed standing there for a few more uncomfortable seconds, his eyes hazing over, before he seemed to come back to his senses and walk away suddenly.

'Fucking weirdo,' Sidney thought before hitting the send button. He quickly moved on, forgetting about Mike, and continued preparing the slides and information packages. He didn't see Mike close his office door or pick up the phone.

CHAPTER 13

Indian Ocean

Danny looked out the window of the Seahawk as it approached the USS John Basilone. The Indian Ocean looked calm from above, with only the slightest hint of white tops appearing across the ocean. The ship looked almost stationary against its backdrop. The USS John Basilone, or DDG-112, cut an impressive sight, a relatively new variant of the tried-and-tested Arleigh Burke destroyer. It was equipped with an array of the latest radar and weapon systems, classed as a Flight IIA. It was technically a technology-insertion vessel, designed to test new tech on the older design before the eventual Flight III was launched.

It had all happened so fast, the sleepless night and early morning call from Tim, then Maia. Danny had almost no time before a car had turned up at Maia's and driven him back home, where, offering the best explanation to Leah that he could, he was ushered back to the car with a hurriedly packed bag and driven to a military hangar at the Canberra airport. Jesse had met him there, looking more awake and better packed than he was. A short hour or so later, they were soaring through the air in the back of a C-

130 Royal Australian Air Force transport plane. Danny had fallen asleep miraculously on the uncomfortable, fold-out fabric seats lining the cargo holding in the back of the loud aircraft. The sudden jolt of the landing had woken him suddenly, the vibrations of the engines replaced with the firmness of being on solid ground. Rubbing his back, he felt sore and arguably worse than he had when they first took off. Stretching his legs out and yawning, he gazed out the small window next to his head. Lush jungle seemed to encroach upon the airfield. It hadn't occurred to him to ask where they were going when they left, but now, he was completely mystified.

A loudspeaker crackled throughout the largely empty hold. 'Welcome to RMAF Base Butterworth, everyone.'

'*Malaysia*?' Why the hell are we in Malaysia?' Danny asked the cargo hold, a confused, half-asleep look plastered on his face.

'Shit, Danny, how do you think we're going to get out there – parachute?' Jesse replied.

His brain struggled to catch up. 'Yeah, okay … so we're getting picked up?'

'Ding-ding-ding, we have a winner!' Jesse said with a grin.

The aircraft taxied, and before long, the rear cargo bay's doors opened. A wave of heated, moist air immediately invaded the cargo bay, whipping aside the stale, recycled air from inside. Members of the Australian crew worked quickly, unloading the couple of crates onto the tarmac below. As they grabbed their bags, one of the crew directed them out of the aircraft. He had to shield his eyes as the morning sun blasted down on them. An unmarked civilian vehicle sat near the aircraft with a uniformed RAAF member waiting patiently – their ride. After shaking their hands, the young man got them moving quickly enough, throwing their bags in the back of the 4x4 without much concern.

'Trust you had a good flight?' the young man asked once

they were on their way, much more lively than Danny felt.

'It was definitely a flight,' Danny grumbled back.

'Yeah, those C130s are a bitch, that's for sure! Ever been to Butterworth?'

'Nope. First time,' Jesse said mildly.

'Ah, well this is home to the RAAF 19 Squadron. We take care of the base and the 92nd Wing, the P-8s you see over there,' the man said cheerily, pointing to a white station aircraft off to their right.

That explained the number of Australians running about; it was one of their few overseas bases.

The RAAF member gave them a quick, cursory tour before dropping them off at a fairly spartan room just off the tarmac.

'Any idea on our pick-up, corporal?' Jesse asked the man as he handed their bags back.

He shook his head, 'Afraid not, sir. My orders were to pick you two up off the C130 and drop you here. That's it.' He shrugged before departing, eager to get on with whatever duties awaited him.

Without any other clear direction, they moved through the doors into a small waiting area not dissimilar to a doctor's office, but without the smell of medical-grade disinfectant. Instead, they had more uncomfortable chairs, and a half-empty vending machine. The whole room felt like it was dragged from the 1980s, with exposed brick walls and stained windows. Jesse sighed, placing his bag down, and then started doing push-ups. Danny instead elected to grab some water and take a seat. A couple of hours passed, and Jesse goaded Danny into doing some crunches and sit-ups in the small space. He still felt tired and sore, but he had to admit, his far fitter colleague was right – he did feel better afterwards. A sudden distant *thump* announced the next leg of their journey.

'That's our ride,' Jesse announced, pointing at an SH-60 grey Seahawk a hundred metres outside their little waiting area.

A figure leapt out of the now-stationary helicopter and made a beeline directly towards their building. She forcefully opened the glass doors separating them from the outside airfield before storming past Jesse and Danny without even a glance, heading straight for the bathroom and slamming the door behind her. Jesse and Danny shared a quick look, Jesse shrugging in reply.

A minute later, she reappeared, saluting Jesse and shaking Danny's hand. 'Apologies for the wait. Lieutenant Molina at your service. I assume you two are my cargo?'

Jesse took over automatically, 'That's us, lieutenant. Where do you want us?'

'We're on a tight schedule, and we've got a date with a refueller, so let's hustle. Hope you don't mind a tight fit; we're picking up some additional supplies.' The lieutenant had a relaxed and confident attitude – she was someone who clearly knew what she was doing and was proud of it. Out on the tarmac, a bunch of bags and boxes were already being loaded by the Australian ground crew.

They grabbed their bags and followed Lieutenant Molina out into the humid Malaysia air. The grey USN Seahawk helicopter stood out against a greener backdrop, its rotor blades spinning furiously. Danny pushed his head lower as the wash of the rotor blades pressed down on him. Jesse entered first, before grabbing Danny's bag and throwing it further into the aircraft. Molina hadn't been kidding; space was at a premium, and he found himself squished between Jesse and what looked like a box of fresh fruit. They'd barely had a chance to fasten their harnesses and put on headphones when Molina began taxiing. A few short moments later, they were airborne, the green ground dropping away suddenly as the helicopter rose, its turboshaft engines whining as they surged to provide power to the rotors. Soon enough, the ride softened out and the deep greens of Malaysia were replaced with the dark, solid blues of the ocean. Not quite the visit Danny had hoped for.

Lieutenant Molina's voice popped over the intercom,

'Alright, gentlemen, thank you for flying with the US navy today. I'll be your captain. You are joined by my co-pilot, Lieutenant Jones, and Petty Officer Barnes is your crew chief. You do what he says, and we'll all get along fine. Have either of you flown with us before?'

Jesse's voice clicked over the intercom, 'A few times, lieutenant.'

Danny didn't know that, but when Jesse didn't respond for him, he jumped in, 'First time for me in a helicopter, actually – and I guess on a navy ship, for that matter.'

Molina chuckled, 'Virgin, huh? Don't worry, sir. We'll go easy on you.'

'Just call me Danny, lieutenant. I'm no "sir". And don't worry about me, I can take it.' He immediately knew he was going to regret that.

She laughed this time, 'Alright, Danny, so you've never experienced mid-air refuelling then?'

Uh-oh. 'Can't say that I have, lieutenant.'

Another hour later, he had.

Sure enough, with an unannounced roar, the Seahawk was jostled as the large grey body of a KC-130 refueller thundered over their much smaller helicopter. The larger aircraft sat comfortably as the Seahawk approached. Danny knew in theory how refuelling was conducted in air, but he had never seen it done in person. The rear cargo ramp opened slowly on the KC-130, where a harnessed crew member, probably the loadmaster, stood comfortably inside the rear of the now-open hold. The man gave the Seahawk a friendly wave. Danny had to resist the urge to wave back as the pilot gave him the thumbs up. Sure enough, a circular nozzle with a basket attached at the end quickly lowered itself towards their helicopter from the KC-130. A moment of fear hit Danny as he worried about the rotor blades spinning above him, but Lieutenant Molina was clearly skilled, and their helicopter rose, while the boom attached to the front of the helicopter extended to meet the free-floating basket. Molina aligned the boom and basket and, with a small increase in power, pulled the helicopter forward, making the connection on the first go.

'Now, that's how you find the hole, boys,' her voice burst over the intercom. Danny couldn't see her face, but he could hear the grin behind her remark. Only a few tense minutes later and their tanks were all topped off. The Seahawk pilot gave the loadmaster another wave and they disconnected, continuing their flight onward.

'Alright, Danny, whaddya think?' Molina asked cheerfully.

'Remind me never to challenge you to a game of golf; you must have a mean handicap, lieutenant,' he replied, enjoying himself.

'Damn straight, I do. But hey, I just make it look easy. Other pilots, like my copilot here, need more than one go! Lucky for you, you're flying with some of the best in the business!' she replied with a laugh, her co-pilot giving her a gentle punch on the arm.

Another couple of hours later, they started their descent. As he looked through the forward-facing cockpit plexiglass windows, the USS John Basilone appeared only as a grey speck against the blue backdrop. But, as they neared, it grew in size. Lieutenant Molina brought them in low and slow, giving Danny a good view of the length of the ship. He could make out the tiny individuals moving along the outside of the vessel. Numerous weapon systems and antennas covered the grey superstructure, giving it a menacing and high-tech feeling. It wasn't until the helicopter banked and came in to land on the stern of the vessel that Danny could truly appreciate the size of the ship. The landing pad on the stern and its aircraft storage hangar seemed to engulf the helicopter, whereas only minutes earlier, it had seemed like it would barely fit on the back.

The Seahawk touched down smoothly, with only a small bounce as it hit the deck. Danny instantly felt the sway of the ocean. No longer was he being lifted by the aircraft; now, he was at the mercy of the ocean. Luckily for Danny, he was experienced. Years of sailing and rowing in his younger years had given him all the sea legs he'd need. Being on an ocean was in some ways like going home, although admittedly, he was not used to being on such a large vessel, let alone a warship.

'Thanks for the ride, guys,' Danny said over the intercom.

Molina gave her co-pilot a fist bump. 'Pleasure, Danny. Welcome aboard the USS John Basilone; we hope you enjoy your stay,' she said, flicking up her visor and turning to face them so that she could give them a big grin.

They waited until the rotors had slowed before disembarking. There was no need to hurry. Stepping out onto the exposed deck, Danny felt immediately out of place. Numerous seamen and women were busy going about their duties, unloading the Seahawk and prepping it to move into the tight hangar in the stern of the ship. Jesse was at least wearing naval fatigues, but Danny just had a black windbreaker and jeans. He looked and felt like a civilian.

A seaman in fatigues and headphones approached them the moment they were clear of the Seahawk, swiftly saluting Jesse and shaking Danny's hand. Something he'd have to get used to.

'Welcome aboard, gentlemen. If you'll follow me, the captain is waiting for you down in the CIC.'

'Lead on, seaman,' Jesse replied formally. Danny hadn't seen the strict, military side of Jesse before. He'd always just been another member of his team, but here, he was a senior officer, and he acted accordingly.

The seaman led them through the tight helicopter hangar and down into the bowels of the ship. The ship seemed busy, with seamen and women moving around through passageways and doors constantly. Danny felt clumsy and in the way; he had to focus to avoid bumping into people or hitting his head on bulkheads constantly. It would take some getting used to. The smells and noises were all foreign to Danny at this moment. He might be an experienced hobby sailor, but military life on a ship was something of a mystery.

In a surprisingly short period of time wandering through numerous doors, tight stairways and corridors, they arrived at another sealed door. This was slightly different, closed shut with a keypad next to it. Their escort quickly typed in a code before the door unlocked with a gentle *clunk*.

Danny was assailed by the low lighting and soft din of sailors going about their work. Multiple bright screens attached to displays and computers beamed across the room, but overall, Danny was surprised by how compact and tight the entire space was. The room had a space-age feel about it, with different tactical and information displays lit up with different-coloured neon writing and symbols. Looking around, Danny could see multiple different inputs, including radar, ship and mechanical information and weapon system statuses.

Captain Jonathan O'Donnell stood looking stoically at a large wall-mounted display, hand resting on his chin as he remained deep in thought. The seaman stood to attention and saluted the captain. 'Sir, Lieutenant Commander Edwards and Mr Blackburn for you, sir.'

Jonathan, disturbed from his thoughts, gave the sailor a salute in return. 'Thank you, dismissed.' Another round of salutes and handshakes was completed before he gave Jesse and Danny a long, curious stare.

'Welcome aboard the USS John Basilone, Mr Blackburn. I must say we were surprised to hear you were coming to join us. And I have to say, I'd like to understand why you are with us now. The orders from PACOM weren't exactly illuminating.'

'Well, sir, we think we might have a location on the hypersonic prototype. Do you have a good idea of the commercial vessels around us?' Danny replied.

'I mean, we have radar coverage from our AN/SPY-6 radar; it'll reach beyond 170 nautical miles. How far do you need?'

'Well, I'll be honest, sir, I don't actually know our current location, but I'm looking for a particular vessel, named the Huang Shen. Chinese-flagged.'

The captain turned quickly to an operator sitting at a console. 'Bring up AIS, let's see where this vessel claims to be.'

The operator didn't waste any time, pulling a commercial open-source feed displaying thousands of little green and red arrows representing the various ships moving through the Indian Ocean. 'Spelling?' the operator asked.

Danny replied, 'H-U-A-N-G S-H-E-N.'

A couple of keystrokes later, the operator said, 'Got it. She ain't close. Position reads as 6.205426, 92.868838, moving at thirteen knots, heading due east. About twenty nautical miles from Indira Point and the entrance to the Malacca Strait. There's a heap of civilian traffic around as well, but that's to be expected.'

The captain scratched his chin, looking up at one of the displays. 'We're roughly 350 nautical miles to the west, gents. At best, we're at least fifteen hours behind her. She won't be easy to catch. Maybe time you give us that brief? My orders are to assist in any way possible, but I don't want to go off on some wild-goose chase. You understand, right?'

Danny did. He still wished they could get underway immediately, but if he was in charge, he'd want all the information before making a decision as well.

'Also, it doesn't quite explain why you're both here in person – surely this information could have been sent across?'

Jesse shuffled awkwardly, clearing his throat. 'That is something we might want to discuss elsewhere, sir.'

Jonathan nodded, a new, worried look on his face. 'Very well, let's retire to my stateroom.'

***

'That's a new one, Danny,' Jonathan said, eyebrow

raised. They were all in the captain's room, a pot of coffee steaming on the small table in front of them.

'New for me as well, sir,' he confirmed. They'd flown through the brief. Jonathan and his XO, Lieutenant Commander Baker, hadn't taken much convincing. The information was pretty solid. The story about Mike, on the other hand, was much harder to explain, especially as Danny didn't fully understand it himself.

'So, basically, we have a rat, or someone who's breaking the law. They've managed to involve another country, and they have been trying to get others to leak information and spy on our allies. Fucking brilliant,' Baker summed up.

'Pretty much. So, given we needed to pass this information on as quickly as possible and keep the lines closed, getting myself and Danny out of there seemed like a win-win.' Jesse added, 'Plus, our goal is to stay out of your way as much as possible, captain.'

Jonathan shook his head. 'Not a chance, son. Now you're on my ship, we'll put you to work. Especially someone with your history, Edwards. Plus, Danny, I understand you're basically the brainchild behind our missile. I want work-ups for boarding parties and our intel officers.'

'We're going after it then, sir?' Danny asked hopefully.

'You bet your ass, we are. We're going to get that missile back.'

A gentle knock on the door interrupted them. A slightly embarrassed seaman entered, saluting and handing a note to the captain.

'Well, shit,' Jonathan muttered. 'Looks like things are about to get a lot more complicated.'

HQJOC – Australia

Mike barged his way into Maia's office without knocking.

'What the actual fuck is this?' Mike said, throwing a

printed email on her desk.

It wasn't the first time he'd shown himself into her office, and it probably wouldn't be the last. She'd tolerated his little outburst and whinge sessions. But that would come to an end. Hopefully soon.

Maia had been speaking with Ata, not that Mike seemed to care; he appeared to have worked himself up. Maia sighed and, without looking at the paper, said, 'What is it, Mike?'

'Both Danny and Jesse have been transferred to USS John Basilone!'

'Oh? You didn't know?' Maia replied innocently. 'I assumed you'd deployed them. It seemed like a good idea to me, get them out there, using their skills.'

He was only momentarily disorientated. 'Well, yes, it is … but that's not the point! I need to know where my staff are at all times. I make the decisions where they can and can't go.'

'Well, I hate to break it to you, Mike, but they're gone, probably over Indonesia by now.'

'Well, why wasn't I informed?'

Maia shrugged, 'I'm not sure, Mike. The orders come from the American side – not my place to interfere, is it?'

The anger and arrogance in Mike's face didn't know where to go. He could feel that he was being made the fool, but he couldn't understand how. 'It's not goddamn good enough!' he said, storming back out.

Ata whistled, 'Wow, he's unhinged.'

'Yep, and now you understand why we need to be careful and watch him. You and Sidney are now the most exposed to him, but you're also the best placed to keep an eye on him.'

'I don't like it. Why can't we just arrest his ass?'

'Because he's not the one running the show. Mike, as I suspect has always been the case, is just a minion in this affair. The FBI want the big fish, and I'm inclined to agree. Even if it means we have to put up with him. He might not realise it, but his every keystroke is being watched. Anything he does will be tracked, and we'll know about it. If he tries anything on either you or Sidney, let me know immediately, and if you can help it, don't be alone with him.'

A tap on the office door interrupted them suddenly. A fresh-faced airman popped his head around the door awkwardly. 'Ma'am, you're needed on the floor; we have a situation.'

Maia nodded to the airman before mouthing to Ata, 'What now?'

It wasn't a long walk to the large, situational watch floor. The data-flows from Australian, American and other friendly nations all fed onto the operations floor. Ata spotted the problem immediately: a small cluster of vessels heading toward the Maldives. Clearly military.

The airman briefed them automatically. 'At 1040 Zulu, a cluster of Chinese PLAN vessels commenced manoeuvres towards the Maldives. They've announced a NOTAM and started forcing civilian vessels out of the area.'

Maia didn't miss a beat. 'What is the Indian navy's response?'

'They are mobilising a response force, but it looks like they were caught off guard by the sudden move by the Chinese. It'll take them at least twelve hours to respond.'

'Any other justification for their move? Looks to me like they are infringing the Maldives' EEZ pretty heavily there.'

'No ma'am, but some open-source reporting has video of the Chinese lowering RHIBs into the water, and apparently, launching divers.'

'Right …' Maia turned to Ata. 'Could that location be one of the possible flight paths of the prototype?'

Ata knew the answer straight away. 'We'll need to take a look at the latest satellite imagery, but it's highly possible.'

The airman interrupted, 'Additionally ma'am, local US naval forces have been given orders to move to intercept.'

Maia bit her lip. 'I don't like this at all. Putting our forces in close proximity like this has all the hints of a disaster.'

'Plus, Danny and Jesse are out there now,' Ata pointed

out.

'Yeah, that too … Ata, get me a work-up on this as soon as possible, figure out if the missile could be down there in the water. Make sure Danny and Jesse are informed.'

'Got it.'

Ata turned to leave and stopped immediately. Mike was standing quietly in the back of the room, clearly having eavesdropped on their conversation. He gave her a small, cold smile before staring back at one of the large displays in the room. A not-so-subtle reminder they would need to be careful.

CHAPTER 14

Central Military Commission Headquarters – Beijing – China

The PLAAF general hadn't stopped fuming since Chang had handed him a short report. The man kept rereading the report and muttering to himself, making notes in a small notebook. Chang repressed the urge to smile. It was almost too easy to manipulate his military colleagues – although he had to admit, the information in the report had truly fallen from the sky, surprising even himself.

They sat in an armoured limousine, moving toward the Central Military Commission Headquarters, the PLAAF general sitting across from Chang, staring into the pieces of paper that contained the report as if he were trying to set it alight with his rage. Chang had been sure to meet the general in person, sharing an "advanced" copy of the report. The effect was exactly what Chang had hoped for, the man's eyes almost bulging out of his head at the first glance while he was also profusely thanking Chang for the information, the small act aligning one playing piece to Chang's agenda.

The loss of the aircraft was first announced across the open airways, with a video posted online showing a large explosion, then quickly picked up by local media outlets and pushed further. The official announcement took far longer from Iranian authorities. By the time an official call was made to the Chinese Government, a field agent had already been dispatched by the embassy. Acting as a representative to organise the return of the fallen aircrew, the agent had been well placed to gather information from the site. The discovery of a partially intact panel with English wording had surprised them.

Chang hadn't ordered the field agent out to the site; nor had he even been remotely aware of the aircraft's loss. Still, the news worked in his favour. He was sceptical that the Americans would take such overt action, and with a missile that, according to his analysts, wasn't designed to shoot down aircraft. But, regardless, the evidence in the report was enough to spark an emotional response in the man in front of him, and emotional people were easy to use.

The PLAAF general was still furiously taking notes when they arrived at the headquarters. Chang's goal was clear: convince the men inside of the need to take strong action. Chang held more copies for his colleagues in the navy.

A few short minutes later, they were escorted into a meeting room with admirals Tung and Taosing, as well as a host of additional aides and officials. Chang handed them all copies of the report before speaking.

'Gentlemen, I must preface that this information is highly sensitive and still needs to be confirmed. As you can see, our officers have recovered wreckage from the PLAAF aircraft in Iran, and it appears its demise was no accident.' He paused, making sure he had their attention. 'Parts recovered from the site are, according to our analysts, American in origin.'

Admiral Tung spoke up over the growing murmur, 'What are you suggesting, comrade?'

Chang didn't have a chance to respond.

'THAT THE AMERICANS HAVE SHOT DOWN ONE OF OUR AIRCRAFT!' the PLAAF general exploded, slamming his fist on the wooden table and nearly toppling any nearby glasses of water.

Perfect, Chang thought.

'We must strike back!' the general continued.

Admiral Tung stroked his chin. 'Comrade, how certain of this information are you?'

'A part has been recovered directly from the crash site. I am more than happy to pass the details over to your analysts to confirm.'

'And we found this part?'

Chang hesitated. He couldn't lie. 'No, comrade admiral. The Iranians collected the components, but we were onsite to receive them.'

'So, all we really know is that American weapon components were found at the site.' Admiral Tung said. 'Can we be certain that it was the Americans that fired at our plane? Your report here states that the component is used in the Hellfire missile. I believe this missile is not a weapon used to target aircraft, if I am not mistaken?'

'The plane had just taken off. They could have guided it to the aircraft,' the general insisted.

'Perhaps. Either way, we must tread with caution,' Tung said calmly.

Good, Chang thought. *Now, to provide the counterbalance.*

'Comrade admiral, you are correct, but you can see the evidence before you. While we cannot confirm that the Americans are responsible, there is every likelihood they are. We must respond in some way, even if it is not as overt.'

The groundwork had been laid, now all he needed was someone to take the bait.

'What do you suggest?' Admiral Taosing asked, getting in before his boss.

'We must be willing to show our assertiveness. I believe we should take a new, more direct approach to challenging the Americans, and I think the navy is best placed to do it.'

He listed the course of action, receiving many approving nods, yet Admiral Tung's frown only grew larger.

The admiral spoke quietly, 'Comrade, your suggestion, do you mean to change our orders to vessels in the Indian Ocean? They are only meant to be a distraction to the Americans, nothing more.'

Chang nodded, 'It is the most logical course of action, admiral. The forces are well placed. All we are doing is … taking a more forceful approach. We will still achieve our mission of distracting the Americans, don't you agree?'

The general didn't look pleased. 'It's too weak! We should strike them!' he complained.

'Comrade general, their time will come – our patience will see to it. But, for now, we must hold our anger. This option allows us to teach them a lesson while avoiding an all-out war. This is our chance to react: now, not weeks or months from now. We *must* act! For your men, and for China,' Chang said with more passion than he'd intended. His goal was to appear the sensible middle ground between the overly cautious admiral and overzealous general.

The PLAAF general didn't look placated, but he didn't speak any further. It was enough for Chang; he had served his purpose.

'We are agreed then, gentlemen?' he asked.

They all either nodded or remained silent.

'Excellent. I will alert the president of our decision.'

Game, set and match. Not only had they agreed, but he would be the one to present the plan to the president. It would push China in the direction he believed it needed to travel, and he was responsible. The urge to smile was hard to suppress as he turned away from the powerful military men and made his exit.

Type 052D Luyang Destroyer – Indian Ocean

Makunudhoo Island was barely an island. The extremely low-lying reef had just enough landmass to jut out of the ocean and establish a small township. Commander Li ignored it entirely. His orders didn't include the township or its people – not that the Maldivian Coast Guard knew that. The small, white hulls of the aged coast vessels were hard to miss, but they kept their distance. The Chinese vessels dwarfed them, not only in size but in firepower. The coast guard was armed with little more than a mounted deck gun; they'd be easy to swat away if needed. By comparison, his relatively new Type 052D destroyer was armed to the teeth; with a modern VLS, a HQ-10 surface-to-air launcher and a single 130 mm main gun, Li's vessel was no pushover. Plus, he wasn't alone. Two smaller Type 054A Frigates had raced to meet them. Although smaller and less well-armed, they would be useful nonetheless. Plus, if all went to plan, he wouldn't need the weaponry today. He needed cunning, and his exceptional piloting skills.

Holding his powerful binoculars to his eyes, he could see the grey silhouettes of the American vessels approaching in the distance. He counted at least three: two Arleigh Burke destroyers and one smaller, Littoral Combat Ship. He'd hoped for more, but his powerful AESA radar hadn't lied. They would have to do. The Americans had already launched a couple of Seahawk helicopters, which were now patrolling close to their host vessels, not venturing too far from the relative safety of their motherships. He'd need to keep a close eye on them. Their torpedoes were more than capable of splitting any of his vessels in half with a good hit.

'Commence recovery operations,' he barked. The relevant officers immediately relayed his order.

The confirmation that the RHIBs had been deployed came a minute later. *Let's see what they do*, he thought. Li's vessels had created a small triangle-shaped area between them, forcing any curious locals that might try to enter away. The Americans had appeared across the horizon in a staggered forward-facing line.

'Start broadcasting,' Li ordered.

A sailor next to Li immediately picked up a microphone, broadcasting in English on all open radio channels, 'Attention, all nearby vessels. The Chinese navy is conducting operational activity in the immediate area. All forces must maintain a safe distance for their own safety. Do not approach Chinese vessels. I repeat, do not approach.'

'Captain, the American vessels are moving.'

'Good,' he smiled.

Li moved his binoculars left to right; indeed, the Americans were making their move. One vessel remained on a direct course with Li's destroyer; the other two had peeled left and right, looking to encircle the collection of Chinese ships.

'Perfect. They are splitting apart for us.'

His orders had been extremely specific and detailed, which in itself wasn't particularly beyond the norm, but the specifics had come as a surprise. The admirals back in Beijing had clearly been busy.

He signalled to the communications officer. 'Connect me with the Americans.'

He waited until he was given the thumbs-up signal from the officer. *Better worsen my English*, Li thought, holding the radio transmitter microphone to his mouth. *No point making it easier for them.*

He clicked the button on the side of the microphone and, in a heavily accented voice, began to speak. 'American vessels, the People's Liberation Army Navy is conducting a sensitive operation. Leave the area immediately. I repeat: *leave immediately*. Any continued approaches will be considered a hostile act.'

***

'Alright, here we go,' Captain Jacob Langford said to no one in particular inside his ship's CIC. He remained standing, a cup of black coffee in his right hand, the other tucked into his pocket. He'd relished the change of pace from the endlessly boring search-and-rescue mission they'd been on for the better part of a week. The damnable prototype missile was gone; he just wished the genius back in command could let it go.

The thickly accented message from the Chinese was pretty typical. He'd been hearing similar messages increasingly over the last few years. The gist of the message was clear enough: stay out, or else. *Well, I can't do that, bud*, Jacob thought. His orders were crystal clear: investigate the Chinese actions and convince them to leave. He could use all available power at his disposal, short of opening fire without permission. Not that he'd have to worry; the Chinese were the underdogs here. Between his two Arleigh Burke destroyers and the smaller Littoral Combat Ship, he had more than enough firepower to deal with anything the Chinese threw at them.

They'd sailed all the way from Christmas Island, South of Indonesia, following the failed missile exercise, tasked with search-and-recovery operations of that same missile. But the sudden incursion by the Chinese had changed things. No one knew what they were doing there. The Maldivian Government was alarmed, and the Indian navy was scrambling, but not quickly enough. Langford's ships had been in the best position to intervene. Even if it took them off their original mission.

Langford preferred to remain in the CIC, where he had all the information from the Arleigh Burke's powerful sensors and radars available to him in one space. 'Let's get a better picture of what's around us. Order Seahawk 1 to test the water,' he instructed the seaman manning the communications console.

'Aye-aye, sir,' came the reply.

The Seahawk hovering nearby didn't waste a second. Descending closer to the ocean, it released a small, cylindrical device attached to a winch. The device, an advanced sonar, was dipped into the water around the helicopter and all nearby vessels. The active low-frequency soundwaves pulsed outward, allowing Langford's forces to detect, identify and track any submarines in the area. The results were relayed almost instantaneously back to the ships in Langford's force.

'All clear, sir. Seahawk 1 reports only crew noises from the three Chinese surface vessels, no undersea contacts.'

He grunted in reply. That made things easier. If they had a sub out there, they'd have heard it. Chinese submarines had a bad reputation for being loud and easy to pick up. It wasn't often they surprised a US navy captain. Langford didn't want to be one of the few. Still, a torpedo was a torpedo, and not something to brush off.

'Alright, let's get this show underway. All ahead, full and sound, general quarters.'

'General quarters, aye-aye.'

'General quarters, general quarters. This is not a drill – report to your battle stations,' rang the klaxon. Most of the seamen and women were already at their stations; he'd ordered them to heightened readiness a couple of hours ago, but this way, they knew things were happening and prepared themselves for action.

Langford was wearing a set of headphones, allowing him to communicate directly with his XO and the other ships in his force.

'Harry, Jack, you with me?' he asked the two other vessels.

'Loud and clear,' came the near-simultaneous response from the two other skippers in their respective ships.

'Alright. Commence manoeuvres, gentlemen. Keep an eye on your depths; we're dangerously close to brown water here.'

The plan was simple. Langford would maintain a straight course, heading right down the middle, while the two other skippers would move along the flanks of the small cluster of Chinese vessels. The idea was that the Chinese would be forced to respond to the Americans' moves and split apart their little flotilla, meaning Langford could get his own RHIBs in to disrupt whatever they were doing near the reef. The Seahawks would provide observations and coverage.

He'd seen a report suggesting the Chinese could have found something in the water, possibly their missile, but Langford didn't really buy it, and he didn't really care.

He felt confident. The Chinese were outgunned; he knew he could easily win a shooting match, but that wasn't really the goal here. He was here to deliver the Chinese their marching orders and ensure they didn't have any ideas that they could do this kind of thing whenever they wanted. This was his chance to give the Chinese a bloody nose – something he thought was long past due.

Langford watched the Chinese vessels on a live camera display. The sleek grey lines and structure of their ships was not dissimilar to his own. He switched to his XO station on the bridge. 'Put us underway, let's get the party started.'

A gentle rumble and vibration announced that his Arleigh Burke's four powerful General Electric gas turbines were spooling up, outputting an eye-watering 19,500 kWs.

The gap between his vessels and the Chinese closed rapidly. His eyes remained fixed on the monitor, watching the Chinese vessels. 'C'mon, move, you bastards,' he muttered as they remained stubbornly stationary, maintaining a tight formation, protecting each other and the smaller boats in the centre. They'd have to move; they couldn't allow themselves to become encircled. Radio messages from the Chinese ships continued to flood the open channels, warning the American vessels to keep their distance.

The minutes ticked by. 'Movement, sir,' an officer announced. 'Chinese vessels are responding.'

Sure enough, all three had sprung to action, separating and moving directly towards the American ships. The radio calls ceased at the same moment. The more powerful of the Chinese ships, the Type 052D Luyang destroyer, began moving on a wide arc.

Langford grunted again. 'Alright, they aren't trying to cut us off ... What the hell is he doing – just making way? Thought these guys wanted a fight.'

'Seahawk reports Chinese RHIBs are remaining stationary in the water, sir.'

'Chinese RHIBs are visible in the water, sir,' another seaman announced.

Langford frowned. 'Alright, deploy our own RHIBs, see if we can't shoo them off.'

'Aye-aye, sir.'

The cluster of Chinese RHIBs didn't look particularly hurried, despite the departure of their protection. A camera feed showed men in diving equipment sitting around on bobbing inflatable boats.

'Jack, Harry, keep an eye out. Not sure what they're up to. We're deploying our own RHIBs,' Langford relayed.

'Sir, that destroyer is coming about. Moving fast, probably at flank speeds.'

The Chinese vessel was moving, alright. Still a few hundred metres from his own, but moving quicker and closer than Langford felt comfortable with. They clearly hadn't intended to peel away. Every second, the Chinese destroyer closed the gap, coming around on Langford's port side.

He wouldn't be bullied. 'Maintain course. Keep an eye out for any sudden movements,' he ordered to the bridge.

'Where are our RHIBs?'

'Three hundred metres and closing on the Chinese, sir.'

A video feed showed three American RHIBs moving against the two Chinese. The crew held on as water sprayed around them.

A sudden movement amongst the Chinese RHIBs caught Langford's eye, with a seaman needlessly repeating, 'More movement, sir.'

'Direction?' he asked. Maybe that was it, the Chinese were making a run for it. He still wanted to get a good look into the RHIBs.

'All three are heading straight for us, sir, closing fast.' The lookout's voice betrayed his uncertainty.

Sure enough, Langford watched as the two Chinese

RHIBs completely ignored the approaching American ship, blasting past them in a shower of water.

If they wanted to play a game of chicken with a 9500-tonne destroyer, they'd not come off on top. 'Get Seahawk 1 to buzz them, see if we can't get a good look at whether they have recovered anything.'

'Aye-aye, sir.'

Langford took another sip of his coffee. This was turning out to be more interesting than he'd expected. The sound of his XO piped through his headphones, 'Sir, Chinese destroyer has moved parallel to us off the port side, still increasing speed; 150 metres distance. Recommend we take evasive action to maintain safe distance.'

'Negative. We won't have them dictate our heading. Maintain course.'

He'd seen this game before. The vessel would edge closer or overtake his own before slowing and turning into their heading, forcing them to take evasive action. Not this time.

'Sir, RHIBs have reached the previous location the Chinese held; they report nothing of interest.'

'Okay. What's Seahawk 1's report?'

'Still moving into position, sir,' the seaman replied.

Langford eyed the Chinese destroyer on camera. Chinese sailors could be seen manning points around the vessel, groups of officers on their bridge staring back at them, a couple holding cameras. *What are they playing at?* he wondered.

The voice of one of the other skippers entered his earpiece, 'Sir, this Chinese frigate is making aggressive moves; taking evasive action.'

He was about to ask what kind of move when the XO's panicked voice washed over. 'Sir, Chinese destroyer is moving closer, recommend we move away. I think they mean to ram us.'

Jacob looked back up at the monitor. Sure enough, the Chinese destroyer, slightly smaller than his own, had moved closer, closing the parallel gap between them by another few metres and edging their ship slightly ahead of their own. Both ships were suddenly within less than 100 metres of each other – well beyond what was considered safe and professional operating standards.

'The devil is he playing at!' Jacob shouted angrily. 'Tell this fucking idiot to back off,' he ordered one to no-one in particular.

They didn't get a chance.

The seaman at the helm of the Chinese destroyer yanked the vessel hard to starboard, putting their vessel on a direct collision course with the American Arleigh Burke. Langford heard the XO yell, 'HARD TO STARBOARD!' but it was too little, too late. The pointed bow of the Chinese destroyer loomed into view of one of the cameras as Langford's ship sought to pull away. He watched in horror as the Chinese bow ploughed into the steel port side of Jacob's ship just near the focsle.

A group of seamen manning a .50 cal. machine gun was forced to scramble and abandon their posts as the unstoppable weight barged into the ship, crushing the machine gun like it was paper. The world inside the CIC flashed black, and sparks flew as the painfully loud screeching sound of metal on metal reverberated throughout the ship. Glass shattered and people yelled in alarm, their world tilted by the impact. Emergency lighting flashed on as the tilt lessened suddenly. More scraping noises echoed throughout the ship but less than before. They couldn't see inside the CIC, but the Chinese destroyer had begun to pull itself free of the American vessel, tearing a massive chunk of torn metal and debris free. Their own bow was bent and torn, not unlike that of the American vessel.

'Damage control!' Langford ordered before checking in with the bridge, 'XO, report!'

'They rammed us, sir! Still assessing damage, but we've got multiple systems down.'

'Un-fucking believable.' This couldn't go unanswered. 'Do we have weps?' he asked one of the officers.

'Negative, sir; systems are down.'

'What about EW?'

'All down, sir.'

'Fuck,' he swore again, the sense of impotence impossible to ignore.

Alarms sounded throughout the ship, at least one of them meaning fire.

'Get systems back online and give me DC reports as quickly as possible. If that bastard comes back, I want the five-inch ready to sink the fucker.'

The shaken officers and sailors in the CIC looked at him. He knew his face was bright red, his fury visibly seething from his every pore. He'd just been outplayed, and he knew it. They all did.

He almost forgot about the other two ships in his command. 'Harry, Jack, we've just been rammed. Keep an eye out, we might need assistance over here. If any of the Chinese approach with the intent to ram, you have permission to fire to protect your ships.'

The other vessels in his group had fared slightly better, taking only glancing blows. Luckily, they'd had time to respond, as Langford's ship had suffered the first blow.

Even before he saw the first damage report, he knew the game was over. His ship would have significant structural issues and would have to return to port. There was no doubt the Chinese vessel was in a similar state, but that probably didn't matter. It occurred to him too late that this had probably been their intention all along.

Somewhere in all the chaos, a seaman reported, 'Sir, Seahawk 1 reports Chinese RHIBs appear to only contain sailors and divers; no additional equipment observed.'

'What the hell was this all about then?' Langford muttered to himself as he looked down at his coffee-stained uniform, his mug shattered, along with his pride.

***

Commander Li grinned as he looked back at the crippled American destroyer, smoke pouring from the gash in its side. *Just like opening a can*, Li thought. His own ship had suffered considerable damage, with multiple systems offline and the bow undeniably bent and crunched. But he'd completed his mission and done it well. It was time to head east, back home. Somewhere in the back of his mind, he wondered how the Americans would react. This had been an overt act. But those thoughts faded quickly, as the fantasy of his own promotion and glory upon returning home flashed through his mind.

Huang Shen – Andaman Sea

Ming scrolled through the various news stories and threads spreading through social media like wildfire. Footage and analysis of the incident between Chinese and American ships was everywhere. He knew this would have something to do with his mission, and he felt uneasy – this was a risk. The Americans would respond to this one way or another. They might start searching vessels at random or challenging Chinese military vessels more openly. His ship was an undefended commercial vessel. He just hoped they didn't come looking; hopefully they'd be distracted enough.

'Not long to go now,' he said to himself, but the knot in his stomach wouldn't subside. They'd just entered the Andaman Sea, and they would enter the Malacca Strait soon.

CHAPTER 15

HQJOC – Australia

'Any word on casualties?' Ata asked quietly. The floor was a frenzy of activity as everyone tried to make sense of what had happened.

Maia shook her head, 'Not yet, but there will be.'

'Fuck me! What a shit fight that turned into.'

Maia nodded with a grimace on her face. 'Yeah, talk about a bloody nose; the Americans are going to be furious.' Footage of the incident was playing on a loop on one of the massive wall-mounted TVs on the watch floor.

An intrepid journalist with a camera and telescopic lens had managed to catch the moment of collision and the immediate aftermath. The shaky footage and exclamation from the video only added to the effect of something dramatic being caught on film. Now the footage showed an American simply smoking, another ship alongside providing what aid it could. Panning off in the distance, the Chinese ships loomed, menacingly circling at a safe distance. Already, commentators and experts were hurrying to examine the footage. They all seemed to be in agreement. There was no doubting the outcome of the little tussle. The

Chinese had come off on top.

'What about Danny and Jesse?' Ata asked.

Maia gave a small shrug, 'For now, this changes nothing. But it also means that if the missile is on that ship, the Chinese might be more than willing to defend it. We need to get a good idea of the forces they have available – not just PLAN but coast guard, and even their maritime militia forces.'

Ata nodded, 'Leave it with me. What about our forces?'

'So, HMAS Hobart will stick to the plan for the moment, but it's far more exposed down there now.'

'I mean, it won't be easy to stop them. We have to maintain a presence in the South China Sea, along shipping lanes …'

'No, it won't. And we'll have to follow the Americans' lead on this one. If they start shooting to keep the Chinese away, we could be in a very dangerous situation.'

'Feels like we already are,' Ata replied solemnly.

'Mmm-hmm,' Maia replied absentmindedly as the image on the TV screen changed, with CNN running live coverage of the incident. The broadcaster presented some kind of update. 'The Chinese Ministry for Foreign Affairs has released a statement denouncing the aggressive and unprofessional actions of the United States. The MFA claims Chinese vessels were forced to respond with force but showed restraint by not engaging the United States naval forces with weaponry …'

'That was quick,' Ata said, surprised. The ramming had only happened thirty minutes prior.

'Yeah, ten bucks says this was prepared well in advance. I get the feeling the Americans just got played.'

'You don't think they did this to draw US forces away from the Huang Shen, do you?'

Maia turned to stare at her, thinking before answering, 'It's concerningly plausible, and what's worse, it makes sense … If we're focused on Chinese naval forces, one cargo ship isn't going to come up as a major focus.' She paused again,

'Ata, I need you and Sidney to start feeding directly into the taskforce. We need to know what USS John Basilone and HMAS Hobart could be facing. We'll need to get additional forces ready if need be.'

'Additional forces?'

'Yeah, don't worry about that, just get a look out for the Chinese. Pay attention to their bases in the South China Sea as well – they can sortie from those.'

Ata nodded, 'Does the prime minister know yet?'

'After this? Oh, he'll be getting briefed soon enough. All the chiefs are going into a meeting in twenty minutes.'

Ata bit her lip. 'I don't like this. Everything is happening too quickly. I feel like we're rushing in blindly. This is how wars start, Maia.'

Maia tried to give her a reassuring look. 'It'll be okay, Ata. Focus on getting coverage across the South China Sea. If we know what the Chinese have, or could use against us, we can avoid getting into a situation where the Chinese think they could fight us … And win.'

Ata had her mission, but she didn't feel any better. Meanwhile, Danny and Jesse were sailing rapidly toward the Malacca Strait.

Zhongnanhai – Beijing – China

Chang sat in silence as the president read through the after-action report provided by PLAN admirals Tung and Taosing. They were all in the president's office, a large and dominating room panelled with dark oak and surrounded by high bookshelves full of various texts, both Eastern and Western. A surprising number of plants hinted at the man's passion. Yet, behind him loomed his own image, side by side with that of Mao Zedong. The symbology wasn't lost on Chang, or anyone else who entered the president's office: he considered himself as equal to, if not greater than the creator of the Chinese Communist Party. A few years ago, such a claim would have had him thrown from office, or even arrested, but the president had successfully dispatched his rivals through a cunningly launched anti-corruption drive and managed to remove the term limits on his time as president as set by his predecessors. He was now the true power of China.

Peering over the report in front of him, the president looked directly at Admiral Tung. 'Admiral, what are your plans to counter any response by the Americans?'

Chang wasn't sure how the older admiral would respond; he was often a quiet, cautious man. 'Comrade chairman, we have raised the readiness of all our forces globally and ordered them to avoid any further provocative actions against the Americans until further orders are given. The Americans and their allies will be on guard now. I suspect that if any of our forces were to attempt a similar manoeuvre, the Americans would engage.'

The president nodded, 'Indeed, a prudent command. I must say, I was surprised at the success of our actions; I had not expected you to take such risks, admiral.'

Tung shuffled uncomfortably in his chair, trying to determine whether his command in chief was insulting or congratulating him. He decided on the latter. 'Sir, it was my belief we needed to send a message and distract the Americans sufficiently. I believe I achieved that with only minimal damage to our own forces. The Americans will have to think twice about how they approach our forces and territorial claims now.'

The president grinned, 'Do not worry, admiral. I fully support your more aggressive tone. We cannot conceal our power and intentions forever. The Americans respect strength, much the same way we do.'

The admiral nodded, still clearly uncomfortable with the praise.

The president moved on quickly, slapping his hands together and eyeing Chan, 'Good! Now, Comrade Wonqin, what is the status of our mission? I trust all is well?'

My turn, Chang thought. He wondered if the admiral had

realised how close he had been to meeting the wrath of the president; the president wasn't one to make aggressive, risky moves, but Chang had counselled him prior. Chang had watched the president rage when he had first seen the imagery of the crippled American ship. The Americans would be even harder to deal with now, and they would almost certainly seek some kind of revenge – the president had nearly screamed.

Chang had sought to soothe him. 'Comrade president, this was destined to happen sooner or later. These kinds of events cannot always be controlled, but we can take advantage of them.'

The president had stopped his raging, eyeing Chang, 'What do you suggest?'

The power dynamics between the two men had shifted ever so slightly. 'I don't believe we need to do anything, but we make it clear that China's policy is that Americans, and their allied vessels and aircraft, are not welcome near our bases or vessels. We can rebuild ships faster than they can. It is not a dynamic they will win. And hopefully, it is one we can uphold largely without bloodshed.'

The president had gone silent for a brief moment, mulling over Chang's words. They didn't call for any major changes – at least, not ones that had already occurred. Plus, it would bolster his standing as a strong leader.

'Comrade chairman, you will be glad to know that the operation has so far gone off without incident. We remain undetected by any Americans and allied forces, and we continue to head towards the Malacca Strait. The Huang Shen will enter the strait shortly and, depending on its speed, should pass through the strait in somewhere between thirty-five to forty hours. Once safely past Singapore, it will be intercepted by one of our coast-guard vessels, which will seek to take ownership of the missile and remove the science crew and security personnel.

'And what if the Americans figure out their missile is on the ship? How are we situated?'

Admiral Taosing stirred at the president's question. 'We have placed additional PLAN and coast-guard vessels in the region to provide support as required. But we did not want to amass too many forces, as it may give rise to suspicion.'

The president nodded, 'Which forces?'

The admiral checked a small notebook, 'A Type 055 Renhai destroyer and Type 052D Luyang are patrolling near the mouth of the strait from the PLAN. However, we have three coast-guard vessels in the area as well, including one of our largest ships.'

'And the Americans? What do they have?'

'There is only one vessel that could threaten the Huang Shen. The USS John Basilone. It was last reported off Sri Lanka, but our forces do not have a current location on it.' The admiral paused, clearing his throat, 'There is also an Australian vessel, HMAS Hobart, moving through the Java Sea, heading towards the strait. We have a surveillance vessel shadowing it.' Likely meaning a disguised fishing vessel.

The president raised an eyebrow. 'You are not concerned by this vessel?'

The admiral shook his head, 'It is one destroyer, and a weaker one compared to our own. If need be, we can intercept it and force it away from the Huang Shen. Plus, the air force has a number of squadrons available should we require them. It is not a concern.' He was confident. The reality was, they didn't have a clear picture of the USS John Basilone, or the intentions of the Australian vessel.

The president leant back into his chair. 'Good, and gentlemen, I want hourly updates on the Huang Shen's progress and to be alerted if there are any complications. Until that cargo is secure on Chinese land, it remains at risk.'

The three men nodded before standing and departing.

As they left the president suite, Tung grumbled, 'We need more eyes in the region. I don't like not knowing where our adversary is.'

Always cautious, this one, Chang thought. 'Surely you don't doubt our seamen and their ability to succeed, admiral?' A not-so-subtle jab.

The older admiral smiled, making Chang feel uneasy. 'But of course not, comrade. However, one of the first rules of warfare is to know your enemy. I know from experience not to underestimate the Americans and their satellite networks. We would be wise to expect the worst and prepare; it is what I have done … Have you made similar preparations?' the admiral eyed him carefully, ready to judge his response.

Chang brushed aside the comment, 'We have plans in place should they seek to take the Huang Shen. Do not worry, admiral. Just make sure the Americans and Australians don't get close enough, and we won't have a problem.'

The admiral smiled again. 'Time will be the ultimate judge, comrade.'

Chang hadn't realised it, but they had reached the entrance of the building. The two admirals stepped smoothly into their armoured vehicle without saying another word to him, although Chan caught the lingering eye of Taosing before he stepped inside.

Chang watched as it pulled away. Cunning old admiral indeed. Perhaps a powerful enemy, or ally. Time would tell.

The White House – United States of America

Quinton felt good. The last few days, he'd put the prototype mess behind him. He'd successfully dealt with that, and there was no point focusing on the past. Sure, he had taken some extreme steps, but in the end, it had been worth it. The Chinese hadn't managed to steal it away, and the joint chiefs and, most importantly, the President, were none the wiser. For Quinton, there was no greater satisfaction than handling a crisis, and handling it well. Plus, there were new, exciting distractions. The scuffle between the US and Chinese forces in the Maldives had given

Quinton a new line of effort to push his agenda of stronger actions against the Chinese. He'd spent the last day in near-endless meetings and discussions, always driving a strong American response.

Quinton's world had all come to a screeching halt from a simple request to provide a brief. One of his aides had organised a time in his busy schedule, and before Quinton knew it, he was getting a brief by a military intelligence analyst on the Huang Shen and the suspected theft of a hypersonic missile, all from a report pulled together from Australia.

Trying to conceal his panic, he started probing, 'How confident are we in this intel?'

The analyst, supported by a rear admiral, didn't hesitate. 'Very confident, sir. We've run further spectral analysis over the vehicle identified as travelling from the suspected crash site, and we have confirmed it is the same vehicle pictured. Additionally, the creation of a special task force within the Chinese establishment has been confirmed through HUMINT. At least four individuals that we know of, specialising in rockery and aeronautics, have disappeared suddenly. We can confidently tie those individuals to the PLAAF flight seen entering Bandar Abbas and subsequently arriving at the port.'

'But how can we be sure the missile is on that ship?' he persisted.

'We can't be 100% sure, but given the available information and the possibility that the missile could have flown that far, we cannot see any other explanation as to why the Iranians would establish a fortified military encampment at that location at such short notice.'

The analyst was supremely confident. A feeling of unease started to grow in Quinton's gut.

'Okay, thank you,' he replied curtly to the analyst. He'd heard enough. Turning to the senior officer, he said, 'What is the plan for this?'

'Sir, the USS John Basilone is currently enroute to

intercept and board the Huang Shen. In addition, the Australian vessel HMAS Hobart has been assigned to provide support and cut off any escape on the other side of the Malacca Strait.'

'Admiral, how come this is only coming to my attention now? I haven't agreed to this "operation"!' He slammed his fist against his desk for added emphasis, faking his own anger.

The admiral didn't budge. 'Sir, the joint chiefs presented this plan to the secretary of defence, who informed the President a short time ago. The operation has executive approval. It does not need "your" approval.'

The man might as well have punched Quinton in the face. He was behind the ball. The President had been briefed without his knowledge. There was an operation underway – and all searching for the missile he had believed destroyed and gone. He'd look like a fool if they recovered the missile. And that would make him disposable.

That couldn't happen.

'Thank you, gentlemen, I've seen all I need to,' Quinton said, dismissing them both.

The men had just left when there was a gentle knock on the door. His secretary poked her head in. 'Sir, the President would like to know if you have time for a quick chat.'

Quinton was surprised. It wasn't often the President wandered down for a "quick chat". He replied hurriedly, 'As in now, Maggie?'

'Yes, sir, he's waiting in the Oval Office.'

'Shit,' he muttered to himself.

'What was that, sir?'

'Nothing, Maggie. Let him know I'm on my way.'

The President of the United States was an interesting character: Boston born and raised, with an Ivy League education; charismatic and, most importantly, popular. But, as Quinton had learnt, he didn't hold particularly set political beliefs, preferring to play the field that would give him the best outcome or advantage. The President could also be aloof, concealing his intention and opinion until it suited him best. Quinton saw him as a man playing games, not a true patriot like himself.

He was reading something on his computer behind his large, wooden desk when Quinton entered. He looked up immediately. 'Close the door, would you, Quinton.'

Quinton obliged before taking up his customary position in one of the comfortable chairs facing the desk.

The President barely waited for him to be seated. 'You said the test failed, and that the missile was lost.'

It wasn't a question; more of an accusation.

Quinton nodded sagely, 'It did appear that way at the time, Mr President. But I am sure you have received the same briefing I just did …'

'I don't want to hear it. You told me this was sorted. Now I find out the Chinese have stolen our cutting-edge, decade-defining tech, AND WE DIDN'T KNOW ABOUT IT.' The President slammed his fist down on the desk, staring at Quinton, who stared back.

'Yes, sir,' he replied simply. 'With the information we had at the time. We believed it was gone.'

'And what information was that? It seems this analyst was able to piece it together without much effort! Did you even try?'

'Of cours—'

The President held up his hand. 'I checked, you know.'

Quinton blinked, remaining silent. *Checked what?*

'I checked with Langley, the department of defence. *Everyone*. And guess what, Quinton? They hadn't received anything from you, or this office.'

'Sir, I can assure you —' Quinton started.

'No, Quinton. I don't want to hear it! You'd better hope like hell this intel is spot on and that missile is on that ship, or at the bottom of the ocean. Remember, you're the one that pitched the change in schedule, you're the one that wanted a big show of force against the Iranians. This is your plan, Quinton. Remember that.'

Quinton waited a moment. 'It's not on that ship, Mr President. I can assure you.' He clenched his jaw as he tried to maintain his composure.

'We'll see,' the President replied coolly, waving his hand dismissively at Quinton. Their meeting was done.

As he walked out of the Oval Office, a furious determination boiled inside him.

There was only one solution in his mind now. The President had made it clear enough that Quinton was going to be the scapegoat, even if they recovered the missile. He had to make sure that missile was never found. He cut a beeline for Dick's office. Really nothing more than a shoebox of a room deeper into the admin area of the building. The title on Dick's door was simple enough, reading 'Advisor: National Security.' It was straightforward enough no one would ask any questions, and vague enough to conceal Dick's real role to Quinton.

'Have you seen this?' he demanded, striding through the door of Dick's office. The man rarely missed much and was likely fully aware. He had already opened Quinton's hurried email.

'It just came to my attention. Looks like the missile is still in play.'

Quinton couldn't tell if he heard a slight tone of bemusement in Dick's voice. The man normally spoke in a monotone at the best of times. He ignored it for now.

'I want it dealt with before the USS John Basilone can intercept it,' Quinton ordered, looking into the dark eyes of his minion. Part of him hated needing this man, but he certainly had his uses.

Dick waited before answering, calculating the best response. 'Sinking it? Using conventional means? Probably not – we'd need to send a team in to —'

Quinton waved him away, 'I don't care, and I don't want to know. I want the missile *gone*.'

'It will be risky, but I do have contacts in the region that might be up for this. It won't be cheap.'

Quinton doubted that Dick just happened to have a team available at the drop of a hat in the right location, but he didn't say so. He just wanted the problem solved.

'But the risks are considerable. We don't know if there is a force protecting the ship; nor do we know if the prototype is even there. My recommendation is we let the USS John Basilone handle this.

Quinton balled his fists and stared savagely at Dick. 'Look, I don't care about the details; this has to be done, otherwise, the Chinese will get a hold of our technology – and then what? We spend the next few decades trying to play catchup and getting our asses handed to us by these fucking communist sons-of-bitches!? Not a chance! America has to be the most powerful nation. It's how we stay on top. Nothing – and I mean nothing – can be allowed to threaten that!'

Dick knew this had nothing to do with saving America or maintaining its might; this was all about protecting his boss's future. He didn't care. The rope Quinton gave him to get the job done, plus the money and power it gave him, allowed him to live a life that had not been available in the military. Plus, his extracurricular activities couldn't be scrutinised as easily when he was linked to the power brokers of Washington. Still, this was the most fired up and unhinged he'd seen his boss before. He had contingency plans in place should it become time to move on; might be time to check on his arrangements. For now, though, he'd go along with his boss's madness.

'I'll get it done and report back once everything is in place.'

HQJOC Carpark – Australia

The sweltering Australian sun battled the air-conditioner in Tim's black car. He was waiting, a camera on his lap. An Australian Federal Police investigator sat next to him in a cheap black business suit with a sidearm on his hip. Tim had wanted more support, but it was still early days. The investigation had only been stood up the day before. In time, they'd get more resources, but for now, it was just him and the man next to him. State-side, a whole team of people would be busy at work, probably supported by a host of lawyers and surveillance specialists. Plus, he was a foreigner here – his powers weren't unlimited. He'd need the Australian feds; they'd do the arresting.

'Here he comes,' the investigator said. They'd parked further back into the carpark but could still see the entrance.

They watched as Mike walked over to a lonely bench and pulled out a cigarette, lit it and gazed off into the distance. He waited only a moment before pulling out his phone and putting it to his ear. Tim picked up his own phone and made his own call. 'We've got activity, who's he calling?'

The agent on the other end was typing rapidly. 'It's a cell number, international, state-side.'

'We recording?' Tim asked, already knowing the answer.

'Every word,' the agent confirmed.

Mike wasn't a master criminal. He was lazy, self-aggrandising and corrupt. From the moment the FBI had agreed to establish the investigation, all of Mike's phones and emails had been tapped. Anything he did electronically was monitored, including on secure systems, and his movements outside of the embassy and HQJOC were being tracked constantly. He couldn't sneeze without them knowing it. Even now, another team was placing listening devices and cameras throughout his apartment.

They hadn't been sure if Danny and Jesse getting deployed would have spooked Mike, but from what they could see, his activity hadn't changed. Although, watching him now, Mike seemed uptight and rigid. Whoever he was speaking to, he either feared or respected. Mike's normal attitude seemed to float between arrogant and indifferent. On the phone now, he looked as though he was out of his element.

Mike hung up, taking a big drag on his cigarette before

throwing it on the ground and smothering it with his foot. He wandered back into the building at a leisurely pace.

'Let's get back to the office. I want to listen to that recording,' Tim said. This would be the first time they'd had a recording of the person giving the orders from the White House.

CHAPTER 16

An RHIB – Malacca Strait

The RHIB's inflatable hull slapped heavily against the light swell of the sea, the roar of its engine mixing with the sound of the wind whistling past the heads of the men onboard. They were practically invisible against the dark night sky and shapeless ocean; only the twinkle of the stars and light from other vessels punctured the inky blackness surrounding them. The RHIB carried no transponders or identification. It would not appear on radar, and only someone paying close attention would be able to hear it. The RHIB cut a direct path, avoiding the numerous container and fishing vessels. Their target lay just ahead. Silence and stealth were critical.

'Stay on this heading for another ten minutes,' one of the men shouted into the ear of the pilot, the dim glow of a small handheld GPS providing only fleeting illumination upon the men's concealed faces. They wore all black, with balaclavas covering their faces, while night vision goggles remained strapped firmly to their helmets. Tactical chest rigs and body armour weighed them down. Each of them had a diverse range of weapons securely clipped to their chest.

They wouldn't lose any kit overboard if they could avoid it. Only the boat's pilot had his goggles down. He scanned ahead, looking for blacked-out vessels or any other unseen threats that could ruin their little mission. The rest of the team held on tightly as their small vessel bounced around, the passing glow of other ships the only indication they were moving in a particular direction.

'Five minutes,' called out the team leader, a slim, wiry man in his forties.

Their team was small by design and necessity; they hadn't had the time to assemble a larger force. But they wouldn't have wanted a larger force for this mission. Everyone started checking their equipment – weapons, radios, explosives and medical tools. They'd all triple-checked everything prior to departure, but it was good practice; no one wanted to be stuck in a firefight without the right tools. They were all heavily armed, ready for close combat. For this mission, the team leader had landed on simple codename convention, simply dubbing himself "Lead". He carried a short, boxy P90 submachine gun, while the rest of the boarding team, "One" and "Two", carried an M4 carbine each, with a backup weapon for tighter quarters, One preferring a small Heckler and Koch MP7 submachine gun and Two taking a larger, more powerful Benelli M4 shotgun.

The pilot, "RHIB", had his own weapons, but he'd stay with the RHIB, their only real escape route. Ideally, they wouldn't run into any resistance, but it was better to be safe than sorry. The intel the team had been provided was spotty at best. The likelihood of armed guards was high, but the overall number of armed men was a complete information gap.

The mission was relatively simple: board the target vessel, locate and identify some kind of stolen tech and, if located, destroy it. Simple, in theory. They'd been given a green light to accomplish the job any way they saw fit; their employer didn't care how it was done, it seemed. But it had to be done quickly and, if possible, quietly. They'd all be given extremely lucrative bonuses upon completion of the mission. A combination of hush money and remuneration for a hurried and dangerous job.

The roar of the boat's engines suddenly eased as the pilot released the throttle, the little boat jolting forward slightly as its wake caught up with the slowing vessel. Each man pulled down their NVGs, their worlds turning from the all-consuming blackness to the glowing green of the view through their glasses. They could make out each other and the features of their RHIB clearly enough, but the ocean itself lacked definition, appearing as an endless pit, interrupted by the occasional movement of a small wave. They sat in silence, letting their ears grow accustomed to the uncomfortable silence, which was broken only by the gentle slapping of the ocean against the RHIB. The pilot checked his nav computer.

'Target is a couple of minutes out. We'll wait for it to come to us.' No one would be able to hear them coming that way.

The small boat continued to bob quietly on the swell. Despite their NVGs, the space around them was largely obscured; without any additional surfaces or light, their night vision was only so good.

'Anyone see it?' asked One. The last thing they wanted was to get run over by the much larger vessel.

'Not yet,' replied Two, who was closer to the bow of the small vessel.

The seconds ticked over, and a distant, dull rushing sound appeared, growing louder. 'How come we can't see the ship?' One asked again, his nerves showing.

'They are running dark,' came Lead's response, firm and definitive; he was obviously not wanting a discussion.

'Don't look directly in front of you. If you look upwards, you can see a faint glow from the bridge,' the RHIB pilot pointed out, keeping his gaze firmly locked on the lights, carefully trying to gauge how far its bow was from them.

One and Two peered outward and upward. The rushing becoming a roar.

Neither of them was ready when the small wave from the bow of the larger ship emerged just to their port side. The pilot kept his eyes locked on the vessel, making tiny corrections, aiming just to the port side of the ship. He teased the RHIB forward slowly, using only the smallest amount of power to reduce the noise. The worn red-metal hull, impossible to see with NVGs, seemed to rise out of the water and disappear into the sky as it slipped past them with surprising speed. The wash of the water made the RHIB bounce, rocking the men who held on tightly. The cascading roar of water began to subside as the bow moved past the RHIB.

The pilot deftly flicked the RHIB around and began to bring it closer to the moving red hull, matching the speed of the ship.

'Ready for boarding,' Lead ordered. Two was ready, picking up a large gun with a hook and a black nylon rope attached to it. Lead tapped his Peltor headset, 'Fire at my mark.' Silently, he counted to five, estimating their position compared to the ship above them.

'Fire!'

A soft *bang* came from the grappling gun, with the rubberised hook sailing up and out of sight. A *clang* sounded somewhere above them, and the rope began to spool out. The man who fired the hook quickly fastened it to the RHIB, creating a lifeline between the ship and the RHIB. With a *thwick*, the rope pulled taut, drawing the bow of the RHIB closer to the ship.

'Get the ladder ready,' came the next command. A second grappling gun was already in the hands of the man who had fired the first one. There was another hook, but this time with a rope ladder attached. The ladder was nothing more than a single rope with loops for their feet and hands. The pilot waited patiently, making sure there weren't any sudden waves or jerks that could throw the men overboard and into the inky abyss of the ocean.

There was a second muffled shot and the hook arched skyward, disappearing into the space above them. One gave the rope a quick tug, and it remained locked in place. Flicking the others a thumbs up, he started to climb.

***

'What was that noise?' whispered the man, exhaling a large cloud of acidic smoke and lowering the joint from his mouth.

'It's a ship, Feng – it makes noises,' his companion replied, uninterested.

'No way. I heard something,' Feng insisted.

His partner stopped and listened for a moment, hearing nothing but the gentle roar of water cascading across the ship's bow. 'I'm starting to think you are smoking too much, man. It's making you paranoid,' came the mocking reply as he took the joint and inhaled deeply.

A second *clang* followed. This time, his fellow shipmate turned his head. 'Okay, I heard that one …'

Both men crept around the container they had been smoking behind.

The deck was poorly lit, but they could see well enough that they could make out handrails and walkways. Feng pointed directly ahead of them. '*The fuck is that?*' he whispered, pointing at two hooks tangled around the side railing of the large ship.

They crept closer. Suddenly, the hook on the left twitched violently. Something heavy was pulling on it. Realisation struck both men. 'Fuck, it's pirates!' Feng gasped. They both took a step back. The hook jerked violently again.

'C'mon, you idiot, let's go!'

Feng's shipmate's footsteps were already quickly receding. Feng could feel his fear rising quickly now. He turned, running towards the large, white superstructure at the stern of the ship, the glow of the bridge like a beacon of safety.

***

Two muffled taps sounded through the headsets of the team as Two reached the top of the boarding ladder. All clear. One watched as his colleague climbed slowly over the guard rail, making every effort to avoid any unnecessary noise. They wore rubberised boots to muffle the sound, and their black clothing made them nearly invisible against the dark night. Even their weapons had been coated black, removing any shiny or reflective surfaces. The rest of the team made quick progress up the ladder, leaving only the pilot behind to guard the RHIB. If need be, he could cut the lines and be away from the ship in seconds.

As Lead climbed onboard, he noted that One and Two had already moved away from the rail, taking up positions near a hatch. Exactly where they'd planned to arrive.

'Open it,' he whispered through his headset, watching as one of the men eased the hatch open, the heavy hatch making only the smallest, almost imperceptible squeak. *Thank God for oiled hinges,* he thought. They had carried a small blowtorch and some thermite charges in case they needed to open any doors, but the quieter they could be, the better.

Moving closer, Lead tapped One on the shoulder. The man shuffled to the side, allowing Lead to get a look down into the space below the open hatch. Dim light met his eyes through his NVGs, slightly washing out his vision. He could make out a metal walkway below them with a ladder leading up to their hatch, but he couldn't see anything down the walkway to his left or right. Taking a leap of faith, he lowered himself quietly down the ladder, dropping with a gentle thud onto the walkway below. He did a quick check left and right; both corridors were empty. He gave a quick hand signal to the two men above him, who rapidly made their way down to join him.

He waited until they were together before continuing forward, his P90 submarine gun firmly held against his shoulder, aiming down the grim, poorly lit corridor ahead. He could see the path they needed to take in his mind's eye. Detailed schematics of the ship had been provided and studied by each team member. The last thing they wanted was to get lost, especially if they were in a firefight. He lifted his NVGs from his face, letting his eyes adjust to the new lighting. After only a moment, he moved forward, the team following closely behind. They held their weapons pointed at doors and corners, scanning, searching and listening for any threats, the walls of the depressing ship surrounding them at all times.

***

The door to the bridge slammed open, hitting the joining wall with a mighty *boom*, startling the late-night crew and making Ming leap out of his chair. His hand instinctively flew to the sidearm fastened to his hip as his eyes searched for the threat.

The two men stumbled through, panting.

'Bloody idiots, you scared the shit out of me!' came the angry reproach from the officer of the watch.

Ming, who'd been lounging in the captain's chair, eyed the two carefully. They both had a panicked look on their faces, and they were panting heavily, clearly exhausted from the exertion of running to the bridge. The hairs on Ming's neck stood on end.

Something was wrong.

'What is it?'

One of the men – Ming remembered his name as Feng – was doubled over, panting. 'Pirates! We … are … being … boarded!' the man finally got out between pants.

Ming's brain took a second. *Piracy*? It certainly wasn't unheard of in the strait, but it was very rare these days.

'What happened?' Ming asked sternly. He needed more information.

The second man stepped forward, a bit more collected than the first. 'We were down on the deck and saw hooks attached to the railing. Someone was climbin—'

Ming ignored the rest of the man's story. Flying across the bridge, he swept up the small handheld radio he used to communicate with Jiang and his team. They had visitors, alright – but there was no way these were pirates. These were far more dangerous than any poor fisherman trying to feed his family with an AK47.

'Lieutenant, come in. We have visitors!'

An unfamiliar voice replied, 'Sir, the lieutenant is sleeping. Please repeat.'

'Wake him *now*. There are hostiles on board – secure the prototype!'

'Yes, sir!' came the immediate reply, the urgency waking the soldier into action.

Ming turned to the officer of the watch, a slightly unhinged look in his eyes. 'Secure the bridge. Don't let anyone in here you don't recognise. Stay on the cameras and tell me if you spot any movement.'

The officer nodded, not quite sure what was happening but understanding the urgency. He went to reply, but Ming had already made a run from the bridge, pistol in hand.

***

The seemingly endless metal corridors were so far devoid of any life. The odd groan and dull rumble from the ship were the only real sign that the ship was alive at all. Still, they remained on high alert. As they neared the final corner, Lead held his fist above his shoulder, telling the team to stop. Crouching down, he moved his hand to cup his ear, the signal for the team to listen. Sure enough, the almost imperceptible shuffling of feet could be heard.

According to the ship's plans, this was the last turn

before a doorway to the central cargo hold, and it was the most likely location they might run into a guard. Lead reached into a small pouch in his chest rig, removing a small telescopic mirror. With practised motion, he delicately eased the small mirror around the corner. The guard was clearly visible, a Chinese QBZ-191 rifle slung across his chest. Panning the mirror slightly, Lead couldn't see anyone else. But the corridor itself was barren, without any cover or doorways. They'd have to take care of the guard to get past.

He quickly retracted the mirror and turned to the rest of the team, holding one hand behind the other. One enemy spotted. Pulling a cynical stun grenade from his rig, he nodded to the others, who nodded back. Flash and clear.

Quietly pulling the pin, Lead hefted the grenade around the corner. The small device clattered as it bounced towards the guard. He made a small yelp just before it exploded.

***

Between the moment the guard spotted the small object flying towards him and the split second later when it clanged on the deck, he knew he was too late, letting out an involuntary sound as his body panicked. His world disappeared in a blinding white-hot flash. The shock wave washed over him, and the sense of heat from the flash made it feel like he was burning. Any sense of control of his body was gone. The blast overwhelmed him completely. A high-pitched screech filled his ears and moved into his head.

He wasn't sure how much time had passed, but the next sensation was a dull impact against his chest. His mind registered it but was unable to process what was happening. Maybe it was the blast hitting him – his death? The pressure seemed to increase on his chest but also his back. Something was pulling his arms backwards. This was followed by a sudden cold piercing sensation on his face.

Slowly, he started to regain his senses. He wasn't dead. Far from it, in fact. He realised he was face-down against the cold metal deck. His arms had been forcibly yanked backwards and hog tied with his legs. He wasn't sure what by, but it felt hard; it was pinching him, cutting into his wrists. Something was shoved in his mouth, making it impossible to speak. He let out a muffled protest as he was roughly dragged to the side of the corridor.

A voice spoke quickly, not in a language he understood, but one he recognised. English. Trying to turn his head, he could see a part of a leg and the waist of someone standing over him. Whoever the person was, they wore black fatigues and had military-grade weapons. Immediate confusion gave way to outrage and fury. They were being attacked, and the attackers had successfully and easily taken him down. He tried to yell out in his rage, but it was impossible. The man on top of him pulled a blindfold over his head and his world went black. Still, his mind raced.

He knew now that he'd been hit with some kind of flashbang or stun grenade. He had to warn his comrades. Maybe they had heard that blast, but it was a big ship. He'd have to wait until the man on top of him left. Why hadn't they just killed him?

Little did he know how out of control events were already spiralling.

***

'Fuck me,' Lead muttered as he watched his men hogtie the soldier on the ground. The soldier's uniform was Chinese, alright. And not just any regular soldier – special forces. No one had mentioned that in the briefing. The whole operating environment had just become even more deadly. Not only were they on a hostile vessel, but the opposing force was Chinese special forces. Whatever the hell was on this ship must be important.

The men finished tying up the soldier, who was starting to struggle. A quick blow to the back of the head would hopefully keep him quiet for long enough. One looked up at him questioningly, clearly recognising the soldier's uniform and wondering the same thing. Lead shrugged. 'We'll deal with it once we're done. Device should be in the next room,' he said quietly to the two others. They still had a job to do, and hopefully, this was the only man they'd encounter. Still, if they'd known of the Chinese special forces before taking the job, there was no way in hell they'd have come with only three men. There could be a whole platoon on the ship for all they knew. *They'll be paying us extra for this*, he promised himself.

Two gave the guard a swift hit with the butt of his rifle, knocking him out cold. Lead pointed to each man, then to the door the guard had been standing in front of. Both men took position on either side of the heavy bulkhead door. Anyone who had been standing on the other side would have heard the blast from the flashbang, but given the late hour, it was unlikely there would be too many people guarding it. Nevertheless, they'd need to be cautious.

The man on the right pulled the door open slowly and quietly, while the man on his left peered into the cavernous hall of the cargo hold. They took their time, scanning the room before entering. It was a big space, bigger than their night vision could see. There were dark, blackened edges across the space, while the low lighting washed out other areas. Far from ideal. The team leader nodded at both men, pointing at them and motioning for them to enter. Rifles up, they moved without a sound, stepping over the threshold of the heavy door and into the cargo hold beyond.

The two men checked their left and right, scanning for anyone hiding in the dark corners or behind something, waiting for them. They didn't raise any alarm or open fire. Nothing. They shuffled forward, separating, one man taking position behind a container and the other crouching beside a workbench. The space was enormous. Containers, tools and random bits of equipment were scattered about. The darkened edges of the massive hold seemed to press in against them.

'Sweep and clear,' Lead ordered in a barely audible whisper.

A small cluster of workstations sat out the front of an open container. The space had been cleared and had obviously been in use recently. Floodlights ringed the space, providing better lighting than the dim overhead lights. The doors at one end of the container were open, with some filthy plastic sheeting hung over to conceal what lay inside.

One held up his hand, a single finger pointing upward, 'One enemy ahead.'

Lead looked carefully at the container, making out the silhouette of a person walking inside, just past the plastic. The only sign of any activity.

Pointing them forward with a sweeping motion, Lead hissed, 'Breach and clear.'

One and Two nodded their understanding. Lead held back, taking up a position behind a desk, trying in vain to scan the walkways above them while keeping an eye on his men. He waited and watched as they approached.

The slightest scratch against metal startled him as he watched and waited, his team moving silently across the metal with their rubberised soles. The noise hadn't come from them; it had come from somewhere above. Flicking his NVGs down, he gazed upward towards the noise. The lower body of a man kneeling against the railing, camouflaged against the black background of the hull, immediately came into view. Lead didn't hesitate, aiming through the holographic sight on his gun. He squeezed the trigger softly, calling out, 'CONTACT!'

The firing pin inside his P90 responded immediately, pulling backwards within the upper receiver of the rifle before using the force generated from the spring inside to slam into the loaded 5.7x28 mm round in the chamber. It all happened in a millisecond. The gunpowder in the round ignited, propelling the full metal jacket bullet from its brass shell and flying from his rifle. Even with the large silencer attached to the front, the sound of the gunshot reverberated around the hold. The single round collided with the man, who fell backwards, disappearing against the black backdrop of the deck. Lead was unsure if he'd killed him, but he didn't have time to find out. The world around him erupted into chaos.

Every corner of the hold around them seemed to explode with the sound of gunfire, flashes from unsuppressed rifles pumping round after round in the team's direction. The two advancing men fell back as quickly as they could, leaping behind a nearby container while trying to return fire. Bullets whizzed and cracked over their heads, the rounds impacting the metal floor with loud clangs, deafening everyone.

Lead pushed away from the flimsy protection offered by the table, running at a full sprint back towards the bulkhead door they'd just come from, the angry buzz of bullets following him the few short metres back. Mustering his strength, he leapt through the doorway, landing heavily in the relative safety beyond the hold. Wasting no time, he turned to gaze back into the hold.

'You two alright?' Lead practically yelled into his microphone, trying to squeeze rounds off towards the muzzle flashes above him.

'We'll survive. Orders?' One replied, panting.

The answer was simple: 'Fall back, cover and move,' he yelled, pulling a smoke grenade from his chest rig. He threw the grenade underhand and it hit the ground, rapidly pouring out thick, grey smoke.

'GO!' yelled Lead once the smoke had spread enough to cover the gap between them and the exit.

Two went first, running at full speed through the smoke while One covered him with long automatic bursts towards the various muzzle flashes above them. Magazines and spent casings built up rapidly around his feet. Two disappeared from his vision. Seconds passed with only the sound of gunfire for company.

'One, you're next!' shouted Lead.

Mustering all his courage, One waited a few seconds before stepping out from behind the container. A whooshing sound overcame the noise of gunfire around him.

Seconds later, the rocket smacked into the container he'd just been behind, sending it rolling over from the force of the blast. Burning-hot splinters of metal flew in every direction as the explosion pushed outward. The man was a few metres away when it hit, sending the shock wave across him and throwing him to the ground, surrounded by smoke, dust and burning debris. Adrenaline pumping, One picked himself up before sprinting towards the open door – towards his team, safety. Rounds smacked into the ground around him. Somewhere in all the chaos, his body registered a dull impact, but his brain pushed it aside, focusing on the task ahead, his escape. The frame of the doorway emerged suddenly through the hazy smoke, and he threw himself through, landing heavily against the metal floor beyond.

Lead slammed the heavy door closed behind the last man as he dived through, quickly spinning the locking mechanism and sealing the hold from their tight corridor. The door vibrated as rounds impacted on the other side, but the thick metal would easily stop most of what was thrown at it. Lead didn't wait around. They moved further down the corridor, not wanting to wait for another rocket to blow the door open.

Two poked his head around the next corner. Nothing. 'Clear here,' he said.

'Keep moving back the way we came,' Lead ordered. Their mission was blown.

'Uh, Lead, I think I'm gonna need some help here,' One groaned weakly.

Lead knelt down next to him, removing a protective glove to feel behind the body armour covering the man's back. His fingers came away wet to the touch; he couldn't see the colour, but he knew what it meant. They couldn't assess how bad it was until they got off the ship. A sudden loud bang echoed from the door they'd just come through, followed by silence. Their attackers weren't going to let them go that easy.

'Two, give me the charges,' he ordered loudly, standing up. 'Take him back out and get him back to the RHIB. I'll buy you both time.'

Two gave him a quick look, knowing better than to argue with the boss but also wondering if this would be the last time he saw him.

'Understood,' Two replied simply, patting Lead on the shoulder. 'We'll be waiting for your signal.'

Another loud bang echoed out from behind the door, this time accompanied by the sound of cracking, bending metal. They were coming through.

Lead stuffed the heavy explosives into his small backpack. The two other men started their slow extraction, Two holding One up and the latter limping along. They made for a sorry sight.

Lead moved up to a T-intersection in the corridor, then waited until he heard the bulkhead door break open loudly. Stepping out from behind cover, he pressed the smaller weapon into his shoulder and squeezed the trigger, firing a long, unbroken burst down the corridor, towards the door. The weapon emptied in seconds.

That should get their attention, he thought, before dropping the now-empty magazine and loading another.

No point waiting around. He sped off down the corridor, heading for the engine room in the stern of the ship. An alarm started blaring over the speakers as he ran, red emergency lighting flashing overhead, further washing out his NVGs. Stealth didn't matter much anymore; they knew they were onboard. He had to run, and fast. There was no telling how many soldiers were on the ship.

***

Ming sprinted down the metal corridor, forgetting his

fear, spurred by the crashing sound of gunfire in the distance. He'd crept quietly towards the hold initially, checking corners and listening for any noises. He cursed his cautiousness now. At least two guards always watched the prototype, but there was no way of telling how many men had boarded the ship. If it was a sizable force and they were already in the cargo hold, he would probably be too late. They could destroy everything with a simple grenade. That would be the end of his mission, and probably his career – but then again, he was assuming he survived that long.

He'd charged down one of the higher levels inside the ship, which – if his memory was correct, and it always was – would put him near one of the upper levels of the central cargo hold. He couldn't hear gunfire anymore, and he slowed as he approached the heavy metal door to the hold. The door in front of him creaked open slowly as he approached. Ming crouched quickly, concealed by the darkness of the entrance, and aimed his pistol towards the opening door, his index finger locked around the trigger. He'd get the first shot off. A figure pushed through the door suddenly. Ming squeezed the trigger slightly, unsure if the figure was friendly or not. The person suddenly swore in Mandarin. A wave of relief washed over Ming as he released the pressure on the trigger and lowered the gun, recognising the voice. He stood up.

'Lieutenant, what happened? Is the prototype secure?'

Jian stiffened immediately, bringing his rifle halfway up before he recognised Ming's voice. He growled, 'Careful, comrade, you almost caught a bullet.'

Ming ignored the comment concealed by the darkness of the entrance. 'The prototype – is it safe?' he insisted.

'Its fine! *I think*. We surprised them and they retreated,' Jian snapped back, clearly wincing in pain.

'But they are still on the ship?'

'Yes, comrade …' Jian replied sarcastically, clearly frustrated and angry.

Ming picked up the radio, calling the bridge, 'Sound the

alarm, and lock the ship down at once!'

He didn't hear the confirmation from the ship's crew; the blaring alarm drowned out the garbled reply. Red lights began flashing throughout the ship, creating a sense of emergency, pumping adrenaline into Ming's veins. He relished the feeling, closing his eyes and letting it wash over him. When he opened them, Jian was kneeling, examining himself.

'What happened to you?'

'They got lucky. It's fine; the round hit my chest plate,' Jian replied, unclipping his armoured vest and letting it hit the ground, grunting in pain but also in relief. Ming shined his torch at Jian's chest. An angry welt was clearly visible where the round had impacted the armour plate. It would hurt, but it wasn't life-threatening.

'You're lucky, comrade. Without that armour, you'd be dead,' Ming commented.

Jian grunted in reply.

Ming didn't have time to deal with the moody lieutenant. He stood, holding out his hand to Jian. The lieutenant looked up at him before taking a deep breath and accepting the offered hand, gingerly rising.

Another burst of gunfire echoed out from the cargo hold, but it sounded distant. The radio crackled from the bridge. 'One armed hostile heading towards the engine room, port side.'

Ming nodded to himself. 'We can't let them stop the ship. Can you help?'

Jian took a single step, wincing. 'You go. I'll keep the prototype safe. Take my men.'

The ship suddenly rocked, vibrating as an explosion echoed throughout the ship. New alarms were ringing – fire alarms.

Ming didn't wait. Turning to Jian, he said, 'Keep it safe. I'll handle our guests.'

He ran off before waiting for a reply. As he ran, he called the soldiers, 'Two men. Meet me at the engine room – the lieutenant will remain with the prototype.'

He could hear garbled replies but couldn't make them out over the alarms. Switching to the bridge, he shouted, 'Bridge, kill the alarms! We can't hear a thing!' into the small handheld radio. He had to repeat himself at least twice before they got the message. A sudden silence descended over the hold. The dull groaning sound of tortured metal replaced the piercing drone of the alarms.

'What was the explosion? Was it the engine rooms?' Ming demanded, still yelling unnecessarily, temporarily deafened by all the alarms.

'Fire portside, not the engine room.'

Ming wasn't sure what that meant but parked the information. 'Copy.'

Whoever was heading for the engine room, he had a head start on Ming. Mentally, he pictured the other person, running parallel on the other side of the ship. He could see himself, the bridge, the guards and Jian. He couldn't let this person win, no matter what. Digging deep, he pushed his legs harder, feeling them burn in angry protest, his radio constantly issuing information. He was panting heavily when he arrived at the heavy metal door to the engine room. He didn't have long to wait before two of Jian's soldiers came stomping towards him, panting significantly less than he was. Ming pulled at the door slowly, trying to avoid making any noise.

***

Lead's mind drifted toward his two teammates as he set the charges against a metal bulkhead in the engine room, trying to picture where they were on the ship and figure out when they'd board the RHIB. He hadn't run into anyone else on his way here, but he had attached one of the heavy charges he'd carried to the side of the ship as he sprinted, giving himself thirty seconds. If anyone had followed him, they'd likely be very dead just about now. At the very least, they'd be confused and probably dealing with the aftermath of the blast.

The explosive charges were technically designed to scuttle ships. Large and powerful, they would punch large holes outward, through even the thickest metal. Typically, they'd be placed at various spots around the ship, ideally below the waterline. But the team leader didn't have the luxury of time. He needed to do the most damage possible in the shortest amount of time. The engine room would have to do. If he could flood the space, he'd bring the ship to a standstill; if he was lucky, it would create a big enough blast to sink the vessel. But he wasn't a demolition expert – everything here was guesswork.

He'd just set the second of his four charges when he heard the smallest clang of metal against metal. Instinctively, he leapt to his right, leaving the small rucksack with the explosive charges in them. It saved his life. A burst of rifle fire smacked into the metal grating where he'd just been crouching. He rolled, putting his body firmly behind a large, solid-looking piece of machinery. Someone cursed loudly on the railing a few metres above him. *Definitely more than one person*, he thought. Pulling himself up, he peeked over the machinery, trying to get eyes on the person who'd taken a shot at him. Another burst of rounds slammed into a spot above his head. Metal fragments splintered off from the bullets fired at his head, piercing the skin just above his eyebrow painfully.

'Fucking Jesus,' he muttered to himself.

Remaining crouched, he took a step to the left, moving around the other side of his cover, and squeezed off a quick burst from his P90. Someone yelled in surprise, but he couldn't hear any groaning. He did another quick burst before trying to dash in the opposite direction and scoop up the explosives, but another burst slammed into the wall next to him from another direction, forcing him back and making him duck down lower. They'd encircle him soon if he didn't move. Eventually they'd get an angle, and then it would all be over. His brain coldly calculated that his mission was over; it was time to make a retreat. He didn't feel anything as he pulled a couple of smoke grenades from his rig and tossed them around his feet, the bitter sense of defeat not yet rising to his mind. The small grenades clattered to the ground, hissing loudly as the room quickly filled with smoke. The men above started firing wildly, unable to see him. He waited, letting the smoke build, before pulling a small lump of plastic explosives from a pouch and slapping them against his cover. He clicked a small button, commencing a soundless countdown on the simple circuit board inside.

Waiting for a lull in the gunfire, he sprinted from his position, hoping to catch the men above unprepared. It was only a few metres. He dashed towards the door. Someone above him yelled rapidly, clearly spotting his attempted escape. There was no point sticking around. He ran, the sound of running feet echoing behind and above him.

***

Ming saw the soldier running out of the smoke and through an open doorway below them. He yelled a warning to the other two men he had with him. Charging down a metal stairway, he caught a glimpse of the enemy soldier disappearing through a now-open door. Adrenaline surged back into his bloodstream and pumped through his body. The chase was on. He paused a split second to let his soldiers catch up, giving himself a chance to think and catch his breath. They'd interrupted their unwanted guest as he was doing something here. What had he been doing? And did he finish what he was doing? They couldn't leave without checking.

He pointed to one of the soldiers as the man came down the metal stairway. 'You! Search this area – he was doing something here. Find out what it was!' Then he turned to the second soldier. 'You, follow me!' He charged off at a sprint, the soldier in tow.

Dashing through the open door, he allowed the noises around him to guide him. The sound of the fleeing man's feet was ringing out against the metal floors and corridors. Another narrow metal stairway loomed ahead of him. The sound of running feet receded.

'He's up there! C'mon, he's trying to escape!' Ming yelled to the man behind him. The stairway would eventually lead to the upper deck if the man kept going upward. Ming came to a hard stop just before the bottom of the stairs, angling his body and head to get a narrow sight line up the tight stairway. He had only just peeked his head around the corner when a shot rang out, smashing into the metal wall next to him and missing him by millimetres. He leapt back quickly. He'd almost been killed, but it had been worth it: it had revealed the enemy soldier's position. He was at least two floors above them, looking down to their level. A quick hand signal to his own soldier alerted him to the threat. Without being ordered, his soldier stepped forward and pointed his rifle up the narrow stairway, firing off a stream of unaimed shots, brash ejected from the weapon hitting the nearby wall. The unsuppressed weapon was deafening in the confined space. The soldier's rifle stopped firing suddenly; the magazine was empty. Ming waited a second as silence filled the corridor. No shots replied from above. Ming risked a glance back up the stairway, his own pistol now aimed upward. Nothing.

He didn't wait, leaping up the stairs two at a time, each step feeling like a lifetime. In reality, only seconds passed. He reached the top of his set, but another three levels remained. He caught a glimpse of movement above and fired off five shots quickly. The sound of Jian's man echoed behind as he came to support Ming.

Working as a team, they could suppress and move, forcing the enemy to retreat further into the ship. They would eventually be able to corner him. The soldier gave him a quick nod as he reached Ming's level. He pointed upward, 'Repeat.' He had begun to rise when a loud clang sounded out on the stairs above them. The small stun grenade bounced into view, landing at Ming's feet. He stared at it only momentarily before kicking it with all his might. It bounced off a nearby wall and around the corner, exploding pathetically out of sight. More heavy steps sounded out from above. The couple of seconds of distraction had been more than enough for the enemy above to flee further upward. Smoke was also filling the space above. Ming cursed to himself, 'How many grenades does this guy have?'

Throwing all caution to the wind, he pushed up the stairs and through the smoke. The enemy wasn't waiting around to ambush them this time; his heavy footfalls were quickly disappearing above Ming. The smoke cleared as Ming charged up to the third level. He didn't bother checking the fourth level – a sudden rush of fresh air had come barrelling down from above. The enemy had clearly opened a door to the outer deck.

Ming charged up the final set of stairs, pushing himself into the wall next to the open door, feeling the cool sea breeze wash over his face. The salty air was crisp and refreshing compared to the stale and recycled air inside the ship. Yet a slight tinge of something acid and burnt invaded his nostrils. Controlling his hard panting, he stopped, listening again: the sound of the ocean and the footfalls of the soldier coming up the stairs behind him.

'Fuck it,' he muttered. He couldn't wait. Pistol in hand, he leant tentatively across the threshold of the door, his gun aimed outward, scanning the deck.

He peeked right and then left.

Nothing. No gunshots, no grenade, no noise. The flat expanse of the vessel's sparse deck spread out before him, the port and starboard sides equal distances apart.

The subtle movement of feet against metal echoed out from the port side of the ship. His mind raced – he must be there. The soldier arrived behind Ming, who signalled for him to follow, quickly and quietly. Clinging to the wall of the superstructure, Ming silently crept to the corner, half expecting the enemy soldier to leap out at any time. The wind across the deck interfered with his hearing, but the discernible panting from the man was impossible to hide. The footsteps around the corner suddenly became faster. The enemy was sprinting.

Gathering his courage, Ming moved out from the corner in one swift motion, gun up and ready. The man darted in front of him a few metres away, near the stern of the ship. In one smooth motion, he leapt over the guard railing, flying from the edge of the ship. Ming squeezed the trigger, firing three quick shots. The man didn't flinch. Ming's rounds had gone wide, while the enemy had disappeared into the inky blackness of the ocean below. Ming rushed to the guard rail, squeezing off more rounds into the disturbed water below. The soldier next to him doing the same but with considerably more firepower from his automatic weapon. The shots rang hollow into the ocean below. There was no point trying to stop the ship or turn around; by the time they did, the man would be long gone. There was almost certainly a boat out there, waiting to pick him up.

The sound of more running feet startled him, making him turn suddenly and bring up his weapon. The adrenaline in his body made him hyper alert but also on edge. He'd loved every moment of the chase, but the failure to catch the man had left him without closure. His heart was still pumping. One of Jian's soldiers came bolting around the corner, and Ming rapidly lowered his gun. The soldier had clearly seen him flinch when he came around and eyed him at a distance. Wary. Ming recognised him as a soldier he'd tasked with checking the engine room.

'Where is he?' the soldier asked, looking around and then back to Ming.

'He jumped,' came Ming's simple reply.

The soldier moved to the guard rail and looked over. 'He probably thinks he succeeded then,' the soldier said smugly.

Ming didn't respond, waiting for the soldier to elaborate.

The man held up a rucksack with a grin across his face. 'I removed two charges, and the rest were still in this.' Ming could hear the sense of pride and satisfaction in the man's voice.

'You're sure you got them all?' Ming queried. He hoped he had, but nothing had gone particularly right this night.

'Of course. I ch—' he was interrupted by a deep, booming noise. The ship's deck vibrated. A new alarm sounded.

Ming eyed the man, anger rising inside him. 'I guess you didn't,' he said flatly, before turning and looking back over the railing towards the water below. The smoke poured out of a gaping hole further up the side of the ship towards the bow. He gripped the railing, his knuckles turning white as he squeezed hard. He let the frustration boil inside him before letting out a guttural roar.

***

Lead bobbed in the water, watching the ship move away from him. He was still panting from the exertion of escaping the ship. He'd used all his grenades and had suffered what he thought was a grazing bullet wound on his left arm for his troubles. The men following him had been persistent and well-trained. The fact that he had managed to get out at all was a testament to his own skill, but also a good helping of luck. He only hoped his men had escaped as well.

He heard the explosion first, knowing instantly that something must be very wrong. He'd set the smaller explosive to detonate the other two scuttling charges as a fallback. He'd set a timer so that it would go off, no matter what, in five minutes. The boom he had just heard was definitely the small Semtex charge, but there was no larger explosion. Even as the ship receded into the distance, he could hear the alarms and what sounded like the scream of a wounded animal. *Someone's not happy*, he thought.

Once the ship had moved far enough away, he signalled

the RHIB, activating a small GPS locator. It didn't take long before he heard the powerful engine of the nimble little boat and flashed a small hand-held torch to make sure they didn't run him over. The boat slid up next to him with experienced precision, and a pair of hands hauled him onboard. Taking stock, he sighed in relief as he counted three of his men. Their mission had been a failure, but given the hornets' nest they had walked into, he felt satisfied with having dived out with everyone alive. He'd be having words with his employer after this. His wounded man, One, didn't look great in the torchlight. He ordered the RHIB pilot to head back to shore. Little did the small team realise what they'd achieved. Down in the engine room, the small wade of plastic explosives had done limited but sufficient damage. The crew on the bridge moved in a panic, alarms wailing. Slowly, the speed of the Huang Shen reduced, knot by knot.

CHAPTER 17

Huang Shen – Malacca Strait

As the morning sun dawned over the horizon, Ming knew they were in trouble. The fire had been brought under control with minimal damage, and the missile was still intact. But the blast in the engine had done more damage than Ming dared admit to himself. Whatever the explosive used, it had completely put one of the ship's massive screws out of action, smashing one of two large gearboxes – at least, that is what the chief engineer had explained to him. All Ming knew was that they had one working screw, effectively cutting their speed down to a pathetic five knots at best. There was no way to repair the damage, and additional damage to the ship's diesel generators kept giving them power issues.

The ship was dying, a slow and painful death. The time it would take to get them through the strait was now doubled. The security force had received a bloody nose, with Jian taking the worst injuries, but they were still alive, and the missile was safe. The mission wasn't over yet.

Ming could feel his body aching for rest and sleep as he trudged up to the bridge. They didn't have a choice; they needed help to get to the end of the strait. They needed to break radio silence. If another attack came, one that was more determined than the last, Ming doubted they could hold out. This small force of unknown attackers had caught them off guard and almost taken down the ship. The question of who the attackers were still lingered in Ming's mind. They'd recovered one of the weapons and the rucksack of explosives, but the P90 sub-machine gun wasn't a weapon of the US military. The explosives were American made, but they could easily be sourced anywhere around the world. So, the question remained, who were they? How did they know about the missile? Ming didn't have the answer, and that worried him more than anything.

Opening the door to the bridge, he was surprised at the silence. Everyone was huddled around the captain, who looked up at Ming. 'What do we do?' the man asked, a look of worry and fear set on his face.

Ming was about to ask about what when he heard the radio crackle. 'Huang Shen Huang Shen, this is the Malaysia Coast Guard, please respond to hail and heave to. We intend to board you.'

The answer was simple. 'Ignore them – they do not get on this ship.' He mustered up his tired body, reaching for the radio to call Jian.

Malaysia Coast Guard – Malacca Strait

The first emergency call had come through Channel 16, the standard emergency channel over VHF. Reports of an explosion at sea – and worse, fire, any mariner's worst nightmare. More calls soon washed into the Malaysian Maritime Enforcement Agency Operation Centre, which was essentially Malaysia's coast guard. The calls all said a similar thing: there was a fire on a ship, they could see smoke, it wasn't responding to hails. Whatever the actual issue, it was serious enough to warrant a response. Using the various coordinates provided by the vessels who'd called in, it didn't take the early-morning shift in the operations centre long to spot the Huang Shen. Sure enough, it had been transmitting on AIS only an hour earlier before suddenly disappearing off the public system. The shift at Malaysia's Maritime Enforcement Agency didn't waste any time; they had procedures to follow and action plans to activate for a whole manner of emergencies, with fires and explosions sitting more on the serious side of the spectrum. Attempts to contact the Huang Shen had ended in failure, further raising concern amongst the staff. There was nothing else for it – they'd need to send someone out to assess. A helicopter could get eyes on the vessel, but it couldn't land – at least, not easily. Better to dispatch a patrol who could load any injured and make a proper assessment.

As the first subtle blues of the morning were just beginning to cut through the night sky, the Penggalang-class interceptor slipped its moorings and powered into the strait. It was a small craft, but agile and fast.

Lieutenant Ismail Teuku half sat in his shock-absorbing chair as his craft glided over the relatively smooth ocean. His knees were bent slightly, taking some of his body weight to reduce the shock of each bounce. Still, every wave inevitably led to a considerable smack against the surface of the ocean. Ismail didn't mind; he'd done this journey thousands of times before. The Malacca Strait was his waters. He'd grown up on its coastlines and dedicated his life to protecting those who navigated through it. His men busied themselves with their various instruments and weapons, all preparing for the unknown the best that they could. They were well-trained, confident and capable. Ismail knew his crew like a family.

Ismail ordered the pilot to slow, pulling his binoculars from around his neck. They were reaching the last known coordinates of the explosion, and it would be nearly impossible to see anything with the boat bouncing along at well over thirty knots. The pilot eased the boat's speed down slowly, avoiding any dangerous rocking. Still, Ismail steadied himself against the now-bobbing boat, raising the high-powered binoculars up to his eyes and gazing out through the dark morning.

Nothing stood out – no burning fields of oil, no ship stranded or troubled. But then again, it was still too dark to see anything in detail. Another ten minutes and he'd be able to see much more clearly. Plus, he and his men were fatigued; they'd been called late in their shift and dispatched. Riding at close to forty knots across the strait had taken its toll.

Before long, the light blues had given way to pinks and yellows, allowing Ismail to see towards the horizon. Pulling his glasses up again, he immediately noticed dark, black smoke in the distance. Something was burning out there. The interceptor raced forward, like a dog on the hunt. Ismail tried to radio the Huang Shen again, receiving only the now-customary silence and hiss of static over the radio. It was odd for a ship not to respond to hails; normally these vessels had satellite phones, and all would have the contact details for the various coast guards in the region. Unless something catastrophic had happened, there were very few reasons why the crew wouldn't be able to get in contact. It didn't sit right in his stomach.

Piracy wasn't unknown to the region. 'Mohammed, make sure the bow gun is loaded and ready. Can't hurt to be prepared.' He watched the man rechecking the mounted machine gun, making sure the ammunition was seated correctly and that the mechanisms were moving freely. The man had a certain confidence and ease to him, seemingly immune to the spray and bumpy conditions.

With each minute, they quickly gained on the ailing cargo ship. The smoke cloud became larger and more pronounced as they approached. Ismail guessed it was only sailing at around five knots, well below the speeds it was capable of. They approached from the stern of the wounded vessel, keeping on its port side. Ismail ordered the boat to slow again.

As he left the enclosed cabin of his boat, the salty, stinging spray of the ocean and rush of the wind assaulted him, even as they slowed. He held on tightly, gazing up at the ship, which was now only a short distance away. A narrow but sizeable hole appeared to be the cause of the smoke. Something was burning, then. Black smoke was never good. But it wasn't pouring out, so whatever was burning was either controlled or dying down. Ismail frowned as he looked out. The damage was in a strange place; there had clearly been an explosion of some sort, but it was amidships, away from any fuel tanks or engine compartments. Volatile cargo, maybe. Based on the jagged, torn metal, the blast had come from the inside of the ship, not outside. He made a mental note to be extra cautious.

As they approached, he ordered the pilot to slow further, allowing him to raise his binoculars to get a better look at the ship. The container vessel dwarfed his own, meaning they had to stay a few hundred metres away just so he could get a better look at the superstructure and bridge. Small specks were moving around on the top deck, and he could see people on the bridge through the glass, pointing in his direction. Not abandoned or haunted, then. He gave them a wave and checked back through his binoculars to see if they acknowledged him. Nothing. He tried the radio once more – again, nothing but silence. The figures on the bridge were hard to see, but they turned when radioed. They could hear him alright.

Ismail frowned again. He didn't like this. But they couldn't leave a damaged vessel with a possibly dangerous cargo moving through the strait. Even now there were more than a dozen other commercial vessels in sight. There was nothing for it; they'd have to board the ship and investigate. He radioed to his commander back on shore, giving him a quick update. He had operational authority out here, but it was better to keep headquarters informed.

The little boat approached the larger vessel with surprising speed. One of his men was already preparing a boarding ladder, essentially a foldable metal frame that could be hooked over the railing of the tall ship. The large reddish-coloured hull of the vessel soon loomed over them, blocking most sight of the bridge and upper decks. Ismail noted a couple of men standing on the ship's superstructure, watching them motionlessly. *What is going on here?* he wondered.

Boarding a ship at sea was one of the more dangerous jobs they had. A simple wrong move or slip, and that could be it – smashed against the hull of the vessel or crushed between the two of them. But it was something that Ismail and his men had done numerous times before. He was confident in his men and the training he'd pushed upon them. They'd have to be careful to watch for movements from the cargo ship, as well as rogue waves and impacts from the wake of the ship. However, the conditions were clear and relatively calm; it wouldn't be the worst boarding they'd ever done.

The interceptor approached closer to the stern, near the superstructure. They didn't want to be too close to the smoking, jagged hole.

Ismail radioed one last time, 'Huang Shen, Huang Shen, this is the Malaysia Coast Guard, please respond to hails and heave to!' Silence again. 'Huang Shen, Huang Shen, we will be boarding you to assess your damage and steer you to the closest port.' Still nothing. He'd be having a word to this captain once on board.

Ismail nodded to his team; time to make a move. They began to manhandle the unwieldy ladder while the pilot eased their tiny boat closer. They'd slowed to match the speed of the cargo ship now. Ismail watched his men carefully: two of them were working as a team to place the top hooks over the ship's rails far above them. He'd seen men yanked off boats doing the same action, and he was hyper vigilant. They had raised the surprisingly light ladder up and had one hook over the railing when a buzzing noise sounded, followed by a loud *crack*.

His head whipped around to look for the source of the noise as another *crack* rang out, this time making him flinch. His mind didn't process what was happening straight away, but as he turned his head back, he watched as the men holding the ladder collapsed, writhing on the deck, blood spilling from their wounds. Only seconds had passed before Ismail's mind caught up. They were under attack.

'Emergency! Turn hard to port!' he yelled.

The pilot obeyed immediately. The little interceptor jerked hard to its left, pulling away from the large cargo ship. The cracks were no longer single occurrences but a stream of angry wasps. A line of bullets continued to follow the little interceptor as it turned, slamming into the fibreglass structure of the ship and creating small explosions in the ocean around them.

Ismail risked a look back at the Huang Shen as they darted away, spotting the small dot of a man tucked away behind some kind of fortification up on the ship's superstructure. A constant hammer of yellow flashes burst from the weapon he held.

'Get those men inside now!' Ismail ordered, pointing to the two bleeding crewmen being thrown about the small deck of their vessel. The harnesses they were wearing were the only thing keeping them from being thrown overboard. Ismail reached for the radio as one of the windows shattered in their cabin, showering them all with glass.

He cursed loudly. 'Keep changing course – don't give these bastards a line on us.'

The pilot, a younger man who was clearly scared and bleeding from the cuts on his face, nodded. They weren't trained for this kind of attack.

Poking his head through the shattered cabin window, he yelled out to the bow gunner, who was holding on for dear life. 'Mohammed! Port-side superstructure, third-storey external decking! I want rounds on that ship. We'll close the gap for you – don't fire until I tell you!'

'Aye-aye, lieutenant!' Mohammed shouted over the wind

and gunfire, grinning back at Ismail as he cocked the large .50 cal. machine gun.

Ismail pulled himself back inside the once-sheltered cabin. Wind and spray freely entered through the many holes that had appeared in its walls. The constant hail of bullets had stopped; they were too far away now for the shooters to reach them.

'Slow ahead!' Ismail snapped. The little boat quickly slowed. The savage manoeuvre of the pilot was brought under control in a second. The two wounded sailors were quickly brought into the cabin, while one of the men tore open a large medical kit and began tending to them. Ismail gave the two a quick glance. They'd need to head back to shore soon enough, but they were both awake and coherent. Looking at the Huang Shen, Ismail noticed their boarding ladder hanging by one rung, sadly diagonal against the large ship's hull. He gritted his teeth, rage bubbling inside him.

'Strap in, everyone. We're not going to let these bastards get away with shooting at the Malaysia Coast Guard so easily. Bring us back around, full speed ahead. Approach from the stern and keep a distance from them,' Ismail ordered loudly. The sailors around him focused on his voice. The shock of the attack was wearing off, soon replaced by anger and determination. 'Weapons up, men!'

The little craft circled wide from the Huang Shen, moving out of the machine gun's range. Ismail had no doubt the people onboard the cargo ship would be watching them closely, but one benefit of being a smaller, nimbler vessel was that they could manoeuvre, whereas the Huang Shen could not.

As they approached from the stern, Ismail could just make out the small, sandbagged emplacements situated around the external decking, disguised behind railings and cladding. Why the hell hadn't he spotted that when they'd first arrived? He cursed himself. Little figures darted across the decking on the Huang Shen, no doubt trying to get an angle against them. Standing behind the pilot, he said,

'Everyone, get ready, we're going to pull to port and engage the vessel. Aim for the bridge and anyone moving outside. Understood?'

Everyone replied instantly, uneasy tension in their voices. 'Alright, start moving onto their portside. No one fires until I give the order!'

Poking his head back out through one of the shattered windows, he eyed Mohammed, who kept his massive deck-mounted machine pointed towards the commercial ship, eyes narrowed, his legs acting as shock-absorbers for each small wave. 'Wait!' he yelled. They sped past the Huang Shen's stern, past the white superstructure. Just a bit closer.

'NOW!' he screamed, throwing his hand down with force.

Mohammed didn't hesitate. Accurate, timed bursts flew from the heavy mounted machine gun. Despite the movement of the ocean and the speed they were travelling, the rounds found their mark, smashing into the sandbags and metal superstructure. Puffs of sand exploded from the impact of the rounds, and Ismail grunted in satisfaction as a splash of red was thrown against the white superstructure. That was a hit. The rest of the boat opened fire with their small arms – mostly shotguns and pistols. It didn't have the same effect as the machine gun, but each man wanted payback. Sparks continued to fly as more rounds impacted the emplacement. A metal door connected to the deck was thrown open.

'Hit the bridge!' he yelled at Mohammed, who somehow heard him over the gunfire. Numerous windows across the Huang Shen exploded inward.

'Cease fire!' That was enough.

Mohammed let off one last long burst into a shattered bridge, shooting a wide, cheeky grin at Ismail.

'Move hard to port. Get us away from this thing.' There would be no boarding the cargo ship in their boat. There was no telling how many enemies were on board, and with their wounded, they didn't have the luxury of finding out.

As the interceptor turned away, one of the doors high on the Huang Shen's superstructure flew open. A man stepped out with a long tube on his shoulder. Mohammed yelled a warning before firing his gun, but the rounds fell wide as the boat turned.

Ismail's eyes darted back to the Huang Shen, just in time to see a grey puff of smoke appear from the ship. He didn't have time to yell a warning, instead simply throwing himself at the helm and yanking the steering controls hard to starboard. A whooshing noise filled Ismail's ears, followed by a deep explosion just off the bow. A wall of water exploded over the little boat and washed into the cabin, breaking more windows and sending the men flying.

The whole cabin rocked back and forth as the pilot lost his footing and the speed of the boat dropped. Ismail spluttered, spitting out seawater, and hauled himself up off the deck. Warm, red blood was oozing out of a cut on his temple. Looking around quickly, he breathed as a sigh of relief as he noted that everyone inside the cabin seemed okay. Cuts, bruises, all soaking wet, but okay. His mind suddenly stopped; he couldn't see Mohammed on the bow. The .50 cal. was pointing skyward without Mohammed there to hold it. He'd been the closest to the blast. His stomach dropped. Leaping through the damaged cabin window, he ran to the gun, slipping as he went. Mohammed's harness was still tied down, but it trailed over a railing and off the deck. Ismail darted to the railing, looking over.

'Beautiful morning for a swim, lieutenant!' Mohammed said, the same grin still attached to his face.

A soggy and dishevelled Mohammed was half in the water, half suspended by harness, but he was seemingly untouched, despite being thrown off the boat.

'You're a lucky one, Mohammed!' Ismail shouted, feeling a wave of relief wash over him.

Miraculously, they returned to port, but this wasn't over – not by any margin.

THE MALACCA INCIDENT

***

As Ismail's emergency radio call echoed towards the Maritime Enforcement Agency headquarters, news of the incident was spreading like wildfire across the internet. Nearby commercial vessels had had a ringside view of the action, and like anyone else in the modern day, sailors had quickly pulled out their phones and recorded the incident. Minutes after the first shot was fired, videos quickly spread around Twitter, Facebook, Instagram and Telegram. Within the hour, the Malaysian media was flooded with the story. Outrage and fury spread across the country as the morning dawned. The call to action was impossible to ignore, the prime minister quickly deciding their only option was to respond in force. Whoever had attacked their vessel would pay. By midday, a sizable force of Maritime Enforcement Agency craft and Royal Malaysian Navy vessels had slipped their mooring, heading for the Huang Shen, which was still plodding its way through the strait.

Intrepid journalists wasted no time gathering camera equipment and hiring helicopters and vessels. If there was going to be a showdown on the ocean, the world would see it. It didn't take long before global news agencies, everyone from Reuters to Al Jazeera, had picked up the story. The country, not used to the limelight, was now on the front page of every news outlet across the world.

Ministry of State Security Headquarters – Beijing - China

Chang pressed his thumbs into his temples. The beginning of a headache was reaching from behind his eyes and up into his forehead. The dramatic footage of an anti-tank missile streaking towards a little Malaysian craft was playing on a loop on the TV across his desk. Sighing, Chang picked up the secure phone next to his computer.

The line rang only once before it was picked up.

'Well, admiral, I hope you have a plan – the president will expect a brief on this immediately,' he said, not concealing the tiredness and stress he felt.

Admiral Taosing was not one to be caught out. 'Comrade, you sound worried.'

Chang gritted his teeth. He *was* worried. The whole plan looked like it was about to collapse in a heap, and the fallout would land squarely at his feet. Ignoring the admiral's statement, he replied simply, 'The president will expect a response.'

'He will have it, Chang, do not worry. We have planned for all contingencies.'

Chang didn't have the patience to play this game, and he sighed loudly into the receiver. 'Admiral, I'd appreciate more detail.'

Taosing seemed to relent, perhaps taking pity on Chang. 'We have a number of options available to us, but there is a contingent of coast-guard vessels moving through the strait as we speak. In addition, two of our most modern destroyers, a Type 055 Renhai and a Type 052D Luyang, are moving south at speed.'

Chang smiled to himself. All was not lost. 'That is a relief to hear, admiral. What of the Malaysians?'

'They will not be a problem. Between our coast guard and our naval forces, we will demonstrate how China is a responsible, global citizen. After all, the Huang Shen is a Chinese vessel beset by pirates, is it not?'

'Indeed, it is, comrade.'

Chang's headache started to ease immediately.

Less than an hour later, he sat in the gilded halls of the Zhongnanhai, patiently waiting for the briefing with the president. A stern-looking soldier eyed him carefully as he waited. Admiral Taosing made a hurried entrance, with a bundle of papers and maps carried between himself and two aides. Chang knew immediately something was wrong. He stood quickly just as the doors to the president's office swung open.

Another guard summoned them, 'The president will see you now.'

Chang's mind started doing cartwheels as they walked in. The admiral had bad news, and he didn't know what it was – he couldn't prepare. He had to stay on his toes.

The president wasn't in a good mood, either. TV screens in his office offered rolling coverage of the incident in the Malacca Strait. 'I want this explained!' he said forcefully.

The admiral gave Chang a quick glance, his eyes begging Chang to take the lead. The admiral's aides were fumbling with the large charts, trying to flatten the ungainly objects onto a circular desk in the room.

Chang cleared his throat. 'Comrade president, last night, the Huang Shen and our forces aboard it were attacked. It appears a small force of at least three individuals silently snuck onto the ship, incapacitating a guard before attempting to reach the cargo bay where the missile was stored. Luckily, our forces detected them and, in the firefight that followed, managed to force them off the ship.' Chang paused for a moment, catching his breath. 'However, in the process of removing the attackers, the ship sustained damage to its engine and across the hull. I have been informed by our forces aboard that the vessel is still seaworthy, but it cannot reach its full speed any longer.'

'How do we not know the identity of the attackers?' the president demanded.

'Unfortunately, we were unable to capture or kill any of them. We did recover a couple of weapons and items, generally European and American equipment, but it is not enough to establish their identity.'

'I see. And do you have an explanation as to how they knew about our operation and the missile?'

'No, sir, I do not have a good explanation at this stage.'

The president wasn't one to dwell. 'Well, and what of this incident?' he said, waving a hand towards the closest TV. An attractive female news anchor was rapidly explaining the incident in detail.

Chang nodded. 'Yes, sir. So, it appears the attack on the Huang Shen was noticed by nearby commercial shipping. The Malaysia Coast Guard deployed a vessel to intercept, board and take control of the ship. Given the damage to the Huang Shen, they would have sought to force it to return to port. Our forces on board decided to resist – and as you have seen, sir, they were successful in forcing the Malaysians away.'

'I am not sure if I agree with your use of "successful", comrade. The whole world is now focused on our ship. I have already seen more footage than I care to, and if the news is correct, the Malaysian navy and coast guard are moving to seize it as we speak.'

Chang was going to reply when Taosing finally spoke up. 'Comrade president, they will not be successful.'

The president raised an eyebrow. 'Please elaborate, admiral.'

'If you'll indulge me, sir, we have some charts that could help explain,' the admiral said, motioning towards the large, unrolled charts on the table.

The president obliged, moving wordlessly around his desk to look over the admiral's shoulder. The charts depicted the Malacca Strait in detail. Numerous vessels had been plotted across the waterway, with a number clearly highlighted as Chinese vessels. The Huang Shen and the incoming Malaysian forces all had circles around them.

'When we received notice of the assault last night, we immediately issued orders for our colleagues in the coast guard to move into the strait.' The admiral pointed at a small cluster of four vessels southeast of the Huang Shen. 'These vessels will arrive in a few hours, and assuming our men can continue to dissuade any attempts by smaller Malaysian craft, should be able to reach the Huang Shen before the Malaysians can. We can then either board it and take control of the vessel, or escort it through the strait under protection.'

Chang could sense there was a "but" coming, but he

remained silent.

The admiral took a deep breath. 'However, there is another problem.' One of the aides pulled the first chart to the side, revealing a second underneath it, two additional vessels clearly circled.

'The first problem is this vessel.' He pointed to the northern end of the Malacca Strait. 'This is the USS John Basilone. It was not transmitting on AIS, so we did not have a good position on it until recently, when it was observed by one of our commercial vessels moving through the region. It is a fully armed and modern Arleigh Burke destroyer, and given its proximity to the incident, will likely arrive at the Huang Shen in the coming hours. Possibly before our forces can arrive.'

'What does this mean for the Huang Shen?' the president asked quietly.

'Well, sir, they cannot resist … At least, not for long. The Americans will be able to board and overpower the crew without much of a problem. But we do not know what the Americans will try to do. They may just sit back and observe.' Both Chang and the admiral knew that was extremely unlikely. Americans weren't the type to sit around and wait.

'I doubt that,' the president said simply. 'What was the second problem, admiral? As if the Americans are not enough.'

Taosing paused, collecting himself. 'Yes … towards the southeast, we have spotted a second vessel.' He pointed to the other end of the strait. 'This is the Australian vessel, HMAS Hobart, a similar class of vessel to the Arleigh Burke, but with a smaller amount of firepower. We have been tracking it for a while; however, a day ago, it made a rapid change in course and headed towards the strait.'

'Your point, admiral? It doesn't appear to be anywhere near the Huang Shen.'

'No, sir, that is correct, but between it and the Americans, there are enemy vessels at each end of the strait.

However, that is not what concerns us. The USS John Basilone was last spotted near Sri Lanka, and given its current position, it has made the best possible time to reach where it is now. The same can be said of the Hobart. Both these vessels commenced their moves well before the attack on the Huang Shen and the incident with the Malaysians. I believe they are aware of our plot.'

Silence hung over the room before the President broke it. 'How certain are you? Do you think they attacked the Huang Shen last night?'

The admiral shrugged. 'We cannot know for sure, but comrade president, I do not believe in coincidences. The arrival of these ships at this time – they must know something.'

The president turned to look at Chang. 'What do you make of this?'

Chang felt backed into a corner, with no escape. 'I agree with the admiral. I do not know how, but they could be aware of our operation.'

The president's eyes seemed to dig into Chang, scanning his face, looking for some sign of deception. After a moment, he looked away and then back to the chart. 'So, gentlemen, what are our options?'

'None are great,' the admiral replied quickly, sweeping his hand across the chart theatrically. 'Our closest forces are the coast-guard vessels; however, they are greatly outmatched by the Americans. If it comes to a fight, I am afraid they are likely to lose, sir. Our more powerful vessels are moving at their best speed towards the strait. At their current rate, they will be within missile range by the end of the day. That will tip the balance firmly back into our favour. But it will all be for nothing if the Americans board the Huang Shen before we can do something about it.'

The idea formed in Chang's head out of nowhere. 'Comrades, perhaps we can force the Americans' hand. They will surely be wary of us following the bloody nose we gave them in the Maldives. If we can surround the Huang

Shen, the Americans will be forced to fire on our vessels first. With the world watching, I doubt they would be willing to act so rashly. Meanwhile, we have our PLAN vessels move into place, and if we combine it with support from the air force, the Americans will be unable to threaten us. We can escort the Huang Shen through the strait.'

'Could it work, admiral?' the president asked.

He gave Chang a thoughtful look. 'Perhaps. Much could go wrong, but if we do not engage the Americans first, we can appear the victims if they strike us. It could work.'

'What of the Australian vessel?'

'We will keep an eye on it, but I doubt they will get involved. Their military is far smaller and weaker than our forces,' Taosing stated confidently, almost dismissively.

'Very well, gentlemen. We are in agreement. I want a situation room set up so we can monitor the progress of our forces – and make sure our forces know not to strike the Americans, even if provoked.'

They both nodded before heading for the door.

'You stole my thunder, Chang,' Taosing said, a slight grin at the edge of his face.

'I apologise, admiral. I admit, it came to me just then.'

'I bet it did. Let us hope the Americans are not desperate for revenge. A lot can go wrong with your plan, comrade, but it is your plan, after all.'

'Indeed, admiral,' Chang replied, a sense of unease rising inside him. Had he exposed himself too much? He mentally shook his head; there was no point doubting himself now. He had to take charge. 'I will make sure our air force colleagues are up to speed, admiral. Today will be a great day for China.'

He stepped into his armoured limousine, leaving the old admiral to watch him drive away.

CHAPTER 18

The White House – United States of America

Quinton could feel nervous energy building up inside of him, clawing to get out. He felt caged, alert and anxious. The last twenty-four hours had been a total disaster. The embarrassing damage to an American naval ship in the Indian Ocean and the failed raid on the Huang Shen had come as a nasty shock. Quinton felt like his back was against the wall in a war where he had to hide his hands and stay in the shadows. Dick had made himself scarce after the failed raid, knowing full well his boss would try to lay the blame on him.

The attempts to hide the loss of the hypersonic prototype were becoming harder to hide, and the questions being asked about Chinese actions were increasingly being pointed his way. Quinton knew he wasn't liked by the joint chiefs; they didn't trust him, or his views, and generally tried to avoid interacting with him as much as possible. But his interference in the missile test only a few days before hadn't gone unnoticed or forgotten. He was now a liability – an enemy, in their eyes. He was sure they'd try to find a way to blame what was happening on him. It didn't occur to him in the slightest that they might be vindicated in believing so.

As he turned a corner on his way to a meeting with the President and Joint Chiefs of Staff, a man suddenly bumped into him, sending the folders he was carrying flying.

'Watch it, you fucking idiot,' Quinton hissed at the unfamiliar man.

'Sorry, sir, let me get that for you,' he replied hurriedly, scooping up Quinton's dropped property.

Quinton snatched it back. 'Be more careful,' he scolded, before marching on, his mood darkening further.

Taking his seat midway down the long table, Quinton cut a lonely figure. Without allies and with many enemies, the hostile stares were commonplace. Pretending not to notice, he organised his notes, but the discomfort he felt wasn't from their stares. The meeting was to discuss the events occurring in the Malacca Strait. The vessel, one Quinton was inherently familiar with, was the cause. That was his fault as well, but they didn't know that.

Everyone suddenly stood, announcing the entrance of the President. He waved them all to sit, not one for formality. 'Alright, everyone, take a seat. So, what is the deal? Someone want to explain to me what the hell is going on?'

The chairman of the Joint Chiefs of Staff beat Quinton to the punch. 'Mr President, as you have probably seen on the news, there was a gunfight that broke out between unknown assailants aboard the Chinese-flagged cargo ship, the Huang Shen, and the Malaysia Coast Guard. Based on the news reports, and reporting out of PACOM, the Malaysians had a number of their crew injured, and in response are deploying additional naval and coast guard forces to intercept and likely board the vessel.'

'Right, hang on – CNN is saying there was an explosion aboard the Huang Shen.' The President had a confused look on his face.

'Yes, sir. Unfortunately, we have no intel to explain that, but that explosion drew the attention of the Malaysians. As for what caused it though, we simply don't know.'

'Right … well that's not ideal. Do we still think the Chinese might have our tech onboard?'

'Impossible to know, sir, at least until we board and search the vessel ourselves. The USS John Basilone is currently moving into position to intercept and board the vessel as we speak.'

'But we'll beat the Malaysians there?'

'Yes, *just*. But that isn't what we're concerned about,' the general replied ominously.

'Go on, general,' the President ordered.

'As you know, sir, twelve hours ago, three of our ships intercepted a group of Chinese naval vessels blocking access to an area in the Maldives. The outcome of that event was decidedly not in our favour.'

'I am aware, general. One ship crippled and two damaged is not what I call a good day.'

'Those vessels are on their way back to Diego Garcia as we speak. However, with those three ships out of action, it leaves the USS John Basilone very alone. We do not have any American vessels within range that will be able to support its operation against the Huang Shen. The Australians have offered their support, and one of their destroyers has been assigned to assist, the HMAS Hobart. Other tha—'

Quinton cut the chairman off. 'And you're worried about what, exactly? Surely the two ships can handle one cargo ship? Hell, we don't even need the Australians here.'

Everyone looked at Quinton and then back at the chairman, who was making a poor attempt to conceal his disdain towards Quinton. The chairman continued on, ignoring Quinton's question, 'As I was saying, what concerns us now is that the Chinese are mobilising. PACOM is warning of increased activity across the board.'

One of the general's aides turned on the screens around the room, all of which now displayed maps of the Malacca Strait with different nations' forces represented in coloured arrows: allied in blue, Chinese in red and everyone else in yellow or grey.

'You can see they have moved four of their coast-guard vessels into the Malacca Strait. We estimate that at their current speed and course, they'll intersect with the USS John Basilone and Huang Shen in two, maybe three hours' time. In addition to this, at least two PLAN destroyers are moving to take up position at the end of the strait. These vessels haven't been tested in combat before, but they are modern and pack a lot of firepower. Lastly, we also have heightened activity from their bases in the South China Sea, meaning we can't discount Chinese airpower either. In other words, sir, we do not have the advantage here; if this becomes a fight, we'll have our backs against the wall. Even with HMAS Hobart's support, we are under-gunned.

A silence hung over the room for a short moment, everyone waiting for either the President or Quinton to say something. The President spoke first, 'Alright, what options do you have for me?'

'Well, sir, there aren't many – good ones, that is. Our first, and arguably safest, option is to pull the USS John Basilone back. Leave the Malaysians and Chinese to sort out the Huang Shen.'

'That, of course, would mean abandoning any chance of recovering our tech, if it is on the ship, sir,' the chief of naval operations interjected.

The general gathered pace now. 'That's right, and given the forces the Chinese have deployed and the incident at the Maldives, I think it's safe to say the likelihood of the missing missile being aboard that freighter is very high.'

Quinton wouldn't admit it, but he secretly hoped the President would take the safer option and avoid any kind of offensive action that he'd normally recommend. If they never searched the ship, they would never find the missile, and his secret would be safe.

'Right, what else do we have, then?'

'Simply put, we call their bluff. We board and secure the

vessel and hold our ground. If they want to start shooting, we force them to be the ones who pull the trigger first. There is enough press out there at the moment that we could use it to our advantage.'

'At the risk to the USS John Basilone and all the sailors aboard it though,' the chief of naval operations added, a slightly worried look spreading across his broad face.

'And the third, general?' Options always came in threes.

'We strike first. Keep the China Coast Guard out of range of the John Basilone and force the Chinese destroyers on the defensive.'

The President paused for a moment, letting the final option linger in the air while the room remained silent. Shaking his head, he leaned forward suddenly, a focused intensity in his eyes. 'Okay. Here's what we won't be doing. We will not abandon our tech on that ship – America doesn't run away. Secondly, we will not start the shooting. We're the good guys here. However, I don't want to be alone in this.' He turned to the secretary of state. 'Amy, I want to make sure the Australians give us confirmation of their support, and see if we can get any additional forces to support us. They owe us that much. See if we can't get the Malaysians to throw in with us, create a unified front. Happy to share any information that will muster their support. Lastly, I want to be on the front foot with the press. Let's make sure all the channels, internationals included, know what we are doing and why. Keep mention of any stolen tech away from them – no leaks! Let's play this smart, people. Is that clear?'

The President was a man of action when he needed to be. The room around him was a flurry of yes-sirs and nods. Quinton felt dejected. The sense of power was slipping from his hands.

The General wasn't finished yet. As if pre-empting the President's decision, he said, 'The Australians are currently running a military exercise with the Malaysians, they've got a squadron of F-35 fighters, KC-30 air tankers and E-7A

Wedgetail AWACS craft in the area ready to go in the strait.'

'Make it happen, then. I want their support, no matter what,' the President ordered, looking directly at the secretary of state and chairman.

The President called an end to the meeting, standing and looking down at Quinton. 'You know I don't like surprises,' he growled quietly, pointing his index finger at Quinton. 'Your job is to head these kinds of scenarios off before they happen. Now it's too late, and we don't have a lot of options. You told me everything was sorted, Quinton.' The accusation in his voice was impossible to ignore.

Someone else called out to the President, drawing his attention away. Quinton felt hot in the face; his ears were burning. A sense of shame and anger washed over him. He wouldn't be discarded like this. He had to find Dick.

As Quinton hurried from the room, a lone secret-service agent watched silently, taking note of the national security advisor's barely checked emotions and haste. He noted the time mentally before continuing his watch.

HQJOC – Australia

'Jesus Christ. This is escalating,' Ata said, leaning back in her chair.

'Yep, I think the exact words from the prime minister were something like "Fuck me sideways". Surprised he didn't shit a brick,' Maia replied, a grin across her face.

'So, what's the plan? I mean, what do you want us to do?' It was barely seven in the morning, and the watch floor around them was filling up fast. Additional officers and soldiers in uniform were arriving by the minute, including more than a few Americans.

'You and Sidney keep sourcing satellite imagery and data; feed it to the watch floor so we keep ahead of any changes. In particular, focus on the South China Sea islands. If we see aircraft being prepped for launch, we need to know ASAP. As you can already see, we're going to be a full house soon. There are liaisons between us and the Yanks at every level and every branch. Anything you get, we feed it back through the liaisons to PACOM.'

'Gotcha. So guess that means we are supporting the Yanks completely?'

'Honestly, we don't have much of a choice here. If we want to keep our access to advanced US tech and gain privileged access to US equipment under AUKUS, we need to show up to the party.'

'Right, but what do we have that can help them?'

'Well, HMAS Hobart is all we have as far as naval assets go. HMAS Fremantle is on the way, but it's seriously under-gunned for a fight – plus, it'll probably arrive far too late anyway. But we have a flight of F-35s and Wedgetail flying out of Butterworth from Exercise Bersama Lima in Malaysia; that'll give us some eyes.'

'Far out – really throwing the kitchen sink, aren't we?'

Maia nodded, 'That's not even the best part. The chief is talking about spooling up the Loyal Wingman program to support.'

'The new drones? Aren't they still in development?'

'You betcha. Gives you a sense of the seriousness of what's happening here. The hope is, if we throw enough equipment into the field, the Chinese will back down.'

'Will they?' Ata asked, unsure that the Chinese would be so willing to back down, given the prize.

Maia shrugged in reply. 'Time will tell.'

An awkward silence hung in the air for a moment.

'Anyway, I'll join you two out here. No point being in my office. I'll work as the link between our team and everyone else. Now, we are less than an hour away from the USS John Basilone attempting to board the Huang Shen. Get some food, caffeine, toilet breaks. Whatever you need, do it now.'

'You got it, boss!' Sidney called out, clearly excited. Ata wasn't so sure. The pieces of the chess board were moving too quickly, and with too much surety from the people around her. Their confidence felt more like a wishful hope than a true analysis.

HMAS Hobart – Western Java Sea

The Chinese surveillance vessel had shadowed them for the last couple of days. Little more than a small fishing boat, covered in sensors and other listening equipment, the poorly concealed boat was like a parasite, always nearby, always listening and waiting. Currently, it was keeping a safe distance from the starboard side of the much larger and heavily armed HMAS Hobart. Kate didn't like having their movements watched; no doubt everything was getting reported back to Beijing. But that wasn't the real threat. That lay thirty nautical miles ahead, in the shape of two modern – and powerful – Chinese destroyers. They could easily outshoot her if they wanted to. Her ship was one of Australia's largest and most modern, packed with the best American technology. But it had one critical flaw: its ammunition capacity. The single-use missile pods were one use only, and there were only forty-eight vertical launch cells. Once the missiles inside were fired, that was it. The Chinese ships used a similar launch system but with a much greater number, if it came to a shootout, her ship would quickly find itself at the mercy of the Chinese. Hopefully it wouldn't come to that. But, as a precaution, she'd ordered her ship to close with the Chinese. At the very least, she could use her deck gun.

As she chewed the end of a cheap pen, her mind churned, calculating the possibilities and outcomes from every action she could take. The two Chinese destroyers had separated, taking different patrol routes near the exit of the strait. She hadn't taken long to choose which ship to follow. While both ships were destroyers, they were of entirely different classes. The ship she wanted to follow, a Type 052D Luyang destroyer, had less armaments and was smaller than the newer, and much rarer, Type 055 Renhai destroyer. The Renhai had at least triple the number of missiles she did. But then again, if it came down to it, either one of the two ships would be able to pick her off without much trouble. Kate only hoped that it wouldn't come to that.

Her orders were simple enough: support the USS John Basilone, remain in the area of operations (AO), watch for interference from foreign (Chinese) vessels and, if necessary, use lethal force. Her subordinate officers had paled at the orders; it was the first time they'd seen the use of force authorised against a potentially hostile nation. They weren't chasing drug smugglers or pirates in small wooden dhows and fishing boats here.

She was busy writing her standing orders when the communications officer interrupted her, 'Captain, connection established with the John.'

'Excellent, patched in now?' she asked, pointing to a nearby headset.

'Yes, captain, the CO is already linked in.'

He must be eager, she thought, swooping up the headset. 'HMAS Hobart calling USS John Basilone; confirm copy, over.' She didn't have to wait long for a reply.

'Copy loud and clear, how's it going Kate?'

'Well, I've got two angry-looking Chinese destroyers down here and a pesky surveillance ship monitoring my every move – how about yourself?'

'Ah, just a container vessel smoldering away. Oh, and three Chinese coast guard ships making their best speed towards me, but otherwise, everything is just peachy.' A small chuckle came through Kate's headset. Jonathan was always calm in stressful situations; this one was no different.

'So, what's the plan? We've both got our hands full, it seems.'

'We'll commence boarding in T-minus sixty minutes. Hopefully we get inside the ship, take control without much fuss – but, after seeing what happened to the Malaysians, we'll see. By our math, those coast-guard ships will get here in just over two hours, so not much wiggle room. My plan is to keep them away from the Huang Shen for as long as I can, but my hands are tied. Unless we are fired upon, we do not have permission to engage.'

'Copy that. What do you need from us?' Kate asked.

'Keep an eye on the destroyers. You see them doing anything hostile, let me know. Between our two ships, we are more evenly balanced against those two. The coastguard ships put us at a disadvantage though. Hopefully we can make them blink.'

'Alright, copy. Looks like we have all the data links open. Anything you see, we'll see. Give 'em hell, Jon!'

'I always do … beers on you afterwards,' he replied, clicking off the line before she could protest.

She bit her lip, frowning. They were in a bad position. Outnumbered, and potentially outgunned, surrounded by civilian shipping. A lot could go wrong, and quickly. But at least they'd have a good understanding of the battlefield. HMAS Hobart and USS John Basilone shared numerous systems, and most importantly, could share data between each other. Their Aegis fire systems would get shared radar images and, at the very least, Jonathan would have early warning of any incoming threats. Canberra and Washington would be watching as well. Dedicated satellites in the space above them tracked their every move, transmitting an ungodly amount of information back to watch floors and command centres in the two countries. Every shot, every missile, all communication and whatever miscellaneous datapoint their ships generated would be shared, analysed and stored.

Kate put the headset down before turning to her 2IC. 'Let's get everything squared away; we're one hour from the John commencing boarding ops. Make sure everything is prepared and ready for whatever comes. Make sure everyone gets some food while they can.'

'Aye-aye, captain.'

She paused. Her lips formed a thin line. The comfort of

knowing that everything that could be done was already done was underwhelming. Her crew and ship were ready, yet a sense of worry remained. There were a lot of weapons in a small area, and even more things that could go wrong. All it would take would be a single mistake, and then they'd all be in it. Could they really claim to be ready? Could anyone? Kate frowned at herself. She had to be strong and confident. No matter what, she would lead the ship and crew. Yet, no matter how much she tried to talk herself into a positive frame of mind, the small voice of doubt remained, whispering from the dark recesses of her mind that disaster was coming their way.

CHAPTER 19

Huang Shen – Malacca Strait

Ming must have nodded off. The gentle kick from Jian startled him awake. Bleary eyed, confused and groggy, he gave Jian a dumb look, unsure where he was or who Jian was for a second. Jian didn't show any kindness or remorse.

'C'mon, you'll probably want to see this,' he grunted at him.

Shaking his head to remove the fog of sleep, Ming gathered his thoughts, quickly remembering where he was and what was going on. He was in the recreation room of an old cargo ship, a damaged one, one that was threatened by enemies.

Jian led him past the bridge, heading towards one of the walkways facing the stern of the ship. The salt air further woke Ming, who rubbed his eyes and took a long, deep breath. 'Look at this,' Jian said, handing him a pair of binoculars and pointing towards the horizon.

Ming could indeed see something as he squinted into the distance. It was midday now; the humidity had climbed, and the heat with it. He wiped his forehead before peering into the binoculars, driven now by his own curiosity.

'Shit,' he muttered. The shape on the horizon was easily distinguished now that it was magnified. The imposing grey superstructure of the warship gliding through the water was impossible to miss. It appeared to cut cleanly through the water, almost unhindered by the friction. All the while, its numerous radar dishes, towering antenna and forward-mounted gun edged closer and closer. Ming knew what ship it was immediately, but the fluttering American flag only confirmed it.

'How long do we have?' he asked, already working the calculations in his head.

'Less than an hour. They are making their best speed towards us,' came Jian's reply, matter-of-fact as always, no hint of emotion.

'Are all your preparations ready?'

'Almost, but as I've said, we can't hold out for long, and we can't oppose their attempts to board like we did before. The Americans will come at us from the sea and air, and in much larger numbers.'

'I know,' Ming replied tiredly. 'But we don't have a choice. Beijing has told us we have to hold out as long as we can, that "help" is coming. I don't know when that is exactly, but if we can delay for an hour or more, we will have at least shown that we tried.' The truth was that Jian's men would be shredded by the warship's weapons if they were exposed on deck. Their only real choice was to use the tight corridors, stairways and access points around the ship as choke points to lure the superior American forces into killing fields or create detours to slow them down.

Jian was still injured from the bullet he'd taken earlier in the night. One hand clutched his chest gingerly. Ming gave him a quick look. 'Will you be alright?' he asked, less concerned about his actual wellbeing than his ability to lead his men and fight.

Jian gave him a hard look. 'I'll be fine. You just worry about the missile and the scientists; they are your problem.'

Ming nodded. 'The chief scientist says the download

from the missile hard drive should be complete soon enough. Let's just hope we get everything. The data is more important than the actual missile now.' They wouldn't be able to get the full missile out now anyway, only key parts and data, so they needed to extract every piece of information they could from it. They'd already taken detailed 3D scans, determining its dimensions, piecing together the parts that were broken or missing.

'Let's go inside and deal with the captain and crew,' Jian suggested, the wind blowing against his face, his right hand resting on his hip-mounted sidearm.

Ming sighed. Yes, he'd forgotten about them. They needed to be out of the way, but they wouldn't be coming with them.

The device in his pocket dinged. It was his secure sat phone. No doubt the message was from Beijing.

USS John Basilone – Malacca Strait

The day had turned out beautifully. It was midday now and the ocean was calm, clear-skied without any dark clouds threatening to ruin what would be perfect holiday weather. The only real blemish was the greyish smoke still pulling skyward from the ugly red container ship ahead. Numerous other container ships moved around them, seemingly unaware or uninterested in the events unfolding before them. A lone civilian helicopter had started following from a safe distance a few miles back and wouldn't leave, despite the stern warnings issued from the crew of the USS John Basilone. No doubt some enterprising journalist had hired it out.

Danny couldn't help but wish he was back in Canberra, despite all the excitement and action occurring around him. A level of anxiety and unease sat uncomfortably high in his gut. He hadn't eaten breakfast, and despite the occasional twinge of hunger, he couldn't eat. He missed Leah, more than anything.

'We don't have enough goddamn time to do this properly!' complained the XO loudly. The captain and the rest of his officers all sat in the officer's wardroom, looking over the final plan of attack. It was too late to change anything seriously, but they had to be as familiar as possible with the plan, especially with so many unknowns at play. Danny was there to provide any last-minute advice, but really, he was more of an observer.

'We don't have a choice, Chris. If we don't go in now, it's going to get a lot more crowded around here. More than it is already. And those Chinese coast-guard vessels are going to outnumber us quickly. Last thing I want is to be fending off angry ships that are trying to ram us while we try to provide protection to our men and women boarding the Huang Shen. We go now, or we don't go at all.'

'But we don't know what's waiting for us, captain. We could be walking into an ambush. Or there mightn't be anything for us to find at all. I mean, hell, she's a big bitch; even if we don't encounter any hostiles, I don't think we could search her effectively in a day, let alone an hour!' the XO said, a little less anger in his voice now.

In some ways, Danny felt guilty for bringing their attention to the Huang Shen. People's lives would be put at risk for the intelligence he had pulled together. The sense of ownership was impossible for him to hide. Internally, he'd decided to own his role in this whole ordeal, any and every way he could.

'We don't have a choice,' Jonathan said again, sighing.

Danny took the silence as an opportunity to speak. 'It's likely they'll have the missile and its components stored together, ready to transport. The satellite imagery we have shows a large container being lifted into the ship. Assuming they deployed a crew to examine the missile in transit, they'd need a clean space to avoid any additional damage, especially if the missile is in a worse condition than we expect.'

Everyone turned to look at Danny. 'What would it look like, Mr Blackburn?' the XO asked.

Danny thought for a second before replying, 'If they are smart, they have loaded it into a specially designed container. It would have a secondary airlock, ventilation. They'd also need a heap of separate analytical equipment. Expect computers, and diagnostic machines – probably in close proximity to the missile itself.'

The XO raised an eyebrow and gave the captain a silent look. Danny looked between them both, unsure what unspoken conversation they were having. Jonathan nodded in reply, and Danny felt the hairs on his neck raise.

'Danny, we need you to accompany the boarding party,' the XO said gently, but in a matter-of-fact way that didn't seem to leave a whole lot of room for discussion.

Danny stood dumbfounded for a couple of short seconds. 'Sir, I-I'm not trained for combat,' he responded weakly.

Jonathan nodded, 'I know, Danny, but listen, we don't have a lot of time here. We don't know where this thing is – we don't even know if it's on the ship. I can't have my men exposed. You're the expert here; the missile is your baby. You'll know what to look for and what we need to prioritise.'

There was finality in the captain's voice. Danny knew there was no point arguing.

Jonathan gave him a kind smile. 'Don't worry, Danny, our guys will keep you safe. We'll send Lieutenant Commander Edwards with you. You won't be alone, and you won't be the first in. You'll be in and out. Find the missile, figure out what we can recover, destroy the rest. And do it before the Chinese get there.'

Danny didn't give a verbal response immediately, just nodded his head dumbly, his brain processing the information thrown at him. He was backed into a corner, and he knew it. He was scared, but he also felt responsible. It was his missile, and it was his intelligence that had led them here. He had to do his part.

'You can count on me, sir,' he replied with more

confidence than he felt.

The captain and XO smiled knowingly, the conversation moving on quickly, 'Right, next we need to figure out what to do with prisoners …'

Just like that, Danny had been recruited – far beyond anything he was comfortable or even trained to do. He could refuse. He knew he could. But he wouldn't. Not only would the sense of shame never leave him, but others would be put in danger. He had to step up.

Jesse gave him a thumbs up as he tried to focus back on the conversation. At least he'd have a friend.

***

Danny awkwardly tried to secure the velcro strap of his body armour. The heavy vest felt cumbersome, but it was firm and provided some sense of security. Numerous sailors were busy equipping themselves around him, donning helmets and other protective gear, checking firearms. He must have looked as lost as he felt when Jesse came over.

'Hold your arms out to the side,' he ordered simply. Danny did as he was told. With practised skill, Jesse tightened the straps around Danny's waist. 'Feel better?'

'Ah, yeah,' he replied dumbly.

Jesse grabbed a helmet and a pair of gloves. 'Take these. You'll need 'em.'

'Thanks,' Danny mumbled in reply.

He felt completely out of place. Jesse, by comparison, was fully kitted out – dark-grey chest rig, body armour and matching helmet – his field experience providing him a sense of confidence and capability that Danny knew he himself was lacking. Jesse looked like a warrior as he hoisted up a short-barrelled M4 carbine, checking the safety as he chambered a round. A large, powerful-looking handgun was strapped around his lower thigh. Something told Danny that Jesse had been here and done this type of work before.

By comparison, Danny only had a small medical kit,

some pliers and a handheld flashlight, reinforcing that he was a tourist amongst warriors.

'Do I need one of those?' he asked, pointing to Jesse's carbine.

'This guy? Nah, you need to be trained up, man. Plus, you won't need it. We'll just be searching containers; a gun doesn't help much with that.' Danny nodded again, but Jesse could see the uncertainty written all over his face. 'Don't worry, Danny, we've got your back. You tell us what to look for, and we'll make sure no one interrupts us. We'll be in and out, quick smart.'

'And what if it takes longer?' Danny asked.

'We pull out,' Jesse said simply.

'Unless we find our missile.'

'Unless we find our missile,' Jesse parroted.

Everyone started to file out, moving towards the RHIBs or waiting Seahawk. They'd be going in three distinct teams. Danny, luckily, was going to be in the safer team, Charlie. Teams Bravo and Alpha would take on the more dangerous work.

Jesse moved towards the exit; only he and Danny remained in the almost-empty space. Danny's feet seemed frozen, indecision and fear mounting.

'You'll be fine, Danny. Just stick with me. Who knows? You might even enjoy yourself,' Jesse said, a broad, warm grin across his face. Danny couldn't help but grin back as he followed Jesse's lead.

The bright sunshine blinded him momentarily as they exited to the exterior of the ship. The noise of the ocean and the ship seemed loud and chaotic. Everyone moved purposefully around him, all with jobs to do. Danny just followed, staring into Jesse's back.

Before he knew it, he was clasping an offered hand and climbing into the small, black inflatable boat, crowded with armed sailors and equipment. Danny moved awkwardly into the next available seat, which was nothing more than a narrow plastic platform with a handle. Rows of helmeted heads sat in front of him, while the one person manning the wheel of the craft stood.

Someone yelled out, 'Ready to drop!' and before Danny could brace himself, the pilot shot a thumbs up and they plummeted to the ocean below.

'Next lesson, Danny: we're going in by RHIB, meaning we'll be climbing up the side of the Huang Shen. Now, we're climbing up in a relatively safe spot amidships. We'll be hooking one of our boarding ladders to the ship. The hardest part of the whole affair is moving from the RHIB to the ladder. Once you are on the ladder, just climb it like you would any ladder. But the important part is, when you grab that ladder, grab on tight – and don't let go until you have all feet and hands on there. If you fall, it won't be pretty.'

Danny didn't entirely understand what Jesse meant by "it won't be pretty", but he guessed getting dragged between the RHIB and the huge container vessel wouldn't be great. Just one more thing to worry about, he guessed.

'Hold on with both hands and feet, gotcha.'

'See, Danny? You'll be fine. Now, let's get the rest of your kit and get you squared away.'

RMAF Base Butterworth – Malaysia

The mission alert seemed to have come out of the blue for the No. 75 Squadron.

The Wedgetail AWACS was the first aircraft to depart, followed shortly by an enormous KC-30A air-refueller, the exercise with the Malaysians officially cut short. The No. 75 Squadron F-35 Joint Strike Fighter pilots sat under their shaded hangars as the order came in. They were fully loaded with an offensive strike package, complete with air-to-air AIM-9 Sidewinders on their wings and larger AIM-120 AMRAAM air-to-air missiles to attack targets beyond visual range. Each F-35 was partnered with two smaller aircraft, slick and pointed like the larger F-35 fighters but smaller, with no room for a human pilot. Each carried a full set of its own Sidewinder and AMRAAM missiles. The Ghost Bat autonomous drone would accompany the pilots of the No. 75 Squadron, increasing their striking power. These drones were state-of-the-art – they wouldn't sit floating in the clouds like the current generation of standoff weapons. They would fly with the F-35s, watching their backs and giving their enemies two more aircraft to fight for each F-35.

'So, we're finally going to test these babies?' one of the pilots asked his wingman.

'Looks like, but they'll probably just want us to fly them around. Don't want to risk their new toys.'

'Either way, gents, we're in for a long flight. You heard the mission briefing: Timor Sea and Malacca Strait,' a third pilot added.

The other two pilots shrugged. They were bored, and despite the cool air inside their cockpits, they were baking in the brutal Australian heat. 'Better than sweating our asses off here!'

The green light for the mission came minutes later, with the waiting ground crews scrambling to remove any remaining covers and blocks holding the aircraft in place. The F-35s taxied, Ghost Bats following on each wing. As they sat on the tarmac, heat waves rose from the ground, blurring the horizon. The pilot was glad they had air-conditioning inside their small glass cockpits.

With final approval from the air traffic control tower, the F-35s pulled forward, speeding down the runway before lifting off the ground and climbing skyward. Six Ghost Bats followed, two on the wing of each pilot, moving in perfect unison with their aircraft.

CHAPTER 20

Malacca Strait

The RHIB's engine roared to life seconds after hitting the water. The pilot wasted no time in spinning the small boat away from the USS John Basilone, spraying water in its wake. Danny gripped the handle in front of him tightly. Any feelings of fear and anxiety were quickly washed away in the excitement of the moment.

Despite the relatively calm ocean, the small swell combined with their blistering speed meant they felt every wave. The engine grew louder every time it left the water. Only a minute into the ride, Danny's backside was killing him, and he found himself gasping involuntarily at a particularly rough bounce.

'Take some of the weight on your knees,' Jesse yelled into Danny's ear, noticing his discomfort.

Doing as he was told, but keeping his hands locked firmly on the rail, Danny lifted his backside off the chair, bending his knees. It wasn't comfortable, but it was slightly better than having his spine shatter with every hit. He could feel the power behind the engines on the RHIB; even the smallest touches by the pilot saw them leaping to a new heading.

The Huang Shen seemed to loom in the distance. They'd left the USS John Basilone a couple of miles back but were eating up the distance now. As Danny looked around him, he noticed that everyone seemed quietly focused, eyes forward or scanning off their port and starboard. The little boat certainly felt full; each seat was occupied by sailors with equipment. He could see what looked like a plasma cutter, some kind of ladder device and a range of shotguns, pistols and carbines – and that was just on the people around him. He guessed the second RHIB and Seahawk would be just as well prepared. No point doing something dangerous in half measure.

Another noise seemed to overtake the roar of the RHIB's engine. A louder whine mixed with the thumping of helicopter blades filled Danny's ears, cutting through his helmet and headset with ease. Turning his head towards the sound, he watched as the grey Seahawk swooped into view. Flying low and slow, it moved smoothly across the line between the ocean and the sky, doors open, sailors packed shoulder to shoulder. One of them manned a heavy-looking machine gun attached to the side of the helicopter.

The other RHIB came into view just to their starboard side, showing the full might of the landing party. Three teams: Alpha, Bravo and Charlie. At least ten people per team. Danny couldn't help but smile, a big stupid grin.

'Having fun yet, Danny?' Jesse yelled into Danny's ear.

He yelled back, 'This is fucking awesome!'

Jesse gave a wider smile in reply but said nothing.

The microphone in Danny's headset crackled to life. The communications of not only his team but of the broader force echoed into his ear.

'All teams, standby. Alpha team has the lead and will insert via Romeo 1. Teams Bravo and Charlie to follow. Let's do this quick and clean. Secure the ship, find the cargo, and come home safely.'

Danny didn't recognise the voice, but it was definitely

one of the senior officers. The Seahawk seemed to get louder as it started its approach, increasing its height and pushing its powerful turboshaft engines hard. It moved ahead of the RHIBs, aiming for the Huang Shen's bridge.

The Huang Shen seemed to grow in size the closer they got to it. From the bridge of the USS John Basilone, it had appeared small in the distance. But now, gazing upon it from the water level, it towered above them.

'Ready for a climb, man?' a sailor to Danny's right asked.

'Whaddya mean?' he asked, confused.

'We're going up.' He pointed to the red wall of the ship's hull.

'We're going all the way up?'

Danny groaned as the man laughed, nudging him on the shoulder. 'Just don't fall off; you'll do fine.' This was going to hurt – he knew it – but the thought didn't last long. The jagged hole marking the port side started to come into view, the grey smoke no longer concealing the damage this close up. Danny had spent more time playing with explosives and determining their impacts than he cared to admit. His previous role as an engineer had started with a bang, literally, and followed with a few years trying to figure out a way to make more effective explosions and weapons for the US military.

Now, staring up at the wound on the Huang Shen, the hole stood out against the aged but otherwise smooth metal hull. Appearing almost as a horizontal tear, it looked a good ten feet wide. Points of sharp-looking steel pointed outwards from a central point. The overall damage, at least externally, didn't look that bad, but it was strange – an explosion powerful enough to tear a significant hole but small enough to remain localised. It was also high along the hull, almost closer to the upper decks. Unless it had done major damage, he wasn't sure how it could threaten to sink or even slow the ship. He tried to estimate the amount of force required for the explosive, but the closer they got, the larger it looked. There weren't any fuel tanks or lines built into the walls, to Danny's knowledge. He'd scanned the blueprints of the ship in detail, deciding not to ask how they had acquired this information. Something else must have caused it – cargo, maybe? Or could it have been deliberate? Were there other forces at play? Could pirates actually have taken the ship? All these questions distracted him as they sped towards the Huang Shen.

'What're you thinking, Danny?' Jesse asked, noticing Danny's eyes on the Huang Shen as they continued to bounce across the water.

'The damage; it's weird,' he yelled back over the roar of the engine and the wind.

'How do you mean?'

'The hole – it's small but powerful, almost like a shaped charge or something similar, but there isn't anything in that part of the ship. No fuel tanks or explosive material.'

'Could be the cargo?' Jesse offered.

'Maybe …' he replied, unconvinced and getting drawn back into his reverie.

A particularly big bounce pulled him from his thoughts. He grunted again, his legs and knees protesting the constant strain. 'Looks like we need to get you out on more runs, Danny!' came a shout from Jesse. Was it that obvious that he was struggling?

'No way, this is all the exercise I need,' he shouted back, flipping Jesse off with one hand and grinning.

'Two-minute warning,' rang out in his ears, likely from the pilot of their RHIB. All the tension and anxiety returned in a second. The reality of what he was about to do assaulted him. What if he fell? What if it was a trap? What if there was nothing at all? He took a big breath, focusing his mind, stopping his thoughts before they ran away entirely. He was here to do a job, and he wasn't about to let anyone down. This wasn't the time to panic.

They were only a couple of hundred metres away now. The sailors on Danny's right had raised their rifles, scanning each entranceway, doorway and potential hiding spot. A noticeable tension settled over them suddenly. Now wasn't a time to be curious or get lost in thought. Now it was real. The Seahawk had come to a stop above the bridge of the Huang Shen. Large ropes were flung out, with sailors quickly and smoothly rappelling down.

The RHIBs turned in towards the towering wall of the Huang Shen's outer hull. The difference in speed became apparent immediately as they got closer. The Huang Shen wasn't moving fast, not at all. The RHIB started to slow, matching the larger ship's speed.

'Bravo making approach now,' called the other RHIB, which had vanished from view, taking up position opposite them on the starboard side of the ship.

'Prepare to board!' someone ordered across Danny's RHIB. Two sailors at the bow of their small craft were ready, poised for action.

'Ready ladder!' someone else shouted.

He watched as one of the sailors hoisted up what looked like an extendable pole, but with metal plates jutting out along its edges. He'd pictured more of a regular garden ladder, not considering the need for lightweight and flexible tools in this environment. The logistics of boarding a ship on the move from their tiny boat started to hit home.

'Shit, Jesse, you didn't tell me anything about this!'

The sailor at the front pointed the ladder upward, the second man holding him steady.

'What's that?' Jesse asked with feigned innocence. 'It's just like a regular ladder, just smaller! You'll do fine!'

The pilot skilfully eased the RHIB closer to the slow-moving cargo ship, then slowly nearer the hull. The disturbed white water of the ship's wake bounced them around. The sailors were keeping their rifles aimed towards the white superstructure, looking for anyone who might try and take a shot.

Danny couldn't help but feel impressed by the skill and professionalism of the men and women around him. He felt out of place by comparison, an ex-engineer turned intelligence analyst. But here he was, preparing to board a ship, looking for a piece of military technology that may or may not be onboard. Nothing felt right or normal in Danny's mind, but the simmering excitement of the moment was impossible to ignore.

As he watched, the sailor with the climbing ladder moved with surprising grace, extending the pole skyward and letting it dart past the safety rails way above them, before pulling it downward quickly and latching the two hooks firmly onto the rails. He gave it two big yanks, then, satisfied that it was secure, let it rest against the hull.

'Charlie, commence boarding,' the team leader announced.

The second man on the bow of the small RHIB wasted no time. With the confidence of someone who had done this numerous times before, he stepped across to the ladder, locking his hands and feet into place. He tested his weight on the ladder, giving it a small bounce, before starting his climb, not rushing but moving with confidence. His rifle swung against his back as he ascended. Two more sailors quickly joined him. Danny had thought they'd go up one at a time, but clearly the ladder was stronger than he'd anticipated. The RHIB quickly emptied, with everyone boarding in order from bow to stern. Before too long, it was Danny's turn.

Jesse gave him a gentle nudge. 'I'll be right behind you, Danny. Just one step after the other, hands and feet. Just like a regular ladder.'

He knew he was trying to be encouraging, but looking up the length of the ladder and hull in front of him, it felt like he was about to climb a skyscraper. Edging forward, he stumbled slightly, only just managing to keep his footing. Multiple pairs of eyes watched him warily, looking for any deadly mistakes he might make.

'Wait until we line up with the ladder, then just step off onto it. Keep a firm grip. You don't want to fall between the hull and us!' the pilot yelled.

Danny nodded, watching the rhythmic movement of the RHIB and the ladder, counting the seconds between each bob of the RHIB. He leapt forward, stepping off the little boat in one smooth movement. One hand, then the next, locked around the rung in front of him as his feet found a purchase on the rungs below. He tried to ignore the churning water just centimetres below him. Falling into that water could mean being smashed against the rusty, barnacle-covered hull, or squished by the RHIB scraping against it. The only way was up.

Shaking his head, Danny forced his gaze upward. The men who had leapt on before him seemed miles above him. 'Let's go, Danny!' came the call from Jesse. How long had he been holding onto the ladder for? For him, it had felt like seconds.

Reaching up with one hand, he grasped the rung above him and began pulling upward while looking for the next step with his foot. Slowly but surely, he started to ascend. A small wobble on the ladder below him signalled that another person had joined the queue. His mind seemed to focus and fall into a trance as he climbed, trying to block out the fear he felt. It wasn't until Danny went to reach up to the next rung and found another person's boot that he realised how far he'd climbed. He was nearly at the top of the ladder. A glimmer of pride flickered inside him as he realised what he'd done.

As he waited for the men above him, Danny realised how tired his arms felt. The strain had been building in his arms and legs, but he'd ignored it while climbing – or rather, he hadn't noticed it. He wasn't sure why they had stopped. Trying to ignore the growing ache in his arms and legs, he took in the sight around him. The USS John Basilone loomed in the background, guns pointing menacingly towards the Huang Shen, although he doubted they'd open fire with friendlies onboard.

Further in the distance, a myriad of commercial ships floated by slowly, obviously curious to see what was happening in their sea lanes, the drudgery of another day on the ocean interrupted by some real action. Danny didn't doubt they'd been told to keep clear, but he guessed a few captains had been willing to risk a slap on the wrist to get a better look. The Seahawk continued to thump away, nearby but unseen. As far as he could tell, there hadn't been any trouble yet. There were no urgent messages in his headphones.

A shouted order came from somewhere above Danny. 'Move up!'

He sighed with relief. His arms and legs had seriously started to hurt in the short time he'd been hanging off the side of the ship. He'd lost all sense of how long he'd actually been on the ladder. It felt like an eternity, but in reality, it had been less than a couple of minutes.

He moved up again, watching the man's feet above him disappear over the railing as the others pulled him off the ladder and onto the deck. It looked easy enough. Eyeing the railing carefully, he reached up with one hand and pulled himself higher, coming eye level with the deck and seeing for the first time the barren metal expanse before him. Mimicking the swift movement of the man before, he gave one final pull, vaulting over the top of the railing.

He almost succeeded. The edge of his boot clipped the top of the railing, throwing him off balance. What would have been a graceful landing transitioned into a stumble and a crash as he landed on the deck. *Ouch* was the first thing that flashed through his mind. The second was the sensation of being hauled up off the ground.

'Careful there, buddy! Don't think you'll win that fight,' a sailor holding an M4 called out, helping Danny up with his free hand.

The remark burnt his pride a little. Still, he felt more relieved than anything; he'd made it, and without serious injury or death, although there would probably be many more opportunities for that soon enough, he mused darkly.

The men and women ahead of him had spaced out,

kneeling and aiming down their sights. Danny found a small metal exhaust pipe to sit behind. The deck seemed to spread out before them. They were close to the midship, but even closer to the bow. Other than some crane equipment, the deck was largely flat. Large doors took up the majority of space along the deck, with walkways either side. Danny felt suddenly naked, being surrounded by so many armed people while all he had was his wits.

Jesse was next, smoothly making the jump over the railing and drawing his M4 carbine from behind his back in one motion. Danny couldn't help but feel impressed at his colleague's apparent experience and skill. It occurred to him that he didn't actually know all that much about Jesse's military history. A part of his brain made a mental note, the analyst inside him finding a curiosity for his colleague.

Jesse gave him a thumbs up before taking up position near the head of the team. They'd begun stacking up next to an entrance way of some kind.

USS John Basilone

'How we looking, XO?' Jonathan asked the microphone in his hand as he watched the live feed from one of the USS John Basilone's high-resolution cameras.

'No sign of enemy resistance so far, sir,' the XO replied promptly. His voice sounded far off as it echoed through the speakers on the radio in the bridge.

Jonathan preferred the bridge, while the XO managed combat systems in the CIC. He knew he'd have to head down into the CIC at some point, but for now, he wanted to see everything with his own eyes.

'How are our friends tracking?' he asked the XO, referring to the encroaching China Coast Guard.

'Still an hour out, sir, but they are moving at their best possible speeds. We've got a pretty good radar picture on them. Definitely two lighter escorts and one big boy. Probably a Zhaotou class. We'll be able to see them soon enough.'

Jonathan instinctively scanned the horizon, knowing he wouldn't be able to see anything yet but checking anyway. Numerous commercial vessels dotted the waters around him, but the tell-tale white hulls of the China Coast Guard were nowhere to be seen. At least, not yet.

'Alright, XO, let me know when they get into visual range. We'll assess their intent from there. Keep them on passive radar for now. No need to let them know we're watching.' It was an unnecessary order, but he was the captain, and sometimes the most important orders needed stating, even if it was just for the record.

'Aye-aye, sir,' came the calm response from the XO.

Jonathan felt like his hands were tied. They'd have no problem taking on the coast guard. They were relatively lightly armed and could be sunk at a distance with only a couple of Harpoon missiles loaded into the John's vertical launch cells. But it wouldn't be that easy. His orders were clear. He might be in one of the world's most powerful warships, but unless attacked, he could not engage. The problem was, they just didn't know what the Chinese vessels would do, and with every minute, the striking distance between the opposing ships lessened. The incident in the Indian Ocean was certainly a good example of what they might do, but surely they weren't stupid enough to try it again?

The packed shipping lanes put a lot of obstacles in his way, reducing his ability to manoeuvre freely. Once the coast-guard vessels were in range, they had enough close-in weaponry that they could pose a real threat to his ship. He was particularly concerned about their bow-mounted guns. Or, they might just simply try and ram them. But if it came to that, Jonathan had promised himself that, for the sake of the crew, they would use all force available to keep the Chinese away. He wouldn't be dishonoured like the sailors in the Maldives had been.

Then there were the two destroyers, a type 055 and a

type 052D. Even if they handled the coast guard, those destroyers could simply outgun the Arleigh Burke. Jonathan didn't like the odds one bit.

He looked down at a lone dot on his display. The HMAS Hobart was making its best speed to their position, but Jonathan knew they couldn't help with the coast guard. Nevertheless, they might be able to help tip the balance away from the destroyers. *Hope you're ready for a fight, Kate*, he thought to himself.

There was one other card he hadn't played yet. Maybe it was time to consider it. 'Comms, connect me with the Malaysian forces.'

Huang Shen

Danny waited at the end of a line of sailors, keeping out of the way but watching with keen interest. A tourist amongst the highly trained and well-armed men and women.

'Door's welded shut – we're going to cut it!' the sailor at the front of the stack yelled back down the line. Another sailor stepped forward with what Danny guessed was some kind of compact plasma cutter. The man knelt down and started working against the door, sparks immediately flying.

The constant thumping of the Seahawk had lessened. The helicopter hovered a couple of hundred metres away, keeping an eye on them and the ship. Clearly, Alpha Team had moved a lot faster than they had.

It seemed strange that they hadn't heard anything from the supposed hostile forces. Could they have ditched? Made a run for it? It didn't make much sense to Danny – how could they just disappear? The ship almost seemed like a ghost ship, but he had to remind himself they'd only been onboard a couple of minutes. Still, curiosity got the better of him. He tapped one of the sailors next to him on the shoulder. The man jerked his head around, surprised at the touch.

'Where is everyone? The guys who were shooting at the Malaysians?' he hissed.

The sailor seemed surprised at first, but an amused look came over his face. 'Probably skipped when they saw us, sir. If they were smart, at least.'

'But what about the crew?' Danny asked urgently, suddenly afraid they were too late.

'If they're lucky, they're just tied up in the crew quarters. More likely they were killed or taken hostage,' the man added quickly.

Danny just looked at him. The man turned around, returning his focus to the sailor with the oxy torch cutting open the door of the ship. The sailor had sounded so confident, Danny guessed he'd done this numerous times before.

'I wouldn't be so sure,' Jesse said, crouched not far from Danny. He'd clearly been listening in. 'It's much easier to defend the ship from the inside. Let's wait and see once we have control of the whole ship.'

A little lump of fear welled up inside Danny, the subtle taste of bile rising at the back of his throat. The fear of the possible enemy catching up with him overwhelmed his logical and curious side. Closing his eyes, he drew a deep breath, letting the nasty taste linger for a few seconds before breathing out, focusing.

His headset crackled to life again, distracting him from his own thoughts, 'Alpha has secured the bridge; controls have been disabled, over.'

'That's not good,' Jesse said, a concerned tone to his voice. Smashed equipment and no control. If anything got in the way of the Huang Shen, it wouldn't be stopping. They'd need to get to the engine room.

'Roger that, Alpha. Bravo Team, status update,' came the familiar voice of the XO from the John Basilone.

A somewhat jumbled reply echoed over the comms network. Crackling interference, likely from the ship's hull. It was still understandable, but not complete; every second word was cut short or removed, making the voice sound strangled.

'Cutting through the pr … bulkhead … oor to the …gine room. Estimate two … m … utes. We expe …'

A high-pitched tone sounded over the entire comm network. Everyone yelped with surprise, grabbing at their headsets or pushing their ears against their shoulders in discomfort. Danny almost yanked the headset off completely, but the sound suddenly cut off. It was now deathly quiet.

'Fucking piece of shit equipment!' the sailor next to Danny yelled out in anger.

'Bravo Team, come in,' came an authoritative voice over the comms.

A garbled, static mess was the only reply.

The seconds ticked by as the numerous calls went unanswered.

'Alpha, keep guard on the bridge, but move some of your team down to support Bravo, and get them back on comms,' the XO ordered.

So much was happening in Danny's ear that he barely recognised the sudden movement around him. With a loud bang, the metal door fell from its frame, freed from its welded prison. Jesse tapped Danny on the shoulder. 'C'mon, let's move in.' Everyone started shuffling forward, and Danny felt more naked than ever.

The drastic change from the beautiful warm day to the dark, cold staleness of the metal corridor was jarring. Flashlights turned on and the space took on a strange semi-illuminated glow as everyone's torchlight danced across the walls of the enclosed space they now found themselves in. Beyond the immediate doorframe, a steep, narrow stairway seemed to drive them deeper into the bowels of the ship.

The rest of the team all seemed to move with purpose, knowing where their colleagues were and where to aim their weapons. He realised again how out of place he was amongst this well-trained team. Danny watched and tried to follow in sync, but without knowing hand signals or procedures, he mostly failed, bumping into the person in front of him when they suddenly stopped.

He was surprised at how slowly the team moved; each doorway, hallway and room was checked thoroughly. Threats could be waiting around every corner, but it seemed impossible they could check every little nook and cranny. The ship was a maze, but it was at least an environment Danny hoped they were familiar with.

Descending stairways seemed to cause the most concern. As they moved down, the lead sailor would be largely blind to any threats on the level below them. Peering around the line of sailors, Danny watched as they crouched down low, scanning the narrow entrance of the stairs before moving down as quickly as possible, taking up defensive positions once they reached the bottom, undoubtedly relieved they hadn't been shot from below.

The constant darkness of the ship's interior suddenly seemed to lift as the team moved down another corridor. More surprisingly, they were met with the sound of the ocean and a slight breeze cutting through the stale air. It didn't make sense to Danny – it wasn't like they could open a window down here. The small mystery played on his mind, but not for long. He got his answer at the bottom of the next set of stairs.

The corridor turned into a T-intersection. The path to their right was clear, but the path right in front of them was a mangled mess. Burnt walls and melted piping hung loosely against the punctured hull. A considerable explosion had obviously blasted through this space, and the confined area had pushed the explosive force in a single direction. Danny hadn't realised it as they'd moved methodically through the ship, but they'd come to the point of the explosion that had seemingly crippled the ship and brought all the world's attention down upon it. Small amounts of smoke drifted upward from a punctured wall opposite the hole, wafting out into the open air. Evidence of firefighting was obvious;

foam residue and hoses lay scattered about the floor. The blackened walls and melted metal described the heat of the fire that had once been there. There had been people here, but where had they gone? The question remained unanswered.

'Keep moving, everyone,' the team leader called out, moving the team down the right corridor. Danny couldn't help himself; he stopped at the blast site as everyone moved forward. The engineer inside him was curious, and the analyst wanted to understand why and what had happened.

It was a weird explosion. Clearly it had come from the inside; the buckled and jagged outward-facing metal sheets of the hull were evidence enough of that. But what had been the source? There was nothing in this part of the ship; there was no additional damage further into the ship to suggest another source. No, the source of the explosion had been here, at this point. There was a roundness to the hole. Yet, despite the melted pipes and bent deck, the damage was still largely superficial.

'What is it, Danny? We should keep up with the rest,' Jesse said, a sense of urgency and worry in his voice.

'This damage, it's wrong,' he replied.

'What do you mean?'

'The explosion was small. The damage here isn't that bad, but it was powerful enough to puncture the solid metal sheets of the hull. Plus, there is nothing here that should have caused that damage.'

'So? What do you think it was?'

'A shaped charge of some kind, but it doesn't make sense – why place it here? We're above the waterline; there is nothing critical here. And a better question, who placed it there?'

Jesse looked down at him, carbine in hand. 'Danny, let's go. I don't like us being alone here, and I don't like mysteries while we're meant to be cle—'

The air pressure seemed to suddenly expand, the space round Danny replaced with a rushing noise, then nothing.

Something under him seemed to rumble and vibrate, knocking him off balance. His brain recognised the sensation of an explosion, and he instinctively covered his eyes, expecting searing pain, but nothing happened. The pressure seemed to release as quickly as it had appeared, the emptiness replaced with a constant ringing. Jesse had dived to the ground next to him but was now looking around. He wore a bewildered look on his face but was otherwise unhurt. Their eyes met, and a look of alarm and realisation spread across his tough features.

'Shit, let's go!' he yelled suddenly, hauling himself off the ground and pointing his M4 down the corridor to the right. He sounded far away through the high-pitched ringing in Danny's ears. Jesse sprinted off, charging towards the sound of the blast, following the path that the rest of the team had taken only moments before. Danny scrambled to keep up.

Jesse paused at a bend in the corridor, peeking around the corner to get a better view before moving around, rifle aimed upward. Danny watched him, wondering briefly if he should follow, then realising he didn't have any other choice. Following Jesse, he stepped around the corner and stopped dead in his tracks. Men and women lay sprawled in a tangled mess of limbs across the floor. Some moved and groaned, while others didn't move at all. Danny stood dumbfounded for a moment, unsure of what to do. His mind froze as it tried to decipher the scene that lay at his feet. Somewhere at the back of his mind, he registered that the heavy door in front of them had been blown square off its hinges, flying into the wall opposite. A booby trap, maybe?

Someone tugged on his pant leg, startling him and breaking his frozen state. A sailor looked up at him from the ground, a shocked, confused look on his face. Danny knelt down, trying to offer some kind of help. He pulled the man up, searching for wounds and injuries. Some blood seemed to be coming out of the man's ear, but otherwise he looked fine. Around him, others seemed to be moving now, seemingly confused, blind and deaf.

Jesse was a few metres ahead, looking at the torn doorway, trying to move an injured sailor out of his way.

Danny was about to call out to him when the shape of a human being appeared in the space beyond the damaged doorway. Time slowed down and Jesse seemed to tense, sensing the movement. The person didn't have the same uniform as the sailors around Danny. His clothing was darker, and the rifle he carried was shorter – some kind of mean-looking bullpup, pointed downward towards the injured and confused sailors on the floor, the intent clearly hostile. The man hadn't expected to see Jesse or Danny in the middle of the corridor and was slow to respond. Jesse wasn't.

In what looked like a practised move, Jesse swept his carbine upward, aiming directly into the massive centre of the man. Jesse's rifle boomed. Five ear-shattering shots echoed out. The enemy soldier had been slow, expecting his targets to be on the ground. He'd tried to bring his rifle up and target Jesse, but he'd been too late. The first rounds from Jesse's rifle hit him squarely in the chest, sending him sprawling backwards and out of sight. Jesse stood quickly, rifle squarely planted against his shoulder, and squeezed the trigger again, letting two more rounds loose.

Someone shouted in alarm through the doorway.

Danny had seen enough violent movies to understand what had just happened, but to see it in real life floored him. The reality of death was far different from the movies. There hadn't been fountains of blood – yes, it had been violent – but this was brutally sudden and, more than anything, real. His body pumped with adrenaline and his mind went into overdrive. He guessed by the way Jesse had moved that the man who'd attacked them was dead. He didn't feel sorrow. In fact, it was the lack of sensation that had surprised Danny, a feeling of sheer nothingness.

Jesse had moved up to the doorframe, flattening himself against its side. He'd barely peeked around the mangled frame before the space next to him exploded into sparks, rounds immediately smacking against the frame. Danny saw him flinch at the sudden impact.

'DANNY, GET THEM OUT OF HERE!' Jesse bellowed from across the corridor.

The urgency of the order sent electricity through Danny, breaking the trance he was in and propelling him into action. He followed his instincts rather than his brain. Grabbing the man at his feet by the arms, he started dragging him back to the relative safety of the corner at the end of the corridor, away from the gunfight. Other members of the team started to recover, and the realisation that something dangerous was happening had begun to set in, but they were still slow to move.

'EVERYONE, GET UP AND MOVE. FOLLOW ME! THIS WAY!' Danny yelled out as loud as he could, his deep voice booming throughout the tight space. More people from Charlie stood up or crawled, following Danny's voice. With one last concerted effort, he pulled the man he was hauling around the corner. Two, then three, then four and five people followed, stumbling and half-collapsing. One, less stunned than the rest, took up a position at the corner, aiming down towards Jesse and the shooting.

Danny moved behind the man, trying to cover Jesse. Poking his head around the corner, Danny could see one last team member laying in the middle of the hallway. He didn't think or hesitate.

Someone tried to grab him, but they were too slow. Danny darted out, fuelled by adrenaline. He could see the body lying face down, helmet knocked clean off. Running, he watched Jesse, who was kneeling down, poking his rifle through the doorway and firing blindly. More rounds from enemies unseen pelted the doorway and the corridor.

He reached the last sailor, quickly flipping the man over and using his chest rig to pull him backwards as fast as he could. Jesse pulled a small round object off his rig. Danny had seen grenades enough times before, and the M67 fragmentation grenade was distinctive. Effortlessly pulling the pin, Jesse held the grenade before letting the latch spring free from his fingers. With surprising speed and strength, Jesse threw the explosive into the space beyond. The blast was an unimpressive crack compared to the one that had knocked out the majority of the team, making just a dull crunching *thunk*. Deadly, high-speed fragments came flying into the wall facing the destroyed doorway. Anyone standing there would have been cut to pieces. Danny wondered grimly what kind of mess would be left of the people who had been on the receiving end.

Another sailor appeared at Danny's side, and together they hauled what he hoped was just an unconscious sailor back around the corner to the rest of the team, who lay in various states of shock and consciousness.

Within seconds of the blast, Jesse leapt back around the corner, panting hard. Danny wasn't sure how he'd made the distance so quickly, but he didn't bother asking. His own breathing was catching up with him.

'Everyone … alright?' Danny asked.

An assortment of replies, groans and grunts was the best he got. The two sailors he'd dragged were getting attention by a medic. They didn't look dead.

'They've got a machine gun set up there. If we'd breached that door, we'd be in pieces right now. They fucked up, trying to blow us up,' Jesse said coolly, his breath rapidly returning to normal, far quicker than Danny's.

'Well, we need to get in there; that's the cargo hold,' one of the sailors replied. Danny hadn't realised it, but they'd taken a very deliberate path. Unfortunately, a predictable and well-guarded one as well.

Jesse nodded, keying his headset. 'Command, this is Charlie. We've just been ambushed. Numerous wounded. Hostile forces are present; repeat: hostile forces present.'

An alarmed but static-filled reply came from the USS John Basilone. 'Understo … d … re … qi … e … ev … a?'

'Negative. Negative. Any wounded will be escorted

topside. Mission continues.' Jesse took charge without being told. Danny hadn't realised it straight away, but the team leader was one of the unconscious sailors.

Jesse paused, waiting for confirmation but getting only more static. 'Fuck, alright, not sure what is playing with our comms, but it's not getting any better. We need to move and secure the hold. Who's still okay?'

The majority of the team nodded. 'Alright, you two, take them topside; we'll get them ready for evac. I want two to hold this spot. The rest of you, follow me.'

Danny's breathing finally started to level out. He started trotting behind Jesse's team, no one stopping him, but something was bothering him as the team moved up a tight stairway.

'Hey Jesse, that guy you shot, what rifle was he carrying? I only got a glance at it, but it looked like a QBZ-191 to me.'

Jesse slowed, 'Yeah … I think it was. That's the new Chinese rifle, right?'

'Yeah, it is, and they have only started producing it; they don't export it. We haven't even been able to get our hands on one yet. I don't think these are pirates.'

Jesse held up his fist and the team came to a sudden halt. Danny almost ran into the back of one sailor. He moved back and crouched next to Danny, speaking quietly, 'Yeah, the same thought crossed my mind. They were well-trained, and their uniforms match as well … Looks like you were right.'

Danny nodded. 'We need to find the missile first, but if the Chinese are here, and are willing to try and kill us for it …'

'They'll probably be willing to do a lot more, I know … Might explain the comms issues as well.'

Danny cocked his head.

'Jamming, most likely,' Jesse said.

It made sense; their comms should get some interference from the ship's hull, but it shouldn't be completely unusable.

'If you're sticking with us, Danny, you're gonna need protection. Take this,' Jesse said suddenly, offering Danny a large pistol from his holster.

The heavy sidearm felt foreign but powerful. He recognised it as a modernised 1911 .45 ACP. It would pack a punch.

'You know how to use it?' Jesse asked.

Danny ejected the magazine and pulled back the slide, checking the chambered round before reloading the heavy pistol. He gave Jesse a cheeky smile in reply. 'Been to a range once or twice.'

Jesse nodded unemotionally. 'Let's go then.'

The diminished team charged down another corridor, Danny pulling up the rear, pistol in hand.

USS John Basilone

The static was becoming a problem.

'Sir, we're losing situational awareness of the team's progress. Alpha seems to have located the crew, possibly in the engine room. But Bravo and Charlie are almost impossible to understand.'

It was an unnecessary statement; the captain had the same channel. What was their next move?

'Understood, XO, we'll keep monitoring channels for now. The teams have their orders and know the timeframes. If we don't hear from them soon, we'll pull them out.' Both knew that would be easier said than done. The Huang Shen wasn't a small ship.

'This could be jamming, sir,' the XO said.

It had occurred to Jonathan; the hull of the Huang Shen wasn't thick enough to cause total communications failures. There just wasn't much they could do about it.

'Agreed, but it must be coming from inside the ship; our external comms don't appear to be affected.'

'Yes, sir, but it does worry me. Our teams might be walking into a trap. We wouldn't know or be able to help.'

'I know, but we have to trust them to do their jobs. The Seahawk will remain on station, and if needed, we'll medivac any wounded. For now, we wait, and we keep providing cover.'

'Aye-aye, sir. And the Chinese? They are only thirty minutes away.'

Jonathan checked his watch, 'They have fifteen minutes, XO, then we start pulling them out.'

'And if they need more time, sir?'

'Then we'll make sure we give it to them, XO.' There was a cold sternness to his voice.

'Aye, and the Malaysians?'

'They're coming, but they'll be late to the party. Once the Chinese arrive, we'll be on our own for a bit. But they should support us.'

'*Should*, sir?'

In reality, he didn't have any guarantees, but the Malaysian naval commander had seemed angry enough; they might just help.

'We'll see, XO.' He checked his watch again, another minute ticking by. 'I'm taking us up to general quarters. We'll need to be prepared.'

The XO's reply was cancelled out by the blaring klaxon sounding throughout the ship, 'General quarters, general quarters …'

Huang Shen

'We're running out of time, sir!' one of the unwounded sailors called out as they sprinted down another grim-looking corridor.

'We'll be fine,' Jesse shouted in reply from the front of their little squad, his voice calm and authoritative. The level of confidence and capability he was demonstrating suggested someone who was familiar with these kinds of environments.

Maybe not just a regular intelligence analyst, Danny mused.

How Jesse had ended up on their little project remained a mystery to him. It was true, he was a good analyst, but Jesse had skills and experience that suggested he was more suited to operational work. Danny made a mental note; another thing to follow up later when all of this was done.

They'd moved well past the ambush, backtracking a decent distance and up two flights of stairs. Danny pictured their route in his mind's eye. If he was correct, they'd be coming out somewhere above the path they'd tried to take, closer to the portside of the ship.

They couldn't feel it, but the Huang Shen was slowing to a stop. Alpha and Bravo had finally secured the engine room. However, stopping the ship in busy shipping lanes wasn't exactly a sure bet that they wouldn't run into trouble. Still, it was better than running uncontrolled. The packed strait wasn't getting any quieter, and the mass of commercial shipping around them was lingering just enough to slowly but surely create a growing cluster of vessels, all watching in anticipation. Already, news helicopters had spotted the encroaching Chinese coast-guard vessels and were eagerly awaiting a front-page-worthy event.

The group slowed as they approached another large metal door. Jesse crouched down, taking small, deliberate movements, keeping any noise to a minimum. In a painstakingly slow moment, he placed pressure onto the turning mechanism of the doorframe, easing the heavy door open inch by inch. Luckily, it didn't squeak or groan, and enough of a gap formed to permit them a look inside. As Danny poked his head through, the expanse of the cargo hold seemed to roll out in front of him. Lighting hung from above, projecting some illumination down towards them, but not much. Beyond the door, a metal catwalk extended across the side of the hold, providing a clear but exposed view around them. He couldn't see below them from his position, but the sound of movement and voices floated upward. They wouldn't be alone.

With the same care he had shown when opening the

door, Jesse eased it closed.

Danny realised he'd been holding his breath and exhaled when Jesse moved away from the door. 'Looks clear. We'll move onto the walkway and provide cover.' Everyone nodded.

His headset crackled into life as Jesse transmitted across the comms network. 'Charlie in position.' It sounded clear to Danny, but he was right next to Jesse. *Wonder what everyone else heard?* A quick reply put the thought to rest.

'Roger, breaching in sixty seconds. Mark.'

Danny wasn't sure who had replied, or what was being "breached". But at this point, he was well and truly along for the ride.

'Alright, we have at least two hostiles down on the deck, two floors below. They're manning a machine gun. We'll take position above them and wait until the guys below us breach. Then we'll take out the emplacement. Got it?'

Everyone nodded.

'Danny, you keep lookout, alright?' Jesse said, giving him a focused look. The message was clear: keep your head down, stay out of the way.

Jesse moved back to the door, quietly heaving it open again, just wide enough for them to slip through. He went first, signalling for the rest of the team to follow and stepping quietly over the threshold and onto the metal catwalk.

Danny found himself at the back of the small team. He closed his eyes and breathed deeply, trying to force his body to relax and slow his rapidly beating heart. Opening his eyes and exhaling, he followed the closest team member through the door.

The size of the hold was the first thing Danny noticed. Cavernous and expansive. Normally, these were stacked to the brim with containers, but this one was largely bereft of its usual cargo; only a small number of containers covered the hold's empty stacking bays. Dim lighting hung from the ceiling, doing a poor job of illuminating the area. Danny guessed there were normally a lot more lights available. Jesse and the two other sailors had quietly taken their positions along the railing of the walkway. By the looks of it, they were on the upper-most catwalk, looking down on the one below. Danny moved to the right of the team, kneeling down to try to make himself small against the darkened backdrop. Even with the pistol ready in his hand, he doubted he'd be able to use it effectively in this space. The distances were too far, and he hadn't done any shooting in a while. Staying out of the way until he was needed felt like the best policy.

Jesse nodded to the two armed sailors, whispering, 'Fire on my mark.'

Their enemy had set up a single light machine gun; bits of machinery and barrels had been stacked together to fortify their position. It was pointed directly at the damaged door they'd been ambushed at; if anyone tried to come through the main entrance below, they'd be forced into a kill zone.

A voice spoke into the team's ear, 'Breaching in five, four, three …'

Another bulkhead door to the left of the machine gun exploded open with considerable force, somehow staying on its hinges but swinging around and slamming into the metal wall next to it. Smoke and sparks showered outwards, obstructing the immediate view of the doorway. The two men below were clearly surprised, the machine gunner swinging his weapon around widely and letting off a quick burst in the direction of the blast.

Danny watched in fascination as Jesse calmly aimed down his sights, aligning the man's head with the red dot of his carbine. He thumbed the fire selector on the gun, switching to single shot before taking a deep breath and gently squeezing the trigger. The recoil was immediate. The bullet met its mark, burrowing into the side of the man's head, just under his helmet. The other sailors in the team opened fire as well, taking down the second hostile next to the gunner. A spray of dark-red blood covered the floor, the last sign of life from the two dead men. Danny was struck by how simply and quickly a life could disappear. They all shot within seconds of the door breach, somewhat masking the noise of their fire.

Danny heard Jesse say, 'Clear to enter,' to the team waiting below.

Danny was about to get up and move when he heard the scrape of a boot on metal below him. Peering through the grate at his feet, he was startled to see a man kneeling below him, looking up, a rifle in his hands. His brain went into a momentary sense of shock as the two of them locked eyes, before he blurted out, 'SHIT, BELOW!'

The man started raising his rifle to point it at Danny; he tried to raise his own sidearm, but he knew he was slower off the mark. Pushing off with his feet, he rolled heavily to his right, half throwing his body along the rough metal of the catwalk.

A mixture of automatic gunfire erupted around Danny. The sound of rending metal and flashes of sparks darted across his vision. Welding his eyes shut, he waited for the expected sharp pain of bullets entering his body. Instead, the world plunged into an eerie silence.

Opening his eyes, Danny could see Jesse reloading and the two other sailors aiming intently at the spot where the man had been only seconds before. The deck just below Jesse was glowing red and yellow where numerous bullets had slammed into the metal. The man was no longer there – had he escaped?

'Fuck me,' he muttered to himself.

'Good spot, Danny. You alright?'

'Other than just shitting myself and seeing my life flash before my eyes?'

'Nothing we can't clean up later,' Jesse replied, a small smile across his face. 'Let's get down there and find your missile.' He checked his watch. 'We're running out of time pretty quickly here.'

Danny had completely forgotten about their time limit.

The team quickly clambered down a metal stairway, every one of their footsteps seeming to reverberate across the entire space in a booming *clang* akin to thunder. As they crossed the lower catwalk, Danny looked up across the hold. Far away, at the other end, he caught the faintest glimpse of movement beneath one of the dull lights. Stopping to get a better look, he watched a second flicker of movement flash past.

'Where are they going?' he said to no one in particular.

'What was that?' interrupted Jesse over the comms.

Danny hadn't realised he'd opened his mic. Embarrassed for a moment before remembering he had valuable information to share, he said, 'Sorry, I just spotted something at the end of the hold. No idea how many people; just some movement near the lighting at the back.'

Danny heard Jesse grunt on the deck below him, 'Good spotting. Bravo, sweep and clear towards the rear.'

That answered one mystery for Danny; Bravo had arrived to support them.

In less than a minute, Danny and the rest of the team had reached the bottom level of the cargo hold. Now, at eye level with the poor offering of cargo containers, the hold seemed to loom over them; the dark corners and edges of the space were more prominent. Part of Danny longed to be back on the elevated railing – he'd had a better view from up there, even if he had been more exposed.

Jesse turned and looked at Danny with an appreciative gaze. 'Alright, Danny, this is your ship now – what are we looking for?'

With all the danger and excitement since boarding the ship, their mission to search for the prototype seemed like a distant memory. Yet, it was something Danny had spent a long time thinking about.

'They loaded a container onto this ship. The safest and most logical way to transport and study it would be to keep it in the container. We need to start ripping these open,' he said, gesturing at the various containers around them.

Jesse nodded. 'Alright, Charlie, let's start checking these containers. There aren't many, so it shouldn't take too long. Bravo Team, once you complete your sweep, move back and help us search. Everyone, look for any containers that are unlocked, and watch for booby traps. Let's get it done quickly; we are late as it is!'

The team members spread out. Danny decided to stick with Jesse. 'You know, I don't think you mentioned the part where you were some kind of special-forces-trained badass, Jesse.'

Jesse gave a cheeky grin. 'Ah, my resume isn't that exciting, Danny. You seem to be handling yourself fine,' he said, pointing to the pistol in Danny's hand.

Danny held his hands up in mock surrender. 'Hey, this is just for show – I'm just the civilian here, remember! But it's fine. You'll have to tell me about your resume one day.'

'Oh, well if I did that, I'd have to kill you,' Jesse said with a broad smile.

'Alright, 007, lead on.'

Might be an interesting conversation one day over beers, Danny mused. His friend was certainly more capable than he'd let on.

Jesse and Danny stayed a bit behind the rest of the team, checking the various nooks, crannies and doorways lining the hold floor. Nothing but storage cupboards and dust greeted them.

'I've got something over here,' one of the sailors from Bravo Team shouted out. Danny, Jesse and a small cluster of sailors all moved in closer to get a better look. 'The doors are open, and it looks like there is plastic sheeting covering the interior.'

Jesse was just about to tell him to hold his position and not touch anything when the sailor moved inside through the plastic sheeting. 'WAIT! STO—' was all Jesse got out before the blast that followed.

Unlike the blast that had ambushed the team only thirty minutes before, this one was short and sharp, almost like someone giving a loud, single clap with their hands. The sailor who'd opened the door was launched backwards ten metres, smacking into the floor with a sickening thud, then lying motionless. Everyone ran towards the explosion.

Jesse was the first to the container. Peering through the smoke, haze and burning plastic, Danny knelt by the motionless sailor. It looked like he was still breathing, but his right arm and right leg were bent at worrying angles, making the sailor's body appear like an oversized ragdoll. A medic rushed in after Danny, shoving him aside gently. 'Let me get a look,' he said calmly. Danny stood there, feeling useless as the medic worked on the man.

'DANNY! GET IN HERE!' Jesse bellowed from the still-smouldering doors of the container.

As he jogged over, the smell of explosive residue and burning plastic assaulted Danny's nose. It was clear that the room was a total loss. A metal table in the centre had a gaping hole down the middle, blasting outward. Danny guessed that was where the prototype had been; it was the logical spot. Numerous hard cases, computers and what otherwise could have been diagnostic tools lay ruined in the small space, burning and shattered. Danny stepped back out of the container so he could breathe.

'We need to put those fires out and secure what we can. Something might have survived,' he said to Jesse. 'If we can find anything that shows the prototype was here, and gives us some indication of whether they got anything from it, this will have all been worth it,' Danny muttered bitterly, a sense of frustration burning inside him. They'd come so close.

Jesse gave the orders to the various teams, organising collection and firefighting to save what they could.

The radio crackled to life urgently. 'This is Alpha Team. We've managed to get internal cameras working and disabled a small jammer. We've got a small group, no more than eight people, making a run from the cargo area towards the upper decks. At least three of the individuals are armed;

the rest appear to be civilians.'

Danny glanced back towards the far end of the cargo hold where he'd seen movement only a minute before.

Jesse sprang back into action. 'Roger that, Alpha. Charlie will pursue.'

'Bravo, keep this area secure and continue recovery operations. Charlie Team, on me!' He looked back at Danny, 'Might be worth having a chat with one of these guys. What do you say? Save us picking through the wreckage. Let's go!'

Danny ran after them, his heart in his throat, the fear and uncertainty of what he was stepping into returning. 'Where do they think they're going to go?' one of the sailors asked.

The answer came quickly.

'Attention, all teams, this is USS John Basilone – our time is up! We have incoming Chinese coast-guard vessels, and it doesn't look like they are here for a friendly chat. Prep for extract!'

'There's your answer. They are making a run for it,' Jesse replied, his voice deadpan.

CHAPTER 21

USS John Basilone – Malacca Strait

The gleam of the white-hulled ships with their dashing red and blue stripes down the forward bow loomed into view through Jonathan's binoculars. They were easily visible with the naked eye now, no longer tiny specks on a radar image or the horizon.

The coast-guard vessels hadn't missed a beat, sailing hard and fast from the moment they'd entered the strait. Their destination was never in doubt; they were headed directly for the Huang Shen and the USS John Basilone. Jonathan didn't like their position. Despite the John's better armaments and capabilities, at this close range, they could easily bring their main guns to bear against his ship. In a warfighting scenario, Jonathan would have dispatched these ships from over seventy kilometres away using an array of Harpoon and Tomahawk missiles, or he would have nailed them with his main gun. But they weren't at war – not yet. He couldn't open fire unless they threatened his ship and people. But now they were so close, if it came to that, it would be a brawl, and a dirty one at that.

Everyone on the bridge had donned helmets and vests.

Sailors were manning machine guns, muster stations and medical posts around the ship. No one would be sleeping or off shift. The call to general quarters put the entire ship's company to work, a wailing call over the speakers sending chills down everyone's spines.

Jonathan wouldn't move from his post. He'd remain on the bridge. He'd be at greater risk personally – the bridge was hardly the most protected part of the ship – but it was a risk he was willing to take. As was standard practice, the XO would man the CIC, ensuring that if Jonathan took a hit, the ship would continue to function.

'XO, I'll remain on the bridge. You have the CIC.'

The XO didn't show any surprise. He'd already figured his captain would want to be up top. His job would be to relay information from the CIC to Jonathan to help him make decisions. 'Aye-aye, sir.'

Turning back to the tactical display, Jonathan saw that the Malaysia Coast Guard and naval forces were still a good thirty minutes out from their position. With the Huang Shen now dead in the water, their location was largely locked in place. The complicating factor for Jonathan was the need to extract his men from the Huang Shen while keeping the Chinese vessels away. If they were able to encircle and block his access to the container vessel, his men could end up being hostages. But pulling them out would take time, especially with the wounded. The Seahawk had grabbed a couple of the more critically wounded, but each flight back and forth took time. The RHIBs would have to take the majority, but they'd be terribly exposed to the Chinese cutters in those small boats. The final complicating factor was the requirement to keep any equipment on the Huang Shen out of Chinese hands.

'How we looking on those Chinese helicopters, XO?'

'Coming in fast and low, sir.'

They had spotted the two Harbin Z-9s the moment they'd taken off from the destroyers. The USS John Basilone's powerful AN/SPY radar wouldn't miss much. Its

X and S bands constantly transmitted accurate tracking information and data back into the John's CIC. If they needed to engage them, they would have everything they'd need to do so. But without shooting them down, there wasn't much Jonathan could do to stop them from landing on the Huang Shen.

Looking down at a display, he watched the Chinese vessels, which were all approaching in a clean line towards him. Each ship was represented by a small red rectangle. They'd need to get in front of the arriving ships and create a buffer between them and the Huang Shen. The longer they could delay them, the better chance his teams would have at returning safely.

'All ahead full.'

'All ahead full; aye, sir,' responded the helmsman, pushing the throttle controls forward.

'We'll close with the coast-guard vessels and run interference. Put us directly between the Huang Shen and the coast-guard vessels,' Jonathan ordered the bridge. He needed his men and officers aware of his intentions. Everyone needed to be on the same page and understand the risks they'd be taking.

Time to warn the crew, Jonathan thought. 'Ship-wide comms,' he ordered a nearby sailor, who gave him the thumbs up when the intercom was active. 'This is the captain. China Coast Guard forces have arrived and look intent on disrupting our operation here. Be on alert and prepared for anything. We still have sailors onboard the Huang Shen, and recovering them safely is our highest priority. But they need time – time we're going to provide. We will not allow Chinese forces to board that vessel until everyone is off. I don't need to remind you of the incident in the Indian Ocean. If they attempt to ram us, we'll take defensive measures. Good luck, everyone. Let's show them what happens when they mess with the United States Navy.'

Huang Shen – Ming

Ming fingered the trigger of his sidearm as he peered through a crack in the open door. Things hadn't gone to plan so far. The Americans had been delayed, yes, but the losses were higher than they'd hoped, and any chance of holding them back was long gone. Ming wasn't actually sure how many of Jian's men were left alive. In fact, he wasn't sure if Jian was alive either. Not that he'd share that information with the scared group of civilians huddled behind him. The soldier with him certainly knew everything wasn't going to plan, but he remained stoic, keeping a close eye on the civilians and anything behind them.

They'd waited in a staff room, listening to the crackle and pop of gunfire for a good thirty minutes. But with the final explosion, everything had gone quiet, and Ming knew it was time to move. The last blast, he knew, was smaller, and expected. A defiant punch thrown at the Americans as they neared their victory. The container, the missile and everything else around it had turned to ash and fire. There would be little to recover, although Ming doubted it would be enough to completely remove any evidence of the missile. The smallest surviving scrap could tell a big story.

The task now was to escape. The men and women around him were some of the brightest and most talented in their respective fields. They couldn't allow them to be captured. The information they held was too valuable, and they wouldn't last long under any interrogation. They were just civilians, after all. Ming was sure the head scientist would be the first to crack.

Still, even their value paled in comparison to the data held inside the hard case Ming now carried. The complete downloaded archive of the missile: its operating systems, specifications and raw telemetry. With this, they could recreate the American missile. Hell, even improve it. He had to get the data out, if nothing else.

The small cluster had made their way cautiously down a

corridor near the cargo hold. Ming had spied a simple security camera as they moved, and he cursed. He'd forgotten to disable the internal CCTV network. A small oversight, but one that could give them away. Hopefully, the Americans hadn't checked the system. There wasn't anything he could do about it now anyway.

A sudden loud *clang* echoed from a door just in front of them. Ming immediately crouched down, holding his sidearm in his right hand, while the case remained firmly locked in his other. The small crowd gasped and tried to push back the other way, but they instead ran into each other, clumsily bumping the next person behind them. The stoic soldier simply stood there, rifle aimed down the corridor in the same direction as Ming's.

The door opened suddenly, banging against the wall, and a curse sounded out in Mandarin. Ming relaxed slightly but kept his weapon trained.

A panting Jian emerged seconds later. Holding his rifle in one hand, he looked down at the little group, somewhat dumbstruck, 'You're still here!?'

Ming lowered his gun. 'Just being careful, capt—'

'They're everywhere!' Jian interrupted. 'We don't have time to wait around – we've got to go!'

'Then let's go. Your men?' Ming asked, knowing the answer already.

'Dead,' Jian replied flatly, his voice devoid of emotion.

Ming nodded. 'Okay, le—'

A door swung open quietly back down the hallway they'd just come from. Ming turned, seeing the face and then full body of an unfamiliar soldier, his dress different from their own. Ming's mind was slow to catch up, until the soldier looked their way and his eyes widened.

'STAY WHERE YOU ARE!' the man bellowed in English. Ming understood him clearly; the stoic soldier, on the other hand, did not.

Spinning around on the spot, he let loose a wild burst at the American soldier. The rounds fell wide and instead pelted the wall near the man. The American leapt out of the way, back through the door he'd just come from.

Ming looked at Jian, who nodded back.

'TIME TO GO!' he bellowed at the group, setting off at a sprint down the corridor. There would be more Americans behind the one they'd just failed to kill. No point going slowly and quietly now. Their enemy knew where they were.

As he ran, a wide smile spread across his face. The sense of the chase, being hunted, outnumbered, filled Ming with a wild thrill. He was lucky he was in the front; no one could see his face. No doubt they'd think him mad, as their own faces were riddled with looks of terror and fear. Like little hunted rabbits.

Huang Shen – Danny

The lead sailor looked pale and shocked but largely unhurt. The burst of gunfire had surprised them all.

Jesse had one small peek around the corner, and another burst hit the wall next to his head. He moved away from the doorway, shaking his head, 'That's a long corridor with no cover; we're not getting in that way.'

'They're not trapped though. That is one of the main arteries in the ship; they can get to any of the decks from the stairway at the end of the corridor,' one of the sailors pointed out.

'Right – most logical escape route?' Jesse asked the group.

The idea seemed to appear in Danny's head, 'Gotta be a helicopter, right?'

Everyone looked at him suddenly. 'Only thing that makes sense; we control the ocean, at least for now ...' one of the sailors said.

'Alright, quickest way to the top deck?'

Another sailor pointed further back into the cargo hold. 'There's another way. If we go up the cargo hold catwalk, we should come out parallel to them; we can cut them off if we're quick.'

'Let's go!' Jesse said, charging off.

They ran up the two flights of stairs in the cargo hold at a flat sprint. Despite his best efforts, Danny started to lag behind the others on the second flight, his breathing increasingly laboured and ragged. By the time he pulled himself to the top of the second set of stairs, he was panting loudly, and the rest of the team were still running towards a far-off door.

Danny jogged after them doggedly, 'I'm going to have to get fit,' he muttered to himself. 'This is getting embarrassing.'

Jesse was waiting at the door when Danny arrived, sweating and breathing heavily. 'Alright, Usain, no need to give us such a head start.'

'Shut up,' was all Danny could muster.

Closing the door behind them, Jesse suddenly became serious. 'Danny, keep your weapon up.'

The order surprised Danny. He might have enjoyed the security and confidence carrying the gun gave him, but he hadn't expected to use it, and certainly not so soon. He did as he was told, keeping it firmly locked in his right hand, safety on and index finger straight.

'Alpha, what's the status of our friends? Where are they?' Jesse asked over the comms.

'Level one. Looks like they are heading for a stairway. They appear to be moving slowly; there are a few unarmed civilians with them, carrying cases.'

'Alright, guys, we are going to have company. We'll head them off at the adjacent stairway, hopefully take them by surprise. Let's go.'

Danny started to move forward, but Jesse put a hand on his chest, looking him in the eyes. 'Sorry, Danny, this isn't for you.'

Danny paused. A short-lived burst of shame and regret moved through his mind, before a larger feeling of relief washed over him. 'Okay.'

'Don't sweat it. But hey, I do need you to do something: watch our backs. There is more than one way out of here, and I need to know our retreat is covered. You cover this stairway and corridor, so if it goes to shit, we can get out of there. Got it?'

Danny nodded. 'Cover your ass, got it.'

Jesse smiled, 'You'll be a pro in no time. See you in a bit, Danny.'

He darted off to follow the other sailors. Danny was alone, surrounded by the grim metal walls and corridors of the container ship. He thumbed his sidearm. No point standing out in the open, he mused. There was a large metal pipe he could get some cover behind while still covering the stairway. *That's my spot.*

Minutes passed in what felt like hours, no new information or noise coming from the direction his team had run off in. Danny fidgeted in the dark hallway. The adrenaline was wearing off, allowing his mind to wearily start processing everything that had and was happening. His ears were filled with updates from the other teams. It sounded like they were all preparing to leave. Bravo team had finished collecting the shattered fragments of whatever had been in the container, while Alpha was making sure the Chinese crew didn't try anything before they had the chance to leave. They'd be the last team out.

A distant noise from down the hallway made Danny look up. The darkened hallway didn't reveal anything. He couldn't see his team. Only emergency lighting seemed available in this part of the ship. He listened intently, his ears met with only an eerie silence that shattered seconds later, as distant but clear gunshots resounded down the hallway. There weren't any flashes, and there weren't any whizzes or pinging noises. So, the shots weren't coming his way. But the gunfire was intense, coming in long, loud bursts. A larger blast sounded out, and the shooting went quiet. The seconds crept by, and panic started to rise inside Danny.

Touching his microphone, he whispered, 'Jesse?' getting

only silence in return. 'Charlie? You guys okay?'

Silence.

'Guys?' The walls seemed to close in on Danny. If something had happened to Jesse, what would he do? What if there were hostiles heading this way? He instinctively aimed his sidearm at the hallway, listening intently and trying to hold his overwhelming sense of fear at bay.

He didn't hear the steps; nor did he hear the mechanism unlock. The wall next to him shifted suddenly, slamming into the left side of his body and hitting his shoulder first before pushing him over. Danny felt the gun slip from his grip, and the ground came rushing towards him. He felt a pulling sensation at his helmet and headphones as he fell; something snapped and came free. He launched himself into a half somersault before whacking his head on the adjoining wall and landing on his ass. The impact hurt. It took a few moments to understand what had happened. The wall he'd been standing next to had actually been a door, hidden in the dark lighting. He'd been so intently focused on the hallway in front of him that he'd failed to notice the door – that was, until it had knocked him over as it was flung open. The person opening it had clearly intended to use a lot of force.

Now, the man standing over him with a pistol in hand was hard to miss.

He had a strong jawline, freshly shaved, and light Asian features. He looked down at Danny in surprise before pulling his sidearm up and aiming it at Danny with one hand in a swift and practised motion.

Danny just looked at him stupidly, hands to his side, sitting on the floor with his legs out in front of him. The man paused, keeping his gun on Danny but not pulling the trigger, not yet. A couple of seconds passed by before the man bent down, placing what looked like a metal case on the ground. *Curious*, a voice in Danny's mind said.

The man took a step forward. Danny looked down, seeing his handgun sitting a foot in front of his feet. He momentarily considered reaching for it, but the man had him dead to rights; he would never be faster than what it would take him to pull the trigger. His only saving grace was that he hadn't pulled it yet.

The man knelt down in front him and scooped up the pistol, keeping his sidearm trained on Danny. With a second weapon in hand, he did something Danny didn't expect. He started grinning mischievously.

'I've always wanted one of these,' he said in perfect English, taking his eyes off Danny to inspect the powerful Colt M45A1 in his hand. 'And taken from an American solider … Not how I expected to get one.'

Despite the gun trained on him, the metal case the man had put down on the floor caught Danny's eye. What was it? Why was this man carrying it? His mind quickly connected the dots – it held something important. Noticing the man's momentary distraction as he sized up the stolen handgun, Danny seized the opportunity, flinging his right foot out, connecting the corner of the case and sending it flying against the wall. By some stroke of luck, he hit it just right, and it snapped open, revealing rows of hard drives neatly tucked into foam pouches.

The man above him, not expecting the sudden move, was slow to react. Jumping back slightly, he refocused his pistol towards Danny.

'I'M NOT A SOLDIER … or sailor!' Danny blurted out, his hand up in a sign of surrender.

The shot never came. The man eyed him carefully. 'Then what are you?'

'Just a man way out of his depths.' It was the truth.

The man seemed to inspect him again, pausing, 'Hmmm … Yet here you are, alone, on this ship, at this moment. Perhaps not so out of your depths as you might think?'

Danny eyed the man's gun, still aimed at him. Somewhere behind him, a distant shout sounded out. A wave of fear washed over him, and he shook slightly. 'What are you going to do with me?' he asked quietly.

The man kept his eyes fixated on Danny. 'What is your name?'

He answered the question automatically, speaking quietly, 'Daniel.'

The man stared at him for a moment longer, the mischievous grin never quite leaving his face. 'Well, Daniel, lucky for you, I am in a rush, and killing an unarmed man is not my style. Perhaps you might consider staying back in your office next time?'

Danny blinked. Why was he having a conversation with this man? What was going on here? 'Okay,' was all he managed.

Another distant yell appeared from behind him. The man looked up quickly before returning his gaze to Danny. 'I'll be seeing you, Daniel. Oh, and I'm keeping this,' he smiled, waving Danny's sidearm in the air. He took a step back, giving Danny a quick two-finger salute and another grin. He picked up the case, snapping it closed once again, and disappeared down the metal corridor at a run.

Danny was still on his ass. *Did that just fucking happen?* was all he could think.

A sudden rattle of feet against the hard metal floor sounded out behind him. Danny jerked his head around towards the growing noise. *This could be it*, he thought grimly. Without a gun, and still sitting on his backside, he didn't have many options. He had started to rise when the first person rounded the corner.

'What are you doing on the floor, Danny?!' Jesse yelled, panting hard. 'C'mon, man, we've got to go! We've been trying to get you on comms.'

For the first time, Danny realised his headphones were no longer on his head. Jesse grabbed him from behind and hauled him up. 'You alright? Where's your gun?'

'I, um, had a bit of an encounter.'

Jesse looked at him, confused and stupefied for a second. His eyes focused past Danny, looking at the open door. 'Shit. Where did he go?'

Danny pointed behind him, 'That way. He was carrying some kind of case. What happened to you guys? I heard all the shooting and an explosion.'

'Some genius decided to chuck another grenade at us.' Danny noticed the soot that had settled on all of the team members. 'Safe to say they failed, but they made a run for it. I'm guessing they're all going the same place your guy went.'

'Yeah, okay,' Danny said, a slight sense of shock moving through his body. Had he just come close to death? Why hadn't the soldier killed him? What was on the hard drives? The questions started to pile up.

'Alright, let's go. Danny, you're with me. We're not finished here yet.'

They went straight back to sprinting, charging up a nearby stairway, heading towards the open deck of the container ship. Unaware of what was happening outside.

USS John Basilone

'Helm, bring us smartly to port, make heading 030 degrees. Commence screening,' Jonathan ordered crisply.

'Aye, sir. Smartly to port, heading 030 degrees.'

Jonathan grasped the nearest console as the USS John Basilone heaved to port. They were close to two kilometres from the Huang Shen now. Further away from it than Jonathan would have liked, but still within range to support if needed. It was more important they gave the teams on board as much time as possible before the Chinese arrived. Every minute would count.

'Weps, maintain solutions against those three ships; prioritise the biggest and work down from there. If any one of them tries to ram us, we'll fire warnings and go from there.'

'Aye-aye, sir.'

'Comms, keep sending out those warnings, and advise if a reply is received.'

'Aye-aye, sir.'

'XO, keep an eye on those two destroyers. You let me know the moment they try anything.'

'Understood, sir.'

Jonathan gave the orders rapid fire, all the while watching the three Chinese coast-guard vessels loom into view. He'd positioned his ship to cut across the front of them, screening them from the Huang Shen. The captains of those ships would have to split up and manoeuvre around the USS John Basilone if they wanted to reach the container ship. The trick would be to constantly pressure the Chinese while keeping them from ramming distance. He had no doubt they'd try to strike him with one of their vessels; it was a classic Chinese tactic, and he'd have to react. For now, though, he'd have to resist the urge to use lethal force against them. A shooting match out here, and this close to enemy vessels, would not be to his ship's benefit. Better to be a constant pest, forcing the Chinese to react to him, not the other way around. The only real problem was the helicopters. The two Harbin Z-9s had been deployed from the Chinese navy destroyers earlier and had flown straight and true towards his position. Now, hovering nearby, they were a nuisance, and there wasn't much Jonathan could do about it. He'd have to shoot them down to stop them, and realistically, there was nothing stopping them from landing on the Huang Shen and dropping off troops.

Jonathan had pointed his main gun, the Mark 45 127 mm, to starboard, aimed directly at the oncoming vessels. It was a clear enough signal: he had the firepower, and he would use it. He only hoped the Chinese blinked first.

His plan was to interfere and annoy, putting the John Basilone in the path of any oncoming Chinese vessel. Hopefully they'd break apart and he could interfere more freely, but if they stuck together, they'd be a powerful and difficult grouping. The Chinese vessels approached directly on, holding a tight V formation, with the largest vessel in the middle up front and two smaller ones on each side.

'Gotta be a Zhaotou-class cutter, sir, at least 12,000

tonnes,' an able seaman said.

Jonathan nodded; it was a big ship, and with a big seventy-six-millimetre cannon mounted on its bow. The Zhaotou could do a lot of damage very quickly. At this range, even the smaller cutter could seriously wound his ship. They were designed for long-range missile duels, not World War 2 slugging matches at point-blank range. If they started shooting, it wouldn't be pretty.

'Commencing manoeuvre, sir,' called the helmsman, a baby-faced young man, barely in his twenties by Jonathan's guess. But he was fiercely capable and an expert at controlling the large vessel. He'd need all of the kid's genius.

Amongst the background noise of the bridge, Jonathan could hear the comms officer throwing increasingly harsh messages towards the Chinese ship, switching between English and Mandarin. 'Attention, Chinese coast-guard vessels! Attention, Chinese coast-guard vessels. This is an active United States naval operation; you are to depart the area immediately. Failure to comply will result in you being designated as hostile and treated accordingly.' The officer kept repeating the call. Normally, the Chinese would play the game, yelling their own orders back. But there was no reply. Jonathan felt a chill run up his spine.

He spotted the movement just before one of the lookouts sounded the alarm. 'Sir, Chinese helicopters are making a run for the Huang Shen!' Both had split around the USS John Basilone, waiting until the John had committed to its turn. All they could do was watch.

'Warn the Seahawk. What's the status of the teams?' Jonathan called, steadying himself as the ship returned to a fully upright position, completing its turn.

'Medivacs are complete. But all three are still aboard the Huang Shen.'

They were taking too long.

'Call a withdrawal, get all teams to return to RHIBs and load anyone we can onto the Seahawk. *Now!*' Jonathan just hoped they'd recovered what they could.

The USS John Basilone sliced through the water, its props churning the ocean below it. 'Passing across the first Chinese vessel.'

Jonathan held up his binoculars, trying to see into the bridge of the smaller coast-guard cutter. They were still at least a few hundred metres apart. Little men in white uniforms could be seen scrambling around the ship.

'No sign of recognition or attempts to avoid us,' the officer of the watch called out.

'Guns are manned!' a lookout yelled.

The tension was building in the bridge. 'Keep calm, everyone. We're trained for this, and we're the big fish here,' Jonathan said loudly. He needed everyone calm and focused.

'Coast-guard ships are increasing in speed,' came another call.

So that's how it's going to be, he thought. Clearly the Chinese wanted to force their way through. Not unexpected, but highly aggressive all the same.

'Increase speed to flank,' Jonathan ordered calmly. 'Maintain speed and commence hard turn to starboard. We'll give them something more to think about.'

Everything started to move faster now.

'Sir, Seahawk is reporting one of the enemy helicopters has taken position on the bow of the Huang Shen, hovering in position. The second appears to be following the Seahawk.'

Jonathan had only just started to consider the information when the officer spoke again. 'Sir! Seahawk reports a large group of people just emerged from an entrance near the bow. Looks like they are running towards the Chinese helicopter … wait … And a second group has emerged. Seahawk confirms it looks like Charlie!'

He could hear the excitement coming from the younger man's voice. A notable buzz was moving through the crew now, the excitement of action filling their voices. He'd have to be careful here, make sure everyone remained calm and professional.

'Keep me updated.'

He wanted to tell Charlie to disengage, but he knew it would be too late. And right now, he needed to ensure the protection of the ship. He steadied himself as the ship leaned to starboard, harder this time under increased speed. His world took a 45-degree tilt.

'Rotate weapons!' the gunnery officer yelled before they'd completed the turn.

'Tracking!' one of the seamen called out.

'Sir! Seahawk is reporting gunfire on the Huang Shen!'

Ah shit, here we go, Jonathan thought.

Huang Shen – Danny

The bright beams of light blinded Danny momentarily as they burst out onto the top deck of the Huang Shen. He covered his eyes, squinting to see anything around him. Slowly, his vision adjusted, and he started to make sense of the shapes and objects around him. The rest of the team must have been better prepared; they sprinted off, leaving Danny to play catch up.

It didn't take Danny long to realise what was happening. The Chinese had a head start on them and were running down the length of the ship towards the bow. The rest of Charlie were chasing.

Danny followed, taking a deep breath and pushing his body on, legs and lungs burning. *Where are they going?* he wondered, but the question was answered for him.

A black, sleek-looking helicopter swooped in across the ship. The large red star of the Chinese military dominated its side. It moved parallel to the Huang Shen, heading directly for the bow. It would be the fleeing group's escape if they didn't get to them first.

The air seemed to buzz with the sound of rotor blades. The ocean met Danny's gaze as he looked to his left. The USS John Basilone wasn't anywhere to be seen, just commercial vessels. But the John's Seahawk hovered nearby, looking fully loaded with sailors. It seemed to be keeping its distance from another black Chinese helicopter that was circling it. Without his headphones, the noise was horrendous; the buzz of blades washed out anything else. He turned his head back, focusing on the increasingly distant figures of his team.

He was slower, tired and not nearly as fit as the rest of his team. Part of him knew he couldn't catch them, but that logical side was pushed aside; they were his team, and he had to be there with them.

As Danny struggled to catch up, he noticed one member of Charlie sprinting ahead of the rest. He could see Jesse reach out to try and hold the man back, but he missed. It took Danny precious few seconds to understand what was happening as he neared them.

One of the fleeing Chinese civilians had fallen behind the rest of the group, visibly limping. Seeing the slowing man, one member of Team Charlie had made a final push and charged forward. With surprising speed, the sailor closed the gap between himself and the limping civilian. In one swift movement, the sailor bent down low and grabbed the civilian around the waist. The smaller man let out a yell of surprise and fear as he was lifted off the ground before being slammed back into it in a heavy tackle.

Danny neared the remaining members of his team, hearing distant, angry shouting from the fleeing Chinese group ahead.

'Ah shit, everyone watch out!' Jesse yelled, furiously calling the other sailor back.

The first Chinese helicopter had just landed twenty metres ahead of them, the side door sliding open to reveal a soldier manning a mean, heavy-looking machine gun. The soldier wasted no time, yelling something unheard to the fleeing group in front of him while aiming the machine gun towards Danny and the team.

Danny watched in semi-shocked fascination as the

fleeing group threw themselves on the ground in front of the helicopter. Jesse and the other member charged back towards Danny, Jesse waving his hands wildly and screaming, 'COVER!'

The other member of Charlie was busy wrestling with his captive and was unaware of his surroundings in all the chaos.

Jesse, Danny and the last team member all crashed behind a heavy, thick metal unit as the Chinese soldier depressed the trigger on his machine gun, letting loose a steady stream of deadly rounds. The heavy booming blasts of the gun washed out the roar of the rotor blades around them.

The sound of gunfire broke the focus of the two men who were wrestling on the ground. Their fellow Charlie team member reacted on instinct. Seeing the machine gunner aiming in his direction, he rolled off the man he'd tackled, hitting the deck and pointing his carbine at the source of danger. It didn't occur to him that if the gunner had been trying to kill him, he'd already be dead. The idea that the shots were warning shots never crossed his mind. He lined up the gunner in his reticule and squeezed the trigger, letting off a short burst of poorly aimed rounds. He didn't wait to see if he'd hit the man, instead rolling again to try and get out of the line of sight of the machine gunner.

The rounds smacked into the side of the helicopter next to the gunner's head, hitting nothing important but making the gunner flinch. It took his mind microseconds to realise someone had just tried to kill him. A surge of adrenaline and anger washed through the gunner's body as he levelled the gun lower, taking aim at the foolish American in front of him.

Seahawk – Huang Shen

It went to hell so quickly.

Lieutenant Molina watched from afar as the landed

Chinese helicopter opened fire on the team below her. Caught out in the open, one member of the group darted for cover, almost making it before dropping still against the hard deck below. The rest of the team took cover behind whatever they could.

'BREAK, BREAK, BREAK!' she called, clearing the comm network to the USS John Basilone. 'Charlie team is taking fire. I repeat: Charlie team is under fire. Requesting orders.' She had already begun to rotate the Seahawk when her headset came alive.

'Protect Charlie, Seahawk. Lethal response authorised.'

She switched to the helicopter's local net, 'JIMMY! LETHAL FORCE AUTHORISED, ENGAGE THAT HELO!'

The door gunner threw her a quick thumbs up, his powerful M240 machine gun already lined up with the sitting Chinese helicopter. He breathed in deeply before squeezing the triggers with his thumbs. There wasn't any serious wind, and the helicopter wasn't rocking around. It was one of the easiest shots he'd ever taken. The belt-fed ammunition rattled against its feeder, while the heavy gun recoiled against the burst of rounds flying out of its long, suspended barrel. It was a short burst, no more than eight to ten rounds, but they found their mark. The gunner in the Chinese helicopter spasmed as he was impacted. There was no blood, but he slumped forward, his own machine gun pointing to the sky, silent.

'Enemy gunner neutralised!' the door gunner called back coolly.

Despite the sudden death of their colleague, the Chinese helicopter seemed to spring to life. A large group charged forward, diving into any empty space they could. A couple of armed soldiers shouldered their rifles and started firing wildly back at the Seahawk, but they wouldn't have much luck hitting them at this range.

'Better luck next time, boys,' Molina muttered.

She'd just begun to press her radio send button when

she noticed something appear in her periphery. Someone yelled from the cabin inside the helicopter, 'WATCH OUT!' Acting out of instinct, she flicked her HOTAS, pulling her Seahawk down. She just caught sight of the other Chinese Z-9 taking aim at them, far too close for comfort.

A whizzing noise filled the crowded interior of the helicopter a second later. The rattle of Chinese machine guns followed shortly after that. Someone yelled in pain, while others called out in fear. The door gunner on the other side of the Seahawk cursed loudly as he tried to bring his own weapon to bear, but the sudden movement made it difficult.

The Seahawk dived towards the sea, riding close to the side of the Huang Shen. Molina hauled her HOTAS back towards her, the co-pilot yelling into the comms while trying to spot the Chinese helicopter.

'This is Seahawk 1. We are taking small-arms fire from a Chinese helicopter. Again, we are taking fire!' the co-pilot yelled, panic filling his voice.

The fully laden Seahawk skimmed the water before its powerful engines pushed its rotors hard enough to claw back skyward. Alarms and warnings sounded throughout the cockpit. The co-pilot yelled warnings and flicked switches as quickly as possible.

Molina tried to level off, keeping the helicopter low against the side of the container ship while trying to maintain some forward momentum and speed. Both the water below them and the wall of the Huang Shen seemed too close for comfort.

'It's coming around!' one of the door gunners yelled, still trying to get a clean shot, but the pursuing helicopter had the advantage of height and speed. Sure enough, the Chinese helicopter was above them, moving parallel to them and giving them a nice clean shot against the struggling Seahawk. Molina saw the muzzle flashes before she heard the sound of rounds impacting the helicopter, making a frightening metal *clang* with each hit. She pulled her controls to the left, trying to get under the other helicopter's firing arch. The barrage stopped, but a bullet must have found something important. The controls felt slacker, but the power remained.

'Losing hydraulic pressure!' the co-pilot confirmed.

She pushed the pedals at her feet, forcing more power into the engines, lifting higher against the Huang Shen and passing its bow. The pursuing Chinese helicopter followed like a hawk, waiting for the right moment to strike.

Molina didn't have many good choices; their only real chance would be the USS John Basilone. She just needed to give them a clean shot.

'Let the John know we're coming in hot!' she yelled, turning the Seahawk towards the American warship, which was at least two kilometres away. The Chinese helicopter followed them, using every chance to fire upon the fleeing Americans.

She wanted to evade, but the controls felt looser and looser as the John loomed into view. 'Hold on everyone, this is going to get bumpy!'

The Chinese helicopter pilot was smart enough to move behind the Seahawk, keeping any supporting fire from the John blocked, but following them this close, with such murderous intent, was madness.

Another spray of rounds impacted the Seahawk, shattering one of the windows near Molina, the glass shards cutting her face. 'Right,' she said simply to herself, a growing rage replacing any feelings of fear. She stayed focused on the warship in front. She waited until she could see the Phalanx CIWS turning to face them. Pushing the Seahawk one last time, she dived suddenly, dropping precious metres back towards the sea, then yanking her HOTAS hard over to the right. The sudden move caught the pursuing pilot off guard.

The Phalanx Close-In Weapon System, or simply CIWS, designed to destroy incoming airborne threats, was a death-dealing weapon capable of throwing huge amounts of munitions towards a target. Pronounced *Sea-Wiz*, it moved in darted motions, tracking the hostile helicopter with robotic speed and cold accuracy. The precious seconds it took for the pursuing pilot to react were more than enough. The crew of the Chinese helicopter never heard the chainsaw like *bzzzzzzt* of the Phalanx cannon. At less than 500 metres, the stream of M56A3 high-explosive incendiary rounds tore the helicopter apart in milliseconds, entering through the cockpit and exiting through the other side. In less than a second, a thousand rounds had been fired at the helicopter. There would be no survivors. To the human eye, it simply exploded in a fiery boom before crashing into the water below.

Without skipping a beat, Molina pulled the damaged helicopter up from the ocean just below, increasing power and banking hard. 'C'mon, baby, just a little bit more,' she willed the helicopter on.

Just as they whizzed past the stern landing deck, she pulled her HOTAS back, slowing the helicopter while rotating it to the right. For everyone inside, their point of view shifted rapidly as the tail rotor span around, bringing them into line with the landing deck.

Something whizzed by suddenly, another round just missing them. Molina didn't bother to look for it. The helicopter was dying. 'HOLD ON EVERYONE!' she yelled out, driving them downward.

She was still too fast and came in too hard, but it didn't matter. With a power crash and thud, the helicopter smacked into the deck, its hydraulic landing gears protesting the sudden impact, buckling under the weight. The passengers gasped as they made contact with the deck, adrenaline coursing through them. The helicopter bounced slightly, edging closer to the stern superstructure of the John Basilone. She could feel it die, the engine whining as it slowed and halted, quicker than it should.

'Thank you,' she muttered quietly to the broken machine.

Another *whizz* sounded out, and another. The noise of the helicopter had been replaced with the loud drumming of heavier automatic gunfire. She recognised it immediately. 'Everyone off the chopper! GO GO GO, people!'

The side doors flung open, Molina and her co-pilot not bothering with the usual checklist and protocols. She unbuckled her harness and leapt out onto the hard deck of the John, taking a quick glance across the ocean.

The Chinese ships were impossible to miss. Only a few hundred metres away, small flashes and puffs of smoke rose from the bow of one of the smaller ships: the source of the whizzing sounds.

'Everyone into the hangar!' one of the flight crew ordered.

Another sailor with a loaded rifle took a knee, lining up the Chinese ship and squeezing off a few rounds.

'Leave it, you idiot!' Molina yelled, grabbing the man and yanking him backwards towards the open door.

The air felt angry, the noise of incoming rounds growing with more whizzes, cracks and metal clangs. Hauling the man behind her, Molina charged through the opening.

She turned, panting, and took one last look out. The cockpit of the helicopter shattered suddenly as a larger round impacted it. Fear and anger rose in her chest as the heavy door was slammed shut, the round of enemy fire lessening but not gone.

They were in it now.

Z-9 Helicopter – Ming

Ming watched with slight bemusement as the last of the civilians piled aboard the bloodied helicopter.

'GO!' Jian shouted at the pilot, who obliged immediately, lifting them skyward.

A few more desultory shots came their way, but they were out and free. They'd beaten the Americans and got out with the case.

Lifting away from the deck, Ming spied the Americans who had been chasing them coming out from their cover. The man Ming had met in the hallway was with them, unarmed and looking out of place. He gazed up at Ming's fleeing helicopter, mouth open.

Grinning, Ming waved at him casually, knowing it was a strange action given the circumstances. But he didn't care; he felt good. *What a thrill!*

A blast rocked the helicopter suddenly, and Ming's head darted towards the nose, spotting a dissipating fireball in the distance towards the American ship.

'Bastards!' Jian cursed angrily.

'What happened?' Ming asked, confused.

'They just killed one of the helicopters!' he seethed. His look of anger shifted rapidly to one of malice. 'We'll get them back,' he said, pulling a small device from his chest rig.

Ming eyed the device, recognising it as a radio transmitter, specifically used for detonating explosives.

'What is that?!' he demanded.

Jian smiled back, 'A little surprise for the Americans,' he said, depressing the trigger.

A deeper blast followed. The Huang Shen seemed to almost lift upward, huge plumes of water, fire and smoke pouring from its sides.

'What did you do?' Ming said furiously. 'The crew is still down there!'

Jian kept smiling, 'A problem for the Americans. They have to rescue their own people, *and ours*, now.' There was a deadly finality to his voice.

Ming wanted to strangle the man, but he knew better than to show his true emotions. He'd make sure Jian's actions didn't go unpunished.

But, for now, the cramped helicopter flew on, the clear blue skies and procession of commercial traffic betraying the chaos below. A sudden deep sadness seemed to wash over Ming. Despite his victory and success, he now felt empty, hollow.

Huang Shen – Danny

Danny watched the Chinese helicopter disappear into a ball of fiery metal in the distance and simply stood there, frozen in a stunned silence. Things had got out of control so quickly. Seeing the helicopters attacking each other before getting shot down was something else. Weapons of war were now doing their best to end each other's lives, and it would only get worse.

The Seahawk had probably saved their lives, but not everyone's. One of the team remained face down, unmoving on the deck. Jesse had rushed to him but realised there was nothing to be done the moment he arrived. The rest of the Chinese soldiers and civilians had managed to flee – even the man who'd been tackled. Watching them fly away left a sour taste in Danny's mouth. The final insult had been the sight of the man who'd spared him, giving him a little wave as the helicopter lifted off. Danny couldn't think of anything more absurd.

The helicopter had flown away fast enough; clearly it had somewhere else to be and didn't want to share the fate of its sister.

'Alright, everyone, I think it's time we got off this ship,' Jesse said to Danny and the other members of Charlie.

'What about the helicopter?' Danny asked.

'Nothing we can do about it now, and considering we just shot down one of theirs, the Chinese are going to be pissed. We're sitting ducks here.'

Jesse didn't wait for anyone to reply, immediately turning his attention to his headset. 'Alpha, Bravo, is there anyone left on the Huang Shen?'

Danny watched him, unable to hear the conversation without his headset.

'Looks like we're lucky last; they're waiting for us below.'

'I've had enough of playing sailor, I think,' Danny said, a weariness starting to drag on his body now that the adrenaline wasn't pumping.

It was a short trip back into the ship and down towards the pilot's entrance: just another airtight door, but much closer to the water. The other member of Charlie had just grabbed onto the ladder when the ship rumbled deeply, vibrating.

'What th—' was all Danny managed before he was knocked over, his world becoming a jumbled mess of sounds and colour.

He could sense something shoving him violently from behind before feeling a sense of weightlessness overcome him, quickly followed by the shock of water smashing against his body. Blackness. Nothingness followed. But only momentarily. Sounds and light returned, but he felted surrounded, covered in … *He was in the water.* His mind panicked slightly as he fought upward, gasping for air. A hand grabbed him from somewhere, and before he knew it, he was face up, spluttering and feeling confused. He could hear voices yelling, but he couldn't make sense of it. Everything felt mumbled and confused. As he shook his head, his blurred vision came into focus, enough that he could see smoke pouring out of the side of the Huang Shen. *What the hell?*

Someone unseen yelled out over the sound of crashing and booming, 'Man overboard!'

Pulling himself up, he realised he was lying in the RHIB. 'How the hell did I get here?' he murmured to himself, still confused.

Another urgent, panicked voice added to the chaos, 'Do you see him? We've got wounded over here! We've gotta go!'

'Not until we get EVERYONE!' someone screamed angrily.

Regaining his senses, Danny realised he could see injured sailors around the RHIB. The few unhurt were trying to fish people out of the water. As he scanned the RHIB, Danny realised that the familiar face of Jesse was missing.

'Where's Jesse?!' Danny called out urgently.

'He went in over there!' a sailor replied, midway through hauling another limp body back into the RHIB. He motioned towards a dark patch of water with his head.

Without hesitation, Danny dived back over, swimming the few metres and duck-diving under, taking a deep breath.

Fumbling around in the dark water, he couldn't see anything, but sure enough, his hand felt the skin of another. Holding on tight and kicking his legs as powerfully as he could, he pulled upwards, dragging the dead weight of the body with him. He didn't feel as though he was very deep, but with every kick, he failed to breach the surface. His lungs started screaming as the urge to breathe began to overcome him. His mind was robotic, '*kick, kick kick.*' Suddenly breaking the surface, he gasped for air, drawing in as much oxygen as he could. Pulling the limp body up, he tried to hold the face of the person upright, giving them a chance to breathe.

'Help him out!' someone yelled, which was soon followed by the sound of someone splashing into the water next to Danny.

Together, they kicked towards the RHIB, hands reaching down to help haul the body up. Danny held on to the side of the inflatable hull, panting heavily, the exertion taking everything from him.

Another pair of hands reached over, pulling him up by the back of his belt. Seconds later, Danny was back in the RHIB.

Jesse was there, lying quietly against one of the chairs, a paleness to his otherwise tanned skin.

Forgetting his breathlessness, Danny moved over quickly, giving Jesse a shake. 'C'mon, man, wake up.' Jesse's head lolled from side to side, his face expressionless.

Danny shook him harder, 'C'MON!'

The lifeless body seemed to shudder before violently coughing up water all over the bloodied deck of the RHIB. A small groan exited Jesse's lips, followed by more stillness.

'Let me in!' another sailor ordered, pushing Danny out

of the way, med kit in hand.

The sailor checked his pulse quickly before tying a tourniquet tightly around Jesse's arm, 'He's alive, but he's in a bad way.'

For the first time, Danny saw a large red patch forming over Jesse's right arm. The sailor tending to him cut away the sleeve of his uniform, revealing a large piece of metal protruding from Jesse's arm. Danny's eyes widened; the chunk of metal was large.

'Hold this. Wrap it around the wound!' the sailor ordered, handing Danny a bundle of gauze.

Doing as he was told, he wrapped it tightly around the piece of shrapnel, the bandage quickly turning red. Danny wasn't a doctor by any account, but that much blood loss could be fatal, he knew that much.

Taking a quick survey around him, Danny saw that some of the panic appeared to have passed. Only a few metres away, the smoking wreck of the Huang Shen was sitting seemingly lower in the water than before.

'Is everyone accounted for?' Danny called out to no-one in particular.

'Yes, sir!' a young sailor replied, not recognising Danny as a civilian.

'Then let's get out of here and back to the John! Cut a direct path!' Danny didn't realise he was giving an order. The call just seemed logical. They had to move. They had to save Jesse and the others.

The RHIBs throttled up their engines, each carrying a load of wounded sailors. Danny felt the power of the engines as they began to move across the ocean, away from the danger of the Huang Shen. The thud and crash of explosions and gunfire surprised Danny. *What was going on?*

USS John Basilone

They hadn't hesitated to open fire against the Chinese helicopter. From the moment it had fired on the Seahawk,

Jonathan had ordered the CIC to protect the Seahawk, the rules of engagement changing in an instant. Watching it harass his own had been difficult, but when the opportunity had presented itself, the XO gave the order rapidly, the operator pressing the "fire" button on their console, taking the weapon into manual fire mode and making the powerful Phalanx blast out death.

The announcement that the target had been destroyed had been wholly unnecessary, as the bridge crew had watched the helicopter's fiery descent. They were in a new game now.

'Hard to port, making heading 290, increase speed to flank!' he ordered the helmsman rapidly.

Jonathan already knew the Chinese reaction; it would be the same as his. The ship began its sudden, vibrating tilt as the vessel powered through, cutting the water below.

'Get the Seahawk on board and secured. Get those RHIBs back to the ship ASAP!' Jonathan yelled at the Boatswain's mate.

'Chinese vessels are increasing in speed!' a lookout called from across the bridge.

'XO, looks like we're going to be in a fight here soon. I'm going to try and put some distance between us, but the moment they move in, hit 'em with EW – blind them,' Jonathan ordered.

The ship was equipped with the standard AN/SLQ-32, or Slick-32, employed on most American and allied warships. The powerful yet aged array of jammers, sensors and antennae could turn even the most sophisticated systems and radars into a blotchy, unreadable soup. In this case, it would hopefully confuse and hamper the coastguard ships' efforts to coordinate, although at this range, they'd have no trouble using more traditional forms of naval communication and weaponry.

'Captain, the other Z-9 is making a direct route toward the Chinese destroyers. It's leaving the area of operations. Do you have any orders?'

Jonathan thought for a moment. 'No, leave it, XO. We've got other problems. I don't want to take any more lives than we already have if we can avoid it. Maintain focus on the Chinese vessels.'

The hard turn finished, and everyone was able to stand upright. The USS John Basilone was now heading back towards the Huang Shen, trying to increase the distance between them and the pursuing Chinese vessels.

'Sir, the two small Zhaoyu cutters are breaking away from the Zhaotou, moving to intercept us.'

So, they want to do this, Jonathan thought grimly, turning his head to get a look at the two ships. Sure enough, the small, quick vessels were closing the gap, well within a couple of miles now. They'd have no problem catching or maintaining course with the larger Arleigh Burke. Luckily, the smaller coast-guard vessels weren't designed for this kind of combat, with their much lighter twenty-five-millimetre chain guns the largest weapons available to them.

The Zhaotou remained further to port, keeping a decent distance between itself and the American ship. Jonathan had just swung his glasses around to eye the ship when he spotted a sudden flash from the Zhaotou's bow.

A lookout screamed, 'INCOMING!' a split second later.

Jonathan heard the sound of the shell closing on them only moments before a large plume of water exploded just off their starboard bow.

'Evasive action!' Jonathan ordered, telling the helmsman to rapidly alter the ship's course, making it harder for enemy rounds to find their target.

Behind them, the Zhaoyus opened up, their smaller guns firing in quick succession.

The world around them quickly morphed into chaos. Smaller rounds were bouncing off the rear of the John's superstructure and hull, while others missed and skimmed across the sea, making small explosions across the water. Every round that impacted the John seemed to vibrate against the ship, sending soundwaves through the metal structure.

Another larger plume of water exploded further to starboard; another shot from the Zhaotou.

Surprise was quickly replaced by anger. The constant *thunk* of the rounds impacting the ship seemed to reverberate throughout the ship, every round causing damage and harm.

'Has the Seahawk landed?' Jonathan demanded.

'Sir, yes.'

Both smaller Zhaoyus followed a couple of hundred feet behind the USS John Basilone, one riding port side, the other starboard.

'Hard to starboard, make heading 360 degrees.'

'Ready Mark 38s and .50 cals. I want a return on these bastards.'

The USS John Basilone turned hard to starboard, the world inside the ship tilting again. The sailors held on to whatever they could. Gunner's mates and weapons operators waited in anticipation, watching their prey come into view as the ship turned.

One Zhaoyu came into view of one of the crew manning a .50-calibre machine gun. The sailor holding the heavy weapon lined it up on the bridge of the vessel, squeezing off a burst of large bullets. The rounds struck lower than expected, slamming against the metal superstructure of the bridge. Readjusting, the man watched in dismay as the smaller, nimble enemy vessel charged out of his line of fire, seeking cover behind the John's own stern and superstructure.

'Having trouble acquiring a clean line of sight, captain,' an officer reported.

'Ready torpedoes, port and starboard. Single fish each, circle pattern and active homing,' Jonathan ordered rapidly.

Further towards the stern of the ship, the two Mark 32 torpedo tubes were already loaded and ready. Hatches along the side of the John slid open. The sounds of battle and gunfire filled the now-open space. Simultaneously, both tubes turned outward before firing one torpedo each in quick succession. They made a soft, hissing sound as they were jettisoned out into the warm seawater below. Just as quickly as they had turned and fired, the tubes turned back inward, the heavy hatch closing quickly behind them as the crew immediately got to work on loading more torpedoes.

The Mark 46s sped through the water, each pulling a wide circle towards the stern of the John. The active sonars pinged forward, hunting the prey in front of them, identifying the two Chinese cutters not far behind the USS John Basilone.

Jonathan watched as both Zhaoyus reacted in almost the same way, darting out from behind the John to get inside the circling radius of the torpedoes.

'Target 1 sighted, clean line of fire from Sea-Wiz.'

'Two-second burst, free fire,' Jonathan ordered.

'Two-second burst, free fire acknowledged, aye sir.'

The forward-mounted Phalanx had a clear view of the Zhaoyu cutter as it approached. The white-and-red-striped vessel cut a dashing image as it pounded over the wake of the John, small puffs of smoke rising from the bow-mounted gun as it fired. The radar acknowledged firm lock on the vessel, and the FC depressed the "fire" button. The forward-mounted barrel of the Phalanx span at an incredible rate, spewing a line of twenty-millimetre death. The port side of the Zhaoyu exploded into an ugly, fiery mess as thousands of high-explosive rounds smacked into the previously pristine white hull of the ship. The burst from the Phalanx lasted less than a second, but the other weapons kept up a barrage of fire from midship-mounted Mark 38 chain guns and .50-calibre gun crews. The windows of its bridge shattered, and black spots covered its previously clean white exterior. It was unlikely anyone on the bridge would be alive. Even if they'd ducked, the high-explosive rounds would have penetrated it cleanly.

The cutter pulled away from the withering fire, moving hard to starboard.

'First Zhaoyu appears out of the fight or disabled. Follow up with the Mark 45, sir?'

'Negative. Focus on active threats. Give me a solution on the other cutter.' Jonathan turned his attention to the Zhaoyu but noted the much larger Zhaotou had moved behind the Huang Shen.

'Target two has returned to our wake, less than 200 feet.'

The smaller vessel was much more nimble, much faster than the larger American destroyer. The captain was clearly savvy to the threats of the USS John Basilone, particularly following the quick dispatch of his sister ship. Jonathan couldn't pull the same trick with torpedoes either; not with the cutter so close.

Cameras mounted around the ship showed various scenes. The rear loading dock for the Seahawk was wrecked. With relief, Jonathan noted that the Seahawk had landed and its crew and passengers had disembarked. But the helicopter would never fly again. Torn apart by the constant fire from the coast-guard ships, it lay crumbled and burning, half on the landing pad and half falling off the side of the ship.

The little Chinese coast-guard vessel made for a dramatic scene. Moving at flank speeds, it leaped through the wash of the larger destroyer, sending white water flying into the air. Its main gun continued a steady stream of fire. Jonathan watched as a number of machine gunners tried to situate themselves on the ship's bow, firing widely. Small yellow flashes appeared constantly from their weapons.

'Damage control reporting significant damage to the rear helicopter bays, sir,' the Boatswain's mate announced.

The entire ship was filled with noise. Alarms ringing, weapons firing, people shouting. Jonathan figured this is what it must have been like to be on a ship in World War Two. This wasn't how his ship was meant to fight.

'Where are the RHIBs with our teams?' Jonathan asked suddenly.

'Keeping their distance, sir, but ready to approach on our

order.'

'Tell them to hold. We need to get rid of this pest first,' Jonathan said grimly. He needed those teams back onboard; the larger Zhaotou would emerge from the other side of the Huang Shen any moment, and they'd be sitting ducks.

In the sky above them, news helicopters hovered well above the chaos, greedily filming and reporting on the deadly skirmish below. Merchant sailors pulled out their phones and exclaimed wildly as the battle wore on in front of them. Captains and officers anxiously radioed out, warning others to stay away. There would be no hiding this from the world.

HQJOC – Australia

Maia and Ata watched on with everyone else in fascinated horror as the events unfolded in the Malacca Strait. The tactical displays alternated with numerous TV screens displaying live reporting from news anchorages across the country. The room was abuzz with the hum of military staff going about their duties. People ran between desks, speaking into phones and headsets, while others tapped madly on their computers. Liaisons kept the key people aware of every update. The Australian prime minister was flying back from an overseas visit and could only listen in. Every minute, another distant boom and explosions sounded through the various newsfeeds. Smoke and water vapour rose in the distance. The scene was confusing and deadly, the state of the USS John Basilone and its crew not entirely clear.

The reality was that there was nothing they could immediately do for the USS John Basilone and all the people aboard it. The ship had to fight, and it had to win. Any decisions made now would take hours to reach the John. The only vessel close enough to support the John was the HMAS Hobart, but its attention was firmly locked on the two Chinese destroyers. Aircraft were taking off from

American and allied bases around the Indo-Pacific, but they still had a long way to travel. The strait was remote enough to put it out of range of most strike options.

Maia fidgeted, 'Any movement from the two destroyers?'

'Still holding position towards the strait,' Ata replied, knowing Maia was nervous and feeling just as powerless as she was.

Maia nodded, processing the information. 'HMAS Hobart is awfully exposed down there. She's the closest ship to those destroyers.'

Ata didn't really know how to respond, so she just stayed quiet, busying herself with the latest satellite imagery from the South China Sea.

The large space suddenly quietened. A tall, important-looking man in military uniform dominated the room at the centre. The chief of the Australian Defence Force, the head of the Australian military – equivalent to the chairman of the Joint Chiefs of Staff – was hard to miss. A number of other senior officers quietly conferred with him and his gaggle of staff. Everyone in the room was straining to hear what was being said.

A two-star general detached himself from the group suddenly. 'Alright, everyone, listen up! We have to assume this is going to spread and escalate. Our forces are going into emergency mobilisation. All leave is being cancelled, all available aircraft and ships are being deployed. We will be responding to this incident with force!'

Ata guessed similar scenes were happening on watch floors and in situation rooms across the US. It was still mid-morning in Australia, meaning it would be a late night for anyone in the US.

'I'd feel a lot better if our people weren't out there, Maia,' Ata said glumly.

Maia nodded, 'Me too.'

Ata was just about to ask another question when her desk phone rang. Relishing the distraction, she picked it up and was immediately disappointed she had. The deep, droning voice of Mike came through from the other end.

'Ata, get down to the security gate. My fucking pass has stopped working, and these idiots won't let me in.'

Having Mike around was the last thing they needed, but she couldn't just ignore him. 'Sure thing, Mike, be there in a second.'

Maia raised an eyebrow and turned swiftly to look at Ata.

'You better hurry,' Mike said ungratefully, hanging up.

'Was that Mike?' Maia asked.

'Yeah, he's locked out. Apparently his pass isn't working. I'll go let him in,' Ata said.

'No need, I'll handle it,' Maia said quickly – too quickly.

'Um … Okay, something going on?' Ata asked, sensing the urgency in Maia's voice.

'I'll tell you after all this. Don't worry about Mike,' Maia said reassuringly before hurrying away.

'Okay then,' Ata muttered to herself, returning her attention to the satellite imagery from the Fiery Cross Reef. Heat bloomed from multiple jet engines appearing over the runways. The Chinese were mobilising.

CHAPTER 22

Situation Room – The White House – United States of America

Quinton was working himself into an excited frenzy. Before his eyes, the new enemy of America was showing its true colours. No cyberattacks hidden by criminal organisations; no corporate espionage stealing American power, technology and wealth. No, this was plain, brutal and violent, for all the world to see.

The situation room inside the White House wasn't a large space, and at present it was packed with every key advisor, aide and bureaucrat the American Government could lay its hands on. The joint chiefs were scrambling, while intelligence officers eagerly awaited more information and watched the newsfeeds from CNN and advisors worried about political and diplomatic impacts on America.

Quinton sat in the middle of the table, not as close to the President as he'd like but close enough to make himself heard. His anger burned deeply at seeing America's assault, but there was also opportunity in this crisis. A chance to reignite America's greatness and finally stand up to America's enemies again. China had to be reminded that the

United States called the shots; they were allowed to exist in this world only by the good grace of America. In Quinton's mind, this could be the first shot in a quick and decisive war to ensure America wasn't threatened again. He just had to make sure everyone in this room – no, not everyone, just enough key people – supported him. He could convince the President to respond in kind, to escalate as required. The Chinese, no doubt, would be foolish enough to strike back, their pride injured. From there, the diplomats would be hard-pressed to stop the falling bombs and guided munitions. Quinton would have his war, a war that would solidify his position and fortify America against all foreign threats. For him, it was the only true way, the pure way, to demonstrate the power of America.

Plus, wars were always good for American industries, and they would help Quinton's own pockets. A few shares distributed throughout the right areas would benefit him greatly. And why shouldn't he benefit? In his mind, the work of remaking America should have its rewards. He didn't want to live as a poor man.

But he had to remain convincing and coherent. The burning rage wouldn't help him here. Controlling himself and lowering his voice to make it sound more reasonable, he said, 'We need to take action now to make sure our forces across the Indo-Pacific are protected. We don't know if the Chinese have other plans. They could be readying attacks on our forces all around the Pacific and Asia.'

He saw a few nods from a couple of key people. But the joint chiefs and the secretary for defence remained stony-faced. The President seemed outright aloof as he watched the live feeds streaming onto the large screens.

'Perhaps, Quinton, but I want to hear our options first. How do we support the John and help our people down there?' he asked the crowded room, barely looking away from the monitors.

The chief of naval operations spoke up quickly, cutting off Quinton before he could launch into another speech.

'Sir, right now the USS John Basilone is engaged in combat with at least three Chinese coast-guard vessels. We're not sure why the shooting started, but it appears that the John felt the need to take out a Chinese helicopter that was pursuing one of our own. We don't fully understand who shot first, or why.'

'So, what *do* we know? Other than the fact that the Chinese are pissed and shooting at us? What are our options?'

Well, sir, there is not much we can do for the USS John Basilone right now. It has to fight that fight and either escape or win. We don't have any naval or aviation assets in the area that can reach the John within the hour, and by then, this will either be lost or won.'

'It does appear that a small Chinese boat just got roasted,' the President pointed out in a mild tone. 'I'd say we're winning.'

The admiral cranked his neck around to look at the screen. One vessel was limping away from the John. 'Yes, sir, that looks right. We'll need to do a full assessment, but I am confident that the John can pull through.'

The President focused his gaze on the admiral. '*But?*'

'But the Chinese have additional naval assets in the area – two destroyers, to be exact. And it appears they are deploying aviation assets from the Fiery Cross Reef nearby, sir. The John is outgunned and heavily outnumbered.'

'So, options? I haven't heard a single one yet, admiral.' There was surprisingly intense focus in the President's dark-blue eyes.

'There aren't many, sir. First option, we could pull the John out, but as they're already engaged, it's probably too late for that. Second, we rely on our allies for support. The Australians are already mobilising and have a destroyer positioned further to the south. They've also got a squadron moving to support from their airbase in the north, RAAF Base Tindal. These forces should provide the additional firepower to back the John. But we don't have a locked-in statement of intent; we need to confirm the Australians will support us.'

The President nodded. 'The last option?'

'Lastly, we could escalate in other theatres, try and force the Chinese to pull back. But sir, that would be difficult to manage; we could find ourselves in a much larger conflict.' The admiral clearly didn't value the final option as much as the second.

It was outrageous to Quinton they'd be reliant upon others for support. 'Why the hell is the USS John Basilone out there alone? It's a disgrace we don't have options to support one of our ships!' He knew he was berating the admiral, but the battlelines had been drawn long ago between himself and the military. He viewed them as too timid and willing to negotiate, when they should do what they were paid to do: find a way to make America's enemies fear them. 'We shouldn't need to rely on another nation, no matter how friendly, to protect Americans!'

The President remained fixated on the TV screen, seemingly ignoring Quinton's statement. 'What are the Australians going to do, admiral? Can we trust in their support?'

'Without a doubt, sir. They have skin in the game like we do. We've been steadily improving our ties through our partnerships and the AUKUS agreement. I've worked with their people and know the commanders over there. They know they have to support us; otherwise, they'll be on their own. Plus, we already have considerable military presence down there in Darwin, with more on the way in the coming years. And as you know, sir, we boarded the Huang Shen looking for stolen hardware as part of a *joint* project with them.' He emphasised the word "joint", giving Quinton a hard look. 'They'll support us and fight to protect the USS John Basilone. I promise you that.'

The President nodded. 'But we don't have strike options from Australia?'

'Not yet, sir. We have plans to establish B-52s and a

permanent naval base, but the facilities aren't built yet.'

'And why is that, admiral?!' Quinton demanded, desperate to stay in the conversation.

The President looked at Quinton, raising an eyebrow before looking back at the admiral.

'The projects are on schedule and under budget; their completion is slated for two years from now. The enemy will always have their own plans, sir. They always get a say.'

The President looked back at the TV screen. 'Okay, admiral. Let's make a note to look at speeding those projects up after this crisis. Alright. Option two sounds like the winner so far – what is happening in the broader region? Anything we need to be worried about?'

'It's all a little early to say, sir. The Malaysians are moving forces into the AO, and we hope they'll be able to route some traffic away from the engagement, but we don't expect they'll engage the Chinese. Everyone else is staying clear for now; Singapore and Indonesia will be paying close attention. If we lose this, they'll seriously start to question our position in Asia. Additionally …'

A junior officer moved quietly up to the admiral, drawing his attention and interrupting his brief. A quiet whispered word and a single sheet of paper were exchanged. The admiral's face dropped slightly.

'Apologies, sir, but there have been some developments. We're seeing heat blooms coming from the Chinese installation in the Fiery Cross Reef; looks like a squadron of fighters and a bomber. This puts us at a significant disadvantage in firepower, sir.'

The President didn't skip a beat. 'Alright, admiral, give me your recommendations.'

'Sir, we don't have many options for the USS John Basilone right now; it has to fight, and it has to win. Its captain, Jonathan O'Donnell, is a tough operator and should have no issues dispatching the coast-guard vessels. But the combination of those two Chinese destroyers and air support means only one thing for us: a lot of dead

Americans, a sunken ship and humiliation on the world stage. We need the Australians' support, here and now. It's the only option.'

The President shifted his gaze, turning to the secretary of state. 'Get me in contact with the prime ministers of Australia and Malaysia, Australia first. ASAP.'

Quinton could see his victory slipping away in an instant. He stood up. 'We should strike the Chinese, hard and fast, show them if they don't back off, we mean business. Their holdings in the South China Sea are easy pickings; we have vessels and a carrier battle group in the area that could level them in minutes!' His voice sounded shriller than he'd intended, but the urgency of the moment had taken hold of him.

The President shifted his gaze to Quinton, giving him a thoughtful look, 'Admiral?' he said, still looking at Quinton, 'give me some strike options for the Chinese holdings in the South China Sea. And I assume you recommend we raise our alert level?'

'Understood, sir, and yes, my recommendation is DEFCON 3,' the admiral responded stiffly.

Quinton suppressed the urge to smile or leap into the air. The Chinese wouldn't be able to ignore an attack on their precious artificial islands sprinkled throughout the South China Sea; they considered them a part of China. This would make escalation impossible to avoid.

Behind Quinton, Dick stood quietly, moving away from the meeting and his boss. Quinton never noticed him leave the room.

USS John Basilone – Malacca Strait

The sturdy glass windows on the starboard side of the John's bridge exploded inward as a lucky twenty-millimetre round impacted the ship.

Jonathan, along with everyone else, ducked down the moment it hit, but the sailors closest to the starboard windows had less time to react. Glass shards and fragments of metal went flying at high speeds, embedding themselves in flesh. Panicked shouts, shortly followed by groans of pain, reverberated throughout the bridge. But his crew were well trained and capable. It only took seconds for the impact to wear off and for the crew to jump into action.

Jonathan looked around carefully, holding onto the console next to him. The bridge was a mess, but it looked like the single round had only caused superficial damage overall. Nothing that would impact their ability to fight.

'Report! Everyone okay?' Jonathan called out.

The helmsman had already leapt back onto the controls, ensuring someone was always driving the ship. They couldn't stop their evasive action; every round that missed them was one that didn't kill or wound.

'Got some wounded here, sir!' called out the boatswain's mate.

'Get them to medical and get that window patched; if the consoles are toast, make sure the backups in the CIC are manned-up and running!'

He could tell some of the officers and sailors were shaken by the sudden and literal popping of their bubble on the bridge. They hadn't been under fire like this before. Then again, neither had he. He raised his voice, 'Let's go, people. That was nothing; we are trained and capable, we are sailors in the United States Navy. Do your jobs and let's kick these fuckers in the ass!'

The faces of the bridge all watched him, signs of determination and pride swelling in their eyes.

Jonathan waited until everyone was back at their posts before announcing his intention. 'Alright, we're going to switch things up. Helm, following the next turn, bring us hard to port, then kill power. We'll see how our friend reacts then. Weps, be ready to fire once you have a clear shot.'

A chorus of *aye-aye* sirs followed.

Jonathan looked up at one of the cameras showing the stern of the ship. They were now travelling away from the

Huang Shen, but Jonathan knew the massive Zhaotou would be emerging from behind it at any moment. They had to get rid of the smaller cutter. It would continue to damage them and, eventually, might hit something important.

'Commencing manoeuvre, sir,' called the helmsman.

Jonathan nodded, feeling the ship heave towards port. The Chinese captain sensed the John Basilone's movement and surged forward, pulling his cutter in close behind the stern of the larger destroyer, trying to keep out of range of the deadly bow-mounted guns. Jonathan hoped the overconfidence of the captain would be his undoing. The fact that the nimbler ship felt comfortable enough to remain so close to the deadly ship seemed insane to him. The constant boom of the cutter's guns continued to sound out, round after round smashing into the John.

'Full stop! Maintain heading!' Jonathan ordered, excitement building in his stomach.

The USS John Basilone seemed to still as its heavy propeller blades suddenly slowed, no longer clawing at the water to push it forward. While not as quick as a car, the loss of momentum was immediate. The Chinese captain hadn't expected the ship to stop and now found himself with little room to manoeuvre as the stern of the John moved closer to his bow. Jonathan watched as some of the Chinese sailors on the bow appeared startled, waving back at the bridge, the speed at which the gap had closed causing concern. A few seemed to step backwards before running.

Good, Jonathan thought.

He watched on the camera as the Chinese captain pulled his cutter hard to starboard, the smaller vessel visibly leaping through the wake of the John. It was close, but the cutter just slipped past the John's stern. With no way to stop suddenly, the little cutter was exposed as it darted past the John, moving amidships towards the bow. The two ships were barely ten metres apart. The John was ready, its weapons pointed starboard; the Chinese cutter was not.

The sailors manning the .50-cal. machine guns along the

ship didn't hesitate, firing in long, continuous streams at anything they could. Lines of tracer fire from the guns and small arms from individual sailors carrying rifles burst from the USS John Basilone along the entire length of the ship. Sparks and smoke swallowed the smaller ship as glass shattered and men fell screaming to the floor beneath them. Small explosions covered the Chinese cutter as round after round impacted against the metal hull, puncturing through the thin aluminium and the flesh of the sailors inside. Anyone foolish enough to try and return fire was immediately cut down by the accurate small-arms fire. In a desperate move to avoid the murderous attack, the Chinese captain made one last, fatal error, pulling hard to starboard and placing the little cutter within comfortable range of the waiting Phalanx CIWS.

The tongue of fire almost touched the fleeing ship, as the high-impact explosive rounds tore into the ship. Jonathan winced as the long *brrrrrrrrzztt* of the Phalanx continued. He guessed the sailor manning the gun wanted to make sure the ship died. The cutter's bridge essentially dissolved under the hail of fire. Glass, metal and people exploded as one. After only a couple of seconds, the cutter had slipped past the USS John Basilone, a smoking, burning wreck of its former self.

'Follow up with the Mark 45, sir?' one of the weapons officers asked.

'Negative. They're done. We'll need it for the next one. Reload the Sea-Wiz – we're going to need it.'

Jonathan had watched with satisfaction as the cutter's smaller twenty-millimetre cannon had been blown off its foundations in the fire blast. The only threat it represented now was the possibility the captain could try and ram the John, but with its bridge destroyed, it could be dispatched with ease if it turned around on them.

'I want damage assessments from that. Injuries and critical systems – who's hurt and what's broken!'

The various officers around the ship would make their

assessments and feed them back to the officer of the watch before handing them to the captain. Already, Jonathan knew there would be unseen damages. Hell, the Seahawk was a complete write-off. What was left of it was hanging limply off the helipad on the stern of the John. A number of sailors already had a hose on it.

'What a mess,' he muttered to himself.

A lookout called out, 'Sir, enemy ship, Zhaotou class, emerging from behind the Huang Shen, heading 350 degrees.'

No time to rest, Jonathan thought as he turned on the spot and brought his binoculars up.

They were roughly a mile apart. 'Bring us about and prepare Mark 45.'

The monstrous Zhaotou-class cutter beat them to it. A sudden flash and puff of grey smoke emerged from the barrel of the large cutter, and someone yelled, 'INCOMING!'

A thunderous explosion burst along their port bow. A wave of water seemed to engulf the John, with crew members making startled yelps or cries. The whole ship vibrated and seemed to move. A single round from that thing would do a lot of damage to his ship. Modern ships weren't designed to take hits from heavy guns; they were meant to fire missiles from long range. This was not a fight Jonathan wanted to be in.

The wall of water subsided. There wasn't any smoke, or fire. They hadn't been hit.

Not yet.

'Weps, commence firing immediately on Zhaotou class. Prioritise guns and bridge!' Jonathan ordered rapidly.

The officer of the watch hurriedly relayed the order to the CIC. Jonathan felt more exposed than ever on the bridge. If one of those rounds hit, everyone would die. Not that it would be much better if it hit the CIC, or anywhere else on the ship. In the back of his mind, he scolded himself. He should have been in the CIC for this.

Jonathan watched as the large Mark 45 bow-mounted gun manoeuvred around with surprising speed. Just below, a small team of four manned the gun. A weapons operator inside the CIC lined the large Zhaotou to his crosshairs, digitally displayed on his screen. With a simple click on his console, the laser range-finder measured the exact distance between the two ships. The Aegis computer rapidly ingested the data, automatically setting the ideal firing position, taking into consideration speed, wind and velocity.

The operator called out, 'Ready!'

'Engage, free fire!' the XO ordered swiftly.

Inside the Mark 45, a 127 mm shell packed with explosive propellant was snatched out of the large, revolver-like barrel sitting beneath the gun. A robotic arm hauled both the shell and its propellant upward before another arm snatched them, pulling them horizontally into the loading mechanism. A piston pushed both the round and propellant into the firing chamber before the breach was slammed shut. The propellant was ignited by a firing trigger, causing the massive ball of expanding gas and fire to fill the small chamber behind the shell. Once the pressure became too great, the shell leapt forward, the fireball behind it pushing it to its destination. *Thunkboom*! The gun rattled, spewing blackish smoke from the barrel. The discarded shell casing was pulled out of the chamber and thrown from a small port above the main gun, making a satisfying *tink* as it fell against the metal deck.

Only seconds had passed. Already, the load crew were pulling more shells and propellant from ranks below the bow and placing them into the insatiable feeding tube that would take each round and load it into the now-rotating barrel. In less than a minute, the Mark 45 would fire over sixteen rounds at its target.

An RHIB – Danny

The spray of the RHIB smacked against Danny's face,

stinging. But he had other problems. Mouth agape, he watched as puffs of smoke, flashes of fire and booming explosions flew from the two ships. The USS John Basilone and the Chinese cutter were firing in near unison, both out for blood. A keen student of history, Danny knew navies hadn't squared off like this in any serious manner since the Second World War. The noise was incredible, the drama of the moment not lost on him.

The RHIBs had only just escaped from the Huang Shen when the Zhaotou had emerged from the other side of the container ship, leaving them awkwardly placed between the John Basilone and Zhaotou as they engaged each other.

The attention of the Chinese may have been on the destroyer, but that didn't stop some enterprising sailors from engaging Danny and the rest of the team with their guns. Rounds started smacking into the water around them, sending small fountains into the air and pushing everyone's heads lower. The sailors driving the RHIBs wasted no time, yelling 'HOLD ON!' as they whipped the small, nimble boats around, trying to avoid any incoming fire. Danny kept a tight hold of Jesse, trying to cradle and protect the larger man from the rapid, jarring movements of the RHIB.

Despite the danger, Danny kept trying to steal glances at the battle around him. Although he was still reeling from the danger he had felt being on the Huang Shen, this was something else entirely. It was clear from the beginning that the Arleigh Burke was superior; its larger gun was able to spit rounds out at the Chinese cutter at an astonishing speed. But the hit rate didn't seem as high as Danny had expected. Most of the rounds splashed harmlessly around the ships, creating enormous fountains as the sea literally exploded around them. He knew that even with advanced technology, hitting a moving target at high speeds on the ocean wasn't a simple task, despite what numerous engineering lectures and manuals had tried to suggest to him over the years.

Another shell rocketed through the air above them,

making a large whistling sound. Danny couldn't see it, but he tried to follow its trajectory and was rewarded with a huge ball of red-yellow fire bursting from amidships on the Chinese cutter. *The first hit*! Danny's mind registered with thrilled surprise.

In quick succession, another two rounds impacted the Chinese cutter, one towards the stern and another amidships. Blackish smoke started to pour from the superstructure, creating dark-black blemishes on the once-white hull. The fire controlman had found his mark. The velocimeter attached to the gun recorded each shot, allowing for adjustments to the targeting matrix.

Despite the impacts, the Chinese Zhaotou kept firing. A sudden explosion of fire and smoke poured from the stern of the USS John Basilone. One of the Chinese shells had also found its mark. The rest of the crew on his RHIB groaned. They were still half a mile away. It was hard to tell the extent of the damage, but some grey smoke was rising, and the crumbled Seahawk seemed to have vanished.

In response, the USS John Basilone turned hard to port, directly facing the Chinese cutter, removing its broadside and making it a smaller target. But if a round hit the forward superstructure – or worse, one of the vertical launch cells – the whole ship could be in trouble.

The RHIBs bounced around as they changed course again to avoid the incoming bow of the John. They couldn't board now, but they could use the ship as cover at least. As they passed the John, the Mark 45 naval gun came clearer into view. It continued belching round after round, *thunkboom* followed by the metallic *ting* of the shell casing being ejected onto the deck.

Danny kept his eyes on the Chinese cutter, where more rounds were finding their mark. The bridge took a good hit, before another two rounds punctured the bow. The Chinese seventy-six-millimetre fell silent. A few more rounds into the broadside of the cutter, and it looked like the fight was over. Fire and smoke billowed from numerous impact points around the ship. Danny could only imagine the hell and devastation occurring for all the men and women on that ship now. He shuddered at the thought of it, a sense of shame washing over him for the excitement he'd felt moments before.

The John slowed, turning starboard against the burning Zhaotou. As they moved past the stern, the fire was still burning, but it appeared to mostly be the remains of the helicopter. Still, the ship wasn't unscathed. Scars from metal fragments and rounds were splashed all over the once-clean grey superstructure. The stern was a mess, having received the majority of the twenty-millimetre rounds from the previous cutter. Danny doubted the helicopter bays would be operable for a while – certainly not with the burning Seahawk still attached. He hoped that was a good thing. Alarms and klaxons wailed, and Danny thought he could hear groaning and a scream. He began to fear he was walking into a new kind of hell.

HMAS Hobart – Malacca Strait

'Coming up on screen now,' an operator in the operations centre, the Australian version of the CIC, called out.

Kate looked up at one of the screens. The picture was crystal clear, lacking the fuzziness expected by long-range flights or when there was interference. The deep, dark blue of the ocean appeared calm, with small white spots marking the waves breaking in nearly uniform patterns below.

The drone was a small ship-launched unmanned aerial system, or UAV, awkwardly called the ScanEagle. Only slightly larger than a regular remote-controlled hobbyist's plane, it was able to fly significantly longer distances and stay up in the air for almost twelve hours. Kate had come to rely on the little aircraft, allowing it to expand her vision far beyond what she could see through her binoculars.

At present, it was flying a good thirty nautical miles

ahead of the HMAS Hobart and was trying to get eyes on the two Chinese destroyers. It sat comfortably under any cloud cover, but it was small and quiet enough that it could get fairly close to its target. Generally, Kate used it to assess fishing boats or commercial craft, but her target today had many more teeth than some unarmed fisherman.

The large grey vessels stood out against the ocean. Sitting a couple of kilometres apart, they didn't look terribly imposing from a distance. But Kate knew better. They were better armed than her ship, although she did have the edge in experience and technology. Still, it was a fight she wouldn't win. She simply didn't have the ammunition.

They'd spotted an airborne target fleeing from the skirmish in the strait. The Aegis system correctly tagged it as a Harbin Z-9. There had been two originally, but the first one was history, a twisted wreck at the bottom of the strait.

Kate watched the screen closely. 'Can we zoom in on the helicopter? I want to see who gets off it when it lands.'

The operator obliged, focusing the camera.

The black helicopter made a low, sweeping pass against one of the destroyers before coming about in a wide turn, approaching the steady, slow-moving vessel from the stern.

As the helicopter came to a rest, a small group of sailors ran out to secure it. The passengers stepped off immediately. The majority appeared to be in largely civilian clothing, but a couple of military figures were present. One was limping rather badly.

'Can we focus on the guy with the case?'

The camera focused. The man was taller than the majority of the people around him; he walked with a certain confidence that gave him something close to a swagger. The case seemed weighted, and it was firmly gripped. When a sailor offered to take it, he pulled it closer to his body, clearly unwilling to part with it.

'Wonder what our friend has in that case?' Kate said aloud.

They'd yet to hear the outcome from the search of the

Huang Shen. The skirmish had kicked off and sent everything to hell. They had listened and watched on, feeling helpless as the John battled it out with the Chinese. But they couldn't engage; Kate's orders were to support as required but to engage only if fired upon or if required to protect the John. Plus, even if she did engage the coast-guard vessels, the two Chinese destroyers wouldn't hesitate to attack them back.

'We recording?' Kate asked, knowing the answer.

'Yes, captain, capturing everything,' the operator confirmed.

No doubt the people back home would want to pour over every frame and detail after everything was said and done.

'Captain! We've got some activity coming from the other destroyer. Weapons and targeting radars are coming online!'

'Targeting us?'

'Negative. It appears to be targeting the John.'

'Shit. Patch me over to the John, we need to warn them.' She knew they'd be getting the same warnings, but it was the proper thing to do.

The drone picture pulled further away from the landed helicopter, focusing on the other Chinese destroyer. Kate had just switched her headset over when the bow of the Chinese ship disappeared in a flash of fire and smoke. She was dumbfounded for a split second before someone called out, 'MISSILE LAUNCH!'

The spell broke as she pressed down the button to send radio traffic. 'USS John Basilone, you have incoming missiles. I say again: incoming missiles!'

The sudden flurry of activity shocked her. Missile after missile pulled skyward, leaving behind light-grey plumes of smoke. Her ship's Aegis system was always tracking the missiles, identifying each one and displaying them on a tactical display, each missile a little red arrow moving towards the John Basilone.

'Confirm missile launch and hostile action back to JOC,'

she ordered. The people back at HQJOC would likely already be seeing the same data, as it was automatically beamed to them via satellite, but it was still her job to confirm.

'How many did they launch?'

'Ten, captain!'

Kate gritted her teeth. There wasn't anything they could do for the USS John Basilone. The first missile volley had surprised them, and even if they fired their interceptors, they were out of position and unlikely to intercept in time. But they'd be ready for the next volley.

'Bridge, move us into position to intercept any additional volley from that ship! Weapons, I want solutions on that ship, active weapons radars. Let's give it something to think about. If it fires another volley, we are firing interceptors. If it targets us, we are weapons free! We're changing to wartime rules of engagement, people.' Her orders came naturally and without any real thought. Her people were already at their action stations. There was a friend out there. An ally in trouble. It was her job to help.

A new set of dots appeared on the tactical display – missiles fired from the USS John Basilone. A lot more dots – little blue ones, this time – formed a swarm and headed towards the incoming missiles. It looked like Jonathan had fired at least double the number of interceptors. Even then, he might not get them all. Intercepting missiles was hard, if not impossible, at the best of times.

The interceptors, the SM-2, short for Standard Missiles, were effectively fast-flying shotgun rounds. The USS John Basilone's Aegis system would identify each threat and select missiles to intercept each one, targeting the highest threats first. Each incoming threat would get at least two interceptors thrown at it, improving the odds of a successful hit. Once the interceptors were close enough, they would deploy a small kinetic warhead that would shoot fragments towards the incoming missile, ideally – *hopefully* – destroying it. But the odds weren't in their favour. A single missile hit could sink a ship. It was now a game of mathematics and pure luck.

USS John Basilone

There was no time to rest. The moment the Zhaotou ceased firing, it was on to the next job.

'Boatswain's mate! Recover RHIBs! Give me an updated damage report! What is the status of the Malaysian fleet?' his orders and need for more information came thick and fast.

The Huang Shen was a pitiful sight, low in the water. The remaining Chinese crew had escaped on life rafts and were now bobbing around near their sinking vessels, flares and SOS calls reaching out to any who could see or hear them. Jonathan wouldn't worry about them now. They'd be rescued in due course. For now, he had to secure his own vessel.

A communications officer turned suddenly, one hand against the microphone on his head, 'SIR! HMAS Hobar–'

She never finished her sentence. The alert, 'VAMPIRE INCOMING!' came screaming through the intercom, something universally feared by all sailors: the alert for incoming missiles. There was no question of where they were heading; they were coming for them.

Jonathan felt his face turn cold, and then a burning rage rose from his stomach.

'Take evasive action!' he ordered the helmsman, before contacting the XO in the CIC.

'What are we looking at, Chris? How bad?' Jonathan asked.

'We count ten vampires, sir. Fired from the Type 055 Renhai Chinese destroyer. Eighty-five nautical miles and closing; ETA nine minutes to impact. Aegis has a firm lock.' His XO sounded surprisingly calm despite the noise and chaos around him.

'Understood. Take 'em down, Chris.'

The powerful Aegis system had identified each missile,

targeting them and giving them designations while determining payload, flight time, arrival time and suspected path. In a lot of ways, there was very little for Jonathan or the XO to do but give the orders. His controlmen were trained and knew their systems. Aegis would automate the selection and targeting of the incoming threats.

Alarms sounded across the bridge and ship as the Arleigh Burke readied itself to fire. The shattered bridge window did little to hold back the noise and smoke as the forward launch cells blasted their payload out: twenty interceptors in total. Jonathan watched them arc gracefully into the air, murmuring a quiet prayer to himself.

If they didn't get the first ten missiles, they'd have time to fire another volley of interceptors. But it would be close. His bigger worry was that they might be expending missiles too quickly. They couldn't reload. Whatever was in the launch cells was all they had. If they fired too many interceptors, they could run out. And then, they'd be easy pickings for the Chinese.

Everyone watched the monitor on the bridge: little blue dots targeting angry-looking incoming red arrows. A deadly dance, high in the skies above them.

An unseen operator from the CIC read out the results as the interceptors went to work. 'One destroyed. Two destroyed. Three – four destroyed. Seven destroyed.'

The little red blips suddenly disappeared, leaving only a couple of spare interceptors with no targets.

'All incoming targets neutralised!'

An audible cheer came through the intercom from the CIC, but it was drowned out by the noise of cheering on the bridge. A momentary relief from the pressure.

Jonathan didn't celebrate, instead keeping his focus on the monitor. 'QUIETEN DOWN, EVERYONE. IT'S NOT OVER YET!' he eventually called out, throwing a damper on any celebrations.

'Hail the Malaysians, see if they can take care of the China Coast Guard, keep them away from us. Then, patch me through to HMAS Hobart; we're going to need her help here.'

Multiple *yes-sirs* followed. Jonathan gritted his teeth, glaring at the pixel that represented the attacking destroyer on the monitor. 'Chris, give me a firing solution on that destroyer,' he ordered.

'Yes, sir! Already set; fifteen harpoons targeted.'

It was a lot of missiles for one ship, but he'd read the capabilities of the Type-055. It could shoot down missiles as well as he could.

'Fire!' Jonathan ordered.

Before the ship shuddered from the missile launch, another wave of angry red arrows appeared on the screen, 'VAMPIRE!'

'Here we go again,' Jonathan said to himself, gripping the console tighter.

Wedgetail AWACS – South China Sea

High above the Southern tip of the South China Sea, a lone Royal Australian Air Force AWACS watched the battle below. The aircraft, known as the Wedgetail, was more powerful and advanced than the ageing E-3 Sentry employed by America.

It had been ordered to keep watch over the boarding operation, departing from RMAF Butterworth hours earlier. The powerful aircraft had many roles, including coordination and control, but for now, it was simply relaying information back to other RAAF aircraft and to HQJOC.

'This is Wedgetail flight. We are seeing active missile launches below, both incoming and outgoing between Chinese and USN vessels. I repeat: missiles are in the air,' the pilot radioed back to Australia.

In the rear of the aircraft, airborne electronics analysts worked furiously to filter and collect all of the data flooding in, sorting the powerful weapons and targeting radars from the missiles in flight. All were a treasure trove of data. But, more importantly, everything they collected gave a clearer picture of the fight on the ocean below them. Their early assessments would be critical to any decision makers defining the next steps.

'USS John Basilone firing Harpoons,' called out another operator. 'I count at least fifteen.'

'Chinese destroyer returning fire. Another volley of ten.'

'New detection! HMAS Hobart has engaged Chinese missiles, firing interceptors!' the operator called in sudden alarm.

'More missile launches; interceptors firing from both USS John Basilone and Chinese Type 055!'

New sets of arrows appeared on their monitors, flooding the picture with a chaotic mess of moving points, all charging towards each other.

The team leader hadn't witnessed nations shooting at each other before. They'd exercised and practised this a million times before, but the real thing was far more chaotic and chilling than anything seen in war gaming scenarios – this was *real*. The cost of a mistake would be measured in lives.

'Sir, I've got what looks like Chinese military aircraft lifting off Fiery Cross Reef!'

'How many?' he asked. They needed only the facts.

'I count at least five, likely fighter aircraft, a bomber and possible AWACS, sir.'

'Track 'em, make sure JOC sees this. We won't be able to stay here for long without support.'

USS John Basilone

Danny's RHIB had only just nestled against the hull of the USS John Basilone when an ear-piercing alarm chimed over the ship's speakers.

'Clear the bow!'

His head turned instinctively, looking down the bow, his

view blocked by the ship's superstructure. The whole ship shuddered suddenly. This was followed by an unbelievably loud whooshing noise, then another. One after another, missiles started to fly. He took a step back and looked up to see multiple grey cloudy lines seeming to merge as one. The whooshing continued; Danny counted at least twenty.

More interceptors, he thought grimly. He'd already seen one launch while they waited, but the second volley meant it wasn't over. They wouldn't fire that many missiles to attack another ship. They were under attack, and the enemy had fired first. He wondered how much time they had. What were their chances of survival? Based on the number of missiles, more than ten of them were coming their way.

Hauling Jesse up with the help of another sailor, they started the awkward movement inside, trying to balance Jesse's dead weight without dropping him back into the ocean churning below the RHIB. The crane above them positioned itself slowly as sailors attached hooks to each end of the RHIB. Progress out on the ocean was painfully slow.

HMAS Hobart

'Interceptors two, three, four and six successful hits!' a warfare officer called out. Meaning the rest of the interceptors had missed or failed. At least they had thinned the herd a little for the John.

They'd largely been ignored by the Chinese vessels so far, but by firing at their missiles, they'd made themselves a target. At least one of the destroyers had turned around, heading away from its sister ship at flank speed. Kate had a hunch that whatever the helicopter had dropped off was valuable enough that the destroyer didn't want to hang around and slug it out. Still, it wouldn't be in missile range for a long while yet.

'Chinese Type 055 Renhai has locked us with weapons radar,' an operator called out.

'Jamming!' another operator announced.

Information was flooding into the operations centre at an incredible rate. Between the numerous sensors and flying ordinance, it was incredible any of the operators, let alone the computers, could keep up.

'VAMPIRE VAMPIRE VAMPIRE!'

'FIVE INCOMING!'

Kate remained calm. 'Deploy countermeasures, set system to automatic targeting.' She turned to the leading maritime warfare officer. 'Target the Type 055, five-round salvo. Keep lobbing missiles at it each time they shoot one down. Don't give them any time to breathe.'

Their own Aegis system had already catalogued the missiles and ships around them, providing targeting solutions wherever it looked. Kate only hoped the other Chinese destroyer kept fleeing. If it turned around, they'd be in serious trouble.

'Ready, captain!'

'Fire,' she replied immediately.

The ship shuddered as the missiles were released. It was the first time the HMAS Hobart had ever fired in anger. Five RGM Harpoon missiles launched out of twenty-four. Only nineteen left, Kate noted. Her interceptors, a mixture of short-range RIM-162 ESSMs, and medium-range SM-2 were packed in the remaining cells. Six ESSMs cells with four missiles each, giving her twenty-four missiles, and another sixteen SM-2s, meaning she had a total of forty missiles to defend the ship.

The Chinese ship had at least 122 vertical launch cells with a mixture of anti-ship and anti-air missiles. They'd have over 200 if the second ship decided it wanted to fight. The USS John Basilone had 112, but it had fired at least forty of its interceptors and fifteen of its anti-ship Harpoons. It was all a numbers game now: one side trying to get a missile through to the other, while that side defended.

HQJOC – Australia

The massive screens showed the now-constant fire of missiles between the three ships. Multiple coloured arrows appeared and disappeared, the new dots representing the small air-wings flying from Fiery Cross Reef. Ata and Maia didn't have a major role to play; they were largely passengers. The machinery of the Australian Defence Force and United States military clicked into place. Combat systems shared information, while soldiers, sailors and airmen of both nations sat side by side, working up intelligence reporting, target packs and plans.

The chief of the defence force remained front and centre, directly connected to the prime minister via secure telephone link. Ata was able to catch snippets of the conversation over the din.

'HMAS Hobart has engaged the Chinese destroyer, sir, together with the USS John Basilone … Yes, sir … The RAAF has been tasked … tankers, F-35 and Ghost Bat … Yes, sir …'

The wheels were moving quicker now. Ata wondered just where'd they end up in all this. The speed of escalation was terrifying. Another, quieter part of her brain wondered where Maia was.

CHAPTER 23

USS John Basilone – Malacca Strait

One by one, the little dots representing the USS John Basilone's outgoing Harpoon missiles blinked out of existence, snuffed out by Chinese counter-fire.

'Fire another volley, twenty-five this time. Swamp their defences,' Jonathan ordered the CIC.

He was doing the maths constantly. Between the John and the HMAS Hobart, they could outshoot the single Type 055. It had only been ten minutes since the first missile had been fired, and he'd already launched half of his total missiles.

The ship continued to vibrate as more missiles were flung skyward. The constant deafening whoosh was almost comforting at this point.

The constant chatter of operators sounded out across the bridge.

'Failed intercept on two vampires. Preparing countermeasures.'

'SLICK-32 active!'

The John's primarily electronic warfare suite would attempt to blast the incoming missiles with enough noise to scramble their guidance. Failing that, they had deployable chaff and Australian-designed Nulka decoys.

'Confirmed kill on two vampires, both ditched in the ocean.'

'VAMPIRE INCOMING! Additional launch, thirty incoming, ETA nine minutes.'

Jonathan clenched his jaw; the Chinese were going for broke.

'HMAS Hobart is being targeted!' an operator yelled.

The ship shuddered as another volley of interceptors rose. They wouldn't have many more.

'How do we look, XO? What state are our missiles in?'

'Less than half, sir, but he'll be running low as well. We'll get him.' The XO's confidence was reassuring.

'Keep at it,' Jonathan said, returning his focus to the organised chaos around him. Someone had finally patched the broken window with plywood board, slightly reducing the noise from the missile launches.

'One vampire has split from the pack! Heading towards a commercial vessel.'

It wasn't that surprising, really. Despite the active targeting and guidance from the Chinese destroyers' radars, the density of vessels around them made a lot of noise. Eventually, one of the missiles was bound to make a mistake.

'Warn them!' Jonathan ordered.

The sudden bright-yellow glow ahead of them told him they were already too late.

HMAS Hobart – Malacca Strait

The small missile blasted out of its tube from the deck of the Hobart, engaging and flying away from its ship. It flew for a few hundred metres before it separated from the rocket, falling towards the ocean before firing a smaller thruster, hovering in position. The small rocket didn't see the incoming missile, but it was vaporised in milliseconds.

The explosion was a few hundred yards from the HMAS Hobart's position, but the shock wave still reverberated throughout the ship.

The missile had been tricked by a Nulka decoy. The clever little mortar-launched missile confused incoming missiles and drew them away from the target vessel.

The constant fire of missiles was starting to worry Kate. She'd lost count of the missiles they'd fired and intercepted, but she knew they wouldn't be lucky forever. Outside of the constant volleys from the Chinese and Americans, individual missiles kept being lobbed over at her ship. The Chinese were focused heavily on the USS John Basilone, treating her as more of a thorn in their side than a primary threat.

'Massive volley from the Renhai!' announced the maritime warfare officer.

The battle was a lot closer for them compared to the John. Every intercept happened in seconds in the sky just above them. The booms from the impacts sounded through the hull of her ship. Kate watched the multiple missiles appear on the combat display.

'John firing interceptors and harpoons!'

'Fire an additional ten harpoons; let's overwhelm this sucker!'

'VAMPIRE VAMPIRE VAMPIRE! FIVE INCOMING! BRACE FOR IMPACT, PORT SIDE.'

More interceptors fired freely, clawing their way towards the incoming threat. Three missiles fell easily enough, with the last two falling victim to the Nulka decoy and detonating harmlessly 500 metres away from the Hobart.

A loud piercing sound echoed throughout the HMAS Hobart seconds after the last incoming vampire had died. Kate had watched it with satisfaction from the operation centre.

But the noise worried her.

'Damage report! What was that?'

It took a few minutes to find the culprit. A large, jagged

piece of metal, likely from the incoming Chinese missile, had been thrown free from the blast and come barrelling towards the Hobart. Despite the distance, it'd had enough velocity to bury itself in the metal of the Hobart's skin, just above the bridge.

Kate felt a small wave of relief that it hadn't hit anyone or anything important. Still, it was a deadly reminder of the dangers of modern naval combat. She knew she had to focus on her own ship, but the USS John Basilone had received double the missiles they had. 'What's happening on the John?'

'They have incoming vampires; looks like a few got through in that last salvo!'

USS John Basilone – Jonathan

'How many?' Jonathan asked.

'Six, sir!'

He nodded. 'Very well.'

They were almost out of interceptors now, the vertical launch cells all but depleted in less than thirty minutes of combat. He had a number of Harpoons remaining, but he was saving them for one last salvo.

'Fire remaining interceptors.'

There was no point saving munitions if even one missile got through; one could be enough to sink them.

The ship rumbled the now-familiar announcement of an outgoing missile. Only eight missiles rose to meet the incoming six.

Jonathan watched the display intently, listening to the results being read out by an operator.

'One trashed, two trashed, three trashed.'

'Three still incoming.'

'Firing countermeasures.'

The softer *thunks* of the Mark 32 countermeasure mortar sounded off somewhere amidships. They'd fire everything now. Part of an idea for layered defence. The last line would be the CIWS.

Clouds of aluminium burst into the sky a short distance from the John. The foil acted to confuse the infrared guidance systems on the Chinese missiles. One fell for the ruse, exploding harmlessly into the cloud. Another went for a Nulka decoy, exploding in a beautiful red and yellow fireball almost simultaneously.

'Two trashed!' the operator almost screamed.

'Sea-Wiz engaging!'

The long tongue of fire accompanying the *brrrrzzzztttt* of the cannon was spectacular, as always. The incoming missile had dropped to skim the ocean. The Aegis system hadn't lost contact and the Phalanx had been readying for its target the moment it had closed within a couple of miles.

The line of high-explosive tracers burst from the cannon, leaving a yellow line of fire that Jonathan and the rest of the bridge could follow.

No fireball appeared. The realisation hit Jonathan like a truck. The cannon was still firing. It was taking too long. *This missile was going to hit.*

Someone yelled, 'Missile incoming, port side. BRACE!' and the world seemed to disappear into sudden darkness.

Jonathan could feel the heat of the blast wash over him. It was sudden and shocking in its intensity. Somewhere to the port side, he could hear the sound of shattered glass and rending metal. Unknown objects whizzed by Jonathan's head, making it sound like they were being shot at. Then nothing.

USS John Basilone – Danny

It had all taken longer than expected. The crane had been slow. The amount of people crammed into the RHIBs meant offloading had to be carefully done, and the equipment and recovered debris had to be brought onto the ship as well. All the while, the constant roar of missile launches and distant booms from interceptions burnt their way into Danny's mind.

The sudden alarm was more urgent than the rest of the noises and klaxons echoing across the warship. Danny didn't recognise it, but everyone else did. In a mad scramble, anyone not already grabbing onto something sturdy rushed to find cover. Danny held onto the railing of the ship, keeping Jesse upright at all costs.

The sound of the Mark 32 mortar firing meant countermeasures were being employed. One or more missiles must have slipped through the air-defence net. A small crowd had formed at the doorway ahead of Danny, with a jumble of people all trying to squeeze through at once. A human traffic jam. A sudden deep explosion sounded off to Danny's left and his head whirled around to look at it. A second followed almost immediately; this time, it was closer.

The tell-tale screech from the Phalanx cannon told him everything he needed to know. They still had incoming. Watching the tracer fire from the Phalanx, he could make out the incoming missile. His body froze in shock and amazement. It was right there. A couple of hundred yards away.

Someone grabbed him and he fell backwards through the door with Jesse. It slammed shut and locked just as the missile detonated.

The whole ship seemed to rock, the force of the explosion moving the thousands of tonnes of steel without much effort. The lights died and the noise was deafening. The door he'd just fallen through seemed to move and bend as the roar of the blast swept over them, prompting the wail of alarms.

In the dark, someone hauled Danny back to his feet.

'You alright, sir? We're not dead yet, but that was close.'

The lights turned back on suddenly, and Danny spotted Jesse lying quietly at his feet.

'Help me get him to medical, Danny,' ordered a sailor next to him. The sounds of battle were now slightly muffled, but the din of alarms and orders rattling throughout the ship was growing.

USS John Basilone – Jonathan

Alarms continued to wail; people were coughing and groaning.

Opening his eyes, he realised he could smell, feel, breathe and see. He was alive. They were alive.

Pulling himself up again for the second time in a day, he thought to himself, *This is getting old fast.*

The bridge was a wreck on the inside. The windows were gone. Its frames were bent and broken. The consoles were utterly shattered. A few crew members were on the ground closest to the port side, some groaning, visibly injured. Some not moving at all.

It took a moment for his mind to catch up to the sights around him. 'Get them to medical!' he ordered, trying to conceal a small break in his voice. This was his crew. Seeing them injured – or worse, dead – almost broke him.

'Give me a status update, and a damage report!' He needed to know if they were operational or not, if the ship was in danger of sinking. He could already see the power on the bridge was flickering on and off.

The officer of the watch put down a handset. 'Sir, CIC reports vampire was intercepted by Sea-Wiz, no more than 200 yards to port. It did not score a direct hit.'

Jonathan nodded; a direct hit could have ended them, but a couple of hundred yards wasn't much better. The whole port side of his ship would be a riddled mess of shrapnel, melted and bent metal, and destroyed systems. They'd be in a bad way.

The officer kept reading out damage reports as they came in. Some systems were damaged, others completely destroyed. There were lots of injuries, no deaths yet. But most importantly to Jonathan, they still had their data feeds from the HMAS Hobart, and they could fire from their midships battery of launch cells. Their AESA array was partly destroyed, but they could still move the ship and reposition it to get a better lock on the Chinese.

They could still fight.

He picked up a handset to the CIC, and the XO picked up immediately. 'You okay up there, sir?' Concern, present and genuine.

'Alive and kicking, Chris. She's taken some pretty serious hits, but no fire, and most of our systems are operational.'

'Good to hear, sir. What are your orders? We have another salvo ready.'

Jonathan smiled; the XO already knew what he had in mind.

'Target the Chinese vessel with everything we've got; make sure Hobart is aware. They will be low on interceptors as well. Once we fire everything, we'll bug out and get out of range.'

'Yes sir, sounds like a plan to me,' the XO responded, fire in his voice.

***

The Harpoon missile pulled cleanly from its dark vertical launch cell. The mid-afternoon sunlight washed over its white, clean panels. With a mixture of fiery heat and smoke, it threw itself free of its prison, leaving the Arleigh Burke destroyer to its own devices. More Harpoons joined its flight, moving in a cluster like a flock of birds towards their intended target. Their turbo fan engines propelled them forward at almost 900 km/h. Other missiles joined too – different missiles, Harpoons fired from another ship. For the first few minutes of the flight, there was peace. Clear blue skies and nothing more.

Without warning, one of the missiles in the group disappeared in a fiery puff, its remains showering into the dark ocean below. Then another met a similar fate, and another. Before long, only three missiles remained in the cluster, the only survivors of the bleak frontal charge. All were locked in on their target a couple of kilometres ahead. Puffs of aluminium appeared in front of them. One missile took the bait and pulled away from the group, exploding seconds later, unaware it had failed its mission. The other two stayed locked on, their active radar homing in and ignoring the trickery. There was a sudden flash from the bow as exploding rounds flew towards them. The missile in front exploded violently, intercepted and destroyed by the wall of metal thrown its way. But the first missile, the original, kept coming, appearing on the other side of the explosive cloud and adjusting to meet its target, turning sharply and moving in. Its final act was to arm its detonation mechanism – just before striking its target.

HMAS Hobart

The cheer went up instantly throughout the operations centre.

The ScanEagle UAV hadn't missed a beat, seemingly ignored or unseen by the Chinese destroyers.

Kate resisted the urge join the rest of her crew cheering, instead watching her monitor intently from her seat, gripping the arms of the chair tightly.

Slowly, a gentle breeze blew away the remaining black smoke, revealing the extent of the damage. At first, Kate felt disappointed; the ship looked fine. But keener eyes than hers quickly picked up the tell-tale signs of damage.

'Captain, we're seeing some hull penetration on the starboard bow of the Type 055 Renhai, and by the looks of it, their main gun is out of action. The drone zoomed in, examining the details.

'Assessment of her fighting ability?'

'She's done. Without her main gun, and with most of her missiles, if not all, spent, she's out of the fight. But we aren't in a much better position, captain. We have expended our own missile storage. In my opinion, ma'am, we're in trouble if that other Chinese destroyer decides to come back.'

He was right. There wouldn't be any pursuit or sinking of the ship that had attacked them. The law of ammunition and distance would make the fight long and difficult – not to mention leave them completely exposed to Chinese reinforcements.

'Understood.' Picking up a handset, she dialled the bridge. 'Set course for the USS John Basilone; she might need our help.'

The ship shifted to a new course. It would still be a couple of hours before they could meet the John; for now, though, there were no missiles in the air.

Their peace was even more temporary than that.

'Captain! RAAF Wedgetail reporting Chinese aircraft approaching our post! ETA forty-five minutes!'

She'd largely forgotten about the reports of fighters departing the Fiery Cross Reef. Without more ammunition and missiles, there was little to nothing they could do. Their only real hope was to make for Singapore or team up with the John. However, despite her ship's speed, it wouldn't be able to reach either in such a small amount of time.

'What is the status of our RAAF backup?' she asked the communications officer speaking with the Wedgetail.

'Thirty-five minutes, captain.'

She bit her lip; it would be close. Too close.

HQJOC – Australia

Maia looked down at her phone as she walked towards the entrance of the facility. She was madly texting, her mind focused on the confrontation about to come.

Looking up, she could see Mike ahead, his face red, hand movements fast and aggressive as he argued with one of the guards. She could already imagine what he was saying. *Don't you know who I am?* or some other obnoxious comment along those lines.

She took a big breath, readying herself, as her phone

dinged comfortingly.

She looked down. It was a short message: *Leave him to us, we just arrived. –Tim.*

Mike looked up at her, raising his arm to wave and finally embarrass the guard, who was clearly in the wrong. Maia stopped in her tracks, locking eyes with him. Mike frowned, a look of confusion spreading across his face.

***

Tim walked quickly.

'Hey, Mike!' he called out loudly as he approached his target from behind.

Mike was busy arguing with someone but spun around to face Tim anyway.

'Mike! We've been looking for you, pal!' Tim said, keeping his tone light and friendly.

Mike's features were still locked in a scowl, but with a slight tinge of confusion. 'You have?' he asked, tone gruff.

'Yeah, we need you back at the embassy – there is some shit going down we need you for!'

Mike didn't budge. 'And you are?'

Tim feigned hurt. 'C'mon Mike, we've met before – Tim Ward, FBI liaison officer out at the embassy.'

'Right, and you said you need me? Why?' Mike asked, still unsure.

'We can't really discuss it here, but the national security advisor requested you. I'm just the errand boy.'

'Quinton Davenport asked for me personally?' Mike asked, his tone beginning to lighten.

'Apparently, you're the man with the answer – and the ear of the big dogs, it seems.' The pathetic flattery tasted acidic in his mouth, but he'd said worse things to get far better people before.

'Well, good. I'll get over there. These idiots seem to have lost my pass access anyway,' he said, giving the guards a dismissive hand gesture. The guard was visibly rolling her eyes behind his back.

'Ride with us! We'll get you there faster – lights and sirens, man. They said they needed you ASAP.'

Mike nodded, 'Right, of course. Lead the way … Tim, was it?'

It never ceased to amaze him how pliable people became when they felt important. The truth was, Tim had never met Mike; they'd attended the same events, but Tim had avoided him, seeing him as a dour and petty individual.

He turned, beckoning Mike towards the car. Mike wouldn't be met with support and open arms but, rather, cold handcuffs and shouted orders – but he didn't know that yet. For now, Mike felt like he was a made man. He gave one quick glance back towards the gates of the facility, looking at something or someone, before following Tim, trotting to keep up.

***

Maia watched the interaction from a distance, unable to hear but seeing Mike's mood lift. He gave her a last glance – a neutral look, a mixture of disinterest and perhaps disdain.

'Bye, Mike,' she said quietly, turning to walk back inside.

Wedgetail AWACS – South China Sea

The large Boeing aircraft was making a straight sprint back towards Darwin, its powerful radar still collecting every piece of information for hundreds of kilometres around. The pilot of the AWACS watched the incoming flight of Chinese fighters closely. They had their own AWACS at the rear of their formation, who were no doubt sending their location back to the fighters. They had to maintain enough distance from the incoming flight while still keeping data feeds available for the incoming support. Without them, the ships down below and the fighters in the sky would lose a sizeable advantage and understanding of their enemy. The AWACS were their eyes and ears.

'Magpie flight, we're bugging out to your post. Once we pass you, we'll take up a support positive behind your cover. Copy.'

'Wilco Wedgetail, ETA five minutes. What's the status of HMAS Hobart and the incoming fighters?'

'Hobart is pushing hard for the USS John Basilone to the northeast. They are moving at best possible speed but will be within firing range in the next ten to fifteen minutes. Chinese bandits are pushing hard to catch Hobart. Note, count one Xian H-6 bomber pulling up the rear. Likely loaded with longer range ordinance.'

'Copy, Wedgetail. We'll sort them out.'

Magpie Flight

'Magpie two and three, we have to keep those fighters out of range of the Hobart and USS John Basilone. I want you both screening the incoming fighters. Engage them with EW, and if they start shooting, we'll light them up. I'll take the bomber, swing around their right flank. Keep it tight, and remember: your wingmen are expendable, you're not.'

'Copy, Magpie lead,' echoed from the other two pilots in unison.

The F-35s were flying supercomputers, in many respects, packed with sensors, stealth tech, communications equipment and various data feeds. They provided a clear view of the battlefield – better than any aircraft ever had before. They weren't the fastest, the most manoeuvrable or the best armed, but when working together, they would be able to outshoot and outsmart even the best enemy craft. Plus, they had the added, if untested bonus of six Ghost Bat drones flying alongside them. One F-35 became three, three became nine. Each Ghost Bat was a slick-looking aircraft, half the size of the larger F-35s and with no space for a pilot.

The dark greys of their paintwork and pointed features cut a sleek and menacing image as they perfectly imitated the movements of their host planes.

Each drone had a slightly different role and weapon loadout. Magpie lead had one loaded for EW. The aircraft was packed with sensors and a radar that, when aimed at incoming craft, would blind their scopes, making communication and the accurate engagement of an enemy plane or ship significantly harder. If they wanted to start shooting, they'd need to get close. And if they tried to get that close, they'd die.

'Powering up EW,' Magpie lead announced. His communications not only streamed to the two other pilots but back to HQJOC and the HMAS Hobart. No one would be out of the loop. However, the American commanders were largely spectators, uncomfortably reliant upon another nation for the protection of their personnel.

The EW equipment on the drone sat on a nose-mounted pod. Radar signatures from the incoming bandits were absorbed into the drones, channelled from the Wedgetail AWACS and pushed by their host F-35. The EW system filtered through the electronic noise, identifying matching signatures and channels before unleashing a flood of its own electromagnetic energy, overriding communications and degrading the radar picture available to the bandits – essentially, making them blind and deaf. It would make their communications network crackle, pop and fill with static, while their screens would be overwhelmed by shapeless blobs. They could still pose a threat, but without accurate radar data, they were easy pickings.

The Loyal Wingman drone received its targets and orders from the Magpie lead. Obediently, it flew out in front of the pack and launched its assault, its graceful lines betraying the chaos it could cause.

Sea Dragon Flight

The five J-16 Shenyang strike aircrafts were relatively modern, yet they didn't hold a flame to the advanced F-35s bearing down on them. But, with five against three, they felt comfortable. Loaded with anti-ship and anti-air missiles, they had considerable striking power.

'Dragons two, three, four and five, take care of our incoming friends. I will target their fleeing AWACS. Keep them busy while our H-6 gets to work on the Americans below.'

The squadron leader felt confident and excited. This was the first time his forces had been sent out with orders to attack their enemy. For too many years, they'd barely challenged the Americans, often reduced to performing shadowing exercises or yelling warnings to their naval vessels, never allowed to shoot, forbidden to defend Chinese land. That was about to change.

They flew in a tight formation, guided by a Shaanxi KJ-500 AWACS loitering fifty kilometres behind them. According to the radar image it provided, the three incoming Australian planes were F-35s: untested aircraft about which there had been numerous issues reported in the news. They had fewer munitions and wouldn't be as fast as his planes. The loss of a few of his pilots would be a small cost to destroy even one of their planes. The cost of the planes, and the pilot flying it, outstripped the cost of his J-16 by many multitudes. If he could distract them for long enough, the bomber could get through and fire its missiles. Based on the information provided by their AWACS, a lot of missiles had already been fired; they wouldn't have many ways to stop another onslaught. This would be their moment.

'Dragons, commence your attack, be ready to—'
ZZZZZZZIIIIIIIIIIRRRRTTTTTT!
An ear-shattering electronic screeching rang out through his headphones, nearly deafening him. 'Fucking hell!' he swore as he dropped the volume on his mic. They'd experienced some interference in training, but never

anything like this. 'All callsigns switch to backup channels,' he yelled into his receiver, unable to hear any confirmation over the washed-out channel.

'AWACS, this is Sea Dragon lead, do you copy?' the line crackled and popped. He repeated his call, a sense of dread wrapping around his throat. Seconds passed as he waited and repeated the call for a second then third time. Nothing.

'All Sea Dragon callsigns, do you copy me?'

'Intef ... sdge, poor ... sgsrs.'

He caught less than half of the garbled reply. 'Fuck me,' he exclaimed again.

Fine. If that's how it was going to be, he wouldn't chicken out now. They still had a good idea of where the enemy fighters were, and they outnumbered them. Comms be damned! He gazed out of his glass canopy at the fighters flying by his side. The men in both planes looked back at him expectantly, no doubt experiencing the same communication blackout. He signalled for them to switch to short-wave communications. They wouldn't be much use once they broke off, but at least he could direct his men now.

Clicking the radio on his chest, he could immediately hear the now ever-present static, but it wasn't as bad. 'Sea Dragon callsigns, do you read me?'

A chorus of replies came over the net, crossing over one another. The sound of relief in their voices was clear, even over the static in the line.

'We are being jammed by the enemy. But our orders do not change. Intercept the Australians, make room for the bomber. I'll find the plane jamming us, and I'll kill it!' It must be coming from the enemy AWACS. They were powerful, valuable planes.

The planes to his right immediately peeled away, swiftly pulling to the side. The planes on his left did the same, but in the other direction. He grinned, feeling his confidence returning. His radar was messy, with large static blotches covering the small screen, making it nearly impossible to see their targets clearly. But he would move away from the group. A lone aircraft. The enemy had only three, and they'd be busy with his compatriots; he could slip by unseen, surprising them.

Pulling down his sun visor, Sea Dragon lead pulled his craft hard over, aiming for the fleeing blob that was the Australian Wedgetail AWACS. He didn't notice his own radar had slowly started to change, the three little dots becoming six, then nine. He also failed to notice that his radar had become increasingly blurry, the jamming slowly ruining his picture.

He didn't know it, but his own AWACS had been trying to warn Sea Dragon flight for the last few minutes. Packed with more countermeasures and a broader electromagnetic range to operate at, its radar and communications still worked effectively enough. It could see the battlefield advantage changing. The incoming F-35s were no longer three but had morphed into nine somehow. It had warned the bomber, but Sea Dragon flight couldn't be reached. It could only watch as they separated and flew directly at their enemy.

Magpie Flight

'Be aware, Wedgetail flight, you have four bandits pushing on heading 205 degrees. Likely seeking to block your advance,' the Wedgetail warned, its operators following the movement of each plane.

Magpie lead smiled to himself. 'Alright, Magpies, looks like our friends don't seem too concerned with the jamming. We've got five bogies incoming on your post. Line 'em up and knock 'em down. I've got number five making a beeline for Wedgetail. Send in the drones and see if we can scare 'em off. They start shooting, take them down. Understood?'

'Copy, lead,' both replied.

They'd done multiple exercises of this exact same scenario. Actually, deploying his men, and now adding drones into the fray, was a new experience. But, with a near-absolute view of the battlefield, plenty of fuel and a swarm of cutting-edge drones, Magpie lead had every right to feel confident.

His only real concern was the warships below. They still had anti-air missiles that could be a problem. So far, though, the shooting seemed to have stopped. One Type 052D destroyer was making a run from the area of operations, the other limping away wounded.

Each F-35 split from their heading, picking clusters of incoming fighters. The Ghost Bats that had been hugging the F-35s also split off, moving to intercept the aircraft bearing down on them. They wouldn't fire without command from the F-35s, but they'd be able to interpret and calculate the path their enemy might take. Without a human pilot, they could bank faster and harder than a manned aircraft, making them nimble and deadly.

The drones blasted ahead of their human leaders. Only the EW drone of Magpie lead remained, constantly blasting and altering its spectrum of attacks to keep the bandits blind and deaf. The reality was that the human pilots would sit back, directing their drones, keeping their fingers on the trigger if they needed to fire. But they were largely out of harm's way in this new form of aerial combat.

Blinded from the persistent jamming, the Chinese J-16s couldn't see the speedy Ghost Bats. The drones blasted past the incoming fighters at speeds over Mach 2, staying high above their human enemies. Smaller than regular fighters, they were hard to see at the best of times. Each drone selected its target before being ordered to activate its fire control radars and locked onto an individual plane by its human master.

Each of the Chinese pilots reacted differently, but all tried to evade as their training had taught them, banking and rolling with increasing g-force. The formation quickly splintered, each trying to shake whatever aircraft was tracking them. If the drones could think, they might have been amused. Without a human pilot, they could easily match the slower aircraft.

'Think they've had enough yet?' Magpie two called.

'Yeah, I'd say so. Maintain pos. Wedgetail, over to you,' Magpie lead confirmed.

The ringing that had started moments before in the ears of the fleeing Chinese pilots stopped as quickly as it had started, leaving an eerie silence behind. But it was quickly replaced by a new sound, a human voice over their headsets.

'Chinese fighters, this is the Royal Australian Air Force. We have each of your aircraft targeted and ready for destruction. Leave the area of operation immediately. You have thirty seconds to comply; failure to do so will result in your destruction. This is your only warning,' the voice said in perfect Mandarin.

The voice was immediately replaced by the warning tone of missile lock, reinforcing the message that they were outmatched.

One by one, each aircraft turned, making a hasty retreat to the northeast without direction from their squadron leader. With a blanked-out radar and almost zero visual on the attacking aircraft that were locking them, it was a simple choice.

At least, it was for four of the pilots. One remained, doggedly maintaining its heading.

'Wedgetail, heads up: you've got one bandit headed right for you. They must have a firm lock on your position. Magpie lead will intercept. Recommend you take evasive action.'

'Copy, Magpie lead, making our move now. Good hunting.'

Rings surrounded the Chinese fighter on the radar picture, representing the known or suspected firing distance of its missiles. The outermost ring was already closer than Magpie lead would have liked, and it was closing in fast. The slower-moving Wedgetail would not be a match for the nimble fighter.

'Magpie two and three, keep pushing forward and drive that H-6 off. If it comes within our AO, take it down. Understood?'

'Copy.'

Magpie lead switched over his targeting feed, bringing up a visual from his Ghost Bat as it covered the encroaching fighters. It was directly sighted into his helmet, making it appear as if he was flying the unmanned drone. Selecting two AIM-9 Sidewinder missiles and targeting them both against the enemy bandit, he checked his timer. As it passed the minute mark, he gently squeezed the trigger on his HOTAS. Unlike firing from his own craft, there was no audio or gentle rock of the aircraft as the missiles launched and activated their engines. Instead, a green confirmation message flashed onto his screen before the two missiles came into view, thin white smoky lines against the clear, blue sky.

'Two away. Fox two,' he announced.

Magpie lead watched from the Ghost Bat's view as the missiles streaked ahead. He could barely make out the bandit, but the small shape suddenly dived, trying to shake the pursuing missiles. No longer in visual range, he had to rely on the little dots representing the planes and the missiles on his screen. He watched them as they edged closer together. One missile closed in on its target before seemingly disappearing in the moments before it was expected to reach the enemy aircraft. The pilot frowned. The missile had either failed or fallen for enemy chaff.

The second missile closed, only to suffer the same early death. The enemy pilot was clearly more cunning – or luckier – than expected.

'Fuck,' muttered Magpie lead. The distance between the enemy bandit and the Wedgetail was shrinking rapidly.

'Two away. Fox two.'

A second volley of sidewinders was unleashed from the drone. The bandit wouldn't survive another round.

They soared towards the target, the infrared nose cones

locked firmly onto the signature of the jet. With each second, they closed, metre by metre. Just like before, the Chinese pilot dumped flares and dove. The first missile fell for the same trick but not the second. It homed in, drawing itself to the plane's right wing.

Magpie lead watched as the missile and aircraft disappeared off radar suddenly. The pilot nodded in grim satisfaction before frowning at his screen. Two small dots appeared within seconds of the Chinese jet being destroyed. Magpie lead checked his screens, seeing that the jet had just reached the edge of the ring representing its firing range to the Wedgetail. The pilot's last action had been one of defiance.

He didn't need to do it, but he did anyway. 'Wedgetail, you've got two incoming missiles! Crank it!'

The pilot replied, sounding strained, 'Copy, Magpie lead, evading.'

Despite being a high-tech military aircraft, the Wedgetail was, in reality, a commercial aircraft fitted with expensive high-tech equipment. It was not nimble, and it was not fast. It certainly couldn't outfly two incoming missiles. It did have some countermeasures, but there was no telling if they'd be enough.

Magpie lead switched back over to the EW Ghost Bat loitering a few clicks back. It was the closest one to the Wedgetail.

'Switching EW Ghost Bat to defence,' the pilot announced.

The radar image showed the enemy missile approaching at speeds of Mach 2. Far beyond that of the Wedgetail.

The drone dutifully followed its order, sweeping in at top speed to cover the fleeing Wedgetail. Gaining quickly, it slowed a hundred metres behind the larger aircraft, waiting for the other incoming missiles to arrive. The drone felt no pain or regret, no fear or sadness; it just waited for its next order, regardless of whether that meant its death.

As the enemy missiles homed in, the Ghost Bat fired its

flares, attracting the attention of one of the missiles. One missile changed course, heading for the distraction. The others ignored the flares and followed the unmanned aircraft. The drone determined its velocity and trajectory, waiting until the perfect moment, before slowing and collecting the missile into its rear. Both drone and missile exploded in a fiery spectacle. It had done its job, loyal to the end.

The Wedgetail pulled hard out of its dive before yanking the yoke towards the left. It wasn't much of an evasion, but this way the missile would have to work for it. All members of the crew were strapped in tightly, white-faced with oxygen masks, as the enormous g-forces pushed against their bodies. They were only passengers now, in the hands of the pilot. The last missile zoomed past the spot where its cousin had just destroyed the Wingman drone. Chasing the large infrared signal that represented the plane and all the lives it held, the missile remained on course for the Wedgetail. The pilot watched his own radar, waiting until the missile closed in for its kill before pulling the yoke over and dumping all the flares he had. Some screamed further back in the plane. The missile sensed it had arrived at its target, exploding violently. The explosion rocked the plane, a sudden yellow and red fiery ball enveloping the right side momentarily. The pilot gritted his teeth, feeling the controls slacken in his hands. But they weren't dead. Their plane was still flying … just. Numerous alarms rang out through the cockpit.

'That doesn't look good,' the co-pilot said suddenly. The pilot unclenched his teeth, the sudden noise from the co-pilot forcing his body to relax a little. The immediate threat of death was gone. 'Looks like serious damage to the port-side wing and engine. No telling if any of that penetrated the cabin.'

'Check the cabin, see if everyone is alright,' the pilot ordered.

The co-pilot opened the door. The fact that they were

met with a sudden blast of decompression was a good sign. He returned a few seconds later. 'All intact and no serious injuries. Wing looks bad though.'

'Wedgetail, this is Magpie lead, I've still got you on radar. Confirm your status.'

'We're alive, Magpie lead, but in a bad way. We'll have to RTB. Grateful if we can get an escort.'

'You'll have it.'

'Magpie two, cover Wedgetail back to base.'

'Copy, lead.'

The pilot nodded to himself. The radar picture still looked good. The Chinese hadn't returned despite the jamming ending; even the larger bomber had turned, but it remained at holding distance, no doubt awaiting orders. They still ran on fuel and would have to return soon. Magpie guessed they'd only have another thirty minutes.

'Magpie three, we'll keep an eye out for any smartasses who get an idea that they can slip through. Once they depart, we'll RTB and meet up with the KC to refuel. I'd say we've won this one.'

CHAPTER 24

USS John Basilone – Malacca Strait

The bridge was a complete mess. The hardened glass windows were shattered and cracked. Consoles were blackened and torn; a good portion of the starboard side had a gaping hole in it. Danny thought he could see some blood pooled on the floor and spattered against the wall. It was a scene of carnage, but surprisingly to him, everyone remained calm and functional.

The helmsman was at his station. Sailors continued working from the few undamaged consoles, while others busied themselves with whatever repairs they could make. The captain stood silently, watching out from his shattered command point. He continued to give instructions and orders, although a quiet spoken word or gentle nod was all he could seemingly muster. The gentle breeze washed through the bridge, hints of sea salt and fresh air mixing with the smell of rocket fuel and smoke. The noise of the ship wafted in; the wash of the bow against the ocean, the clank of tools against the deck. People below were collecting spent shell casings that were littering the deck.

Danny broke the silence, 'Captain, reporting as ordered.'

Jonathan stirred from his quiet contemplation. 'Ah, Mr Blackburn, sounds like you had quite the adventure!' He gave Danny a quick look up and down. The dishevelled state of them told enough of a story.

Danny replied, 'Yes, sir. Looks like you had a similar experience.'

Jonathan gazed around his shattered bridge. 'You would not be wrong there, commander …' he said quietly. Then, touching a damaged console with his hand, 'She did just fine. We had a few close calls, but we're still operational … *just*.' His voice drifted off as he silently worked through his emotions.

Seconds passed before he spoke again, this time with a deep sigh, 'So, give me an update; did we find what we were looking for?' he asked, looking at Danny directly.

Danny swallowed, 'Well, sir, as you probably know, we ran into some trouble. There was an explosion while we were searching the hold.'

'Yes, it killed one of my men.'

'Right, well, we recovered as much as we could, but whatever was in that container, it's a total loss. Once we examine the remains, we can confirm whether it was our missile, but that might not be the end of it …'

'Go on,' Jonathan intoned, sensing Danny's hesitation.

'Well, sir, it's impossible to know if they have taken components or data from the missile. Without knowing the state of the missile, we can only speculate, but there were some serious diagnostic tools and equipment in that cargo hold. Plus, we observed one individual leaving with a large case. We can't know for sure what they recovered, but it stands to reason it would have been something valuable.' Danny explained his interaction with the soldier in the Huang Shen's corridor.

'Doesn't sound like a regular soldier – special forces or something more,' Jonathan mused before sighing, looking around the bridge again. 'Well, I think it's clear we stirred up the hornet's nest here. I only hope the bloody nose we gave them was enough. For now, we are sailing at best possible speed for port in Singapore. As you can see, our ship isn't exactly in top condition, and we're basically out of munitions. We'll meet up with the HMAS Hobart along the way. Hell, the Malaysians are even going to give us an escort.' He smiled to himself, enjoying some internal joke.

'What about the Huang Shen's crew and the Chinese coast-guard vessels?' Danny asked.

'The Huang Shen is making its way to the bottom of the strait as we speak. It appears the crew got off and the Malaysians have picked them up. As for the coast guard, the Zhaotou is that burning cloud you see off our port. We've observed the two other cutters offloading crew. They're done. The Malaysians will probably escort them out of the strait and recover the Zhaotou in time.

'And the ships that were lobbing missiles at us? Did we get them?'

Jonathan smiled, 'I'd say closer to a draw. Injured and killed men and women, empty munitions racks and damaged systems. We've got aircover from some Australian F-35s. So, for now, everyone has called it a truce.'

Danny nodded, a contemplative look on his face.

'You're dismissed. Go get some food and rest if you can. We'll be in port in a couple of hours – where it appears there is a plane waiting for you.'

'For both of us?' Danny asked.

'Correct. VIP treatment, and a medical team for Commander Edwards. I believe you are the only reason he is still alive, Mr Blackburn. You've done good work, but you'll forgive me if I'd rather not have you darken my doorway for a little while. Your mission has taken a toll on my ship and crew.' He made a sweeping motion with his arm towards the shattered bridge.

Danny smiled, reaching out to shake the captain's hand, 'Sir, you'll find I am more than happy to go back to dry land. This has been more adventure than I ever signed up for.'

Jonathan shook his hand. 'You did just fine, Danny.'

Danny turned, leaving the captain to his duties and contemplation.

The ship around him was still a hive of activity, with sailors doing repairs and other tasks. He'd somehow figured out how to navigate the maze of stairwells, ladders and hallways, making his way to medical.

Jesse lay motionless on a medical bed, various tubes and monitors coming from his body, while a large bandage covered most of his right side. They'd apparently done some emergency surgery to stabilise him and mend his arm, but there would be more surgery, and no doubt a long recovery time.

Danny wasn't sure if Jesse could be woken. He knew they'd have him fairly drugged up to ease his pain.

'Hey man, not sure if you'll hear this, but we'll be heading out soon. Captain has sorted us some VIP treatment back to Australia.'

Jesse's eyes flicked open, his gaze momentarily unfocused in his drug haze.

'That you, Danny?' Jesse asked weakly, his voice quieter than normal.

'Right here, Jesse,' he replied, squeezing Jesse's uninjured hand.

'Ah shit, man, not so hard – you'll break my other arm.'

Danny flinched, 'Oh, I'm sorry, I …'

The slim smile on Jesse's lips and almost inaudible chuckle said enough.

'Ah, you dick!'

The little chuckle died quickly, as Jesse's eyes suddenly focused, the haze lifting. 'Hey Danny, seriously though, thank you. One of the guys told me you fished me out of the water. Not sure I'd be here if you hadn't.'

It was Danny's turn to smile now. 'Don't mention it; you'd do the same for me. Plus, I think this makes us even now, right?'

'Not even close yet, Danny,' Jesse said with a weak smirk.

'You get some sleep, man. We'll be out of here soon enough.'

Jesse nodded, his eyes closing again, a slow rhythmic breathing taking over.

For Danny, his only remaining goal was bed. The last few hours had started to catch up with him, and without the constant flood of danger and adrenaline, he was fading fast. Making his way back to his bunk, his last memory was climbing onto the sheets. His world immediately turned black.

The White House – United States of America

Quinton was in a rage. 'We have to strike back! They have attacked our ships, killed our men. This is war!' He slammed his fist against the table.

The rest of the room looked around uncomfortably, Quinton oblivious. They'd been getting a constant flow of data directly into the situation room, each missile intercepted, fighter shot down and person killed. More information was available than ever before. However, they'd been spectators, watching boxers in the ring. For Quinton, the sense of impotence was agonising.

The joint chiefs had become openly hostile, bristling under Quinton's constant attacks. 'What do you suggest we do?! Everyone is disengaging, and you want to start it all up again? Attack the Chinese?' the chief of navy ops growled back across the table.

Quinton wouldn't be put off; he was most comfortable in a fiery debate. 'We need to send a message that attacking America will have severe and immediate consequences. We can't let these upstarts think it's okay to shoot at us!'

'And what, smashing their ships and blowing their planes out of the sky isn't enough?' the admiral roared back, standing with his hand flat against the table.

Quinton stood, squaring up against the bulky man, readying another reply. His anger was hotter than ever. He'd ended up in his fair share of fist fights in his younger years.

The secretary of state intervened quickly, seeking to keep some kind of decorum, or at the very least avoid a fistfight. 'What do you suggest then, Quinton?'

He turned to face the President. 'We strike them hard!' he said, punching his fist into his other hand for emphasis. 'We have the Seventh Fleet up near Japan. Let's target one of their military bases in the South China Sea and wipe it back into the ocean. They claimed those islands weren't militarised, but here they are, launching combat aircraft. Let's remind them how powerful we are and put them back in their place. They need to remember who's the world's greatest superpower!'

'You'll start a war, you fool!' the secretary of defence called across the oak table. 'We need to find a solution that doesn't involve missiles and death. We need to pick up the phone and talk with their president!'

'That is bullshit. You're talking like we're afraid of them – they're the ones who should be afraid of us! We need to make our point known; if they start shooting back, that's on them. Maybe they need a harsher lesson!' He was shouting now, his heart thumping and little bits of spit flying from his mouth. Somewhere in his brain, he knew he was losing control, but it didn't matter. The excitement and rage fuelled him. This was his moment.

Throughout this episode of rage, the President had simply watched on, happy to let his staff fight. Quinton was sure he would back the strongest in the room. The President loved a good show of force. The volume in the room rose as the arguments continued. Quinton grew redder in the face.

Suddenly, a sharp knock at the door broke through the yelling. Everyone stopped and looked at the door.

The President looked at Quinton with a worryingly mischievous grin. Quinton felt a quick jolt of fear.

The doors were pulled open by two secret-service agents as two men with badges and guns strode in, escorted by more secret-service agents. Quinton didn't recognise the new men. Dressed in black and grey suits, they carried themselves like law enforcement, shoulders squared, scanning the room, seemingly unfazed by the powerful people present. Their eyes fell on Quinton, and the rest of the group swarmed in. Two men in FBI blazers approached Quinton.

'Quinton Davenport, you are under arrest. Anything you say—'

'WHAT?! GET YOUR HANDS OFF ME!'

The two agents forcibly hauled him unceremoniously out of his chair. His mind whirled.

'Under suspicion of acting unlawfully and outside of your power—'

'DO YOU KNOW WHO I AM?' he screamed.

Everyone around the room looked totally bewildered – all but the President, who remained sitting, legs kicked outward in a resting position, hands crossed over his chest. The same mischievous grin was still on his lips.

'Anything you say—'

They dragged him towards the door. He struggled against them. 'YOU CAN'T DO THIS!' he screamed back into the room.

They could, and they did. Ignoring his protests, and twisting his arm painfully behind his back, they pulled Quinton across the threshold and out of the situation room. As he took one last look at the President – the man he'd help get elected, whose job he coveted – Quinton saw nothing but the lasting, satisfied smirk across the man's face. It hit him all at once. He'd been outplayed.

The doors closed sharply. The President and everyone else in the situation room were now concealed from his view. Quinton would never again see them, that room, or much else. Handcuffs were slapped on his wrists. The desire to fight was suddenly leaving his body. He gazed across the corner of the next room, and standing quietly in the corner, his errand boy watched silently.

'Dick, help me, please!' he pleaded to the man who had faithfully served him.

The man didn't move; nor did he reply. He simply watched as his boss was hustled on. All Quinton would receive was Dick's uncaring, cold stare.

The President waited until the doors slammed shut and Quinton's pitiful show had come to an end. 'Well, now that that has been taken care of, shall we move on to solving this crisis?'

Everyone else in the room was clearly shocked by what had just happened.

'Madam secretary,' the President began, 'your recommendation?'

'Sir, we'll reach out to the Chinese through our embassy and arrange a ceasefire. I recommend we do the same through military channels. They will no doubt be wondering what we'll do next. However, I recommend you give the Chinese president a call as soon as possible, sir. Knowing how fragmented the Chinese system can be, we want to go to the top as soon as possible.'

The army chief of staff spoke up, 'I second the secretary of state's recommendation, sir. We should keep our forces on alert but make sure they stay out of range of the Chinese for now. I recommend we order a new safe minimum distance for the time being. Give everyone some breathing room.'

'Great! Sounds like a plan – and do we have anything from the John? Any news on whether they recovered the missile?'

A quiet intelligence officer spoke up when no one else answered. 'Not yet, sir. That'll take time to assess, but early reports from Captain O'Donnell indicate there was some kind of explosion. They believe the missile was on board and that it was destroyed or sunk with the Huang Shen.'

The President nodded, pressing his two index fingers against his chin. 'Okay, the missile can be a later problem. Let's get the Chinese on the line and clean this mess up.

Good work, everyone,' he smiled.

Zhongnanhai – Beijing – China

The president faced away from the men, staring at the large bulletproof window of his office. Chang sat with Admiral Taosing. They'd been summoned the moment the shooting had started in the strait, but by the time they'd arrived at the presidential offices, everything was over.

'What are the Americans doing now?' the president asked, still facing out towards the window, hands interlocked behind him.

Chang let Taosing do the military talk. 'It appears they are disengaging, sir. Radar and satellite imagery shows air and naval forces returning to base.'

'Should we expect follow-up strikes?'

'Is it very unlikely, sir. Everything happened very quickly. And we could make the argument our forces were simply protecting their own. The Americans shot first, after all. The rest of their forces do not appear to be making any kind of threatening displays. All the same, we should remain on alert.' Chang doubted it was as simple as *the Americans shot first*, but he kept his mouth closed; there was nothing to gain.

The president nodded. 'Very good. And Comrade Wonqin? What of the missile? What could we get out?'

Chang had been relieved that his aide had run the latest report from his field agent over; without it, he'd have had to find some kind of excuse. It would have made him look incapable.

'A success, sir! As you know, we couldn't take the missile with us. However, our field agent states that they successfully captured the contents of the missile's hard drives and have detailed examinations of its internal workings. It will be easy for our engineers and scientists to rework the data into a weapon of our own.'

'And do you think the Americans know?'

Chang frowned theatrically. 'We can't be certain they are completely unaware of our capture of the missile, but it is doubtful. We destroyed the missile, and the Huang Shen is at the bottom of the ocean with any of its remains. Even if they do figure out that we captured it, they would think it was destroyed. They'll never know we can rival their technology.'

The president turned around, smiling for the first time. He seemed pleased.

'Well, comrades, it seems we have won our first victory against the Americans. Our sailors did well, and our airmen had great courage. The damage we have inflicted on their ships will take months, if not years, to repair. In that time, we will have produced a multitude of new ships and planes. More powerful and better armed than before. We can suffer the loss of a few older planes, and we can train new men. The Americans cannot match us, not anymore.' The smile and passion of the president's voice was infectious. 'I want to make sure your field agent is rewarded, Comrade Wonquin. Without him, this operation would not have succeeded.'

Chang nodded, mentally noting the president's request to reward the man. He hadn't even considered it, personally. His view was that his agent had fulfilled his duty and should expect nothing in return. He also had another thought.

'Mr President, if I may, we will need to reconsider the threat we see from the Australians. They put up stiff resistance against our brave destroyers, and it was their fighters that killed our pilot. Maybe they need to be taught a lesson and remember whose backyard we let them live in? Wouldn't you agree, comrade admirals?' Posing it as a question would make it seem like more of a group discussion.

Admiral Taosing nodded slowly. 'We have some options available to us,' he replied cautiously, unsure what Chang was suggesting.

The president nodded sagely. 'Do you have a

recommendation, comrades?'

Chang spoke first, 'Yes, sir, and if I may use the wisdom of the military.' *A little bit of flattery never hurt.* These men were prideful and, in truth, Chang was as military as any of them, except he didn't wear a uniform. 'The next time the Australians send a plane or ship to our bases in the South China Sea, we should make an example of them. Not use words. The world needs to know how strong China really is. Make sure they understand the costs of working against us.'

Admiral Taosing tried to hide his discomfort. 'If it is the president's wish, we can pull together a plan. No doubt they will be cautious around us for the time being. Perhaps we give them some time to drop their guard?'

The president shook his head. 'No, we need to be strong now. The Americans rely on their allies. If we can pull the Australians away, our chances for the future are much better. Particularly when it comes to Taiwan.'

'If we attack or destroy an Australian plane or ship, the Americans will respond,' Taosing said weakly.

'Over one plane or ship? At worst, we can expect some harmless sanctions or strong words.'

The president turned to look back out of the window. 'Very well, gentlemen. Bring me a plan tomorrow. For now, good work.'

HQJOC – Australia

'So that's it?' Ata asked, looking up at the tactical displays covering the tall walls. Officers, soldiers and aides continued their hurried work, but the constant flow of alarming updates and clenched fists as each rocket was intercepted was gone. The energy and intensity of the room had lifted. The chief of the defence force had made his own quiet exit as the little dots representing Chinese forces continued their northward course. HMAS Hobart and the USS John Basilone were close to joining up and would soon be cautiously moving into Singapore. Magpie flight and the Wedgetail, likewise, had moved towards the circling KC tanker, waiting their turn to refuel before heading back to base. Allied forces remained at heightened readiness, and the HMAS Fremantle was moving into the Java to escort the Hobart if needed. Across the Indo-Pacific, flight crews remained on standby; aircraft patrolled, and ships kept a lookout. They'd remain this way for many more hours before they were sure the Chinese forces were no longer a threat.

Maia nodded quietly, 'I'd say so.'

'What about Danny and Jesse?' Ata asked, still worried.

'We won't know until they send us a message or someone gets a list of killed and wounded.'

'Oh ...' Ata replied before quickly pulling up her emails and shooting off a quick message. *Let us know if you're dead. I call dibs on your desk.*

Maia didn't say anything, knowing it was Ata's own way of coping, of feeling in control.

Ata looked up at Maia. 'What happened to Mike? You take him out back and you know ...' She made a gun with her hand.

Maia gave her a wink. 'Oh, something like that. Safe to say we won't be seeing Mike back here anytime soon ... or ever.'

Ata looked mystified. 'What do you mean?'

'You'll find out,' Maia said cryptically. 'Looks like you have an email,' she said, pointing to the little window that had just appeared on Ata's screen.

'It's from Danny!' she said excitedly. The relief of finally knowing washed over her.

THE EAGLE HAS LANDED!
P.S. Hands off my desk.

Maia smiled as Ata groaned, 'What a dork.'

Mehrabad Air Base – Iran

THE MALACCA INCIDENT

Colonel Rostami watched the live coverage of the incident in Malacca with a sense of grim satisfaction and fascination. The BBC reporter was trying in vain to continue discussing the possibilities of further conflict between the Americans and Chinese, but despite the suggestions by various "experts" that this event could spiral into a larger war, it was clear that the skirmish was over. Both sides had backed away. If they were going to keep fighting, the news would have kept coming, thick and fast.

Still, it was interesting all the same. The Americans hadn't done nearly as well as he'd expected, but nor had the Chinese scored any knockout blows. To his mind, this event would be considered more of a tie than any clear victory.

A gentle knock against the door of his temporary office stirred Rostami from his focus on the small television. 'Enter.'

A tall, slender man in uniform entered. One of Rostami's captains – one of his most trusted men.

'Do you have them?' he asked him, pointing towards the bundle of rolled documents in the man's hands.

'Yes, sir. Everything.'

'Quickly, lay them out on the table,' Rostami ordered eagerly.

The man obeyed, unrolling a set of detailed architectural plans for numerous buildings.

Rostami flicked through greedily as the captain confirmed the locations.

'That is the parliament, president's office, Sa'dabad Complex …'

'Good, good,' Rostami said, already examining the details. 'With these, we cannot be stopped. For the country, we rid ourselves of these oppressive, corrupt religious fools.'

'The men are ready, sir. All you need to do is give the order,' the captain said, feeling confident.

'Soon, my friend. Soon. We must wait until the moment is right; we will need the right allies, and we will need to get the people onside.'

Rostami grinned as he continued examining the documents, noting entry points, secret rooms and other safe places. He'd exterminate the roaches.

All of them.

EPILOGUE

Fiery Cross Reef – South China Sea

Chief Scientist Sun hadn't stopped jabbering away since they'd escaped the Huang Shen and arrived on the destroyer. A certain nervous energy pervaded the little man as he paced around the common room inside the destroyer, switching between whingeing and talking up his exploits as they had made their escape. By his retelling, he'd wrestled valiantly with the soldier that had tackled him, but everyone knew otherwise.

Equally, he'd wanted more time to study the missile and was annoyed that it had been destroyed. Most importantly – no matter what – it wasn't his fault. He threw accusations around freely and easily to anyone within earshot, seemingly oblivious to logic and what would have happened if they'd stayed.

Ming had stopped listening long ago, while Jian had stormed off, hopefully to get medical attention for his likely broken ribs.

The data had been locked away securely after they'd checked to make sure all of its contents were intact after the rather bumpy extraction. Everything looked good, and

Ming had to smile to himself. It had been a fun ride. Hopefully the bosses would see his worth and reward him with more postings, although he doubted anything would live up to his expectations. Already, the excitement of their escape was wearing off.

Plus, sitting here, listening to this small man moan and groan was hardly the ending Ming had longed for after the action he'd just seen. He recognised the melancholy building slowly inside him. The slow-moving, molasses-like feeling of emptiness that always came after coming down from a high. Part of him recognised it as a form of addiction and depression, but another part suppressed those thoughts, choosing instead to focus on finding his next fix. More adrenaline. He just had to go find it, and in Beijing, there were many ways to have a good time. His mood lifted somewhat at the thought. They'd be docking at Yongshu Jiao soon, the Chinese name for the island, in an hour, where he could board a military transport back to China. He'd have to do endless hours of debriefing and cross-examination by analysts. But it was ultimately a small price to pay.

Tapping his leg with his fingers, Ming felt the hard edge of a pistol tucked into one of his pockets. He'd almost forgotten about it in all the action. Certainly, watching the destroyer he'd boarded firing missile after missile had been a new, if not slightly thrilling experience. Pulling out the pistol, he examined its features more closely. It was larger and heavier than what he was used to. He recognised it as a modern 1911. It would shoot a large 45 ACP round, which could easily drop someone with a single shot. It was simple enough, a standard-issue weapon for sure. But it was a trophy, his to win and keep. Plus, the man he'd taken it from sat in his memory. An oddity. His strong features and the somewhat shocked look on his face were still clearly visible in Ming's memory.

Ming stood, leaving the raving scientist behind. There was a secure compartment on this ship, which would have what he needed. The tiny shoebox of a room had space for two people, and he had it all to himself. In the MSS internal system, there would be a list of known foreign officials with top-secret clearances. It was a long list, detailing almost everyone in the Five Eyes intelligence alliance. They'd managed to steal huge datasets of biometric data from vetting servers more than once, meaning they could, in theory, search for anyone.

Filtering the options to Americans, he started scanning the endless number of faces, removing sexes, ethnicities and other features that wouldn't fit the bill. Thirty minutes later, he landed on Danny's face.

'There you are.'

'Mr Daniel Blackburn.' The name sounded funny in Ming's mind. 'Weapons engineer and intelligence. What an interesting combination,' he mused. Ming put a flag against Danny's profile, making an entry for future use. His file was empty for now, beyond the basic data. Ming doubted it would stay that way. Call it a hunch.

An email notification drew Ming's attention; it was from his CO back in Tehran, Liu. *Good work. The bosses want to have a chat back in Beijing. Meet you there.*

Interesting, he thought. It wasn't often he'd been examined by the bosses themselves. But then again, this had been an abnormal operation.

Ming logged off, stretching, and went off to search for a coffee, walking with the relaxed confidence of a man without a care in the world.

Fairbairn – Canberra Airport - Australia

The bounce of the aeroplane woke Danny unceremoniously, and he gripped the armrests of the comfortable leather chair that had seemed to swallow him the moment he'd sat down. He'd had barely any time to appreciate the richly decorated interior of the executive jet, falling asleep and remaining that way for the entire duration of the flight. In the last forty hours, he'd gained a lifetime of experience, most of which he never wanted to repeat.

He relaxed quickly after the sudden jolt. The flight into Canberra was usually bumpy on landing and take-off; he'd clearly slept through the worst of it. Stretching out in the chair, he immediately felt the aches and bruises he'd accumulated over the last few days. His muscles protested the sudden and forced fitness regime; his body was cut and bruised in places where he'd fallen, been thrown or landed. He'd managed a shower and change of clothing in Singapore, but he still felt the fog of travel and the staleness of the same clothes worn for too long.

The plane taxied to the VIP terminal at the airport, normally reserved for government officials and visiting dignitaries. With some regret, he said goodbye to the ridiculously comfortable chair.

The RAAF aircrew said their goodbyes, ushering him out of the cool, air-conditioned interior of the cabin. The assault of the Australian summer heat was as unforgiving as ever, the humidity of the tropics replaced with the baking, dry heat of the land down under. He had to dig around in his travel bag for his sunglasses; the sunlight blinded him immediately.

Despite the uncomfortable heat, Danny felt immediately at ease. Back in familiar surroundings, in a familiar country. A place where he wouldn't be shot at or blown up – at least, he hoped he wouldn't.

A car was waiting off the tarmac. A familiar face looked over at him, smiling, leaning against the car.

'Well, well, well, if it isn't the man-of-the-hour himself, Mr Bond,' Ata grinned.

'Missed me, Ata?' Danny grinned back.

'Not even a little bit. Finally managed to get ahead in my work; no more Danny specials. No more rabbit holes. Plus, I had dibs on your desk.'

'You're telling me the whole place didn't go up in flames without me?'

Ata looked suddenly sheepish, 'Well, I wouldn't say that. Hop in.'

The cool interior of the car was refreshing already. How people lived in this country before air-conditioning was a mystery to Danny. He waited for Ata to drive off, but she just sat there.

'What's up? he asked.

'Just you wait,' she said, before pointing towards a small building just off to the side.

A man was walking out surrounded by three others, his arms firmly locked behind his back and head down. One of the men had a hand on his shoulder. As the figures got closer, Danny's eyes widened. 'Is that Mike? In handcuffs? What the actual *fuck*?' he gasped, mouth agape.

He looked back at Ata, who was nodding with a smirk across her face. 'A lot went down while you were away,' she said. 'Turns out our old friend was playing a game of his own in the background.'

'That piece of shit,' Danny chuckled, shaking his head. He was too exhausted for outrage right now.

Mike looked up as he walked past their car, his eyes briefly locking with Danny's and Ata's. Pure, burning hatred flashed across his face before it was replaced with defeat. Danny gave him a farewell wave.

'Let's get out of here. I have a girlfriend I need to see, and if you try and tell me I need to do a briefing, you'll have to break my legs and drag me in there.'

The car started to move. 'So dramatic! Don't you worry. Maia has you covered and told them to lay off. You'll need to debrief sooner or later, but I reckon a day or two won't hurt.' She drove them out of the security gate. 'But also, good idea breaking your legs. I might keep that in my back pocket.' Once they were through, she stomped on the brake and halted the car. 'Alright, get out.'

Danny was confused. 'What?'

'I'm only here to get you out the gate, Danny boy. Your real escort is waiting for you just there.'

He followed her pointed finger. Sure, enough Leah was sitting on the bonnet of her car, waiting for him.

Danny didn't need to be told twice. 'Cheers, Ata. Catch you in a few days. And hey, thanks for holding down the fort.'

She smiled back. 'Don't mention it,' she said, giving him a fist bump. 'Glad you're back.'

Without another word, he leapt out of the car. The joy of seeing Leah felt overwhelming. He ran up to her, scooping her up in a big hug and swinging her around, his aches and bruises all forgotten.

She laughed, 'Aww, missed me, did you?'

'You have no idea,' he beamed back.

'Tell me on the way,' she ordered, disengaging with him suddenly and wrinkling her nose. 'We need to get you into a shower.'

Danny didn't mind; everything was now in the past. Right here, right now, he was exactly where he wanted to be, with the person he planned on spending the rest of his life with.

As he threw his bags in the back of the car, Leah turned the engine on. The radio was playing 'Everybody Wants to Rule the World' by Tears for Fears.

Danny closed his eyes as they sped off. The comfort of sleep overcame him quickly. Leah smiled to herself, the peaceful look on her man's face filling her with relief and love.

THE END

ABOUT THE AUTHOR

Jack Newman is a first-time author. Having grown up reading stories from Tom Clancy, Wilbur Smith and Clive Cussler, Jack has a love for exciting adventure stories with a focus on real-world history and strong research. His first novel, *The Malacca Incident*, started as a hobby project three years ago while looking for good new books to read. Disappointed with the available options, Jack decided to write his own. Jack studied at the Australian National University in the Strategic Defence Studies Centre and has a master's degree in Strategic Studies. He has a keen interest in international affairs and emerging technology.

Printed in Great Britain
by Amazon